THE SECRET SPIRAL OF SWAMP KID

PROPERTY
OF
RUSSELL WEINWRIGHT

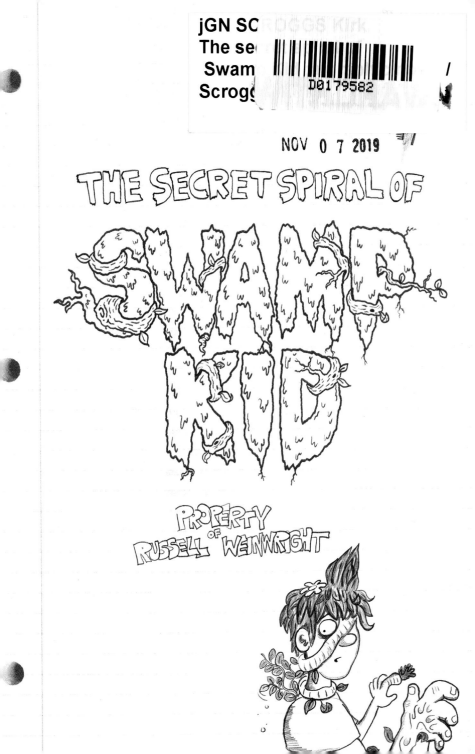

Writer & Illustrator

KIRK SCROGGS

Letterer
STEVE WANDS

THE SECRET SPIRAL OF SWAMP KID

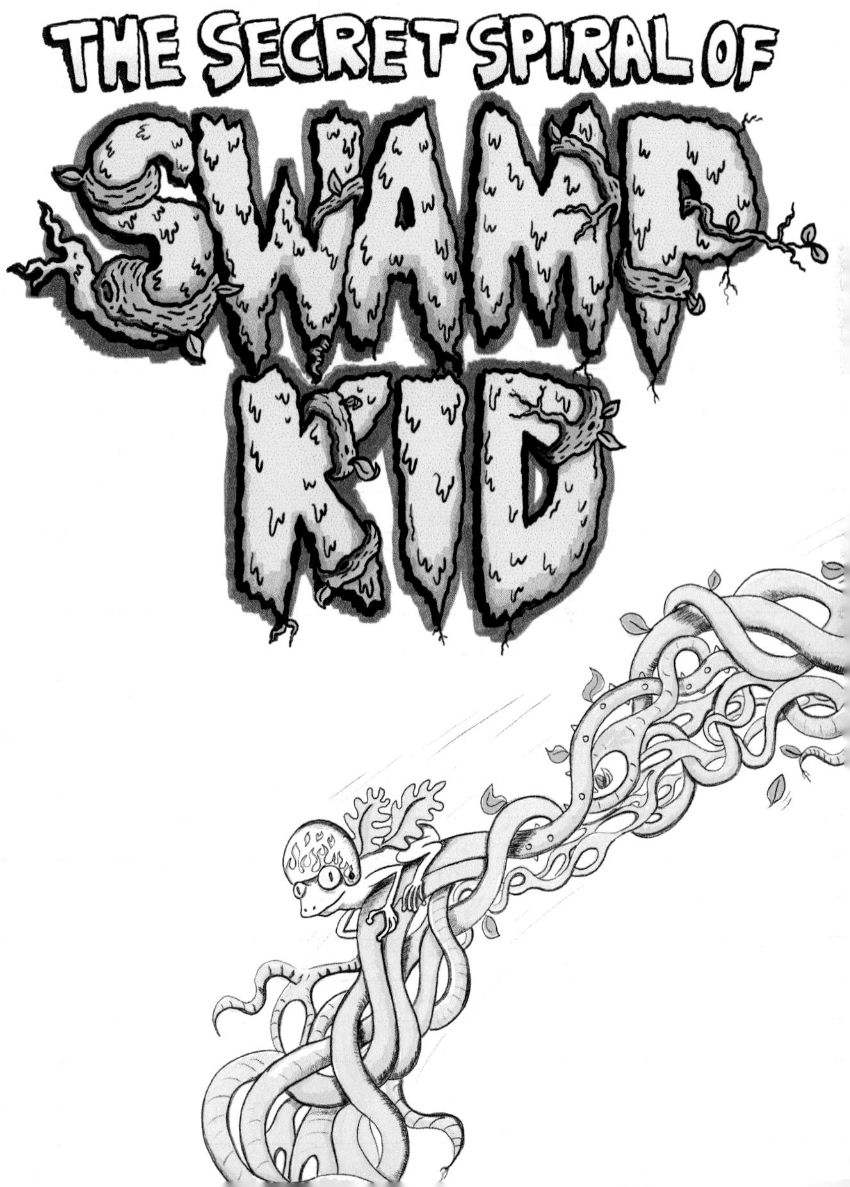

ALEX R. CARR Editor

DIEGO LOPEZ Assistant Editor

STEVE COOK Design Director - Books

LORI JACKSON and AMIE BROCKWAY-METCALF Publication Design

BOB HARRAS Senior VP - Editor-in-Chief, DC Comics

MICHELE R. WELLS VP & Executive Editor, Young Reader

DAN DiDIO Publisher

JIM LEE Publisher & Chief Creative Officer

BOBBIE CHASE VP - New Publishing Initiatives & Talent Development

DON FALLETTI VP - Manufacturing Operations & Workflow Management

LAWRENCE GANEM VP - Talent Services

ALISON GILL Senior VP - Manufacturing & Operations

HANK KANALZ Senior VP - Publishing Strategy & Support Services

DAN MIRON VP - Publishing Operations

NICK J. NAPOLITANO VP - Manufacturing Administration & Design

NANCY SPEARS VP - Sales

THE SECRET SPIRAL OF SWAMP KID
Published by DC Comics. Copyright © 2019 DC Comics.
All Rights Reserved. All characters, their distinctive
likenesses and related elements featured in this
publication are trademarks of DC Comics. DC ZOOM is
a trademark of DC Comics. The stories, characters,
and incidents featured in this publication are entirely
fictional. DC Comics does not read or accept unsolicited
submissions of ideas, stories, or artwork.
DC - a WarnerMedia Company

DC Comics, 2900 West Alameda Ave.,
Burbank, CA 91505
Printed by LSC Communications,
Crawfordsville, IN.
8/23/19. First printing.
ISBN: 978-1-4012-9068-9

PEFC Certified

This product is
from sustainably
managed forests and
controlled sources

PEFC/01-31-106   www.pefc.org

Library of Congress Cataloging-in-Publication Data
Names: Scroggs, Kirk. writer, illustrator. | Wands, Steve, letterer.
Title: The secret spiral of Swamp Kid : a graphic novel / writer &
    illustrator, Kirk Scroggs ; letterer, Steve Wands.
Description: Burbank, CA : DC Zoom, [2019] | Audience: Ages 8-12 |
    Audience: Grades 4-6 | Summary: The everyday life of middle schooler,
    Russell, is depicted in his spiral notebook full of doodles and journal
    entries detailing what it's like being different and how to be
    comfortable in his own skin.
Identifiers: LCCN 2019026065 (print) | LCCN 2019026066 (ebook) | ISBN
    9781401290689 (paperback) | ISBN 9781779500007 (ebook)
Subjects: LCSH: Graphic novels. | CYAC: Graphic novels. |
    Notebooks--Fiction. | Diaries--Fiction. | Cartooning--Fiction. |
    Self-confidence--Fiction.
Classification: LCC PZ7.7.S4145 Se 2019 (print) | LCC PZ7.7.S4145 (ebook)
    | DDC 741.5/973--dc23
LC record available at https://lccn.loc.gov/2019026065
LC ebook record available at https://lccn.loc.gov/2019026066

PRO LOG

WARNING!

Unless you have received explicit permission from Russell Weinwright, this scientific journal (NOT a diary!) is strictly

OFF-LIMITS

To make sure you comply, certain pages have been written in toxic ink.

SWAMP KID

Why did I lick it?

Others may contain lethal booby traps!

ARGH!

SWAMP KID

And should you read all the way to the end you could be pulled into the swamp like this unfortunate kid.*

*Identity withheld pending notification of distraught parents.

Yesterday I finally realized
I am scum. To be specific, I am pond
scum. For those of you who just happened
across this notebook, maybe because you are
snooping where you don't belong (that means
you, Mom!) don't worry. I'm not in a depressed
tailspin, about to lock myself in my room and
devour ten gallons of mint chocolate chip.
I'm just stating the facts—I am pond scum.
Literally: 50% cellulose, 50% human.

When most folks hear there's a half-swamp
monster/half-human student at Houma Bayou
Middle School, they probably picture something
like this:

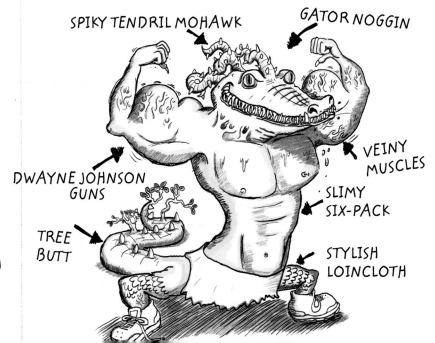

SPIKY TENDRIL MOHAWK

GATOR NOGGIN

DWAYNE JOHNSON GUNS

VEINY MUSCLES

TREE BUTT

SLIMY SIX-PACK

STYLISH LOINCLOTH

Of course, THIS is what I really look like...

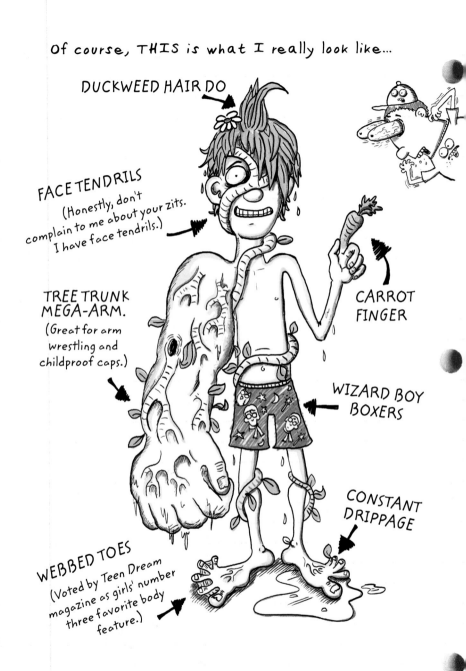

DUCKWEED HAIR DO

FACE TENDRILS
(Honestly, don't complain to me about your zits. I have face tendrils.)

TREE TRUNK MEGA-ARM.
(Great for arm wrestling and childproof caps.)

CARROT FINGER

WIZARD BOY BOXERS

CONSTANT DRIPPAGE

WEBBED TOES
(Voted by Teen Dream magazine as girls' number three favorite body feature.)

That's me. Russell Weinwright. Handsome, huh? I've come to realize I possess what fashion blogs call the Wet Algae look.

I'm used to my veggie physique by now, but yesterday reality hit me like a truckload of fertilizer. Charlotte tried to set me up on a date with her cousin Tonya, and you can imagine how that went.

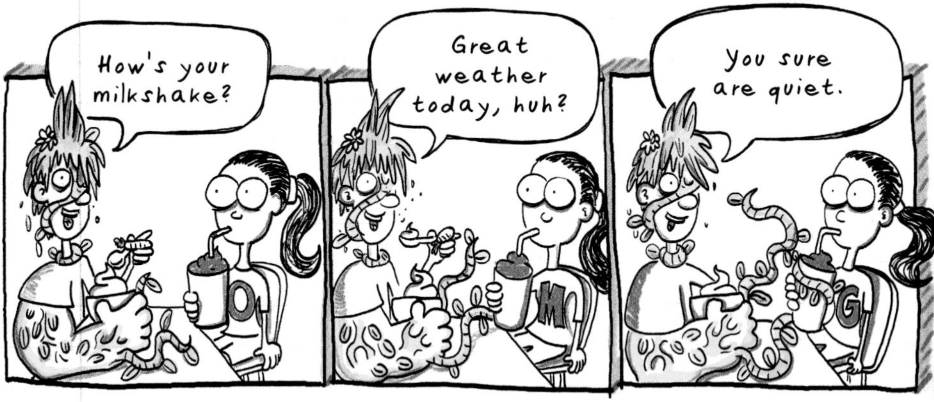

How's your milkshake?
O
Great weather today, huh?
M
You sure are quiet.
G

So, yeah, that happened. Like I said, pond scum. Charlotte was just trying to help, I suppose. She's my best friend at school...uh, scratch that. She's my ONLY friend at school. She's full of Cajun-spiced words of encouragement when I'm feeling sorry for myself.

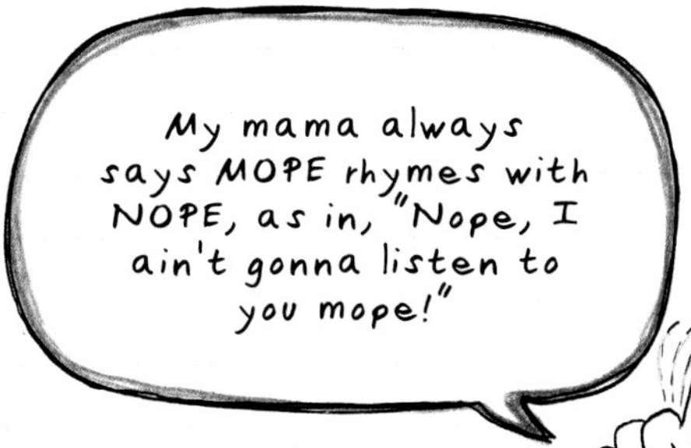

My mama always says MOPE rhymes with NOPE, as in, "Nope, I ain't gonna listen to you mope!"

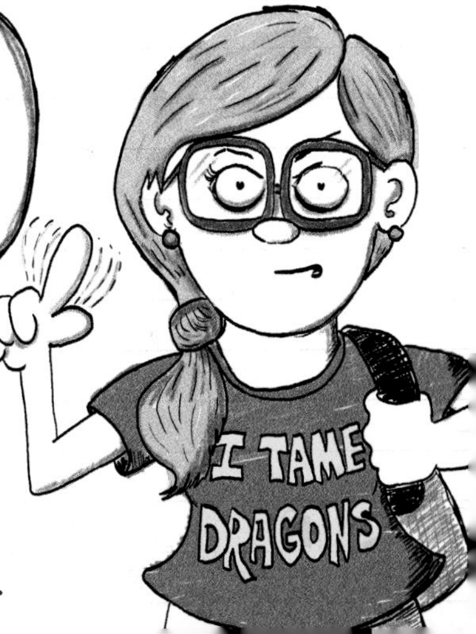

I TAME DRAGONS

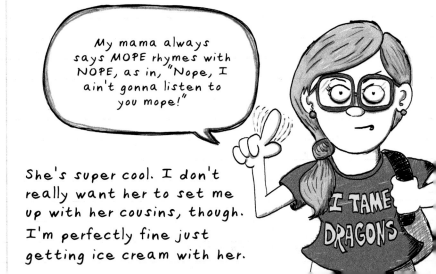

She's super cool. I don't really want her to set me up with her cousins, though. I'm perfectly fine just getting ice cream with her.

Right now, as I write this, Charlotte is totally staring at me from across the classroom, making some weird motion with her eyes.

Oh wait!

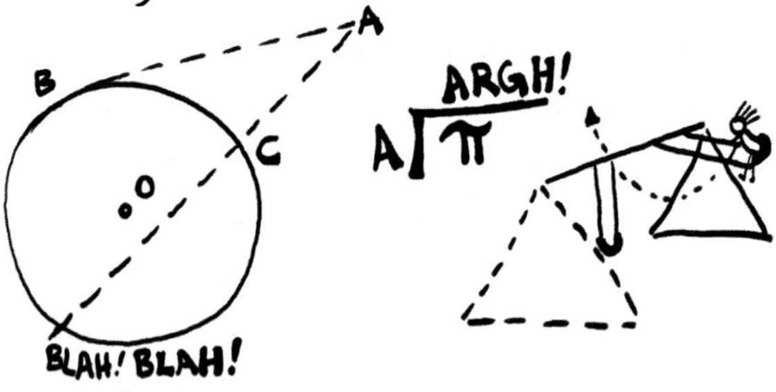
A
B
C
O
BLAH! BLAH!
ARGH!
A π

Sorry, had to pretend to take notes there for a second! Charlotte must have been trying to warn me that Mr. Finneca was walking up right behind me! Dude's always busting me for doodling in science class.

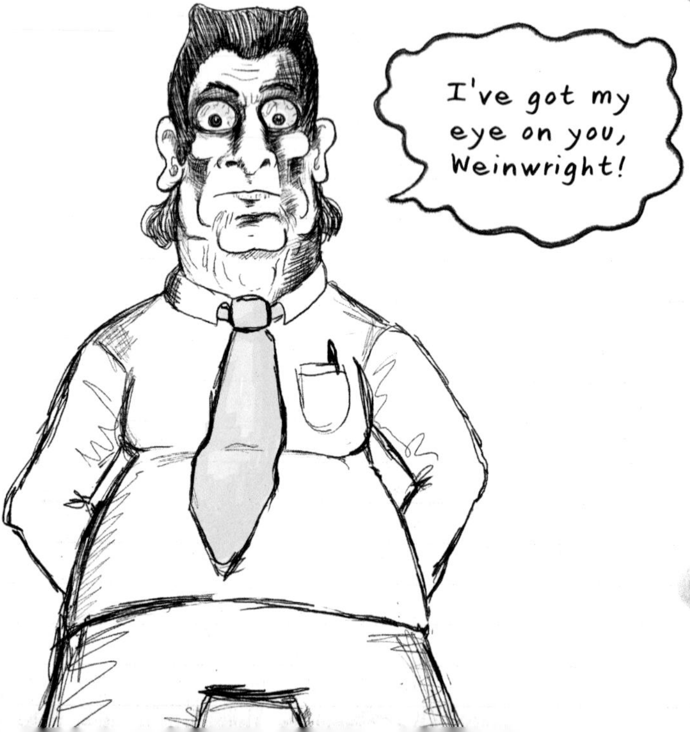
I've got my eye on you, Weinwright!

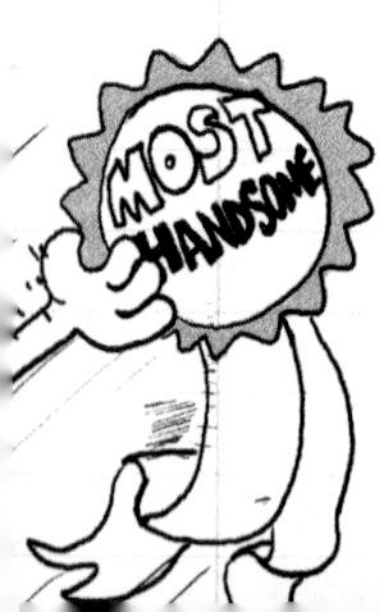
MOST HANDSOME

He's got a right to be cheesed. I do draw in his class 98% of the time, but it's almost always pictures of him. I draw him as evil vampires, evil space lords, deformed monsters... he should be honored!

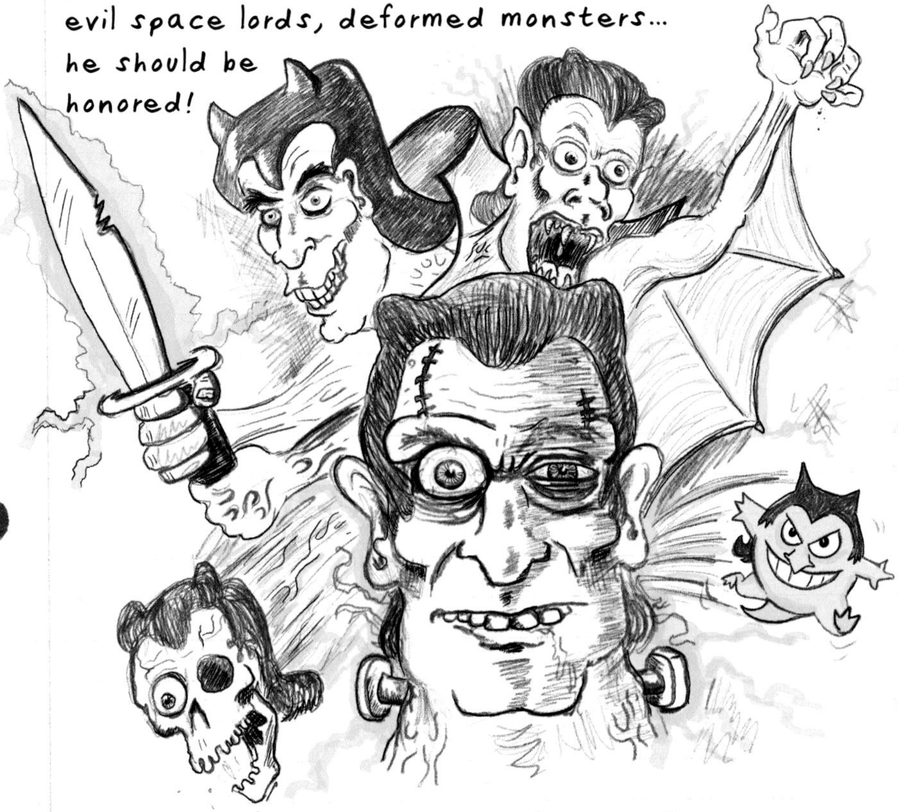

Okay, I guess my pics aren't very flattering, although he did seem strangely impressed when I drew him as a great white shark.

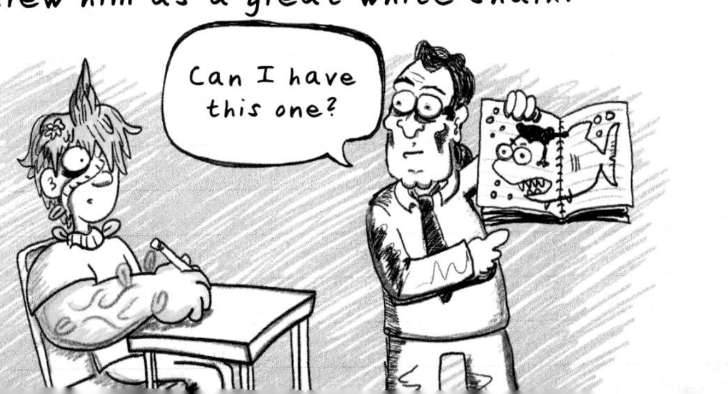
Can I have this one?

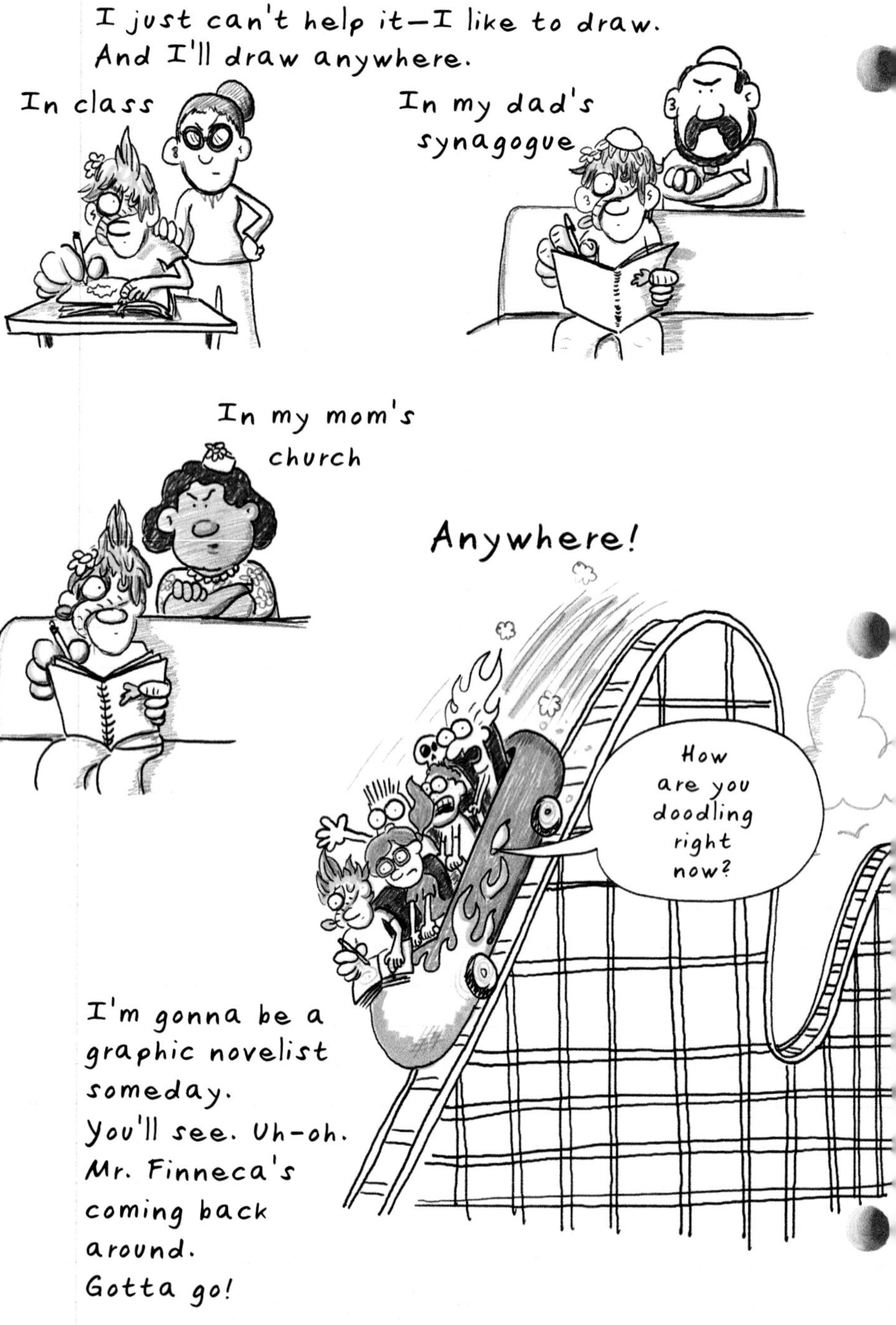
I just can't help it—I like to draw.
And I'll draw anywhere.
In class
In my dad's synagogue
In my mom's church
Anywhere!
How are you doodling right now?
I'm gonna be a graphic novelist someday.
You'll see. Uh-oh. Mr. Finneca's coming back around.
Gotta go!

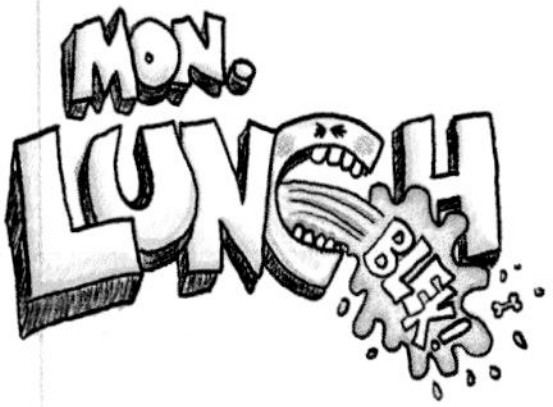
MON.
LUNCH
BLEH!

Lunch period. A.k.a. Last Meal of the Condemned. Dad says my weekly allowance is bigger than the whole Houma Bayou lunch budget for the year, which explains the subpar cuisine. If you don't believe me, just take a look at this pic of today's spaghetti and meatball special...

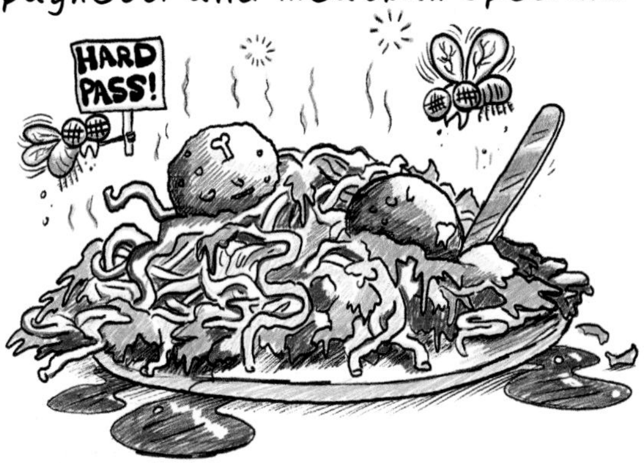
HARD PASS!

Fooled you. It's actually a garden salad.

Today I decided to eat my lunch outside. It's something I do a lot, mainly to escape the stench of the lunchroom, the endless stares from my classmates, the bullies trying to read my spiral without my authorization, and, oh yeah... I eat sunlight.

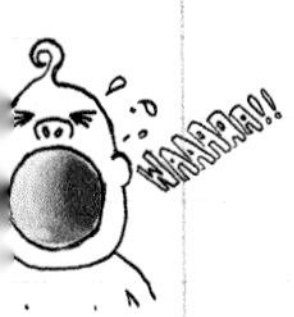
WAAAAAA!!

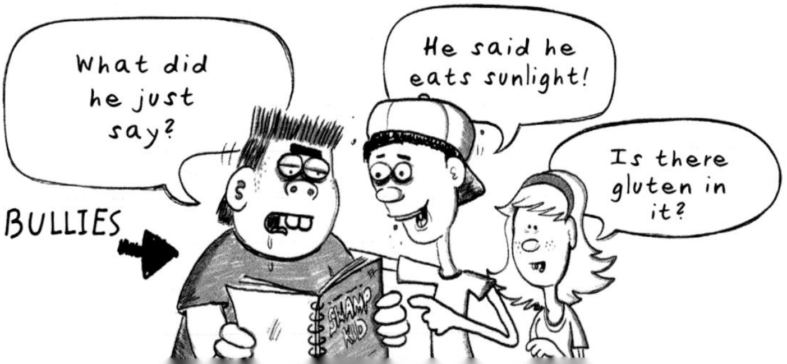
What did he just say?
He said he eats sunlight!
Is there gluten in it?
BULLIES
SWAMP KID

LADIES AND GENTLEMEN, PHOTOSYNTHESIS!

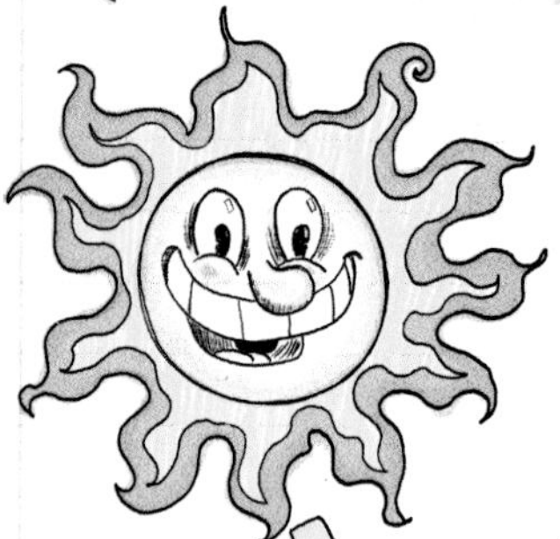

One of the perks of being half plant is that I can get a good meal just by soaking in some rays. Sunlight goes in...

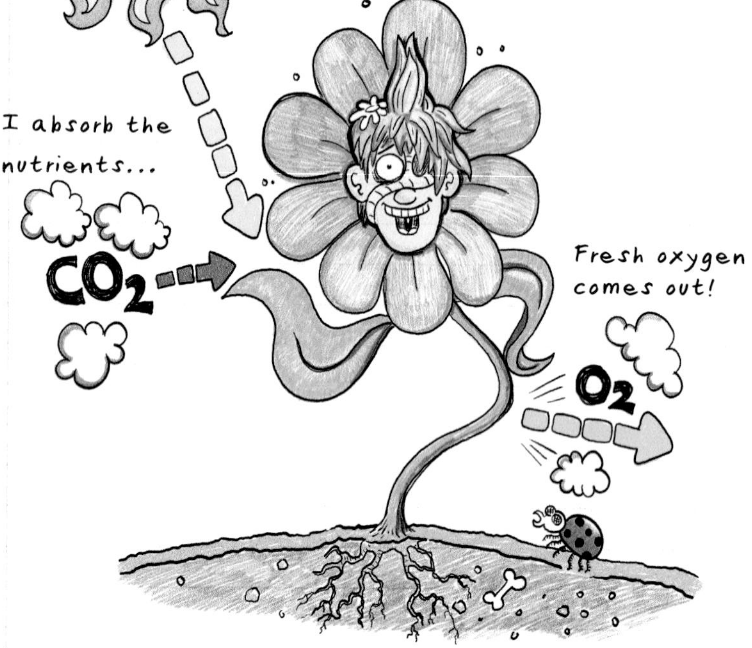

I absorb the nutrients...
CO_2
Fresh oxygen comes out!
O_2

Don't get me wrong, I still like a good pizza, but it's mostly the sun's warm rays that give me energy.

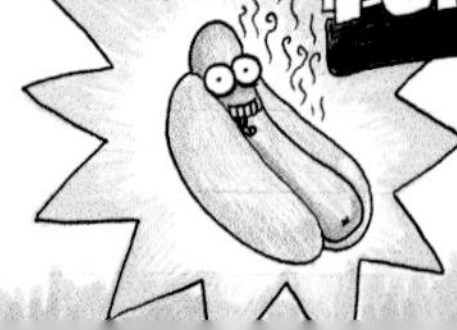

FUN FACT

SUNLIGHT TASTES LIKE HOT DOGS!

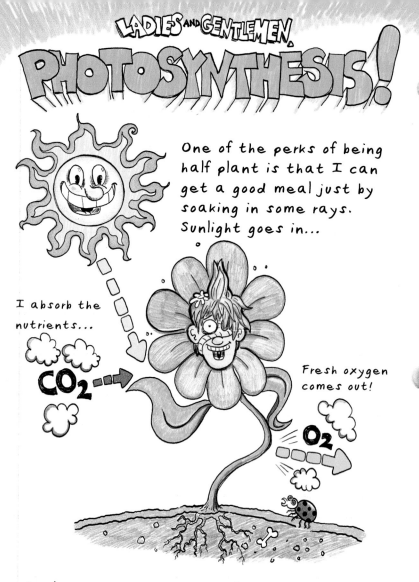

I also convert carbon dioxide pollution into oxygen, which helps you all breathe easily, so...

YOU'RE WELCOME!

Of course, this unique feature can cause confusion. Especially when it comes to my folks...

Be sure to get lots of sunshine, son. You're a growing boy and need your nourishment!

And wear sunscreen. You don't want melanoma!

Okay... Wait, what?

But, anyway, what was I talking about again? Oh yeah, eating outside. It's peaceful out here. I can draw my comics and write in my spiral while I absorb lunch. And I can avoid the other students asking me annoying questions. There's this one kid in particular who keeps following me around with his old-school video camera and pelting me with personal questions that I just don't feel like answering...

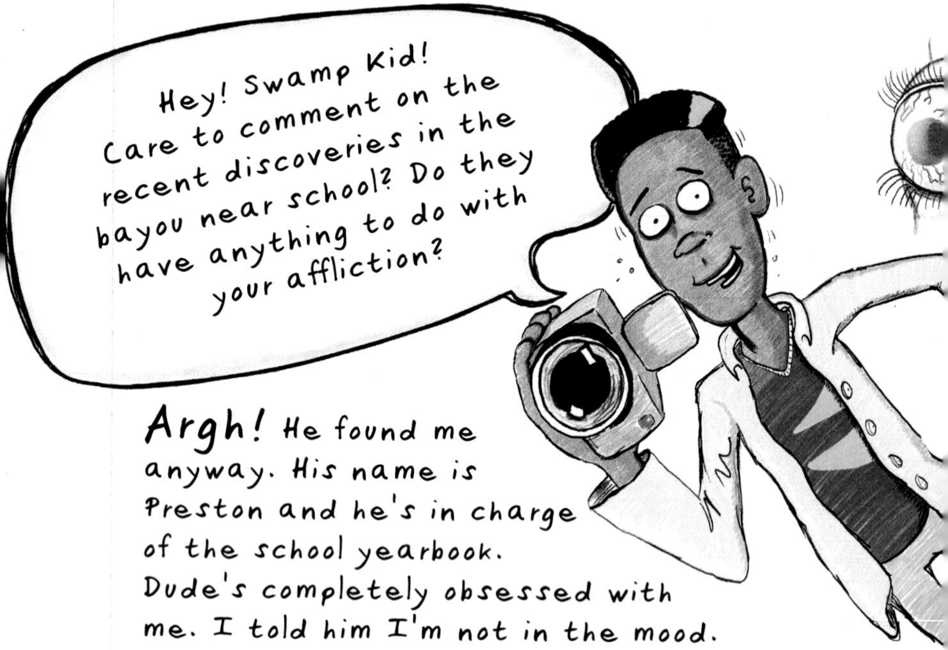
Hey! Swamp Kid! Care to comment on the recent discoveries in the bayou near school? Do they have anything to do with your affliction?

Argh! He found me anyway. His name is Preston and he's in charge of the school yearbook. Dude's completely obsessed with me. I told him I'm not in the mood. But that never deters Preston.

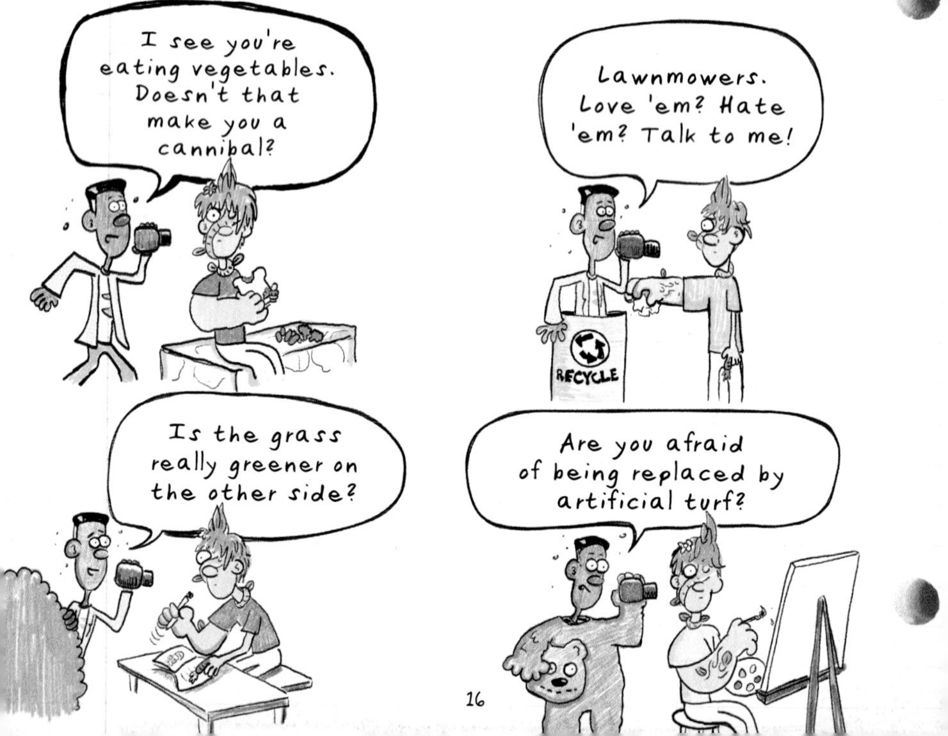
I see you're eating vegetables. Doesn't that make you a cannibal?
Lawnmowers. Love 'em? Hate 'em? Talk to me!
RECYCLE
Is the grass really greener on the other side?
Are you afraid of being replaced by artificial turf?

Luckily for me, Charlotte popped up out of nowhere and took care of business.

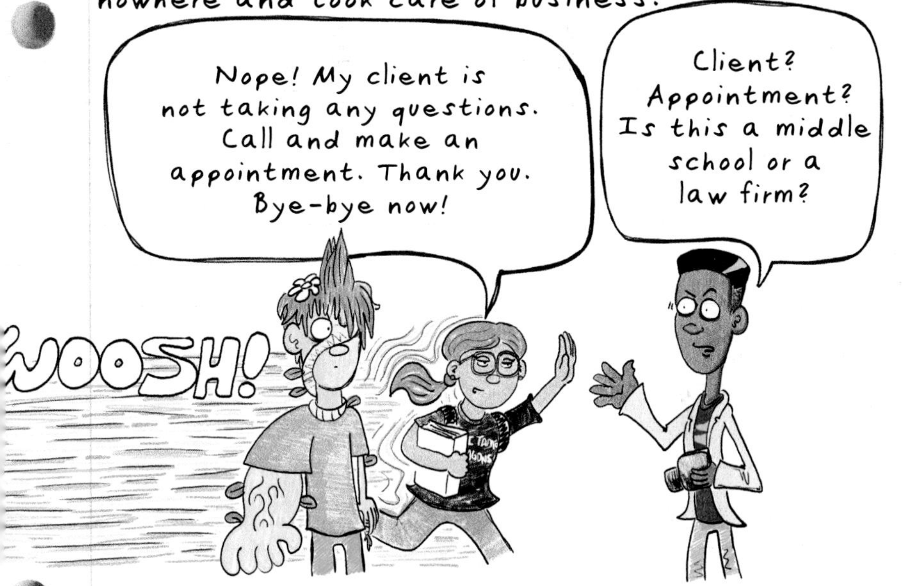
WOOSH!
Nope! My client is not taking any questions. Call and make an appointment. Thank you. Bye-bye now!
Client? Appointment? Is this a middle school or a law firm?

Preston left in a huff. I thanked Charlotte for protecting her "client." She said she'd bill me later.

I couldn't help but think about what Preston had said. You know, about the discoveries in the swamp. It had been all over the news. Remnants of an old science lab scattered about in the bayou. I kinda wanted to go check it out, but not by myself. Good news, though. All I had to do was say one word to get Charlotte interested...

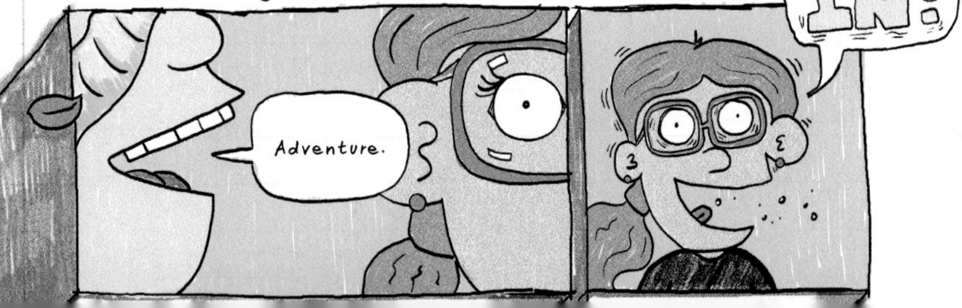
Adventure.
I'M IN!

MON. AFTER SCHOOL 3:47 P.M.

School let out almost a half hour ago and we've already hiked a mile into the swamp nearby. We're taking a break so I can sketch this amazing place in my book.

It's spooky in here, though. There are shadows and weird noises everywhere.

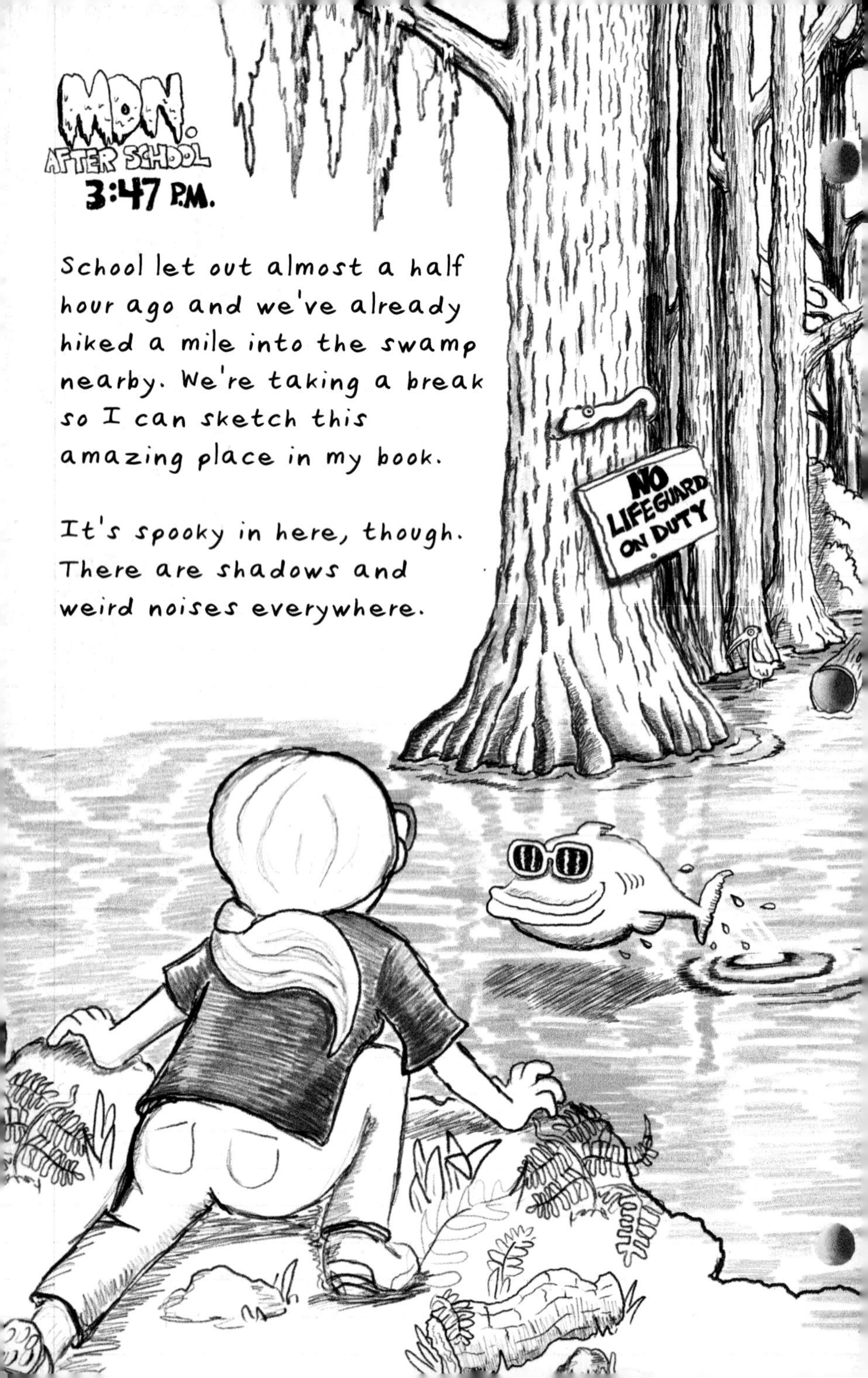
NO LIFEGUARD ON DUTY

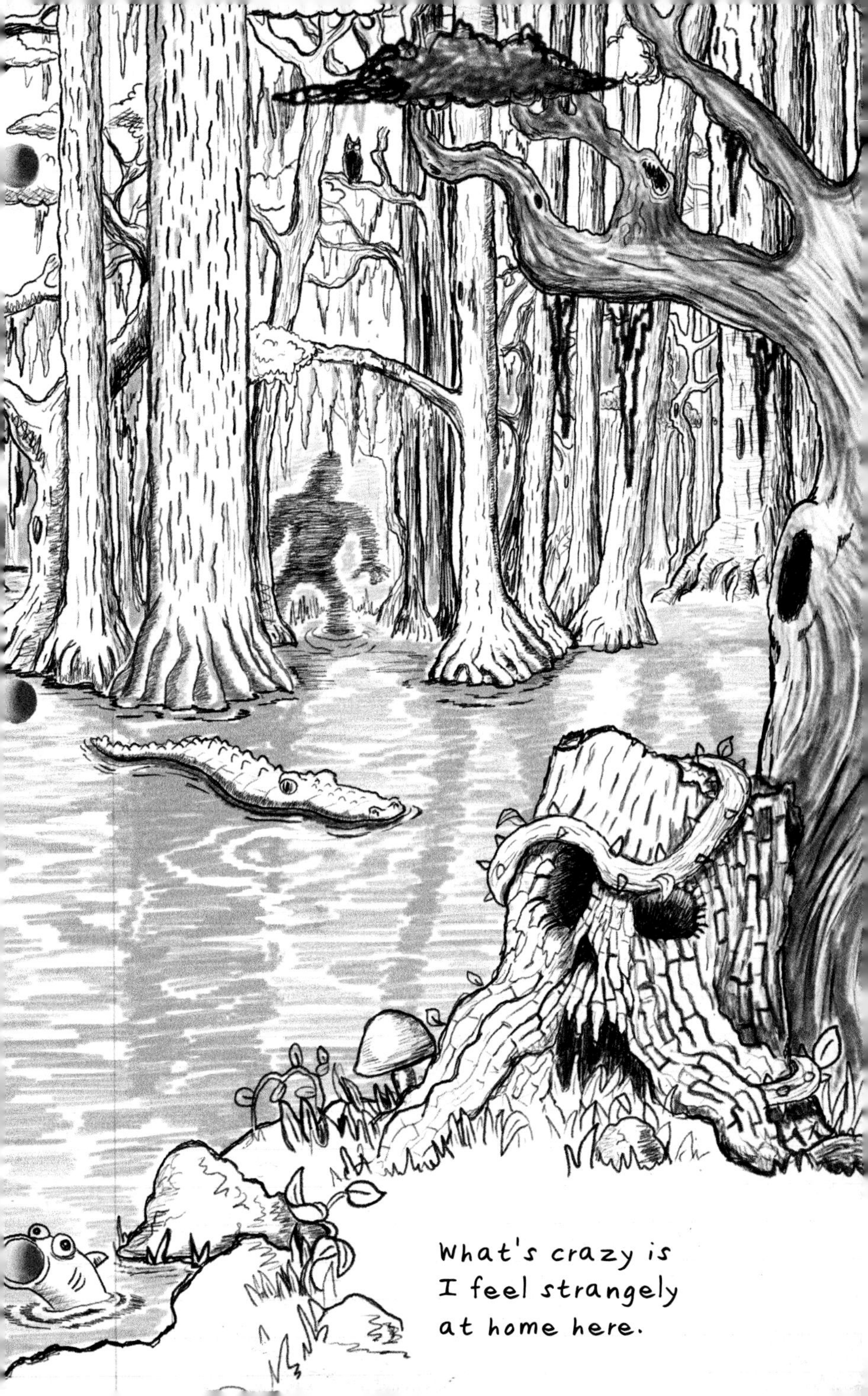
What's crazy is
I feel strangely
at home here.

I guess there's a reason for that...this is where I was discovered as a baby, or a "tiny sapling" as Mom used to call me. Probably just a few miles from where we are now, Dad was working on a gas line when he moved some branches and there I was.

Ain't I the cutest thing? Just chillin' in the swamp. No parents. No explanation. No pants. Dad tried to locate my real folks, but no one ever stepped forward. So, Mom and Dad adopted me. Treated me like I was one of their own. Questions still plague me. Why was I abandoned out here? Why am I like this? It's weird not knowing these kinds of things. Simple things. Oh well, gotta keep going. Gonna get dark soon.

4:30 P.M.

I just had to stop to collect this specimen of plant. I suspect it's a species never before seen by man!

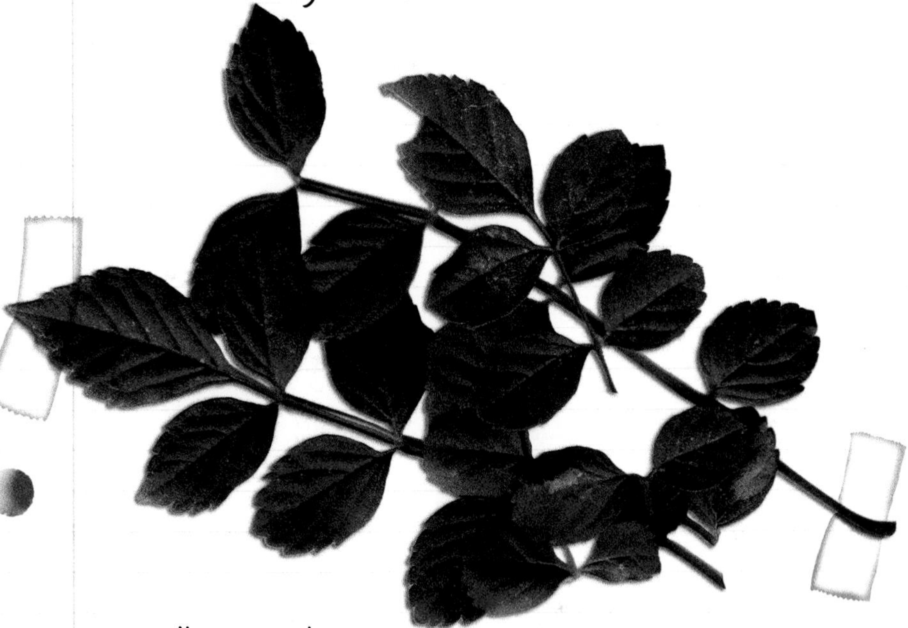

Actually, Charlotte just shot down my theory.

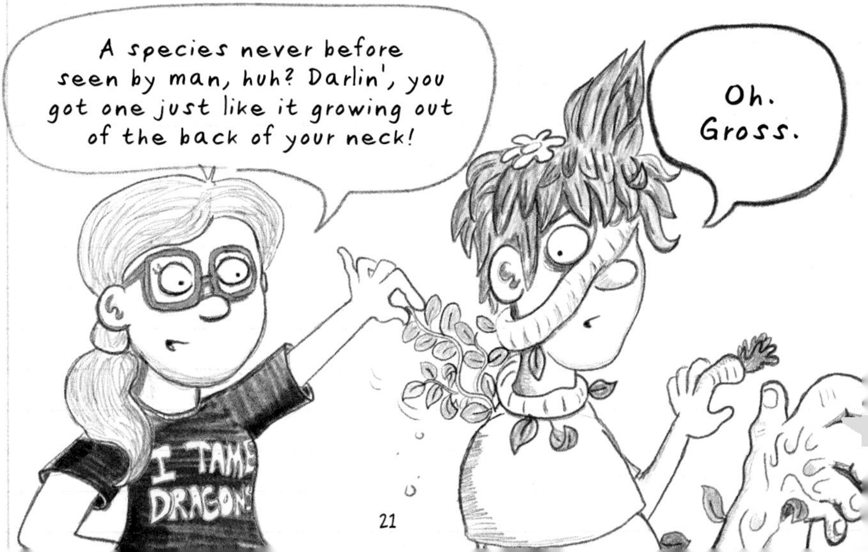

A species never before seen by man, huh? Darlin', you got one just like it growing out of the back of your neck!
Oh. Gross.
I TAME DRAGONS!

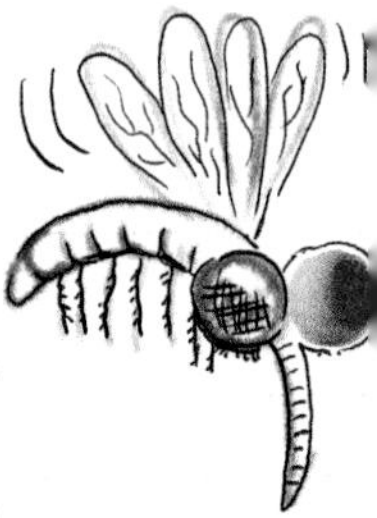

4:47 P.M.

You're not gonna believe this—we just stumbled upon some old gnarled pieces of wood and shards of glass.

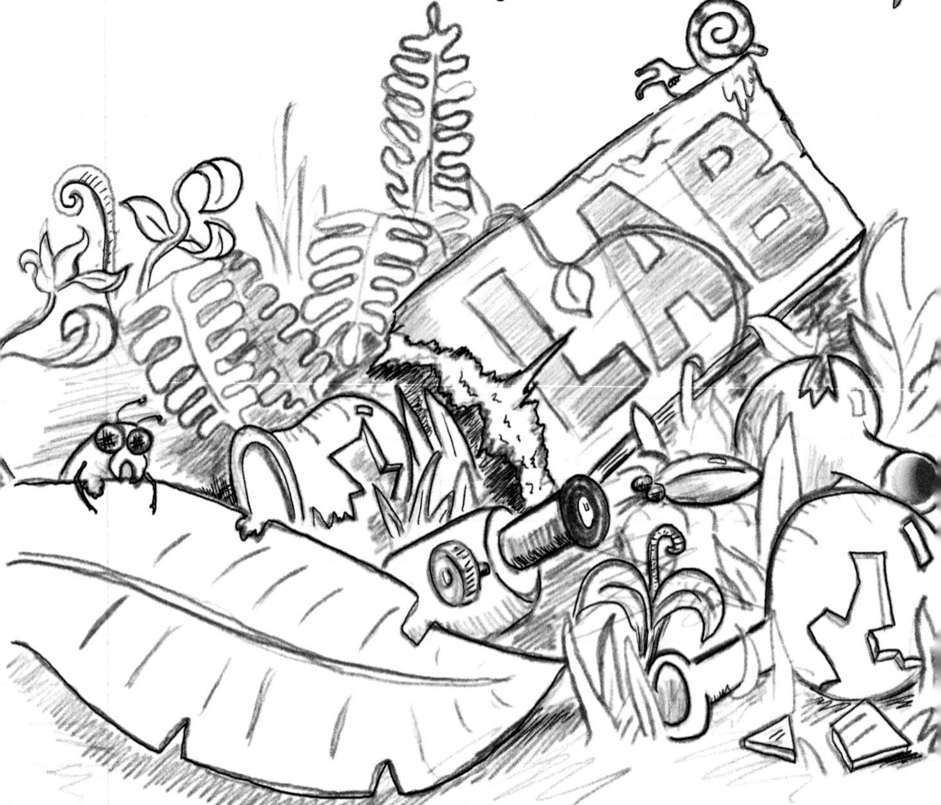
LAB

Looks like under all this thick growth of vines and foliage lie the remnants of an abandoned building. We must be close to where investigators have been uncovering that old medical lab. There are broken beakers and test tubes, too!

But the coolest find of all actually just found us!

This tiny critter looks to be half plant/half frog...
with leaves growing out of its back! It's like the
amphibian version of me, except cuter. I shall
call it a tree frog! Oops, Charlotte just said that
name is already taken. I shall call it
Specimen Number Two!

Well, Specimen Number Two
just sprayed us with specimen
number one and hopped away!

Something spooked it! A noise
off in the woods. We hear it now,
too! Something is out there!

Gotta go! Will update later...
if I'm still alive!

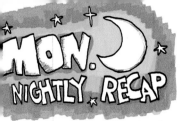

MON. NIGHTLY RECAP

It's nighttime now and I'm still with the living, safe in my bedroom.

I was thinking about just skipping this update or making up something, like the thing that was following us in the swamp turned out to be my long-lost father who looked like a garden shrub crossed with an artichoke and we were reunited and lived happily ever after! Of course, what actually went down was much more humiliating.

Woe is meeeeee!
SWAMP KID
THE MUSICAL
NOT SOLD OUT!

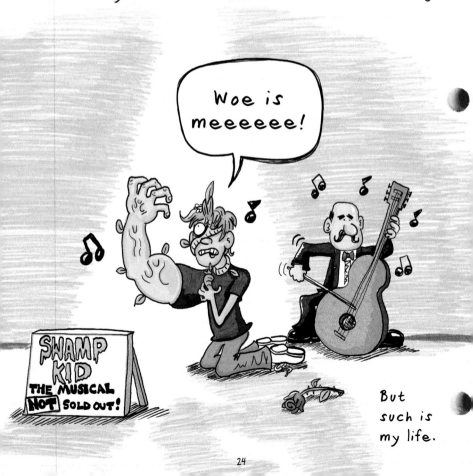

But such is my life.

So, here's what really happened...
Remember when I left off last, there was something approaching us in the woods? A shadowy presence sloshing through the swamp? Well...

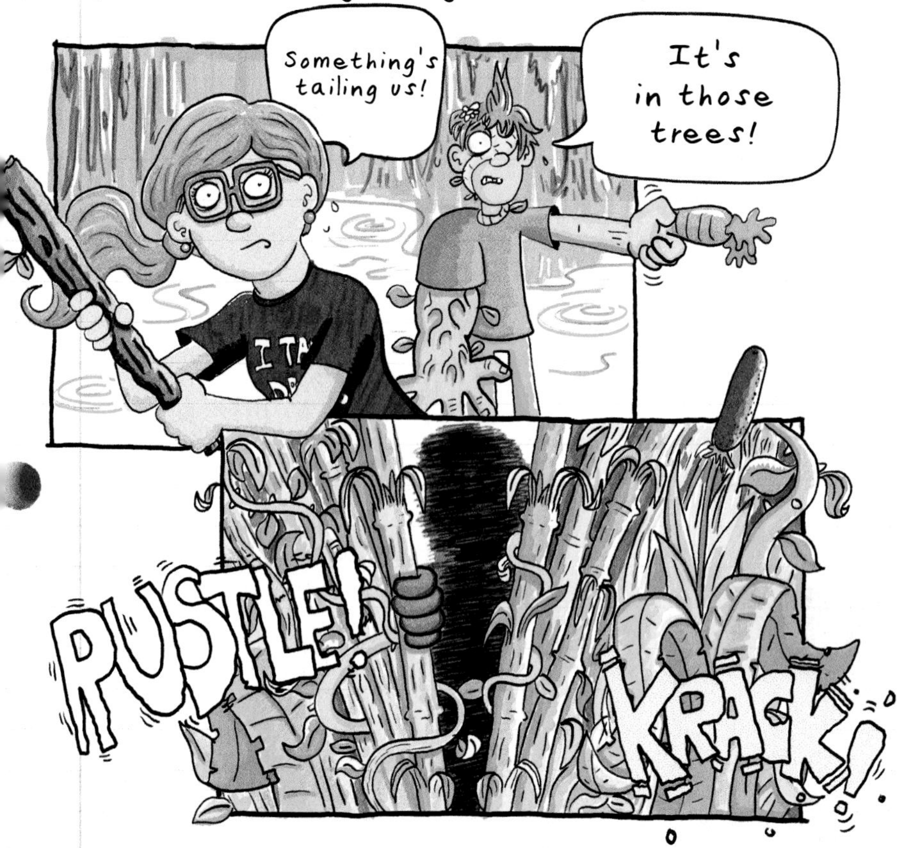
Something's tailing us!
It's in those trees!
I TA
RUSTLE!
KRACK!

The bushes opened up to reveal the hulking, slithery presence of...

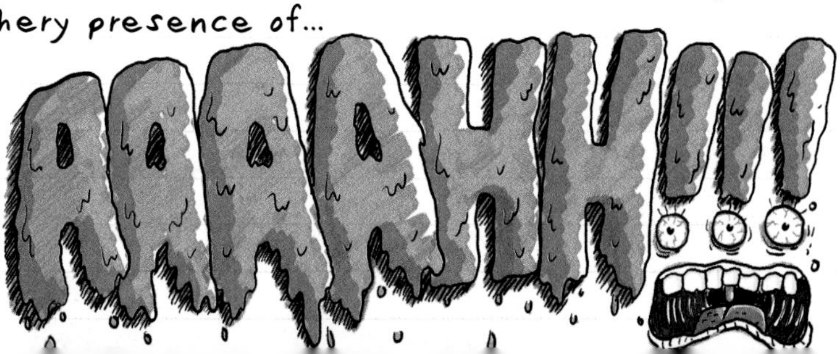
AAAAHH!!!

Hey, guys! Funny finding you here. Heh! Heh! Mind if I stick with you two? It's awfully creepy out here.

It was Preston. He was following us with that stupid video camera but he was pretending it was just a ~~coincidence~~ ~~coincidence~~ stroke of luck.

We let him have it. I demanded to know why he was snooping on us and Charlotte threatened to give him a Louisiana Luxury Mud Bath, which I think meant she was going to push him in the swamp, but I'm just guessing.

Sorry to scare you. Just trying to get a good story for the yearbook... wait a sec, you guys thought I was IT, didn't you?

I TAME DRAGONS

The IT Preston was referring to is a legendary creature that supposedly haunts the bayous of Houma...Swamp Thing! A beast even more freakish than I am. No one's gotten a great picture of him yet, but witnesses say he's hideous. Constant news stories about him keep everyone on edge.

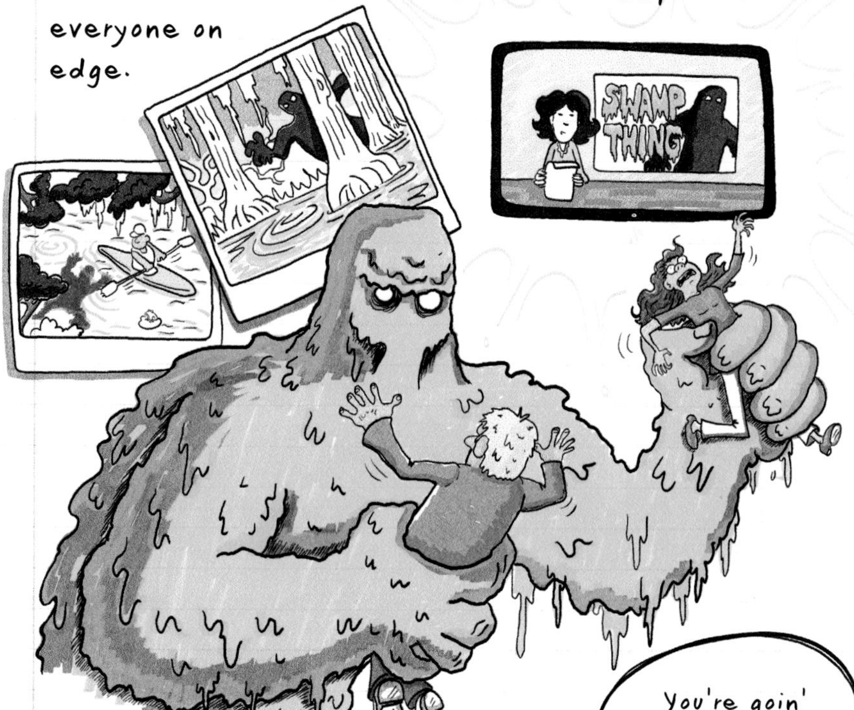
SWAMP THING

He's a bogeyman to the kids around here, though some say he's actually a superhero and that sometimes he's even been known to hang with a certain resident of Gotham City!

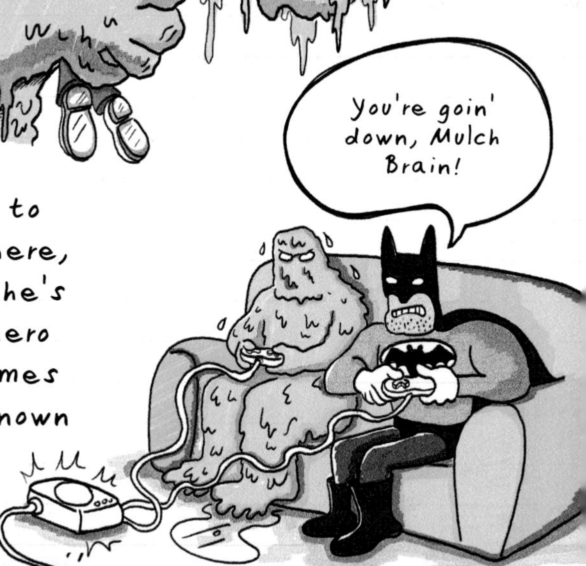
You're goin' down, Mulch Brain!

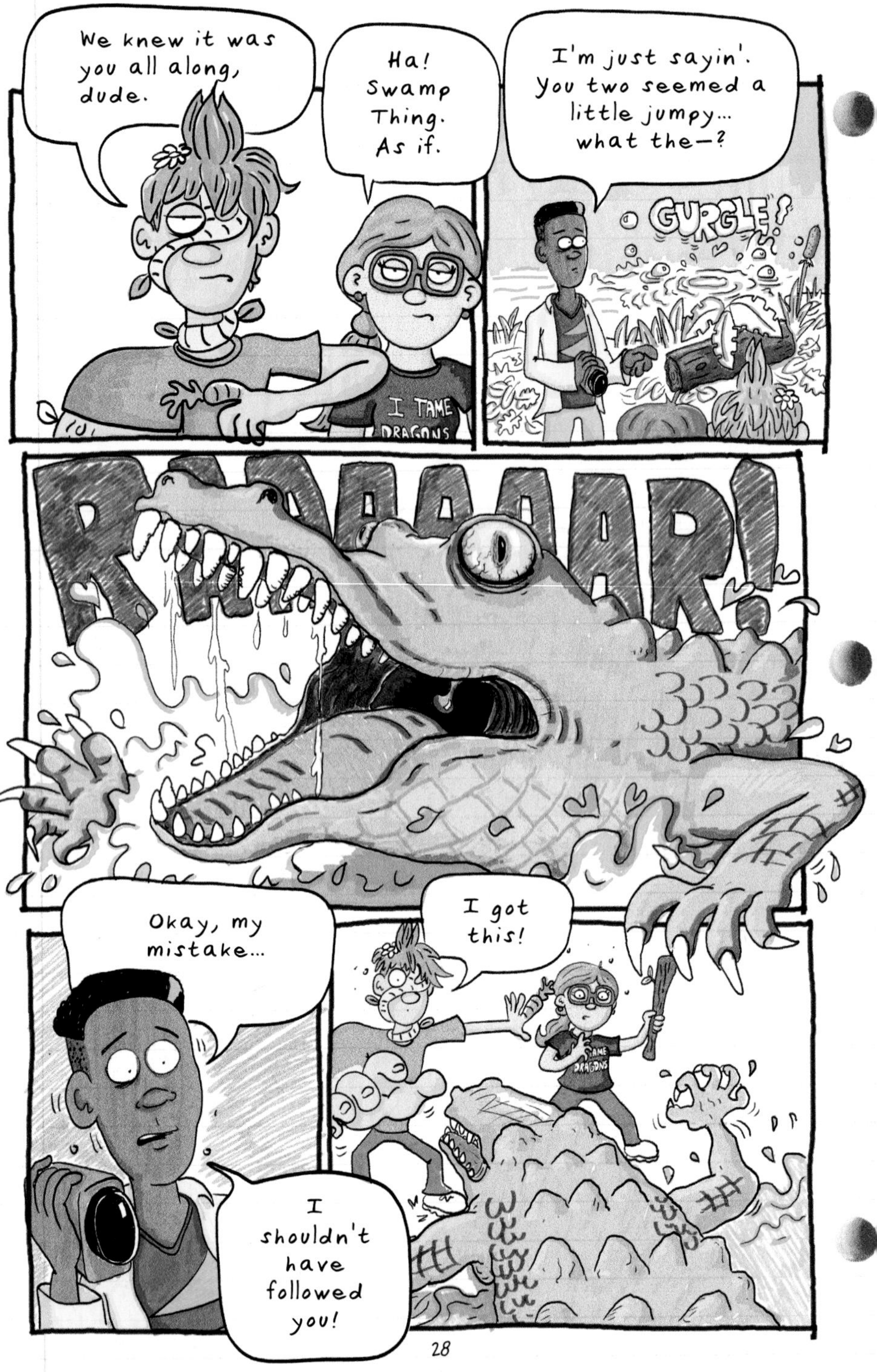

We knew it was you all along, dude.
Ha! Swamp Thing. As if.
I TAME DRAGONS
I'm just sayin'. You two seemed a little jumpy... what the—?
GURGLE!
RAAAAAR!
Okay, my mistake...
I got this!
TAME DRAGONS
I shouldn't have followed you!

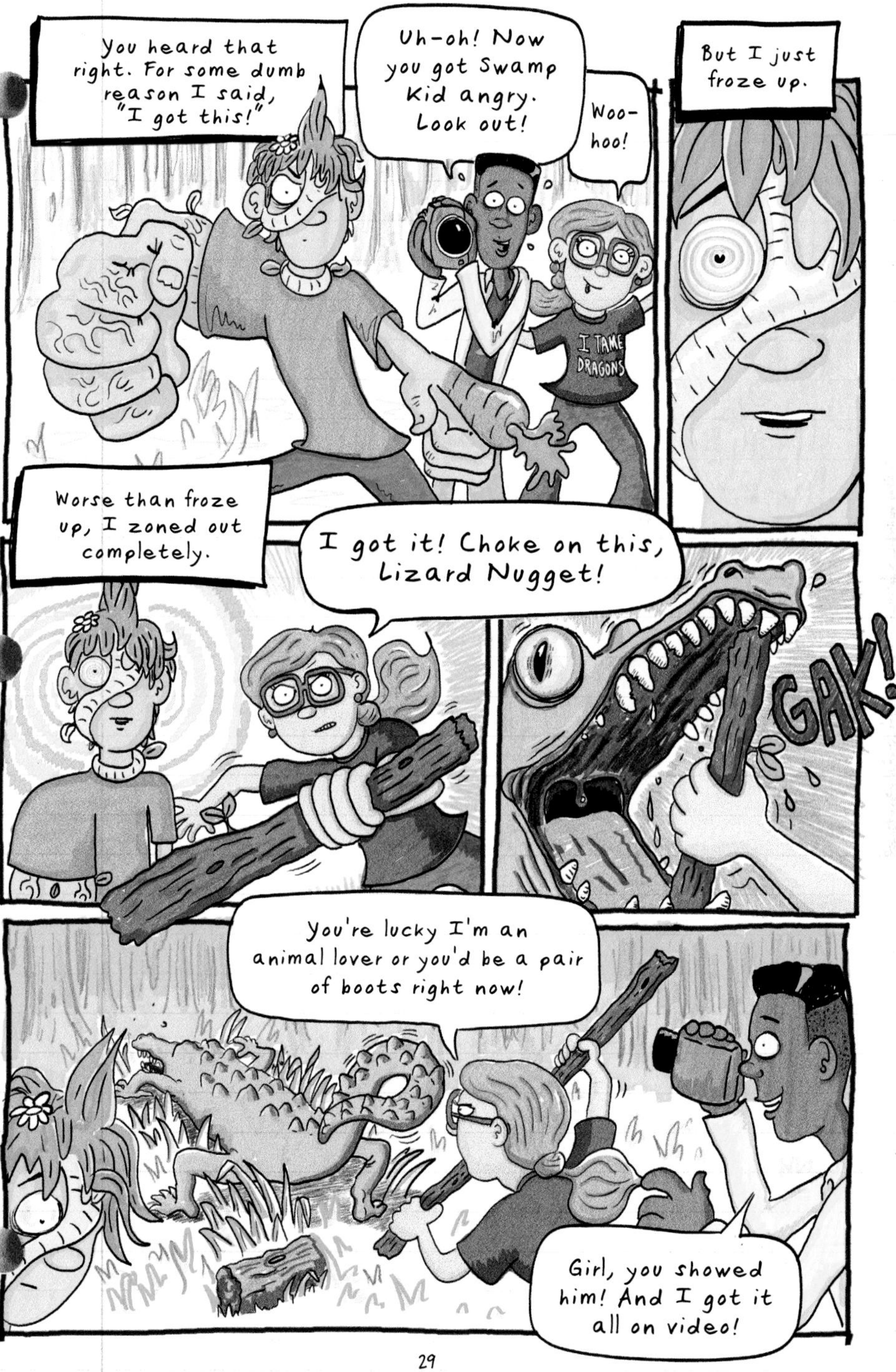
You heard that right. For some dumb reason I said, "I got this!"
Uh-oh! Now you got Swamp Kid angry. Look out!
Woo-hoo!
I TAME DRAGONS
But I just froze up.
Worse than froze up, I zoned out completely.
I got it! Choke on this, Lizard Nugget!
GAK!
You're lucky I'm an animal lover or you'd be a pair of boots right now!
Girl, you showed him! And I got it all on video!

The hike back home was a slog through the bog. I was devastated at my unparalleled wimpitude in the face of a challenge. Charlotte tried to put a positive spin on it.

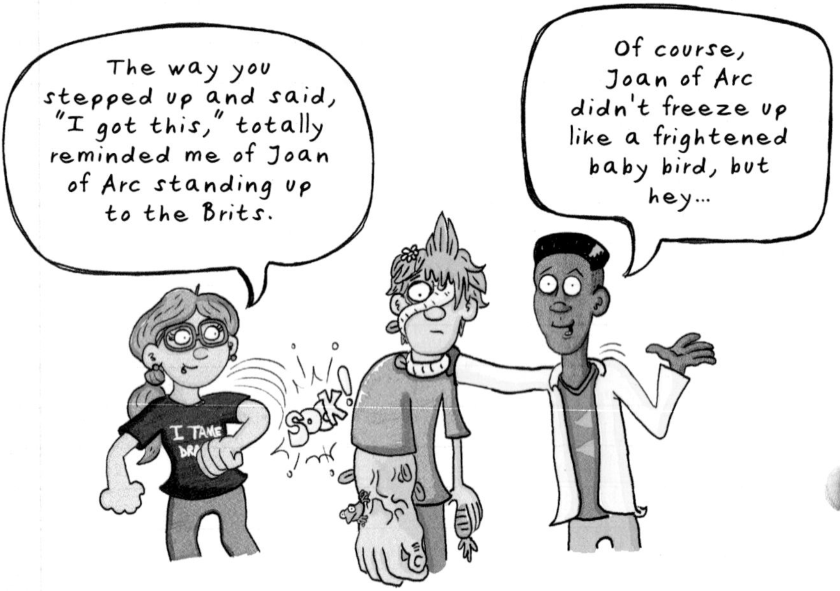
The way you stepped up and said, "I got this," totally reminded me of Joan of Arc standing up to the Brits.
Of course, Joan of Arc didn't freeze up like a frightened baby bird, but hey...
SOCK!
I TAME

Preston was right. Annoying but right. I had wimped out. But something else had happened, something more than just freezing up. I had gone into a weird kind of trance. For a moment, all I could see was green. I kept that part to myself, though. I don't want to sound like I was worming my way out of the embarrassment I richly deserved.

It's late. I'm going to bed.

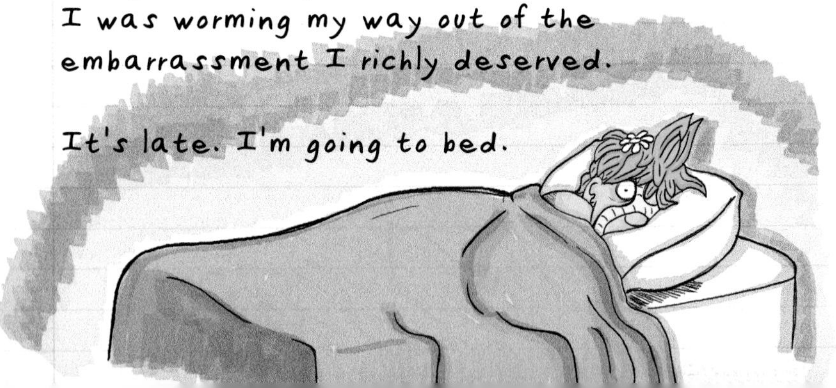

TUES. 8:02 A.M.

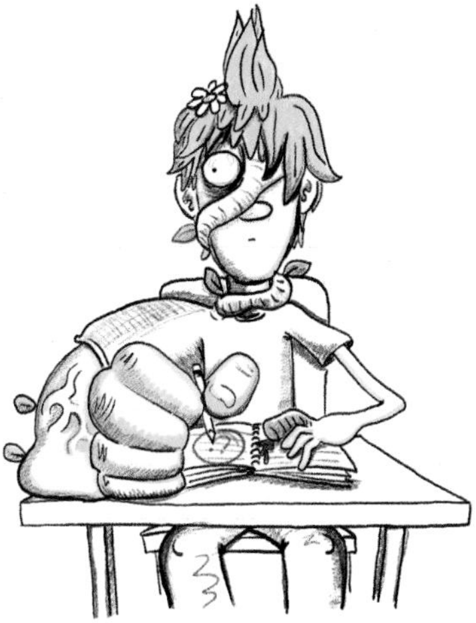

Some odd mojo in the air this morning in science class.

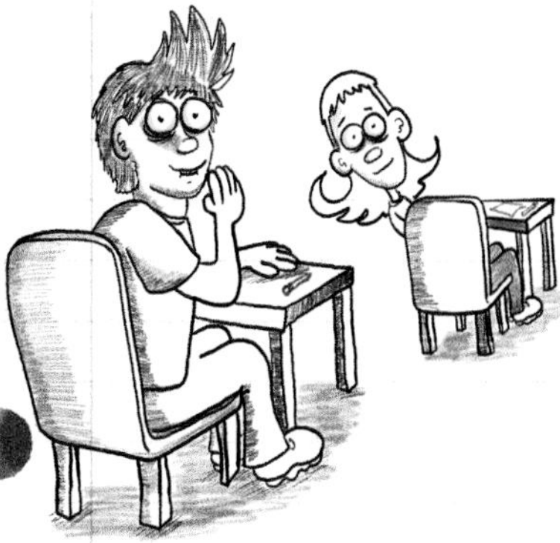

Seems like everyone is staring at me. Studying me. And am I crazy or are they giggling?

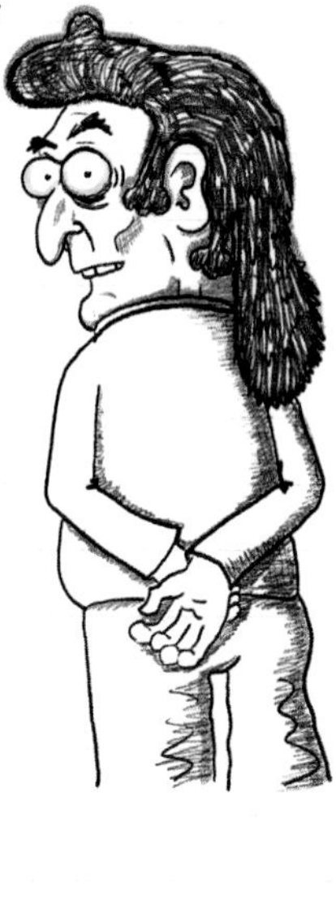

Mr. Finneca is monitoring me more than usual as well. Have you ever noticed that from the back he looks like he has a dead squirrel on his head?

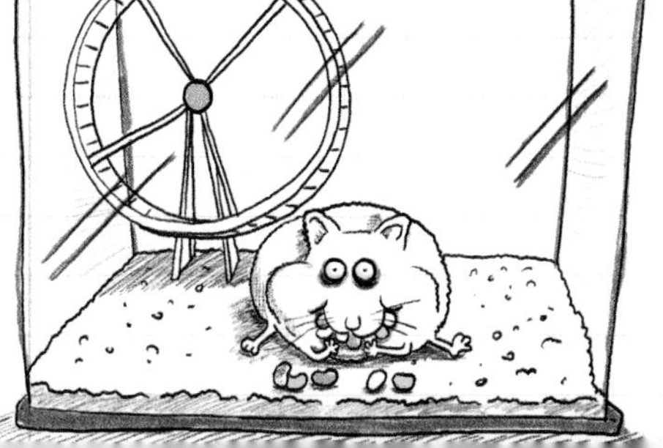

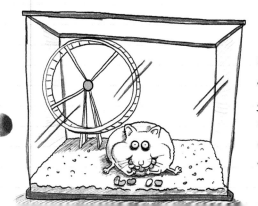

Even Barbeau, the class hamster, is grinning at me. Or maybe her cheeks are just stuffed with jelly beans.

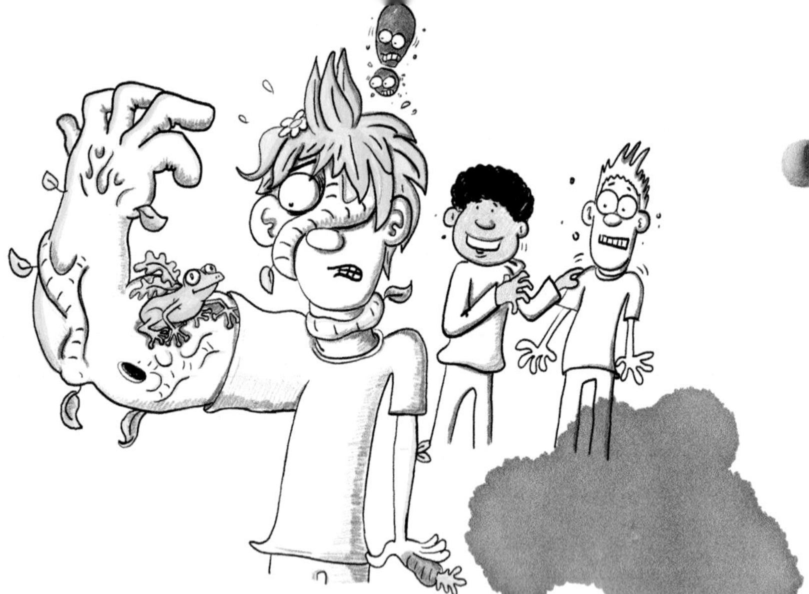

And to top things off,
I just noticed something poking out of my arm. It's Specimen Number Two! That's right, the tree frog must've hitched a ride back at the swamp and now my giganto arm is, apparently, its own ecosystem!

I tried to catch him but he hid immediately. More laughs ensued. Oh, this day.

9:05 A.M.

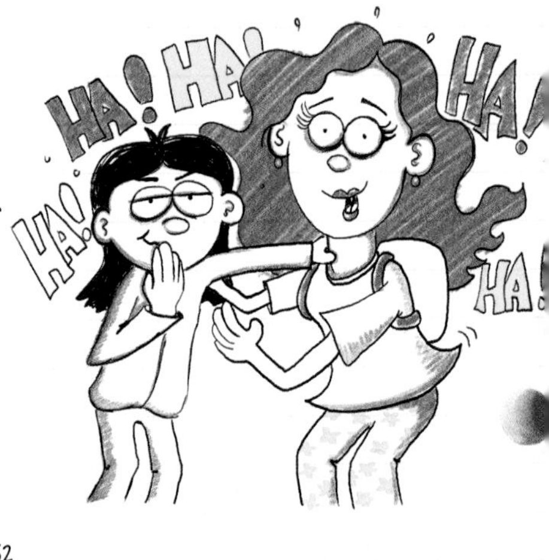
HA! HA!
HA!
HA!
HA!

At my locker now. About to head to P.E. The laughs and stares have continued and I just found out why—Charlotte walked up and handed me her phone and said, "You should see this." Uh-oh.

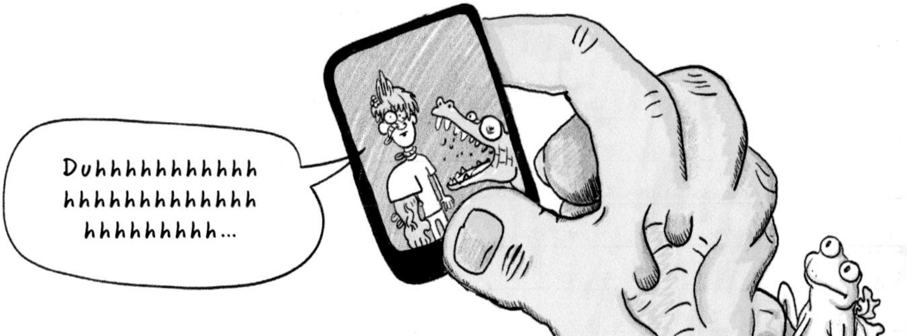
Duhhhhhhhhhhh hhhhhhhhhhhhh hhhhhhhhh...
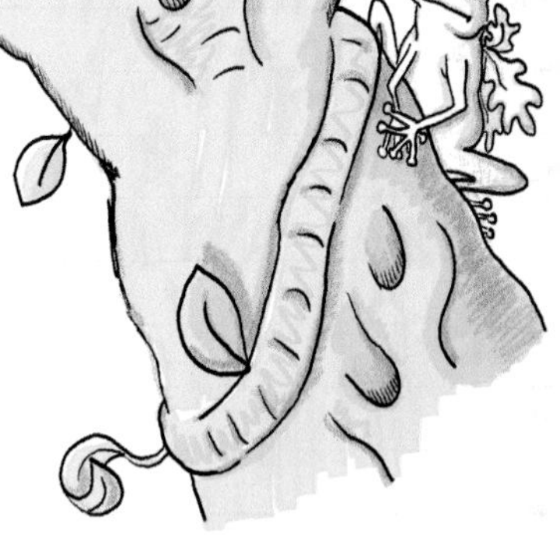

Streaming on Preston's school gossip news site, W.W.H. (Who, What, Huh?) there I was, freezing up in the face-off with the gator for the whole world to mock. I had gone viral. My humiliation was complete.

Okay, my humiliation was not complete. At that moment Nils Canebrake strolled up with his good hair and his pectoral muscles and his skinny jeans. Blech! What a rat! Not only does Nils call me Russ, which I HATE, he has a way of saying terrible things disguised as nice things.

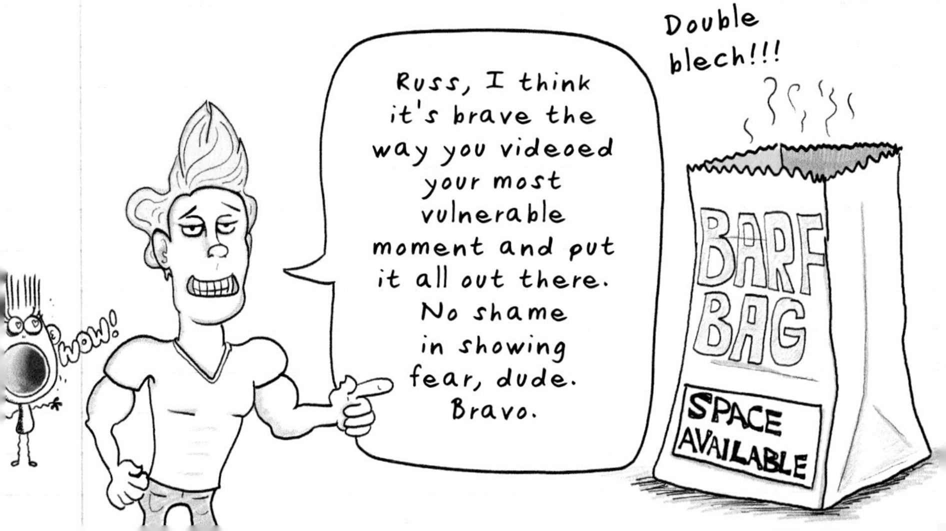
WOW!
Russ, I think it's brave the way you videoed your most vulnerable moment and put it all out there. No shame in showing fear, dude. Bravo.
Double blech!!!
BARF BAG
SPACE AVAILABLE

To make matters worse, Preston walked up all peppy and happy, asking about what everyone was laughing at. My reaction was... well let's just say it might have been detected on several local Richter scales.

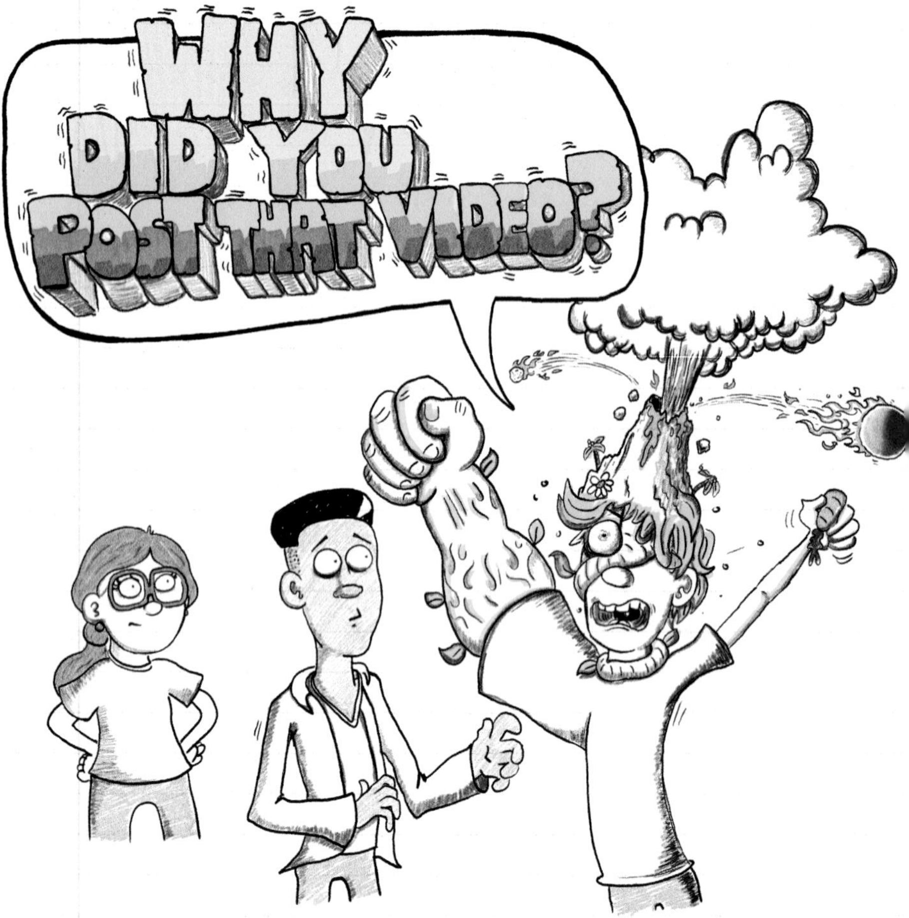
WHY DID YOU POST THAT VIDEO?

I may have overreacted a bit. Preston walked away looking pretty down and Charlotte gave me the eye. That's it—I'm taking a break. Maybe I'll have another update at lunch. We'll see.

TUES. LUNCH

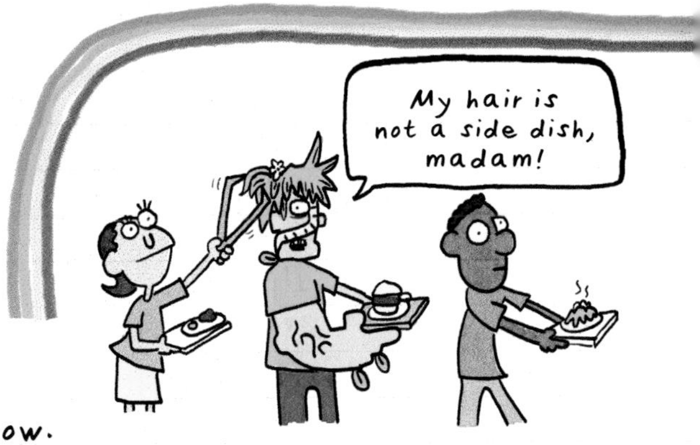
My hair is not a side dish, madam!

OKAY! It's lunchtime now.

Two hours have passed since my meltdown. And my how things have changed. My mood has improved considerably.

So much so that this school meatloaf actually tastes acceptable.

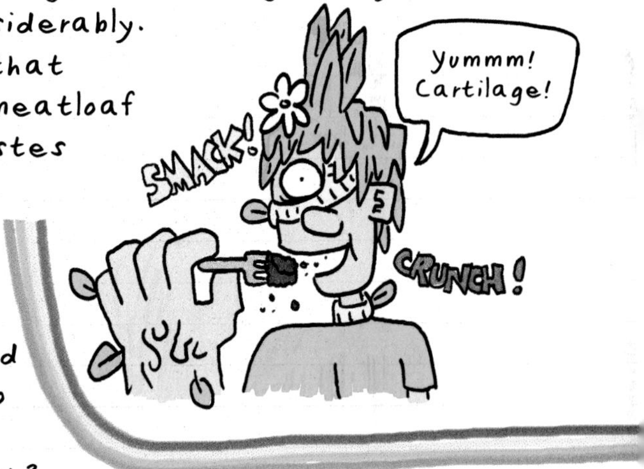
Yummm! Cartilage!
SMACK!
CRUNCH!

What could have happened in two hours to turn my mood around, you ask?

Well, it all started in...

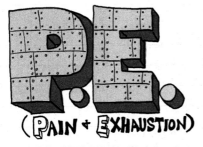

P.E.

(PAIN + EXHAUSTION)

I know what you're thinking: nothing good ever started in P.E., except for maybe a good case of shin splints.

But, trust me on this, today was different.

I was still in a wretched mood at the start of class, and it most def did not improve when Coach Sanchez announced...

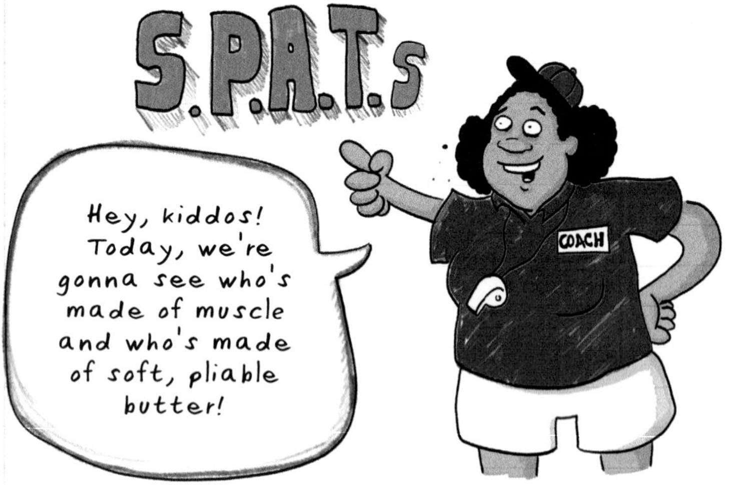
S.P.A.T.s
Hey, kiddos! Today, we're gonna see who's made of muscle and who's made of soft, pliable butter!
COACH

Ugh! I couldn't believe I had forgotten about the S.P.A.T.s, which stands for Student Physical Aptitude Tests! I would have totally prepared for them by, you know, calling out sick with food poisoning.

Preston approached me on the soccer field.

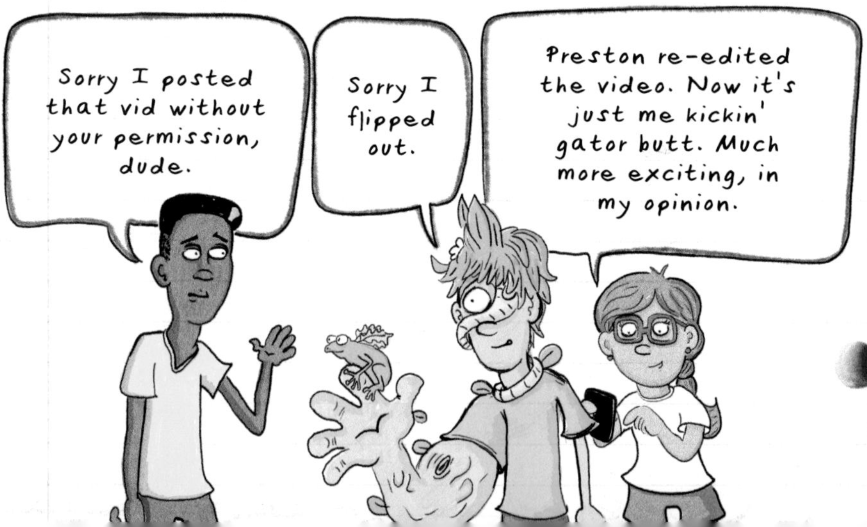
Sorry I posted that vid without your permission, dude.
Sorry I flipped out.
Preston re-edited the video. Now it's just me kickin' gator butt. Much more exciting, in my opinion.

First test, the ten-yard dash. Of course they made me race against Nils, Lord of the Track.

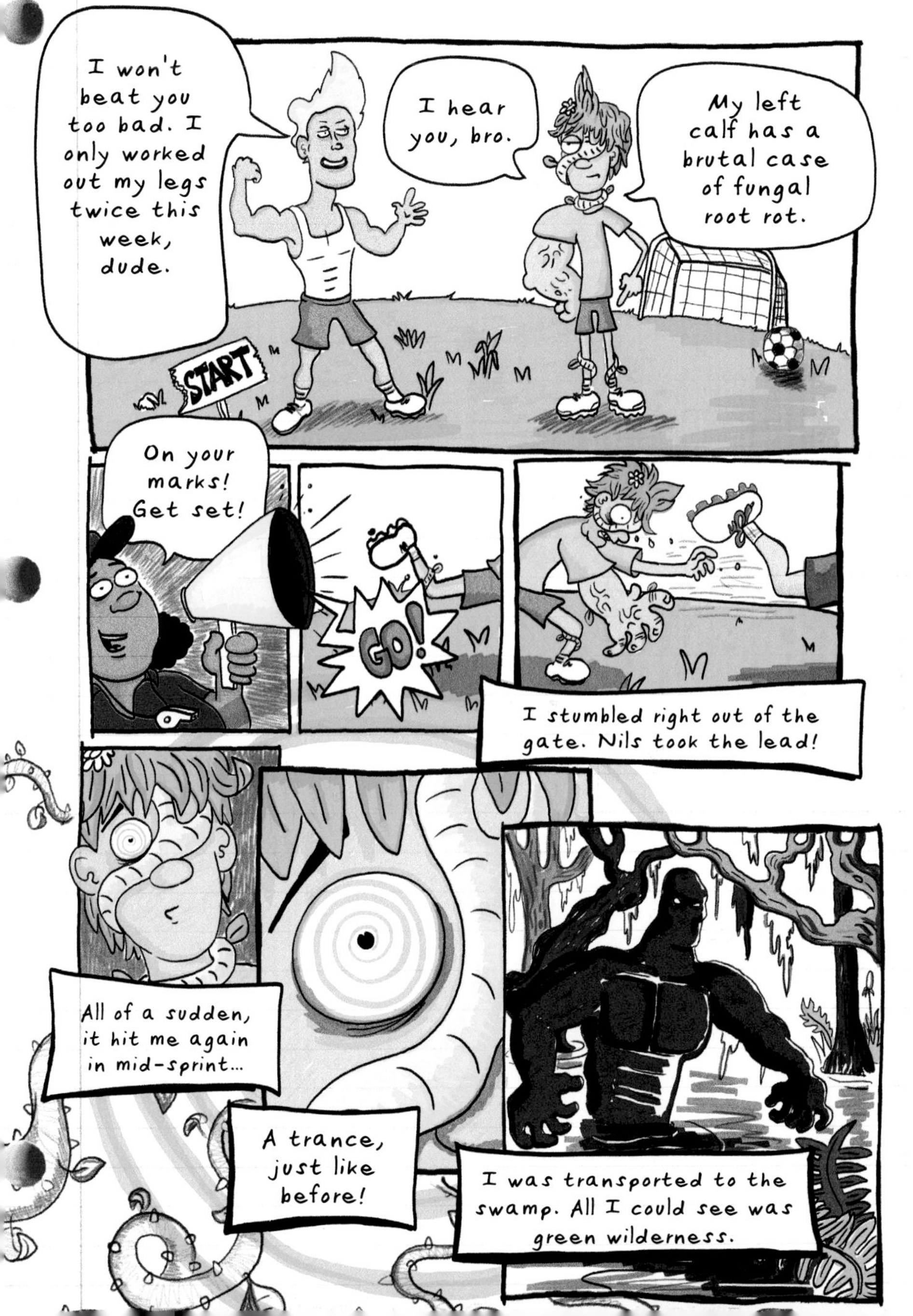
I won't beat you too bad. I only worked out my legs twice this week, dude.
I hear you, bro.
My left calf has a brutal case of fungal root rot.
START
On your marks! Get set!
GO!
I stumbled right out of the gate. Nils took the lead!
All of a sudden, it hit me again in mid-sprint...
A trance, just like before!
I was transported to the swamp. All I could see was green wilderness.

When I snapped out of my daze, people were...congratulating me?

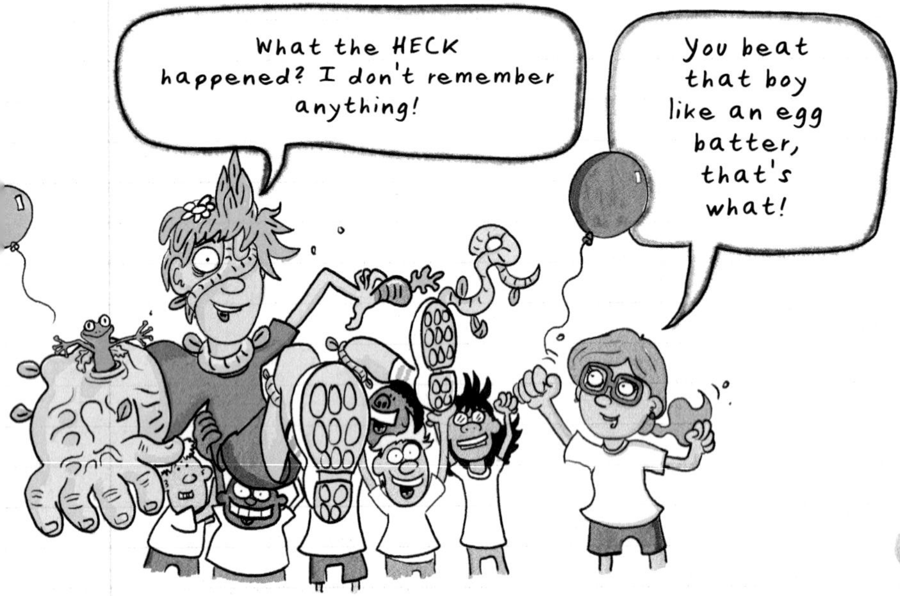
What the HECK happened? I don't remember anything!
You beat that boy like an egg batter, that's what!

Okay, maybe I wasn't actually hoisted up in the air, and maybe there were no balloons or cheers, but I had beaten Nils Canebrake, Mr. Muscles himself! How? Luckily, we had a noted video expert.

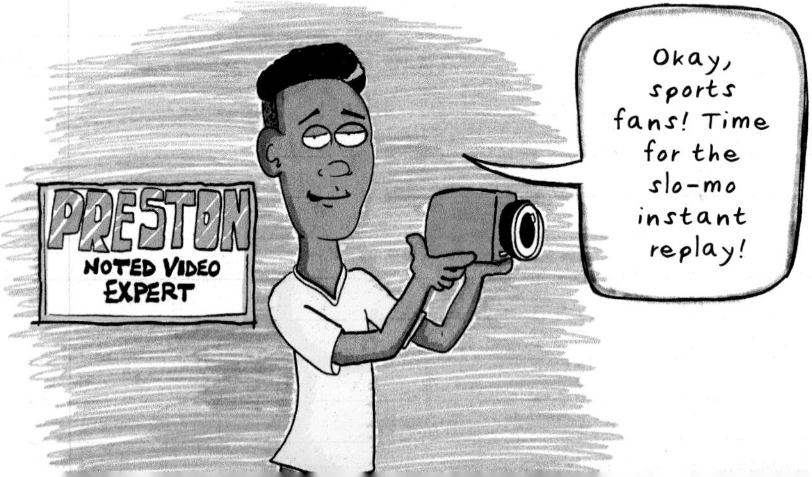
PRESTON
NOTED VIDEO EXPERT
Okay, sports fans! Time for the slo-mo instant replay!

We watched the video in Coach's office. I have to say, it looked like I was pretty far behind Nils at first. But Preston pointed out something I was missing.

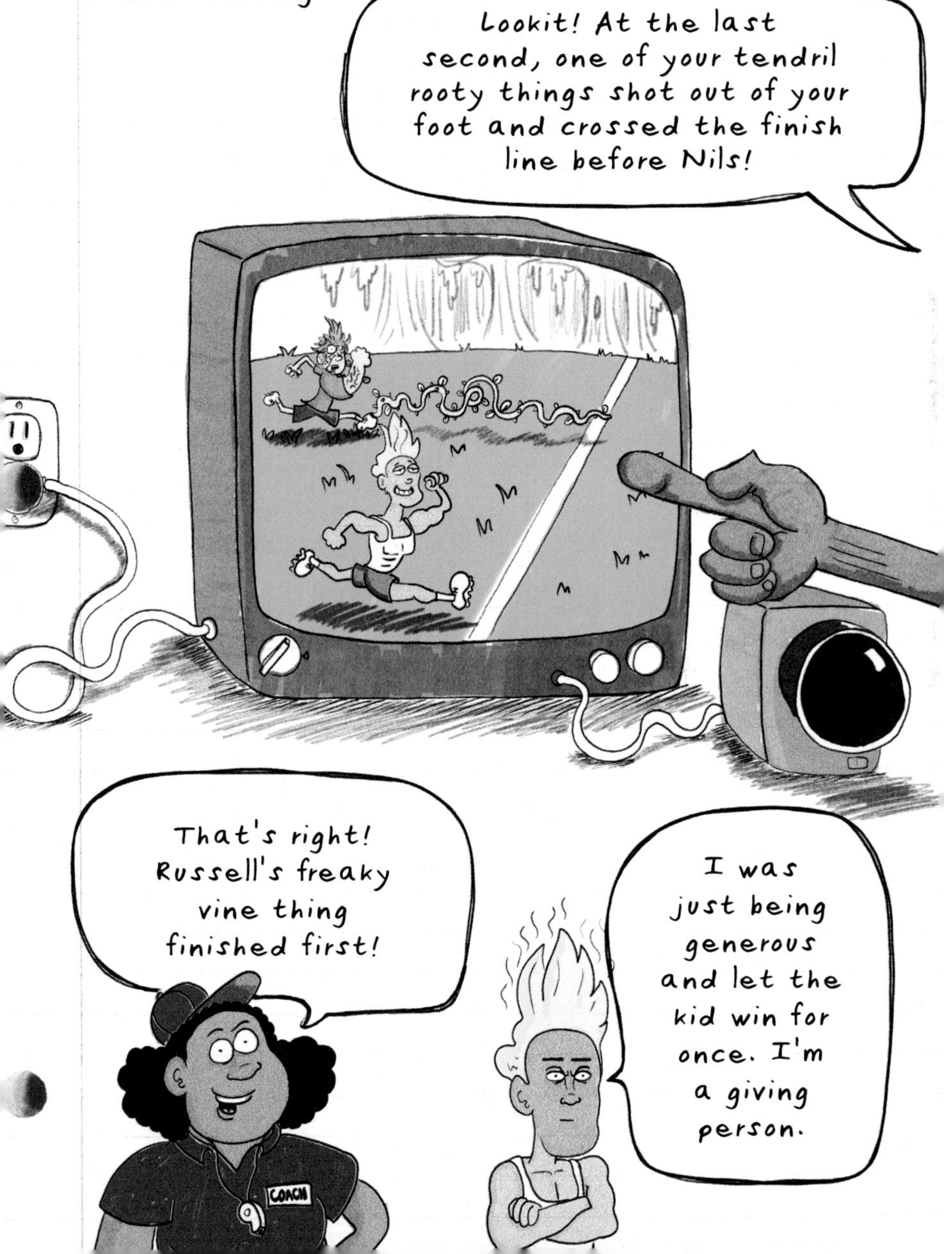
Lookit! At the last second, one of your tendril rooty things shot out of your foot and crossed the finish line before Nils!
That's right! Russell's freaky vine thing finished first!
COACH
I was just being generous and let the kid win for once. I'm a giving person.

There definitely was an extra vine on my big toe. It had shrunk a bit but was still there. I told Charlotte about my trance during the race. And I also mentioned my vision of the swamp.

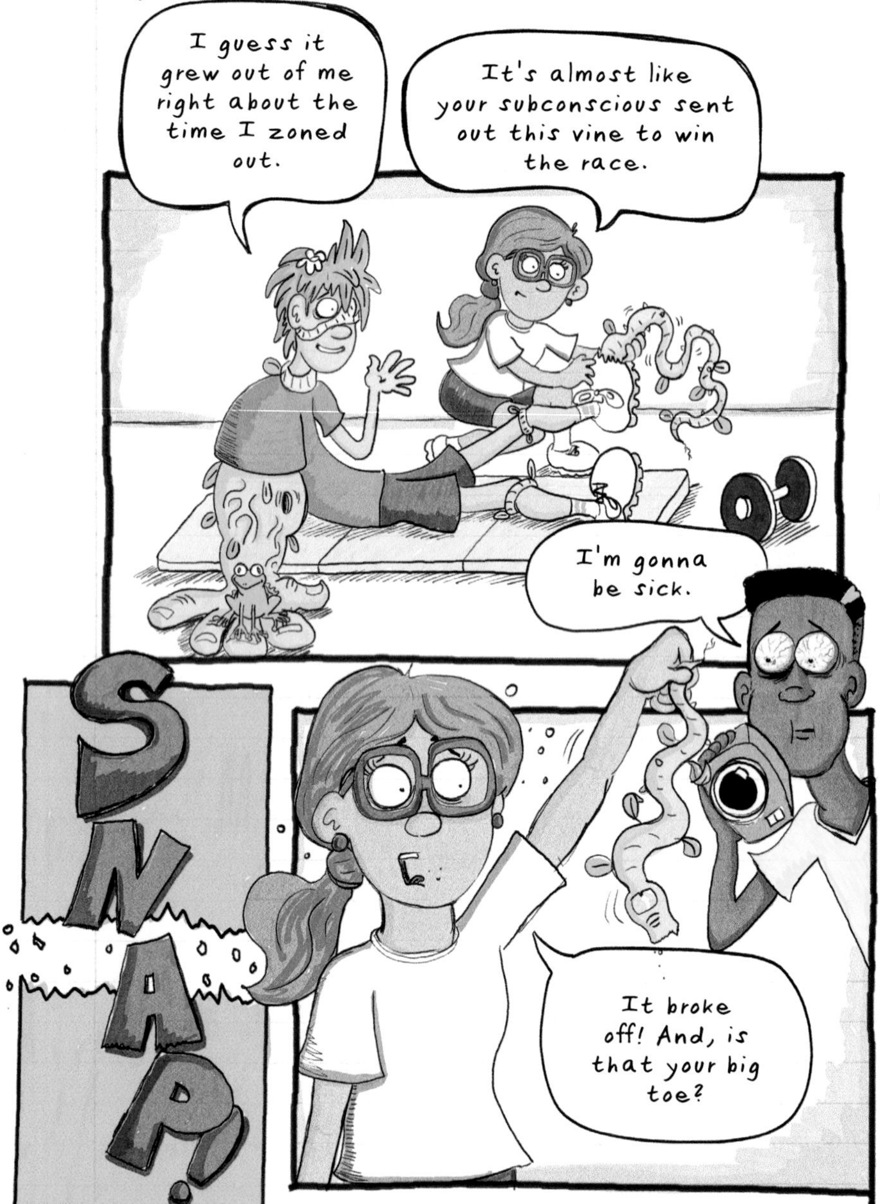
I guess it grew out of me right about the time I zoned out.
It's almost like your subconscious sent out this vine to win the race.
I'm gonna be sick.
SNAP!
It broke off! And, is that your big toe?

Don't worry. My body parts can grow back like a lizard's tail if they fall off. It's one of the few upsides of being half shrub. Most of the time it's a huge bummer...

DRAWBACKS OF BEING SWAMP KID

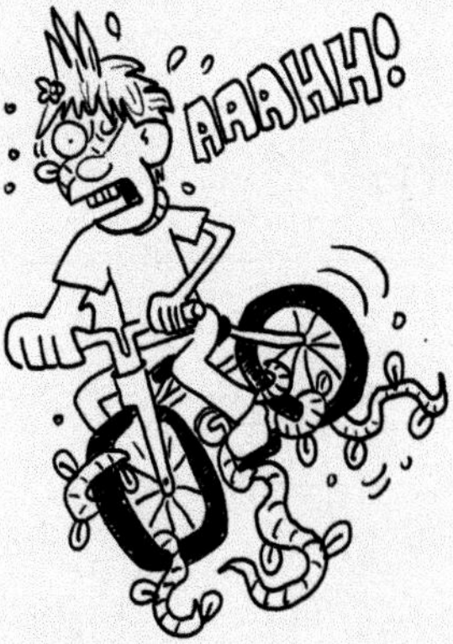
AAAHH!

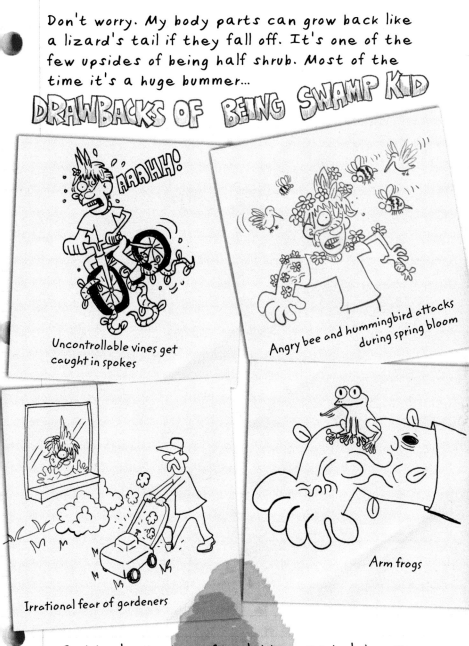

Uncontrollable vines get caught in spokes

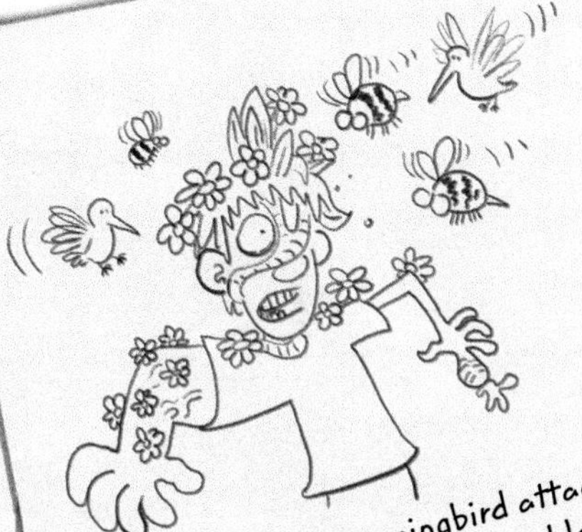

Angry bee and hummingbird attacks during spring bloom

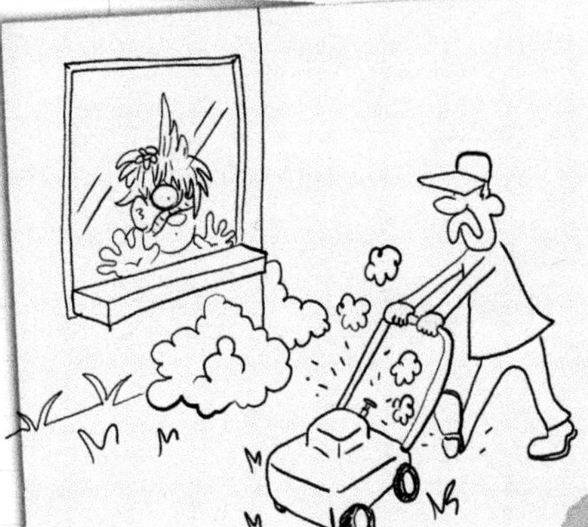

Irrational fear of gardeners

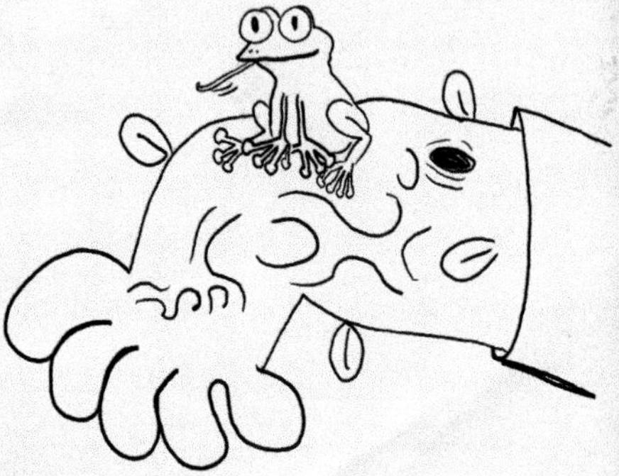

Arm frogs

Suddenly, just as Charlotte was helping me up, we felt a menacing presence behind us...

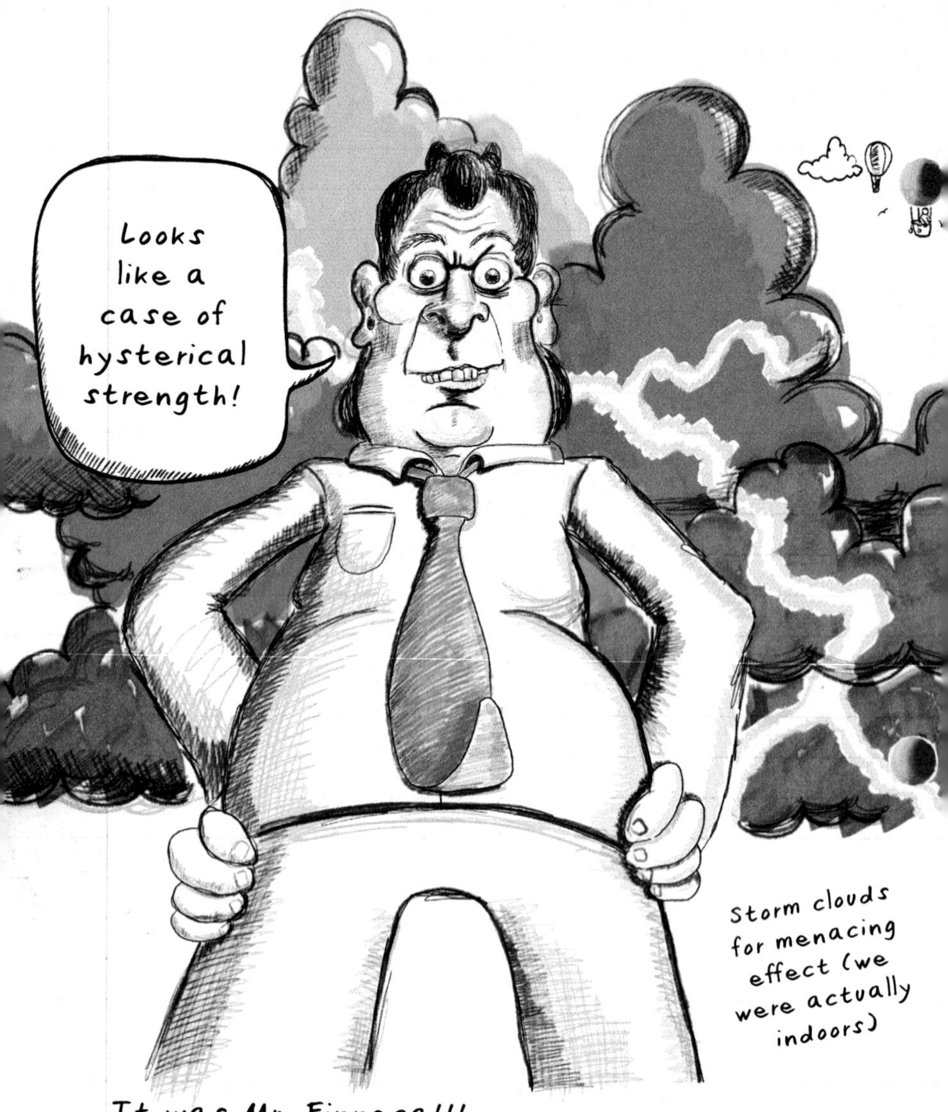
Looks like a case of hysterical strength!
Storm clouds for menacing effect (we were actually indoors)

It was Mr. Finneca!!!
He was towering over us with his freaky squirrel hair and he was going on about something called hysterical strength.
I asked him what's so funny about strength.
He said, "No. The term *hysterical strength* refers to a sudden burst of superhuman ability a person can get when they are facing adversity."

Kind of like those news stories where an ordinary mom lifts a heavy car to save her kid trapped underneath.
I pointed out that I didn't get a sudden burst of strength and I wasn't rescuing anybody.

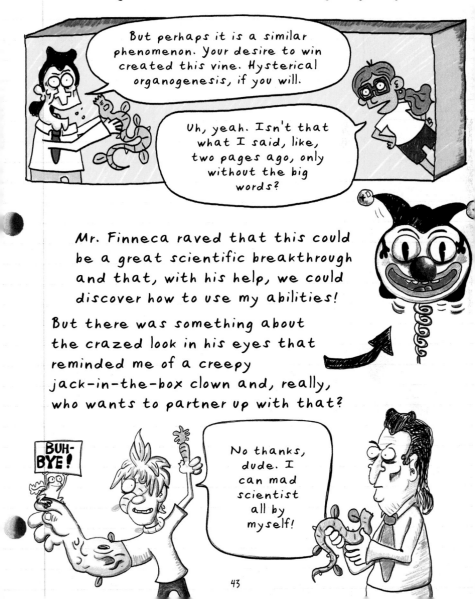

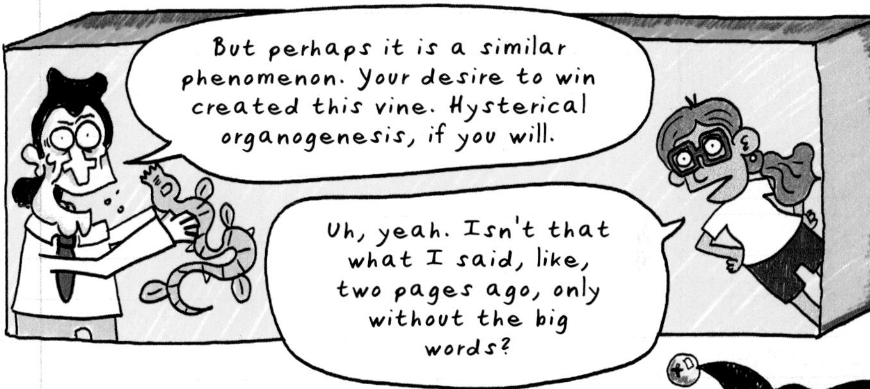
But perhaps it is a similar phenomenon. Your desire to win created this vine. Hysterical organogenesis, if you will.
Uh, yeah. Isn't that what I said, like, two pages ago, only without the big words?

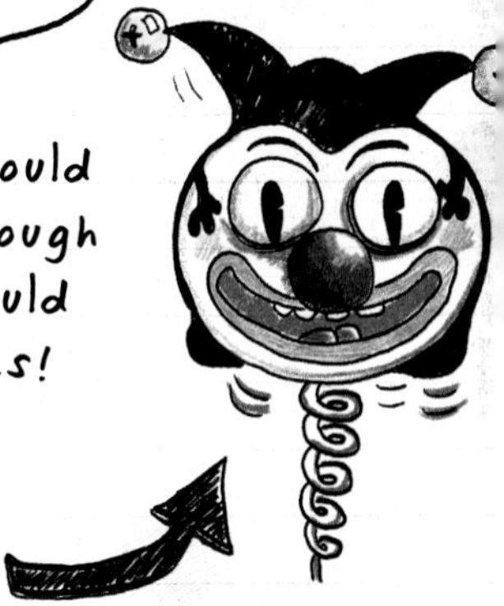

Mr. Finneca raved that this could be a great scientific breakthrough and that, with his help, we could discover how to use my abilities!

But there was something about the crazed look in his eyes that reminded me of a creepy jack-in-the-box clown and, really, who wants to partner up with that?

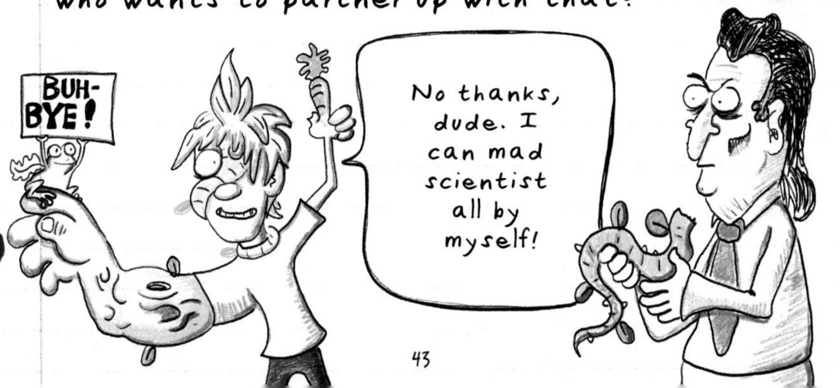
BUH-BYE!
No thanks, dude. I can mad scientist all by myself!

So, that's it.
I'm finally finished with my wild P.E. story and I finished my meatloaf, too, so I'll likely be needing a restroom pronto.

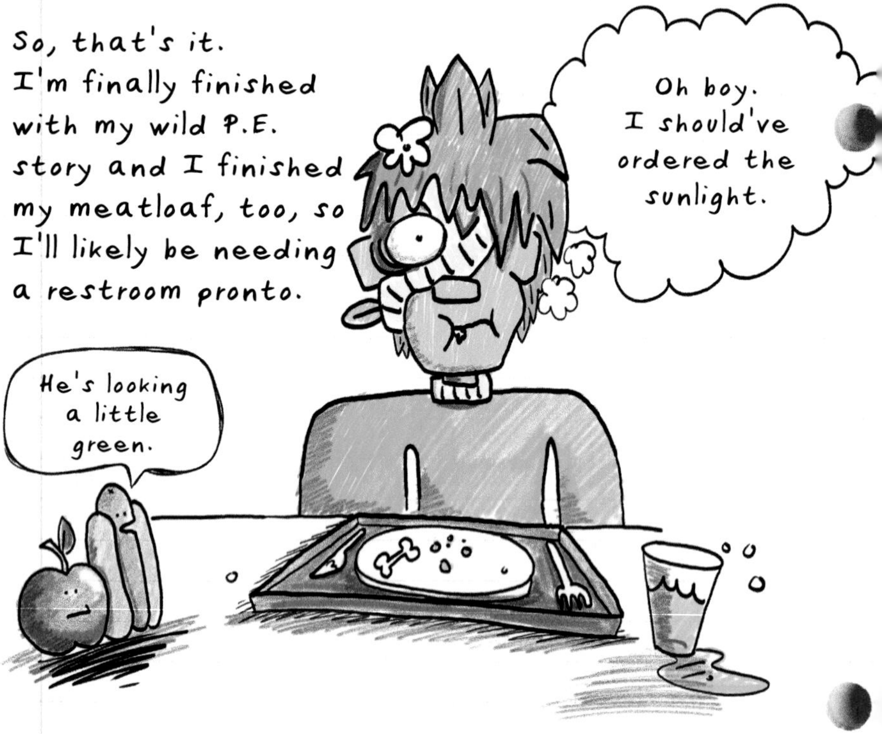
Oh boy. I should've ordered the sunlight.
He's looking a little green.

Oh, wait a sec. Coach Sanchez is motioning me over to the door. Be back in a jiff.

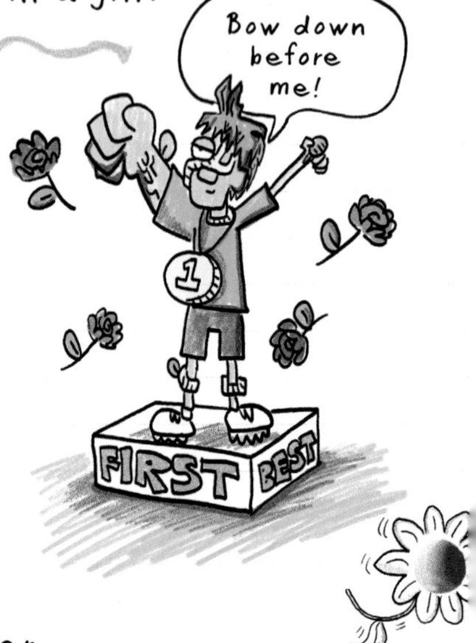
Bow down before me!
1
FIRST
BEST

Okay, how's this for weird? Coach Sanchez just asked me to race in this coming Saturday's track meet! No one's ever asked me to represent them in sports before. It's like asking a three-legged mutt with fleas to enter a dog show. Still, winning against Nils today felt awfully good. I told Coach I'd think it over.

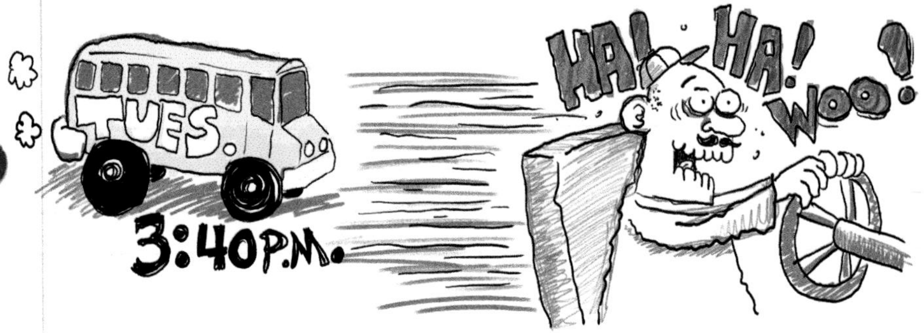
TUES.
3:40P.M.
HA! HA!
WOO!

Please forgive my herky-jerky handwriting. I'm on the bus. Old Pete is our driver and, let's just say Pete was demolition derby driving champion fifteen years in a row and he's having a hard time letting go of the glory days! Nothing much to report, except that Preston decided to sit with me today for the first time. AND he never even pulled out his camera! Maybe I am more than just a yearbook story to him?

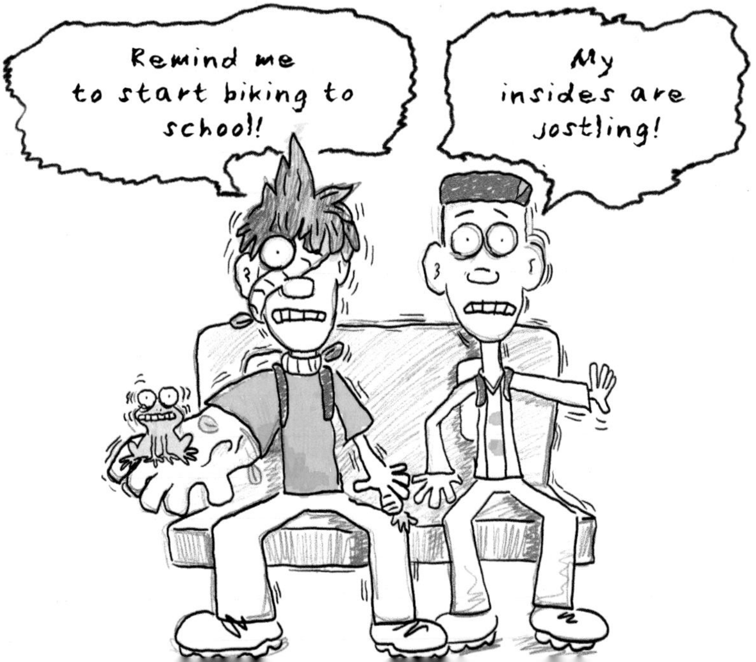
Remind me to start biking to school!
My insides are jostling!

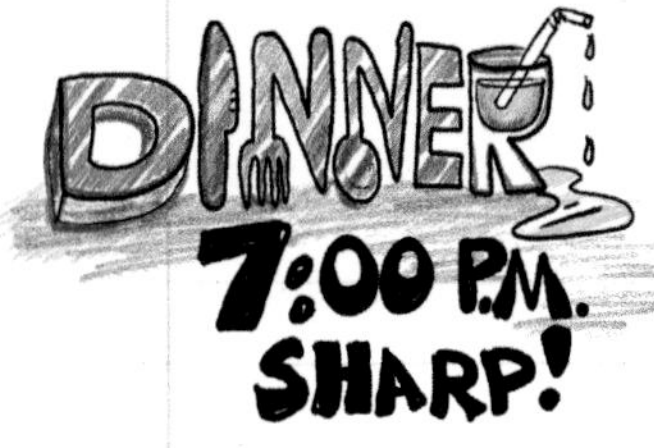
DINNER
7:00 P.M. SHARP!

Mom made jambalaya tonight. As usual, it was on point. I told my folks about Coach Sanchez's offer before dessert.

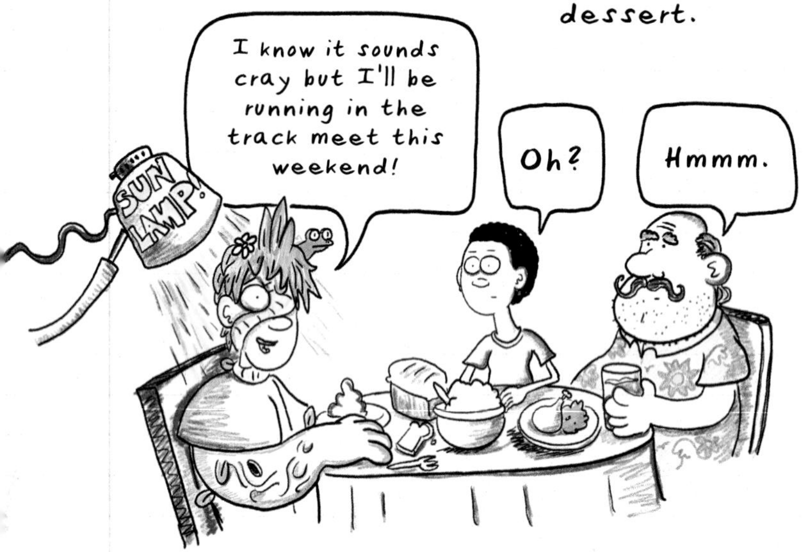
I know it sounds cray but I'll be running in the track meet this weekend!
Oh?
Hmmm.
SUN LAMP!

Can't you just feel the excitement radiating from them? There's a reason they're being a little cautious. They've seen me get burned before.

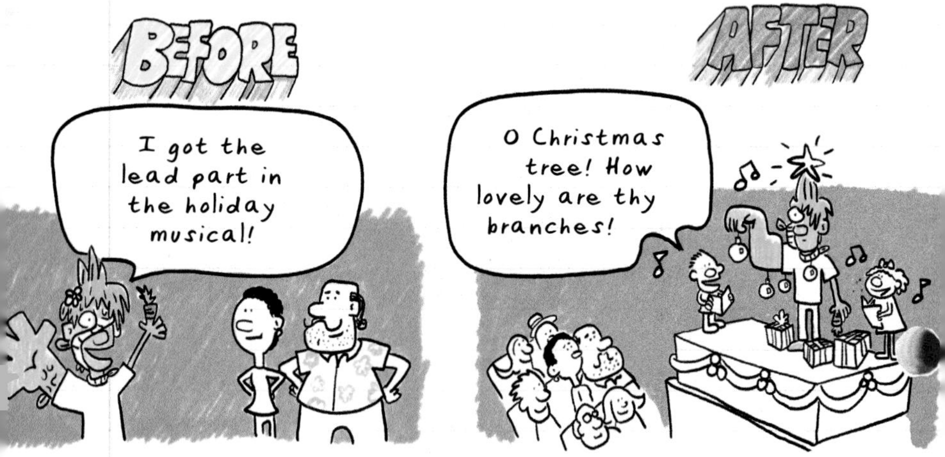
BEFORE
AFTER
I got the lead part in the holiday musical!
O Christmas tree! How lovely are thy branches!

I get why my parents have been a little overprotective of me. When I was first discovered it was a huge deal.

MYSTERY SWAMP BABY BAFFLES AUTHORITIES

HOUMA, LA - Local police and botanists are utterly perplexed by the case of the apparently half-person/half-vegetation sensation locally known as Swamp Baby. The infant was found deep in the marsh of Terrebonne Parish by local couple Adam and Zoey Weinwright, who have filed papers to adopt the bouncing bayou baby.

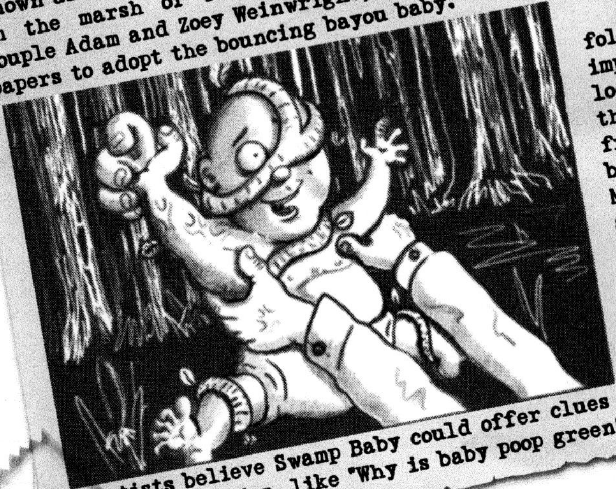

Scientists believe Swamp Baby could offer clues to life's mysteries, like "Why is baby poop green?"

Many in the city of
if the child is some ho
legend of Swamp Thing
thought to be composed
plant matter and possi
disappearance of Profe
years ago.

Sheriff Corey Ever
folks not to give in to
implausible rumors re
local swamps, but many
the theory that the ch
from the same malady
by a link to Swamp Thi
Mayor Candace Bonnavo
advises calm and reas
jump to conclusions.

Several experts fr
of Arcane Incorporate
fly in to conduct tes
on the infant. Samp
leaf and stem plus a
vial of green liqui

I know what you're thinking—they used to print the news on paper? Crazy, I know. But anyway, as you can see, I was all the rage with reporters and scientists. The hubbub died down though. I mean, who really cares about me when we have Superman buzzing around? I'm only pond scum, remember?

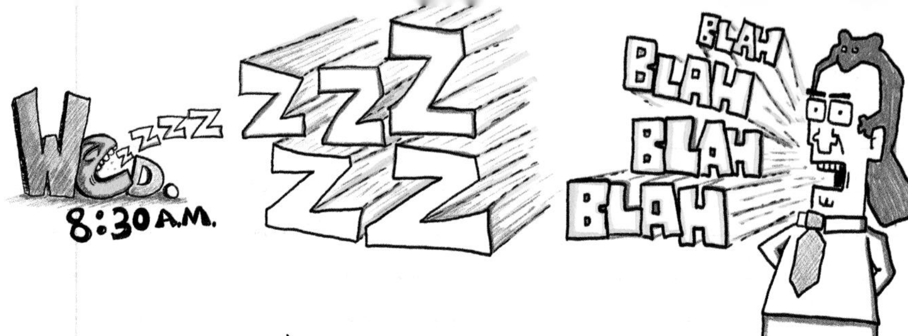
WED.
ZZZZZ
8:30 A.M.
ZZZZ
BLAH
BLAH
BLAH
BLAH

O.M.G., I'm so tired and bored this morning. Mr. Finneca is rambling on about instinct and natural selection. I can tell this is going to be one of those days. It's going to require every ounce of willpower to take notes and not fall aslee

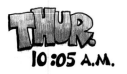

THUR.
10:05 A.M.

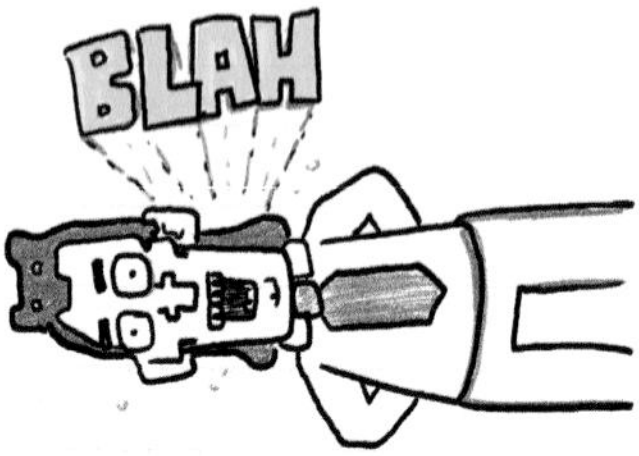
BLAH

I told Coach I'd run in this weekend's meet and she was super jazzed. She had me race the rest of class on the soccer field for practice. To my surprise, not only did I win again, but this time a vine shot out of my giant arm, even after I fell on my face! There's no way I can lose!

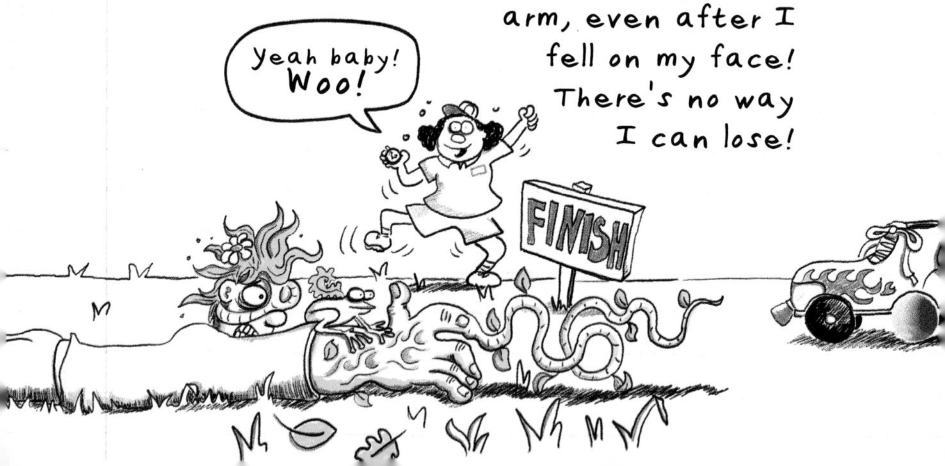
Yeah baby! Woo!
FINISH

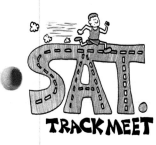

SAT. TRACK MEET

Saturday morning! The big day! Man it's early! Seriously, why am I here at seven a.m. just to sit and wait for my race? Lots of time to sketch, I suppose.

We are at our rival school, Cypress Hollow, and their stands are packed with people. Everybody's here!

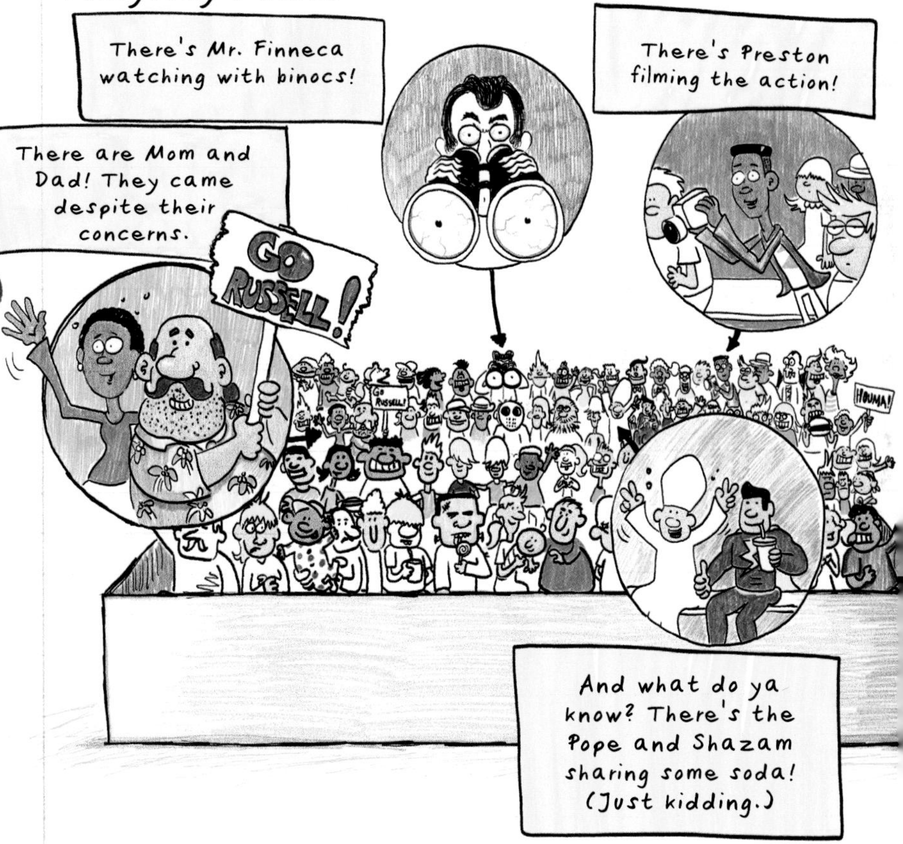

There's Mr. Finneca watching with binocs!
There's Preston filming the action!
There are Mom and Dad! They came despite their concerns.
GO RUSSELL!
HOUMA!
And what do ya know? There's the Pope and Shazam sharing some soda! (Just kidding.)

Welp! I'd better put this away and get out to the track. My race is coming up. I'll fill you in on my glorious victory tonight!

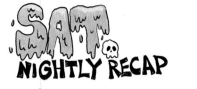

SAT. NIGHTLY RECAP

Sigh...wanna know how the track meet went? Well, how do you think it went?

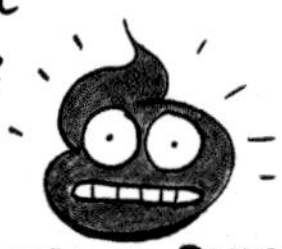

CHOCOLATE PUDDING EMOJI

Charlotte had just placed second in the two-mile run when I stepped up to the track.

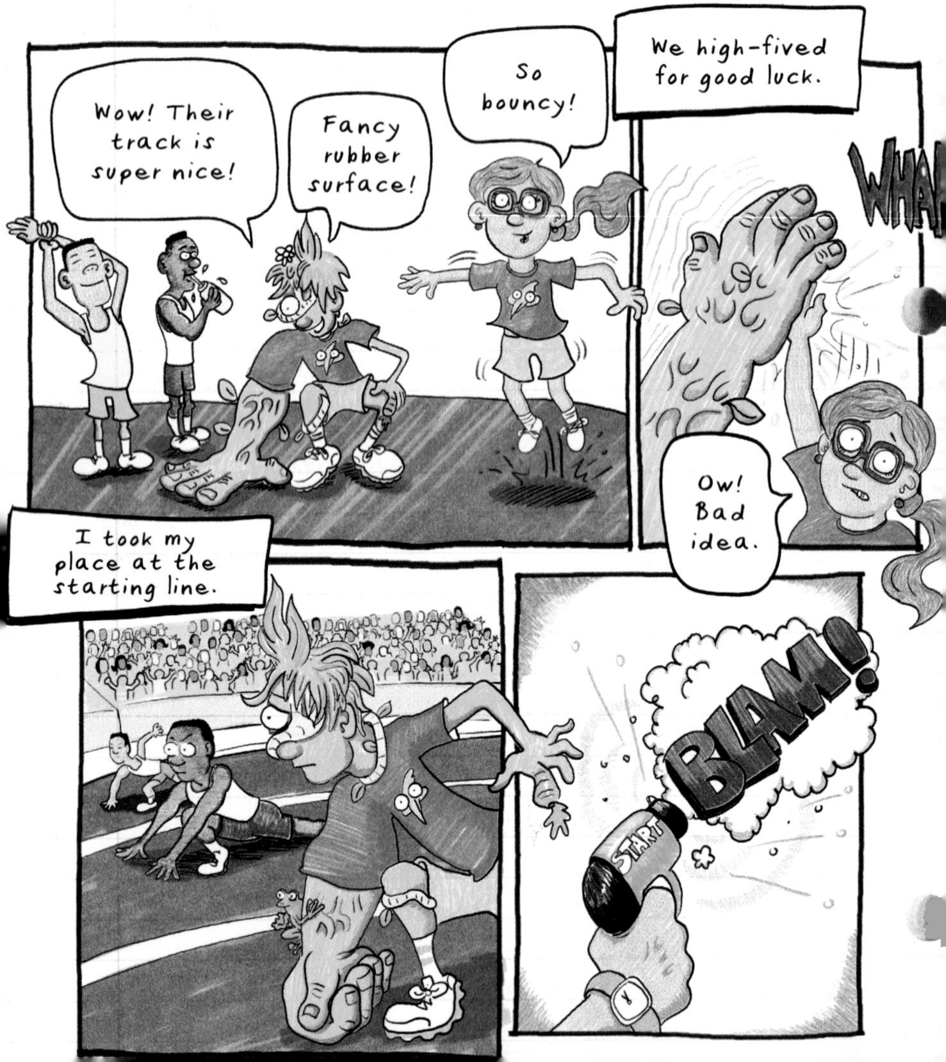

Wow! Their track is super nice!
Fancy rubber surface!
So bouncy!
We high-fived for good luck.
Ow! Bad idea.
I took my place at the starting line.
START
BLAM!

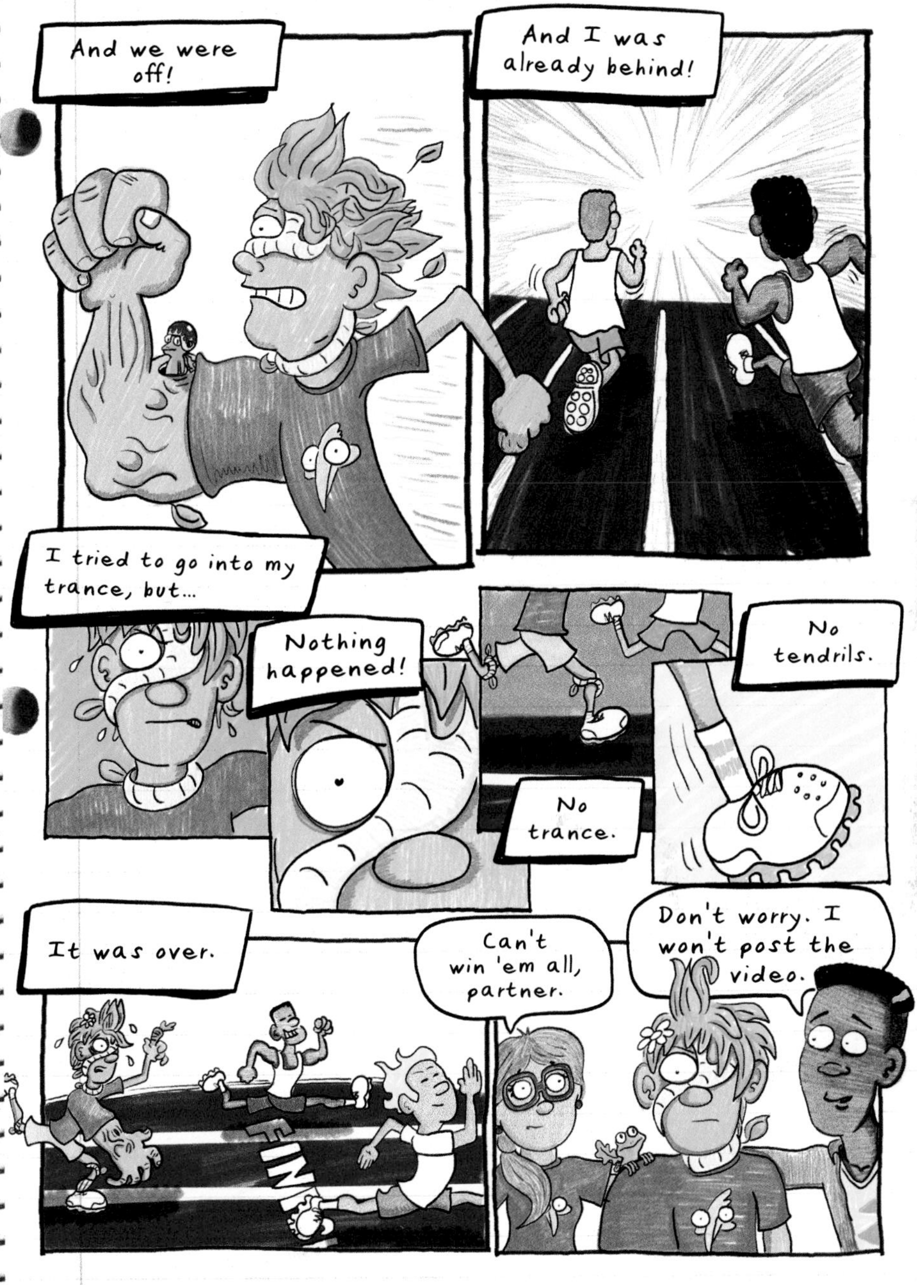
And we were off!
And I was already behind!
I tried to go into my trance, but...
Nothing happened!
No trance.
No tendrils.
It was over.
Can't win 'em all, partner.
Don't worry. I won't post the video.

The shame was unbearable. What had gone wrong? Where were my freakish plant powers when I needed them?

Now I can't sleep. Just lying here, completely bummed. For a brief moment I thought I had control over this embarrassing curse. But I'm still just a freak. And a powerless, disappointing, unimpressive freak at that.

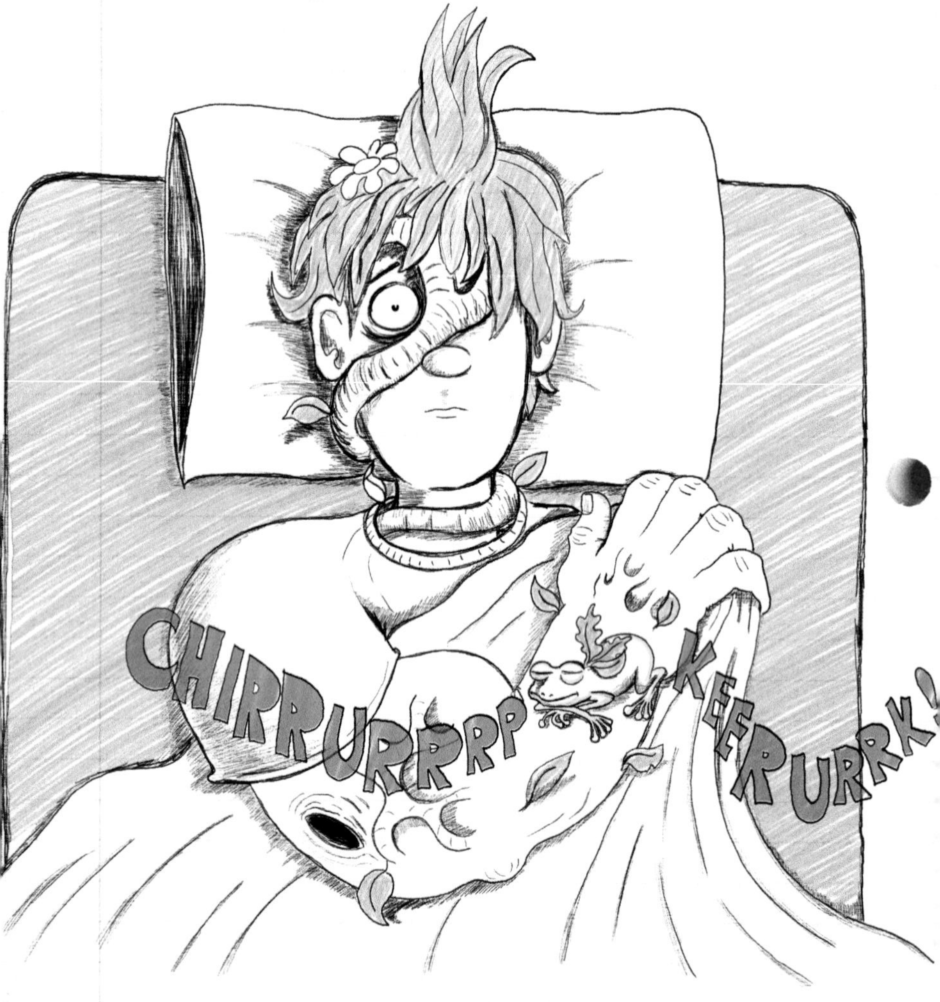
CHIRRURRRP
KEERURRK!

Specimen Number Two is singing his nightly frog song. Most of the time it keeps me awake, but tonight it sounds kinda nice. Soothing. Good night.

SUN. MORN.

Ugh. Still feeling irked about the track meet.

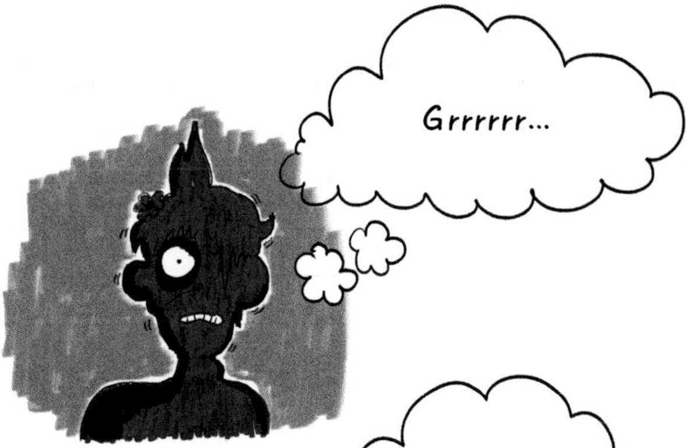
Grrrrrr...

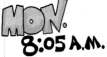

MON. 8:05 A.M.

My rotten mood is worse today.

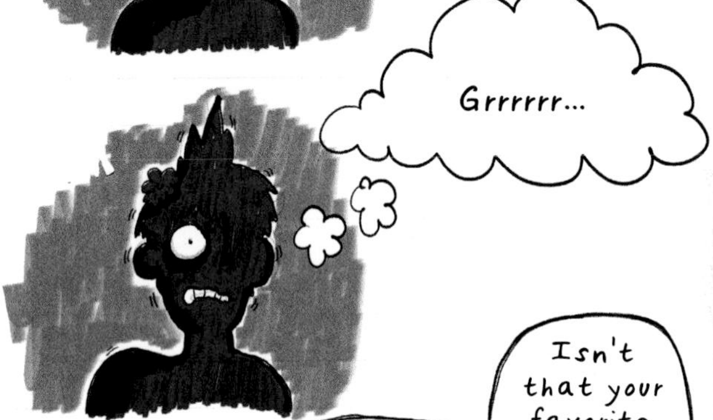
Grrrrrr...

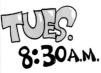

TUES. 8:30 A.M.

Hey! I'm actually feeling better today!

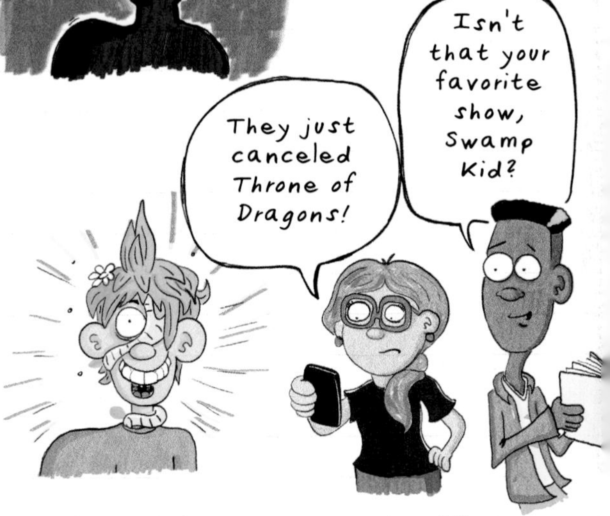
They just canceled Throne of Dragons!
Isn't that your favorite show, Swamp Kid?

WED. 8:05 A.M.

The darkness continues.

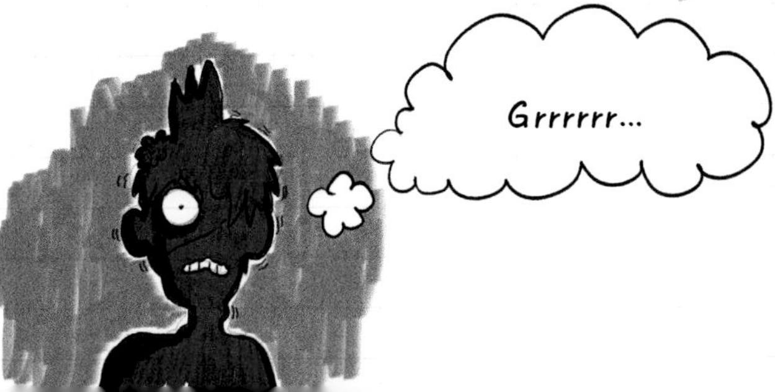
Grrrrrr...

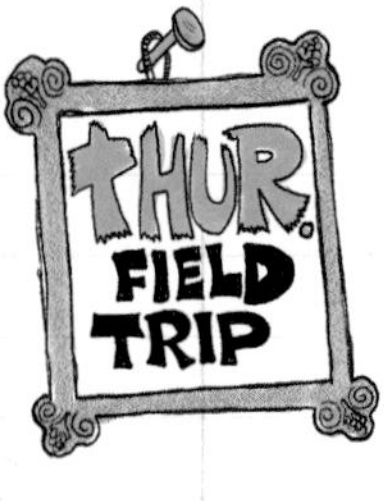
THUR.
FIELD TRIP

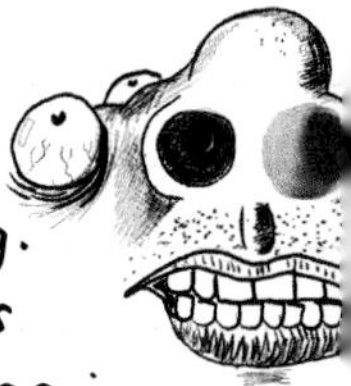

I am definitely feeling less gloomy today, which is a good thing. It's field trip day with Ms. Moss's art class. We're sitting in the grass in front of the Houma Art Museum.

In honor of the abstract art exhibit, I've decided to draw the three of us in the style of Picasso.

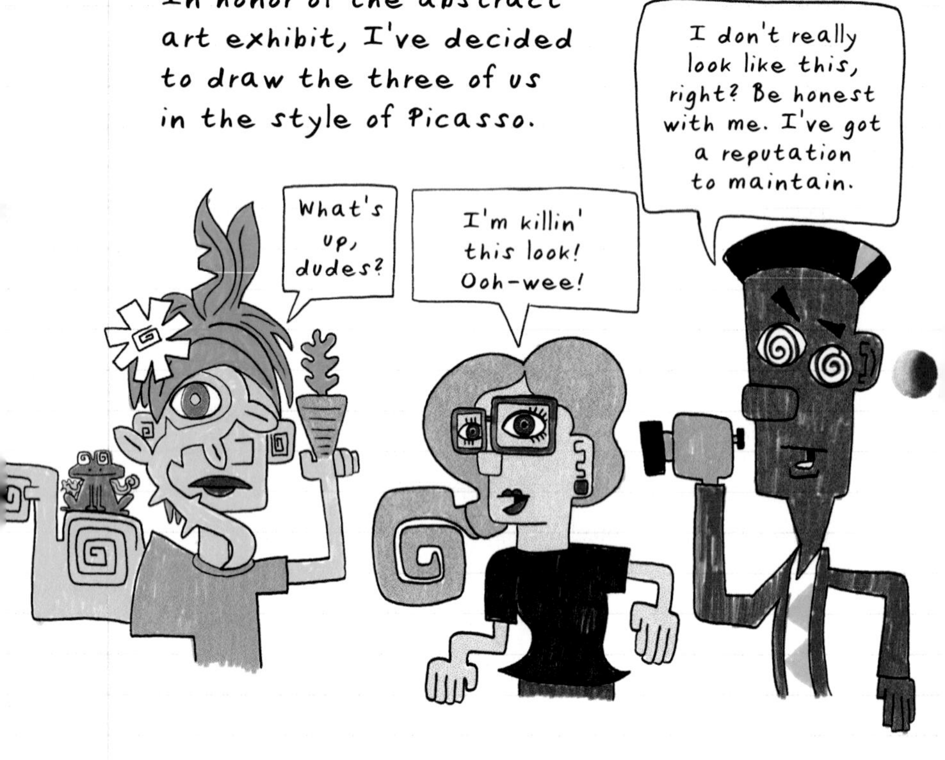
What's up, dudes?
I'm killin' this look! Ooh-wee!
I don't really look like this, right? Be honest with me. I've got a reputation to maintain.

Not that the Houma art museum actually has any Picassos, although there is a painting of a cute puppy by someone named Enrique Picasso.

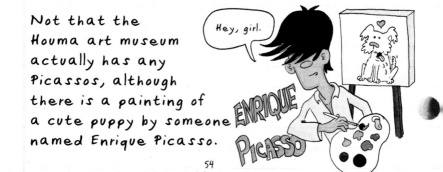

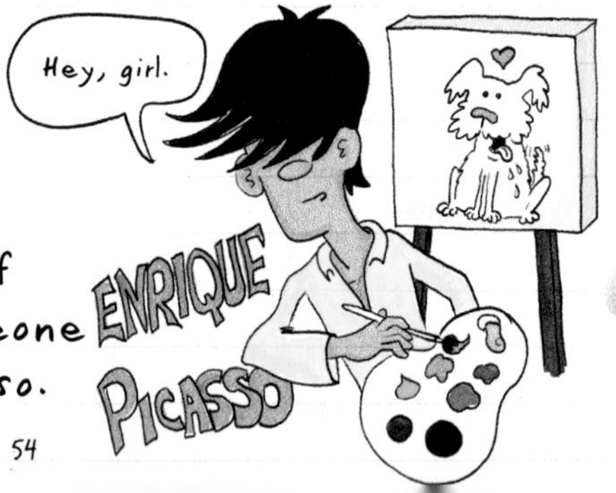
Hey, girl.
ENRIQUE PICASSO

RAINDROP STAIN. (Possibly drool.)

I just apologized to Charlotte and Preston for being such a wet blanket the last few days. They're cool. We've made a pact to figure out the mystery of my plant powers together.

Ooh! Big thunder nearby!
Starting to rain.
Gotta find shelter!

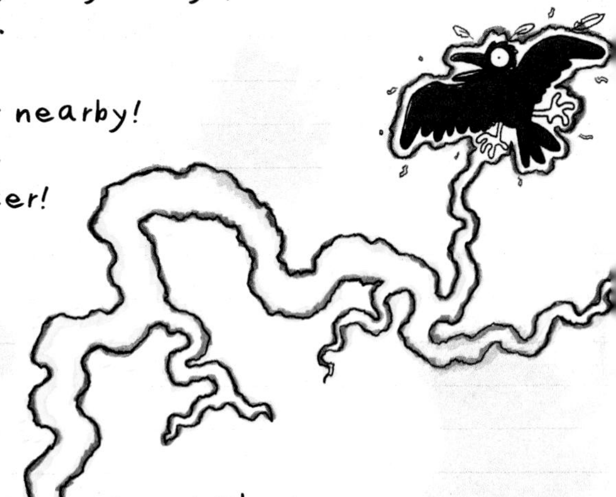

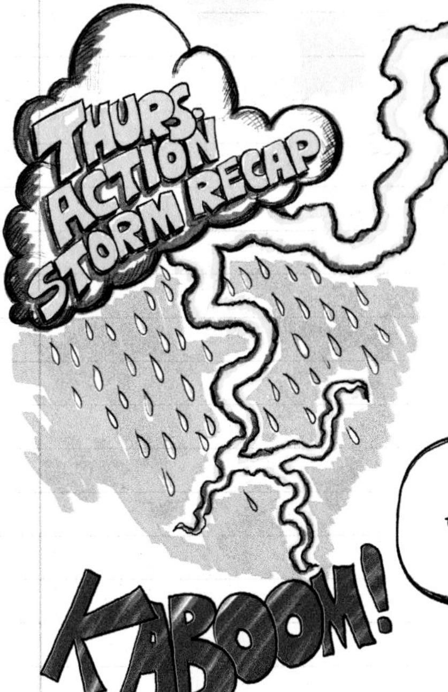
THURS. ACTION STORM RECAP
KABOOM!

Okay! I'm home now, safe and sound, but you are NOT going to believe what happened at the museum!

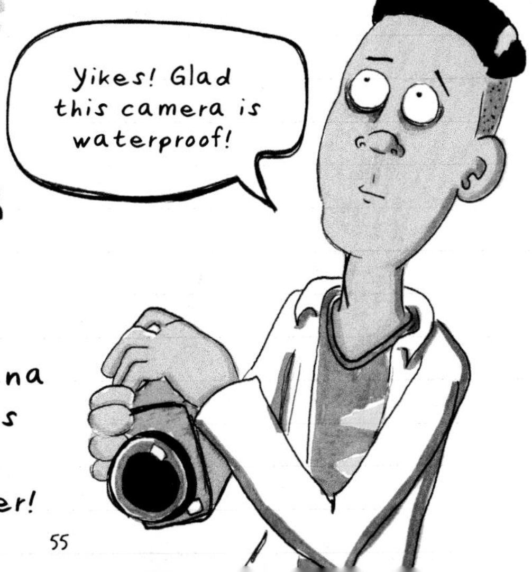
Yikes! Glad this camera is waterproof!

A crazy big Louisiana thunderstorm hit us out of nowhere. We had to seek shelter!

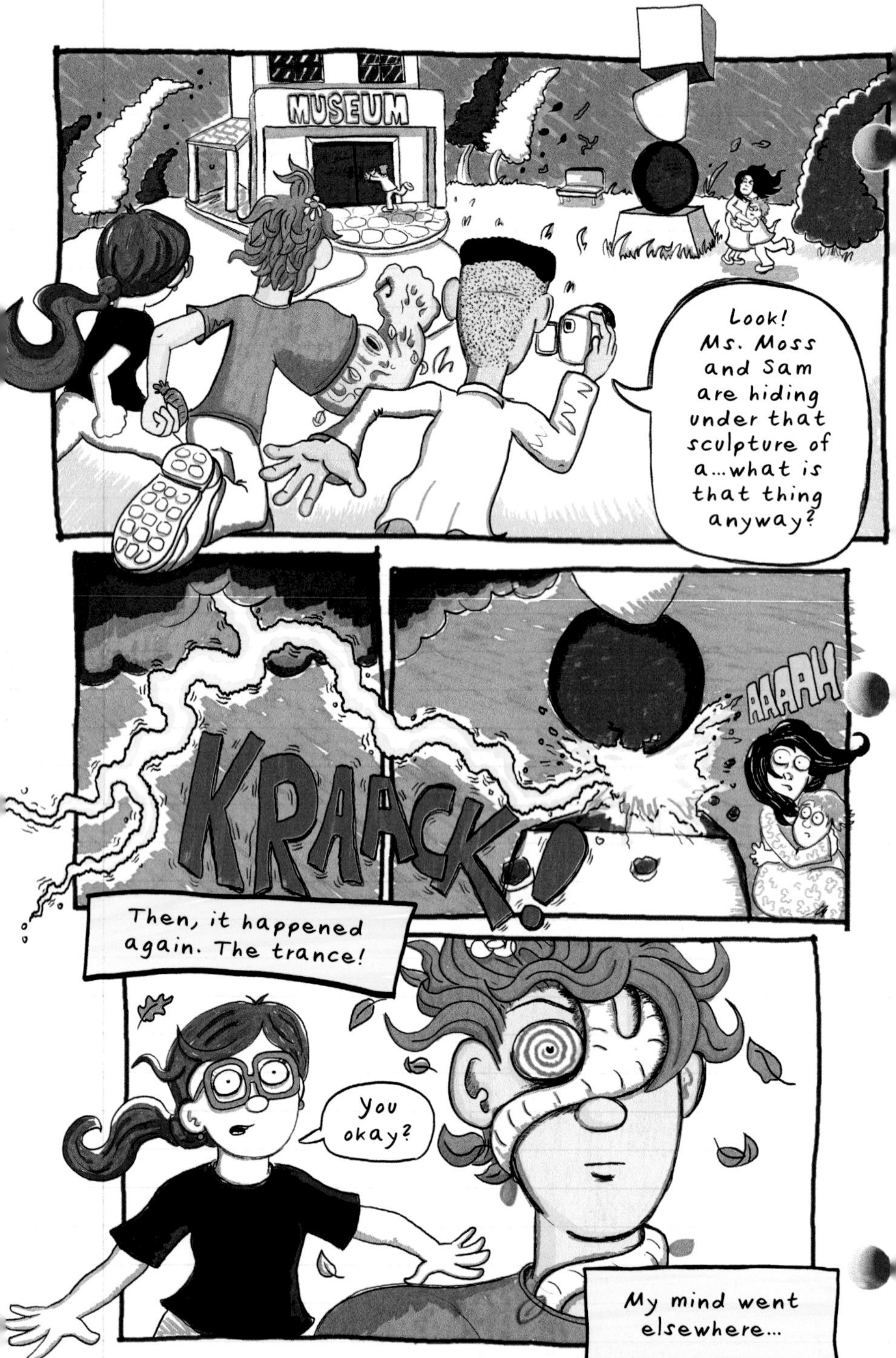
MUSEUM
Look! Ms. Moss and Sam are hiding under that sculpture of a...what is that thing anyway?
KRAACK!!
AAAAH
Then, it happened again. The trance!
You okay?
My mind went elsewhere...

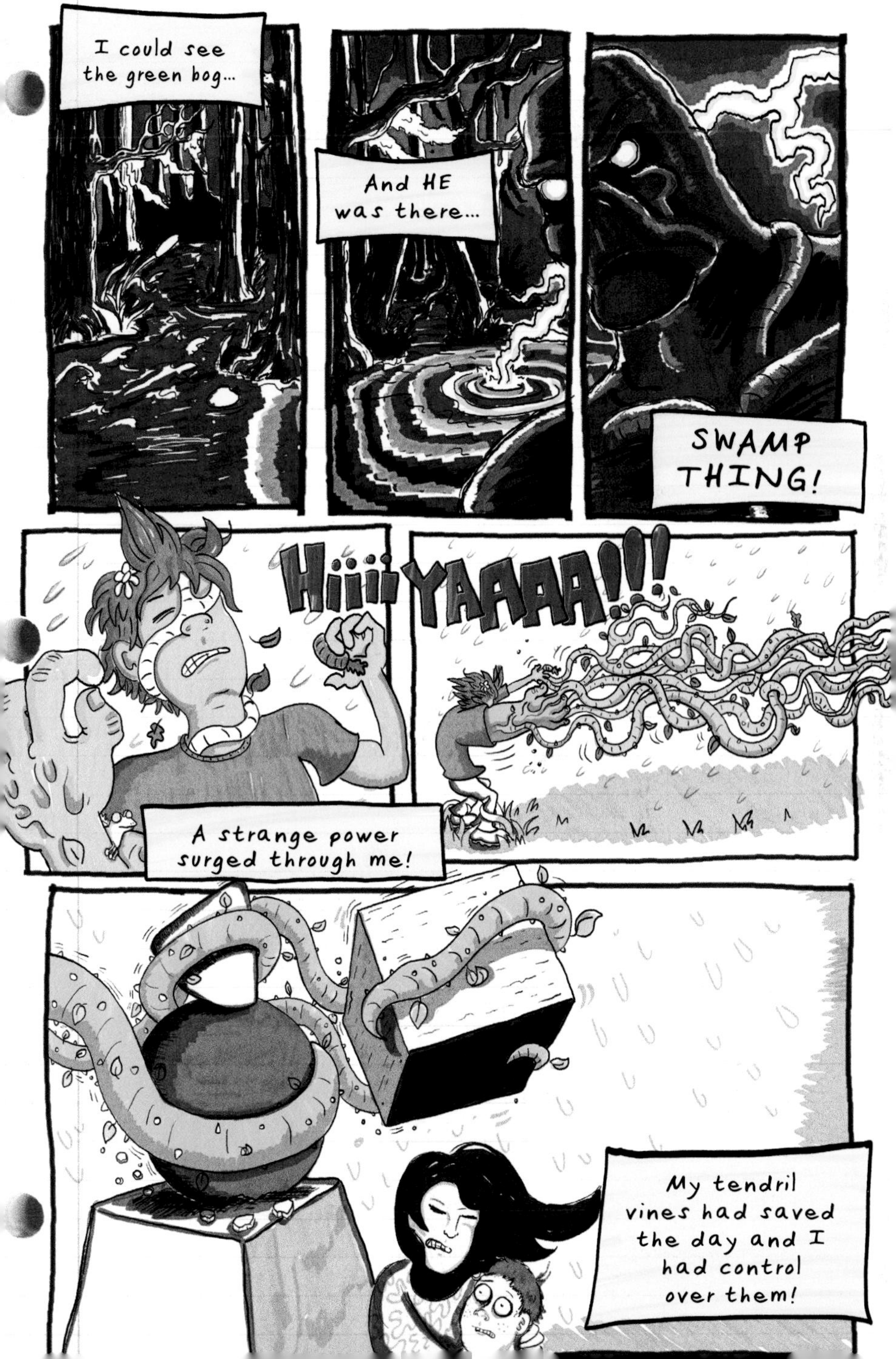

I could see the green bog...
And HE was there...
SWAMP THING!
HiiiiYAAAA!!!
A strange power surged through me!
My tendril vines had saved the day and I had control over them!

The storm blew out just as quickly as it had hit. I begged everyone to keep quiet about what I had done.

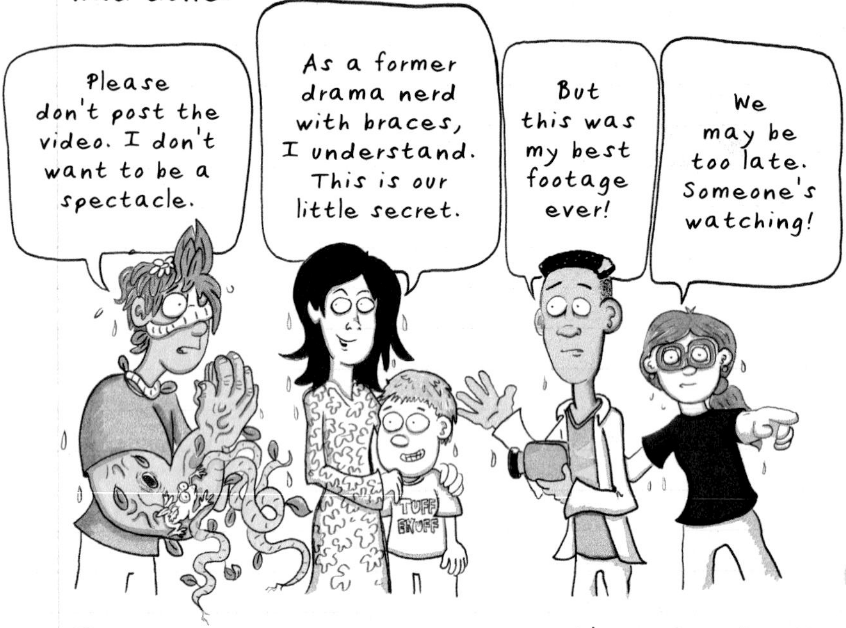
Please don't post the video. I don't want to be a spectacle.
As a former drama nerd with braces, I understand. This is our little secret.
But this was my best footage ever!
We may be too late. Someone's watching!
TUFF ENUFF

In the distance sat a shady black S.U.V. with a dude in a shady black suit wearing shady black, uh, shades. The side of his van said ARCANE INC. on it. Had he seen what happened? Did he know about my powers?

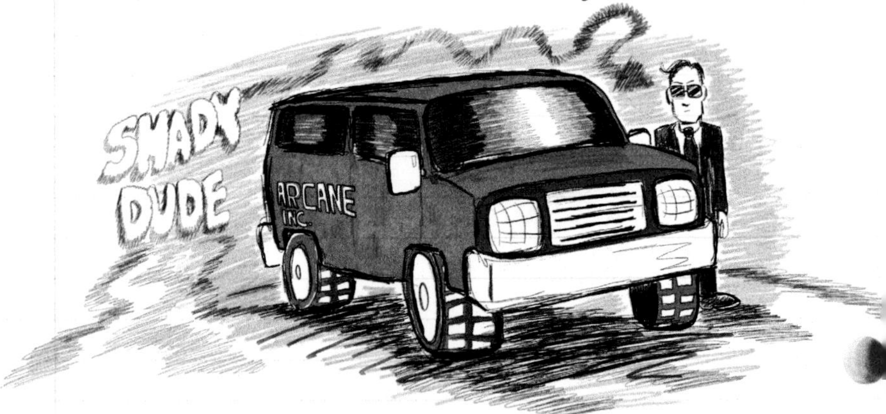
SHADY DUDE
ARCANE INC.

We didn't wait around to find out.
It was time to head back to school.

Fri. Science CLASS

8:07 A.M.

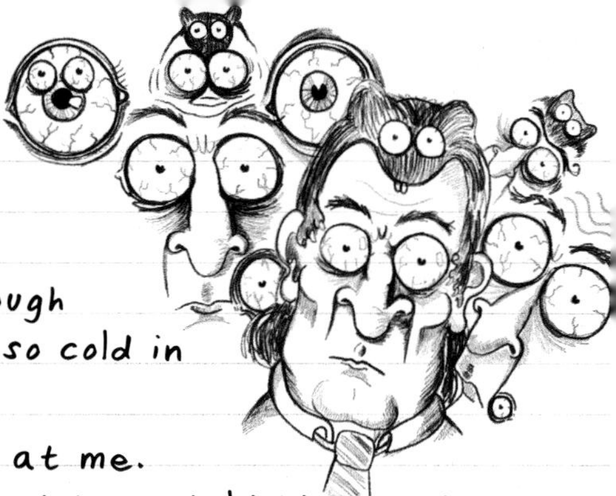

Science class is rough this morning. It's so cold in here.

Mr. Finneca is glaring at me. He knows. Someone must have told him what happened at the art museum. But Ms. Moss would never tell. She promised not to reveal that I saved her and Sam...SAM!!!

How could I have trusted that little blabber munchkin? He's known for his loose lips. Seriously, he should wear a T-shirt that says SPOILER WARNING.

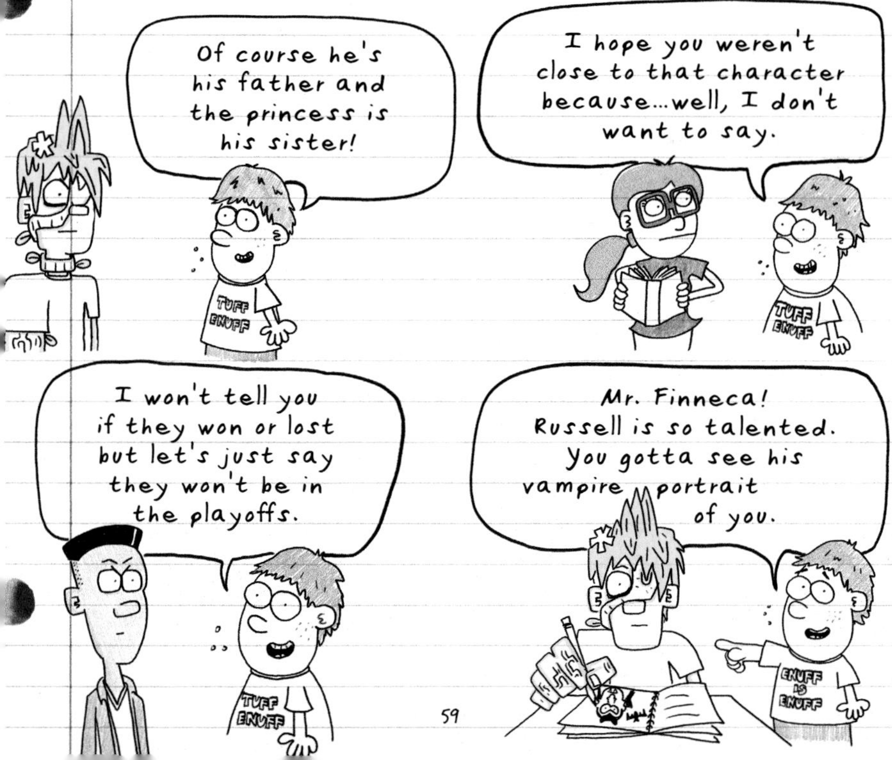
Of course he's his father and the princess is his sister!
TUFF ENUFF
I hope you weren't close to that character because...well, I don't want to say.
TUFF ENUFF
I won't tell you if they won or lost but let's just say they won't be in the playoffs.
TUFF ENUFF
Mr. Finneca! Russell is so talented. You gotta see his vampire portrait of you.
ENUFF IS ENUFF

9:05 A.M.

After class I guilted Sam by flashing some serious hairy eyeball.

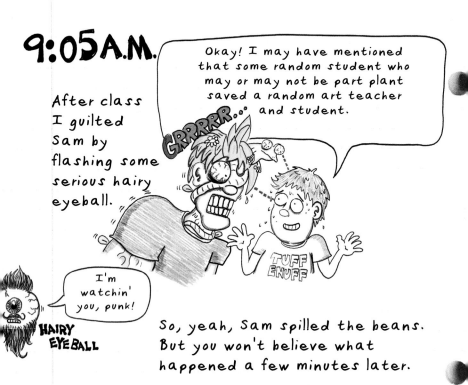

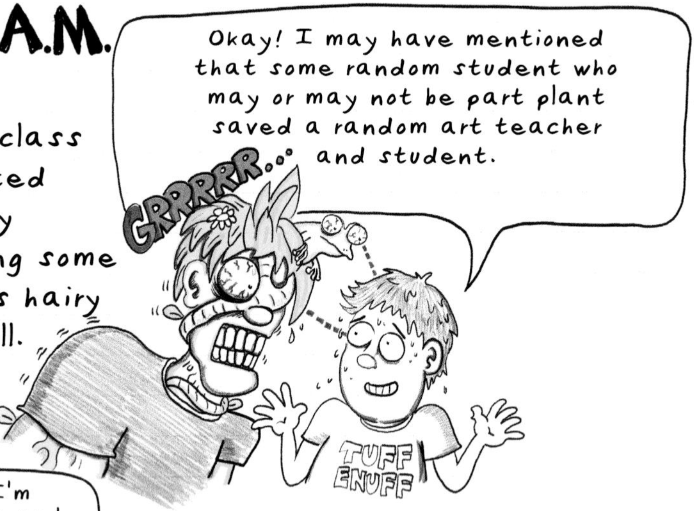
Okay! I may have mentioned that some random student who may or may not be part plant saved a random art teacher and student.
GRRRRR...
TUFF ENUFF

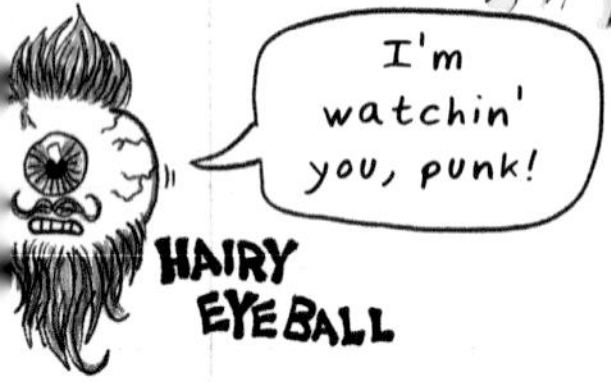
I'm watchin' you, punk!
HAIRY EYEBALL

So, yeah, Sam spilled the beans. But you won't believe what happened a few minutes later.

First, I spotted another shady-looking dude in sunglasses chatting all serious-like with Mr. Finneca outside the classroom.

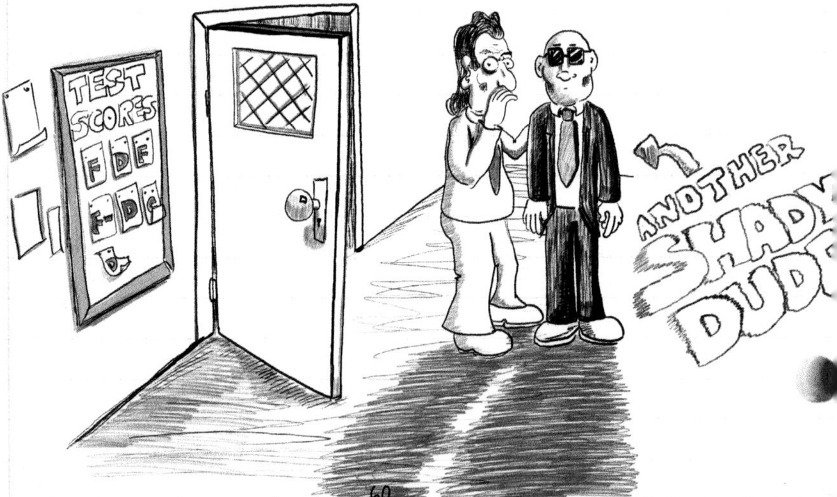
TEST SCORES
F D F
F- D
ANOTHER SHADY DUDE

I don't know what they were talking about but after the dude left Mr. Finneca started bugging me again.

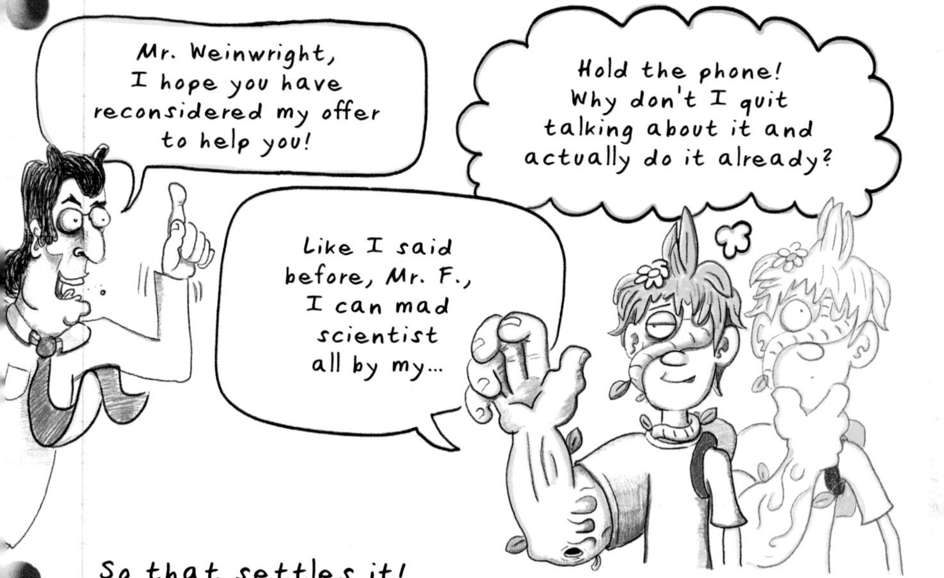
Mr. Weinwright, I hope you have reconsidered my offer to help you!
Hold the phone! Why don't I quit talking about it and actually do it already?
Like I said before, Mr. F., I can mad scientist all by my...

So that settles it! Tonight, we go full Victor Frankenstein and figure out what makes Swamp Kid tick...and sprout disgusting green appendages. I'd better go inform my assistants!

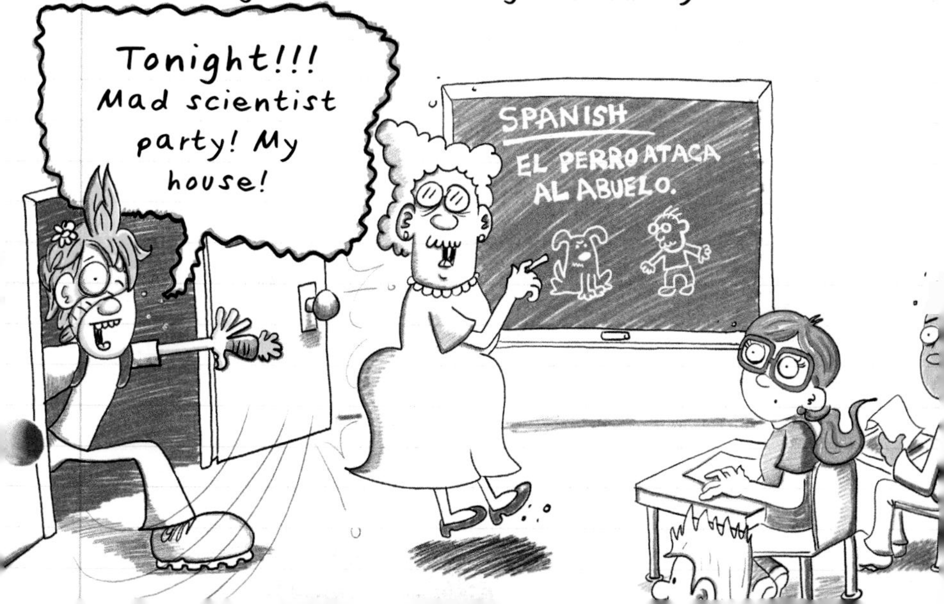
Tonight!!! Mad scientist party! My house!
SPANISH
EL PERRO ATACA AL ABUELO.

FRIDAY NIGHT MAD SCIENCE PARTY

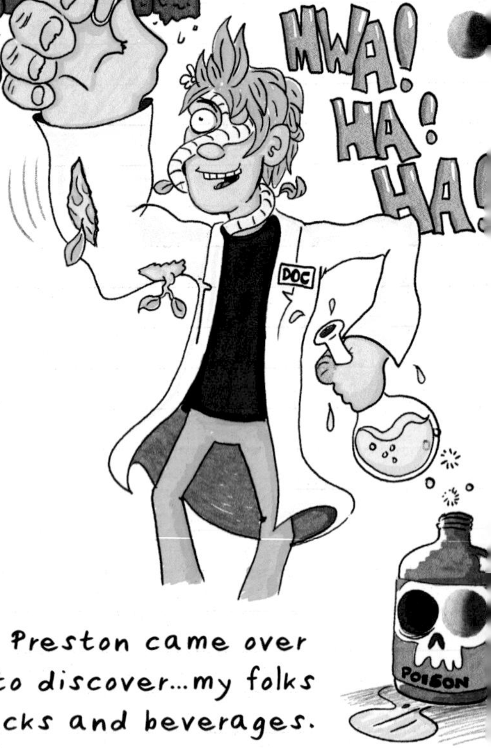
MWA! HA! HA!
DOC
POISON

Whew!
It's late Friday night. The dust has settled from our wild experiments. Or, I should say the slime has settled from our wild experiments.

When Charlotte and Preston came over they were shocked to discover...my folks offering endless snacks and beverages. I couldn't get rid of them!

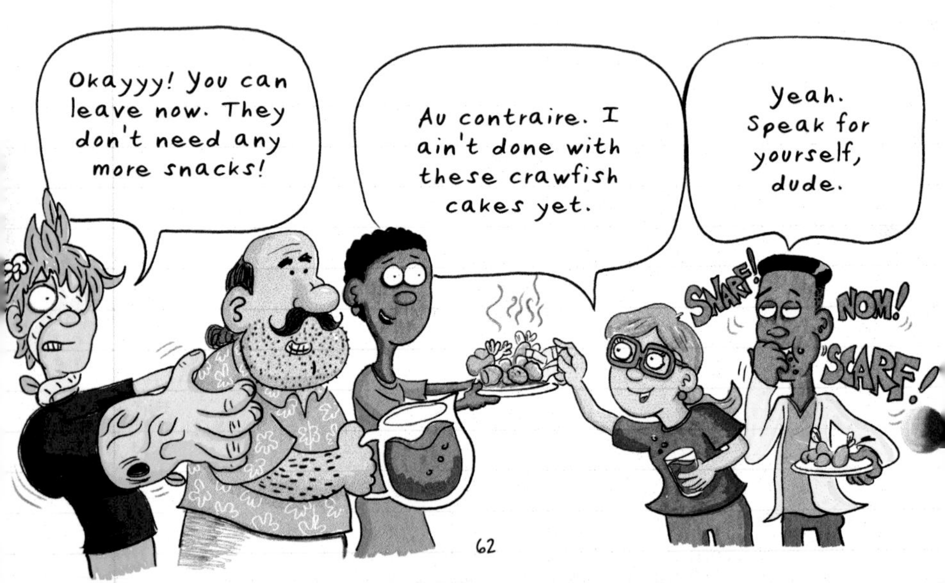
Okayyy! You can leave now. They don't need any more snacks!
Au contraire. I ain't done with these crawfish cakes yet.
Yeah. Speak for yourself, dude.
SNARF!
NOM!
SCARF!

Once they were gone Charlotte threw on her lab coat and took charge. (She's the only one who actually knows some science.)

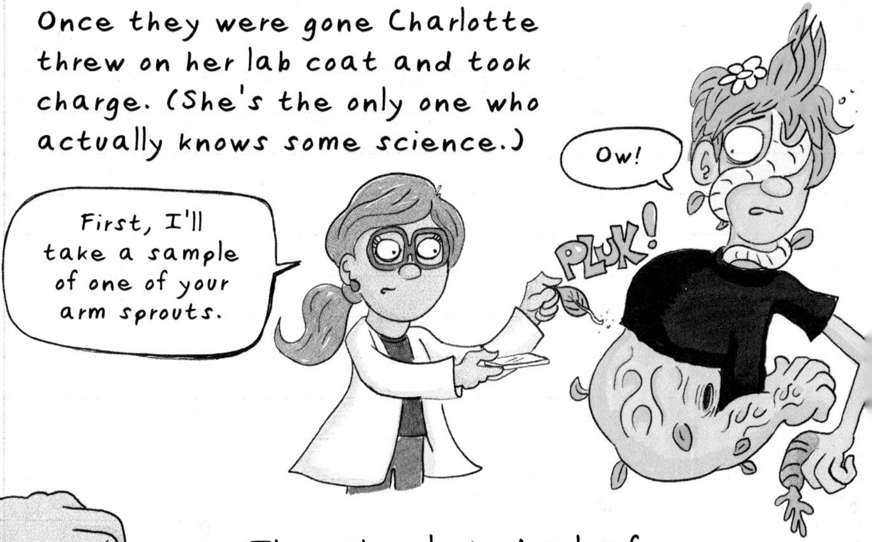
First, I'll take a sample of one of your arm sprouts.
Ow!
PLUK!

Then she plucked a leaf from poor unsuspecting Specimen Number Two.

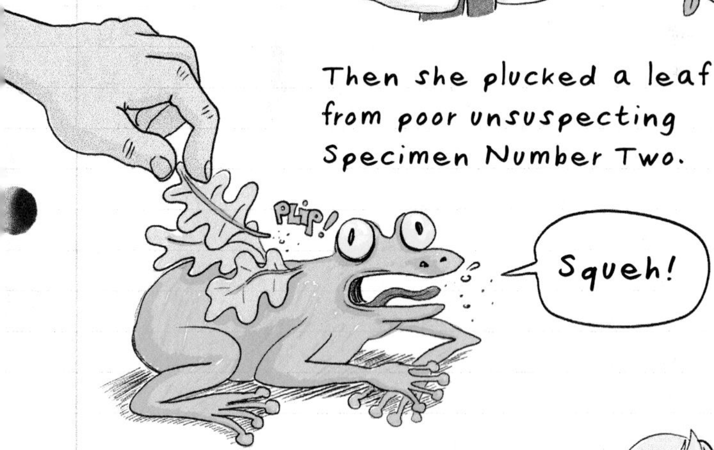
PLIP!
Squeh!

And, finally, she asked for my big toe appendage that had fallen off during my race in P.E. Thing is, I had no idea where it was.

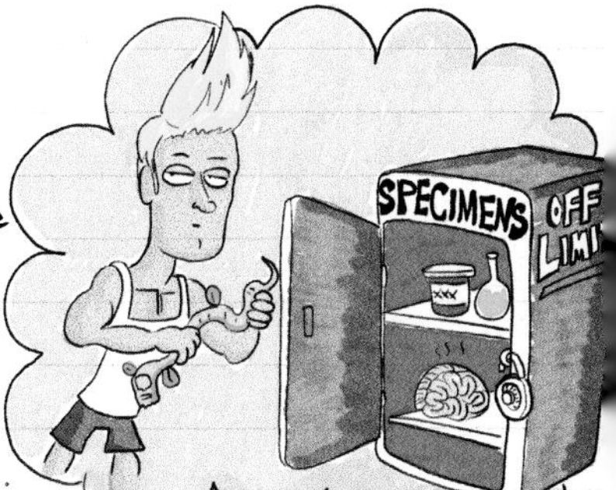
SPECIMENS
OFF

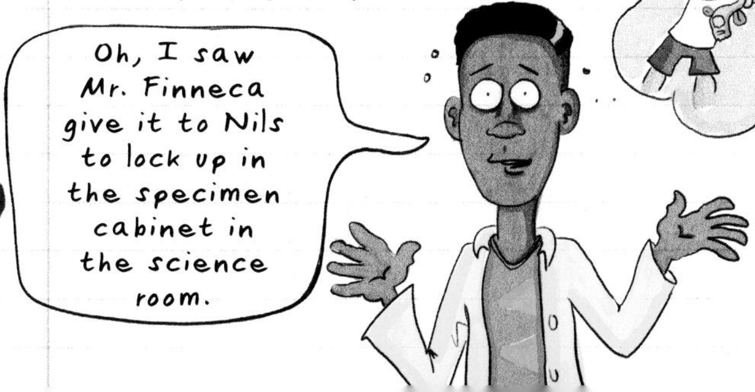
Oh, I saw Mr. Finneca give it to Nils to lock up in the specimen cabinet in the science room.

Hmmm.
Weird.

Charlotte examined the samples under the microscope.

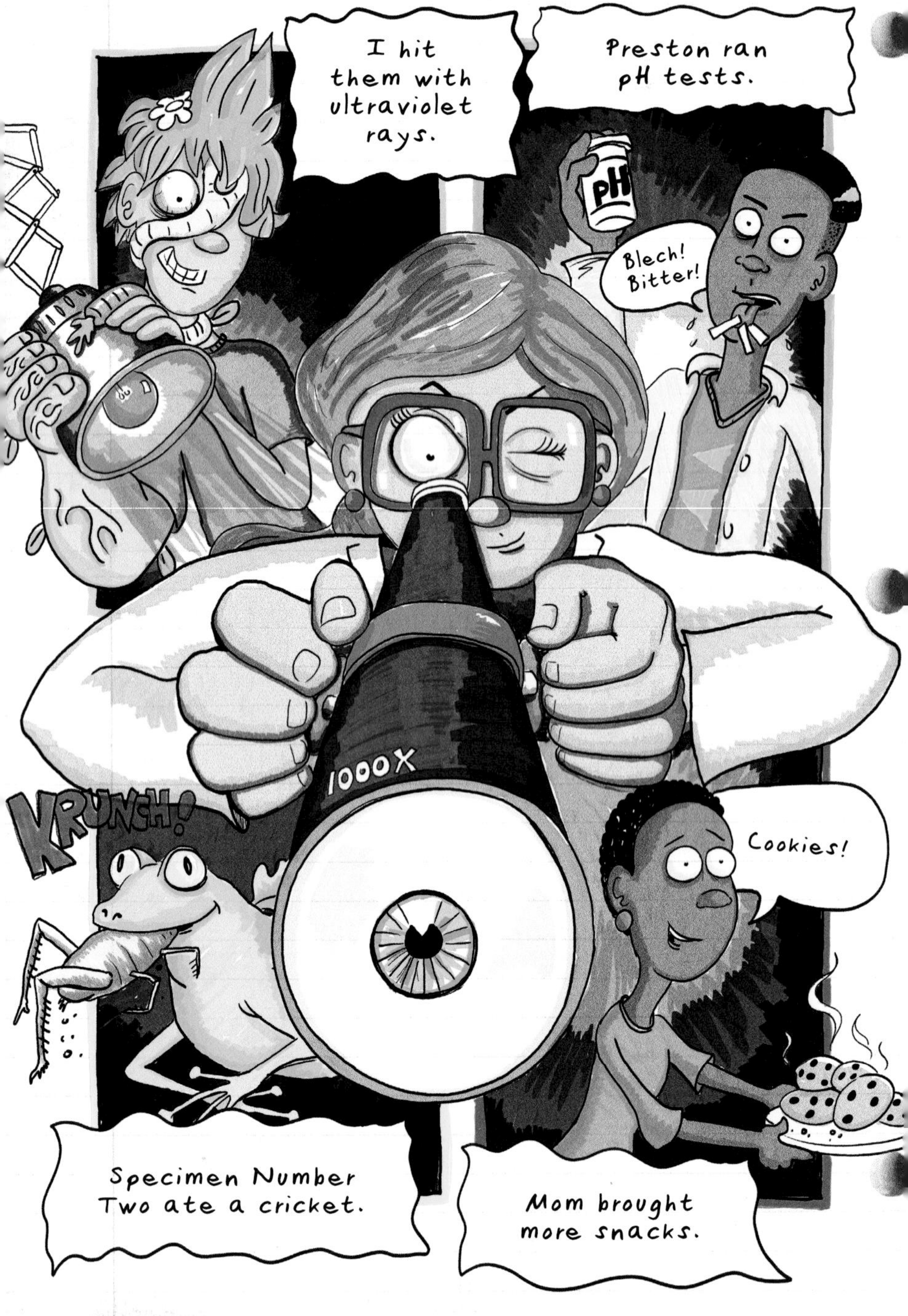
I hit them with ultraviolet rays.
Preston ran pH tests.
pH
Blech! Bitter!
1000X
KRUNCH!
Cookies!
Specimen Number Two ate a cricket.
Mom brought more snacks.

Within minutes the place was trashed! Green goo and broken beakers everywhere!

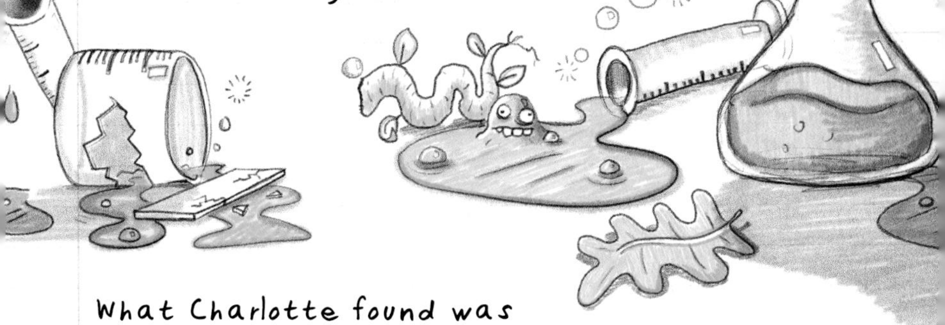

What Charlotte found was both promising and a little frustrating. There most definitely was a common factor in the leaves plucked from me and Specimen Number Two, and from some of the plants I had collected where we found the old laboratory wrecked in the bayou. There was a microscopic component in each one, a component she couldn't find in samples of any other plant or animal life.

Charlotte has kindly drawn the mystery component to the left here. Even though she sketched it in hot pink ink, trust me, it was green. Here's the kicker, we have no idea what the component is, just that it shouldn't be there.

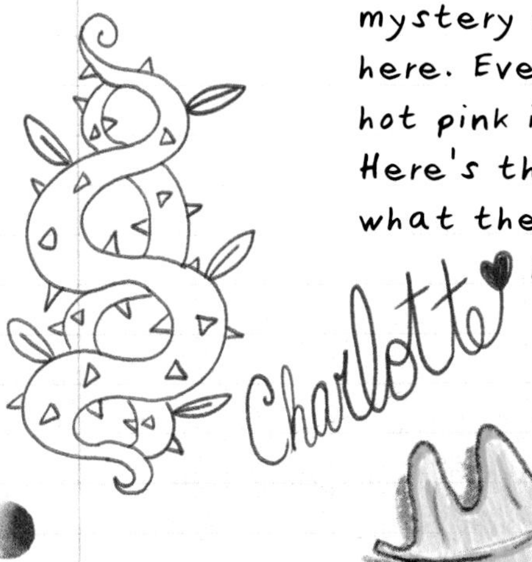
Charlotte

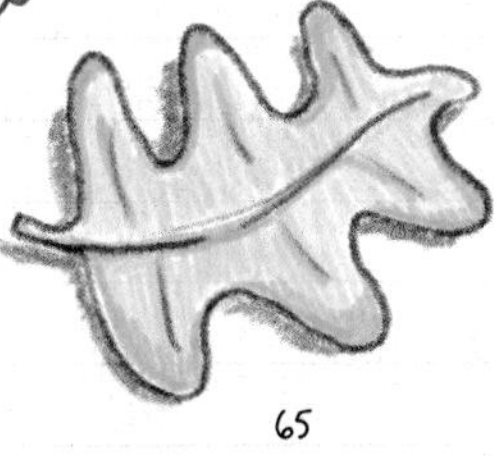

BUNSEN BURNER INCIDENT.

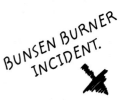

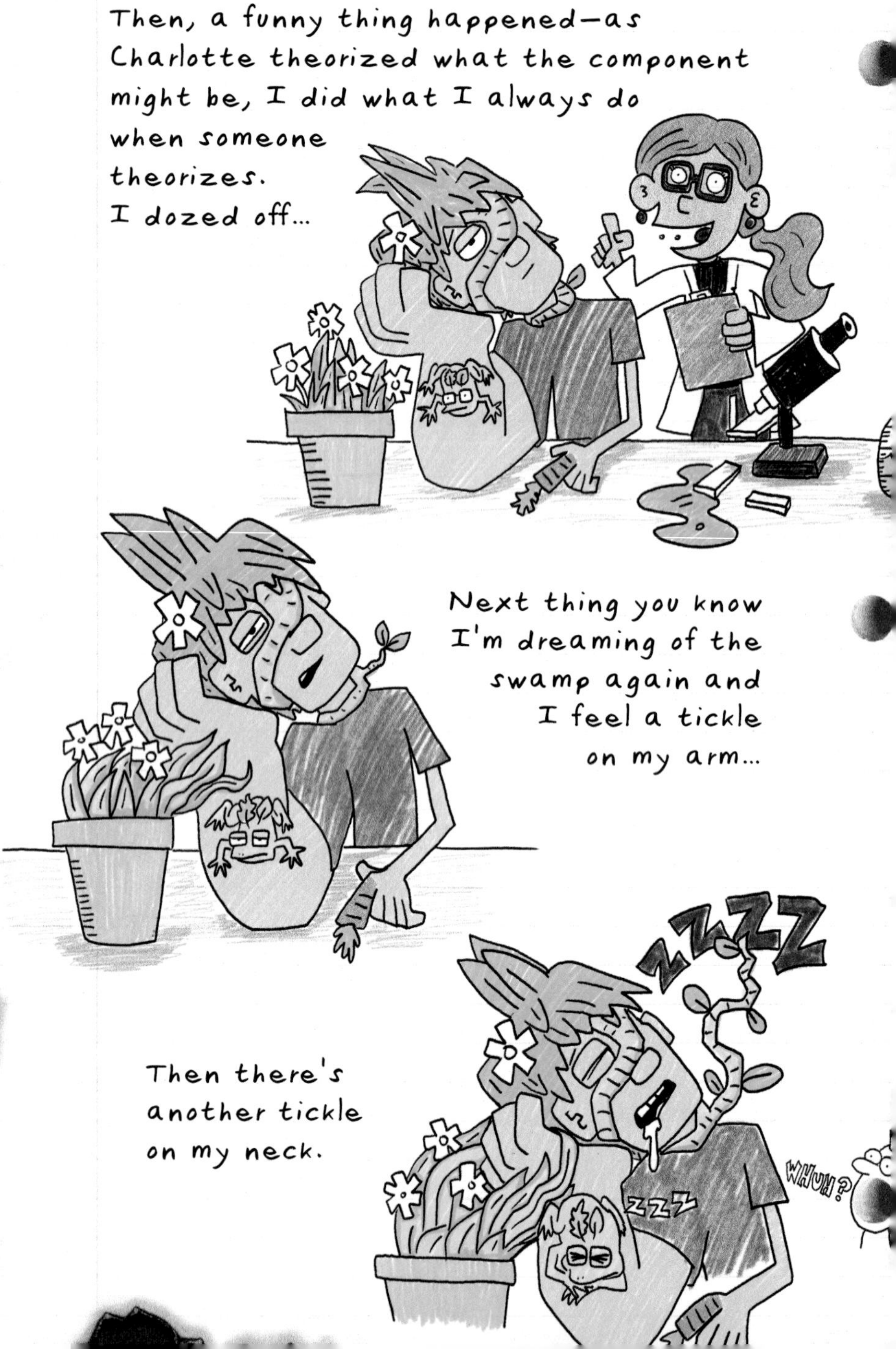

Then, a funny thing happened—as Charlotte theorized what the component might be, I did what I always do when someone theorizes.
I dozed off...
Next thing you know I'm dreaming of the swamp again and I feel a tickle on my arm...
ZZZZ
Then there's another tickle on my neck.
ZZZ
WHUH?

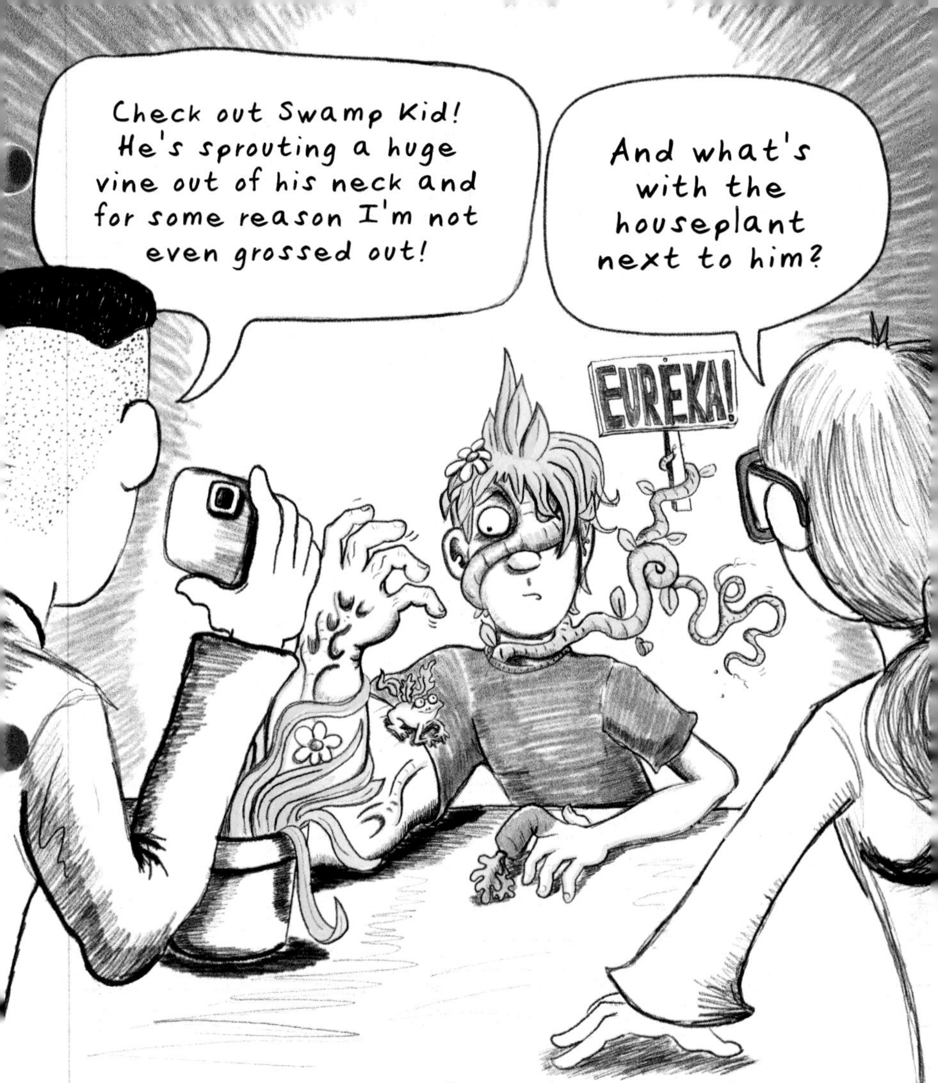
Check out Swamp Kid! He's sprouting a huge vine out of his neck and for some reason I'm not even grossed out!
And what's with the houseplant next to him?
EUREKA!

I snapped awake to find the potted plant to my right was wrapped around my arm and my neck was lush with new foliage. Then a thought hit me like a wheelbarrow full of compost...

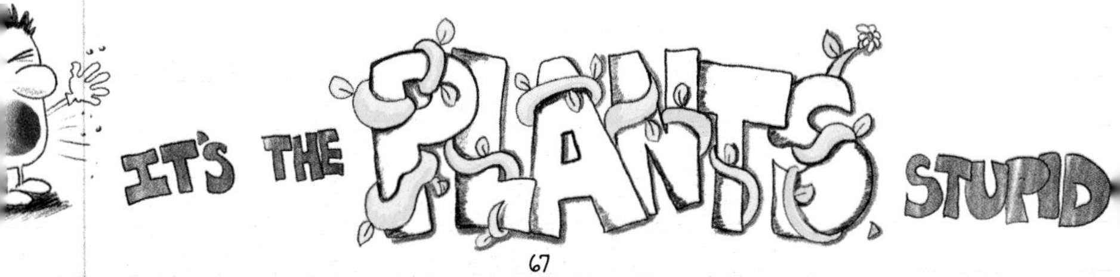
IT'S THE PLANTS, STUPID

Preston was on the same page. He whipped out his camera and downloaded his videos to my mom's notebook.

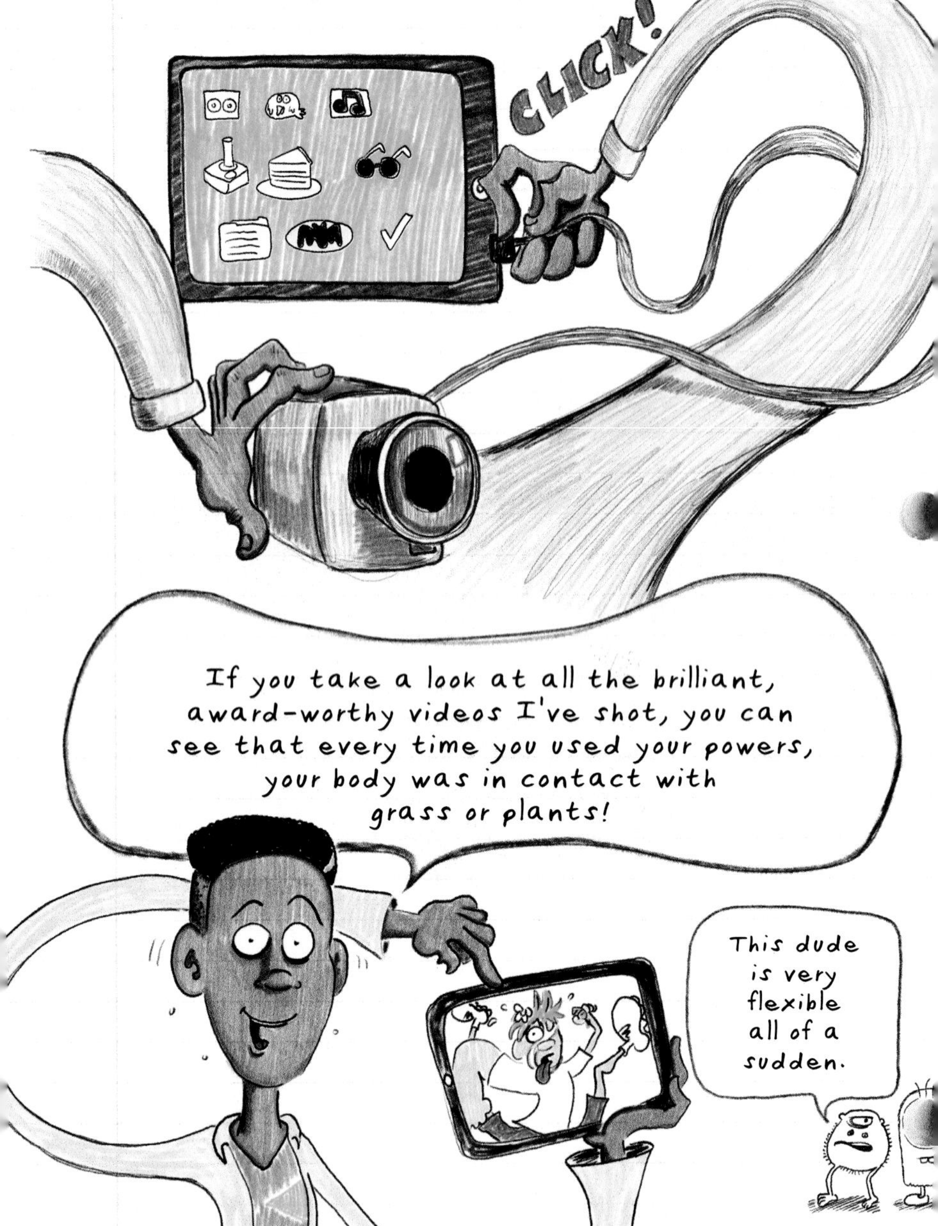
CLICK!
If you take a look at all the brilliant, award-worthy videos I've shot, you can see that every time you used your powers, your body was in contact with grass or plants!
This dude is very flexible all of a sudden.

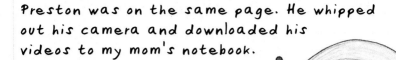

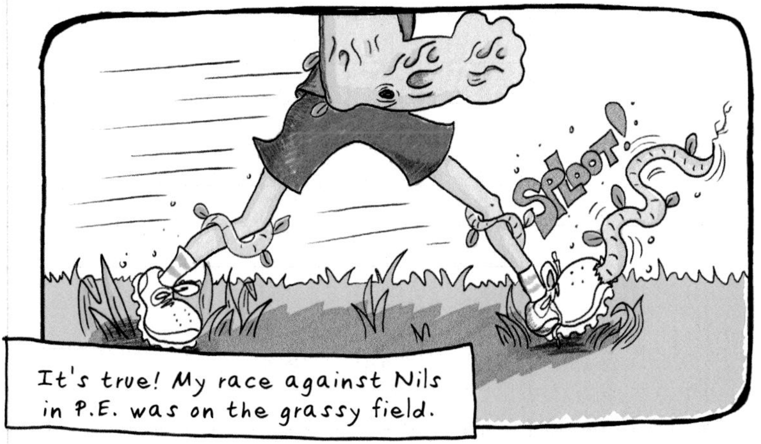
SPLOOT!
It's true! My race against Nils in P.E. was on the grassy field.

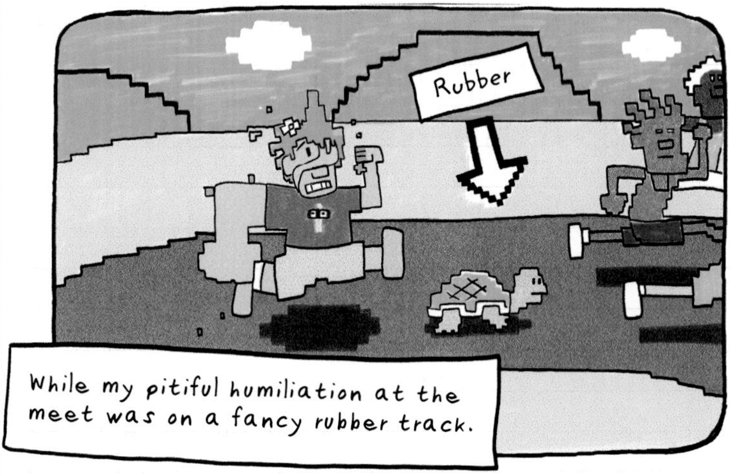
Rubber
While my pitiful humiliation at the meet was on a fancy rubber track.

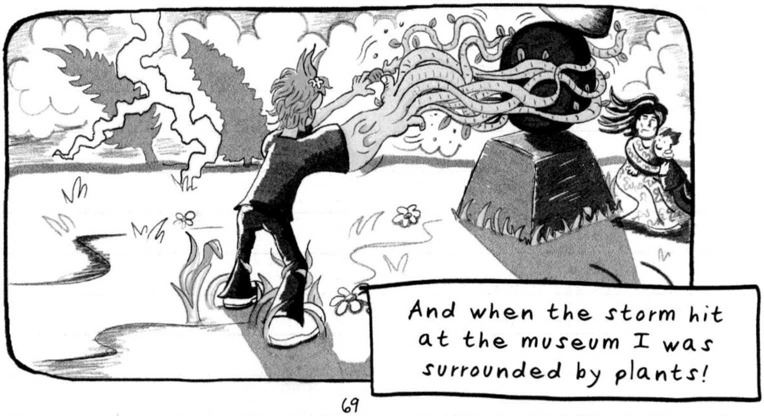
And when the storm hit at the museum I was surrounded by plants!

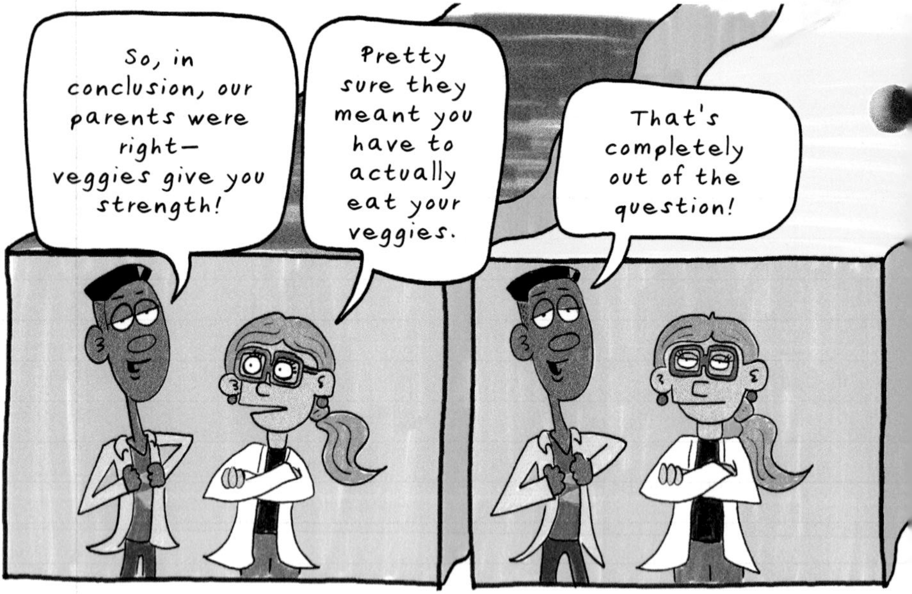
So, in conclusion, our parents were right— veggies give you strength!
Pretty sure they meant you have to actually eat your veggies.
That's completely out of the question!

I had to test this theory, so I darted out into our backyard and shoved my arm into the disgusting, green, slimy, vine-covered birdbath.

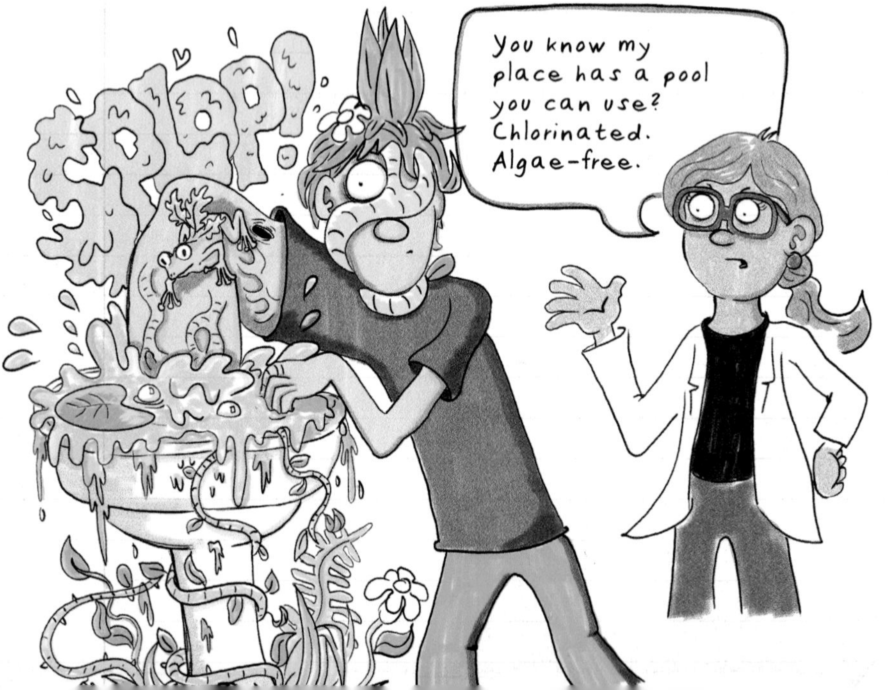
SPLOP!
You know my place has a pool you can use? Chlorinated. Algae-free.

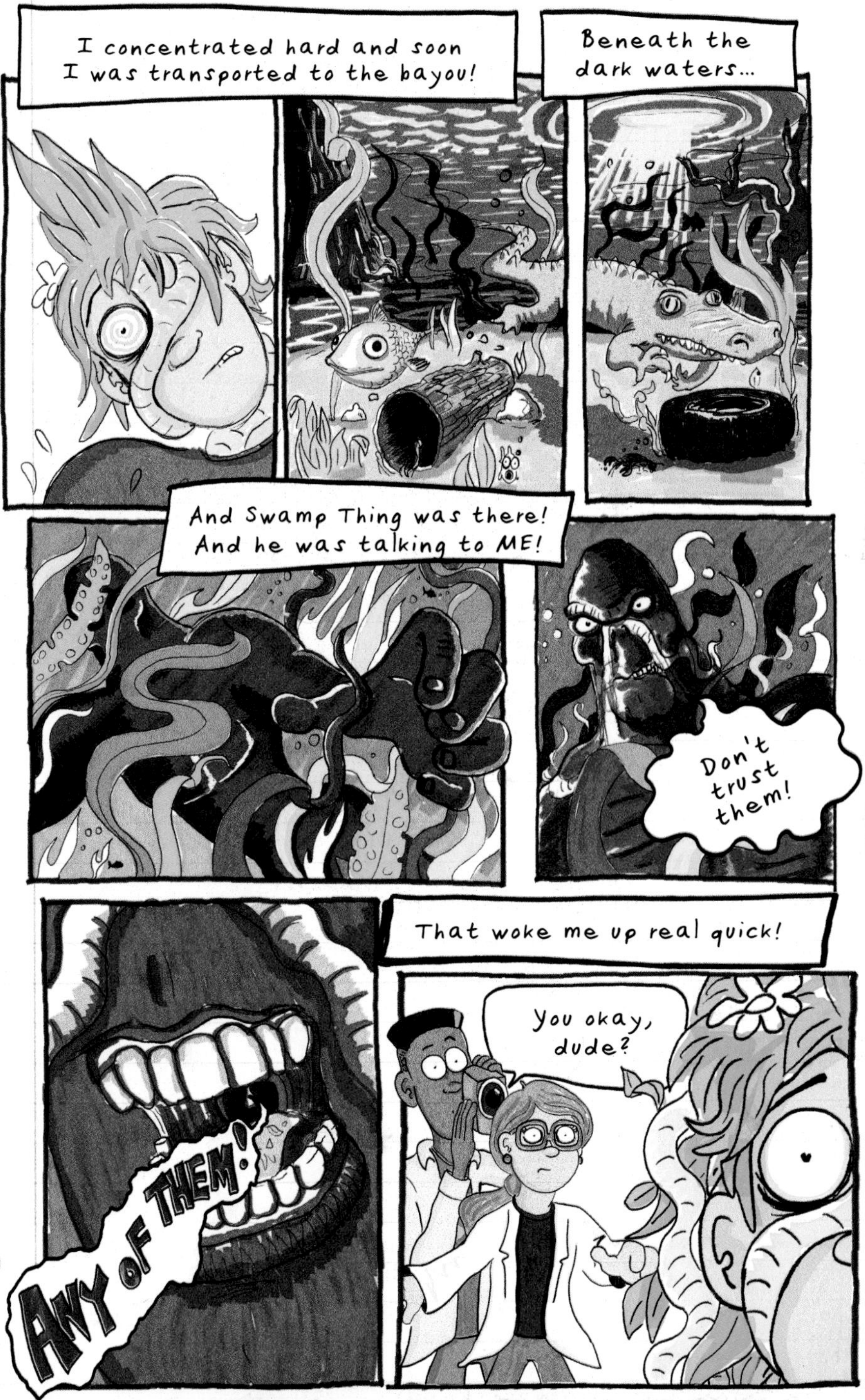
I concentrated hard and soon I was transported to the bayou!
Beneath the dark waters...
And Swamp Thing was there! And he was talking to ME!
Don't trust them!
ANY OF THEM!
That woke me up real quick!
You okay, dude?

When I came to I decided to keep my vision of Swamp Thing to myself. I was a little freaked out about what he had said. Don't trust them! Does that include my friends? Surely not. I was confused and exhausted. Still am.

On the bright side, I sprouted so many vines and leaves while I was under I ended up looking like a cross between a heavy metal rocker and a plate of spinach fettuccine!

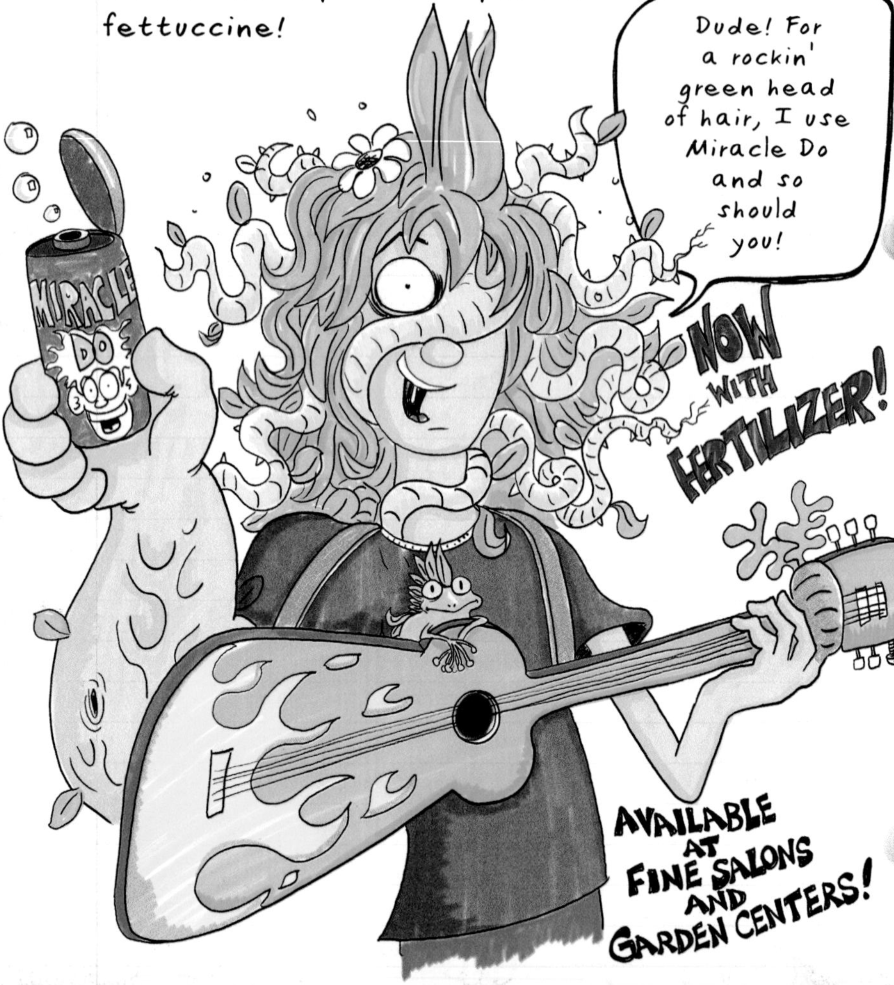
Dude! For a rockin' green head of hair, I use Miracle Do and so should you!
MIRACLE DO
NOW WITH FERTILIZER!
AVAILABLE AT FINE SALONS AND GARDEN CENTERS!

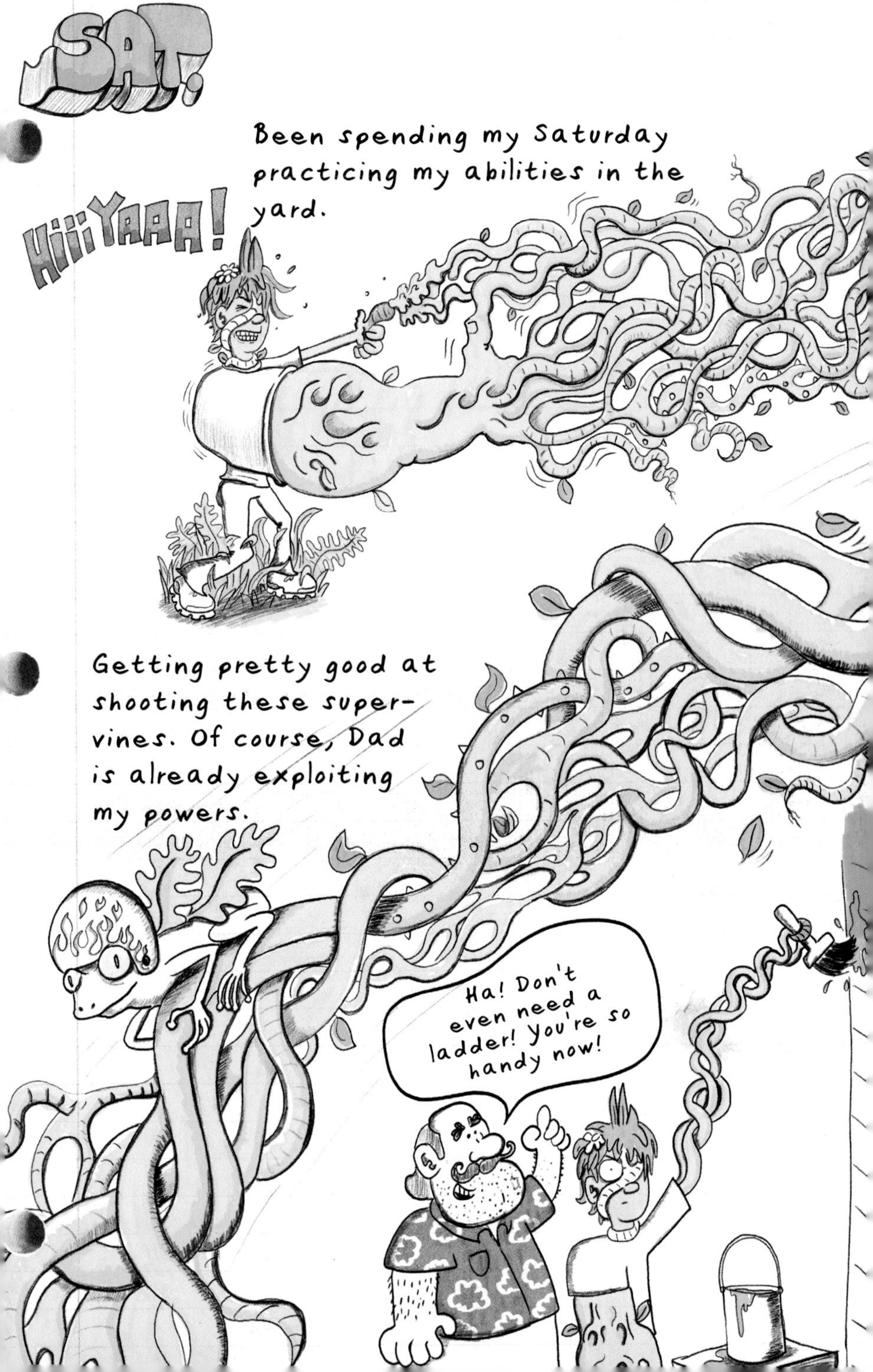
SAT.
Been spending my Saturday practicing my abilities in the yard.
HiiiYAAA!
Getting pretty good at shooting these super-vines. Of course, Dad is already exploiting my powers.
Ha! Don't even need a ladder! You're so handy now!

I told Mom I'd help her with the grocery shopping this morning. It might sound crazy, but I swear the store was filled with shady characters in black watching my every move!

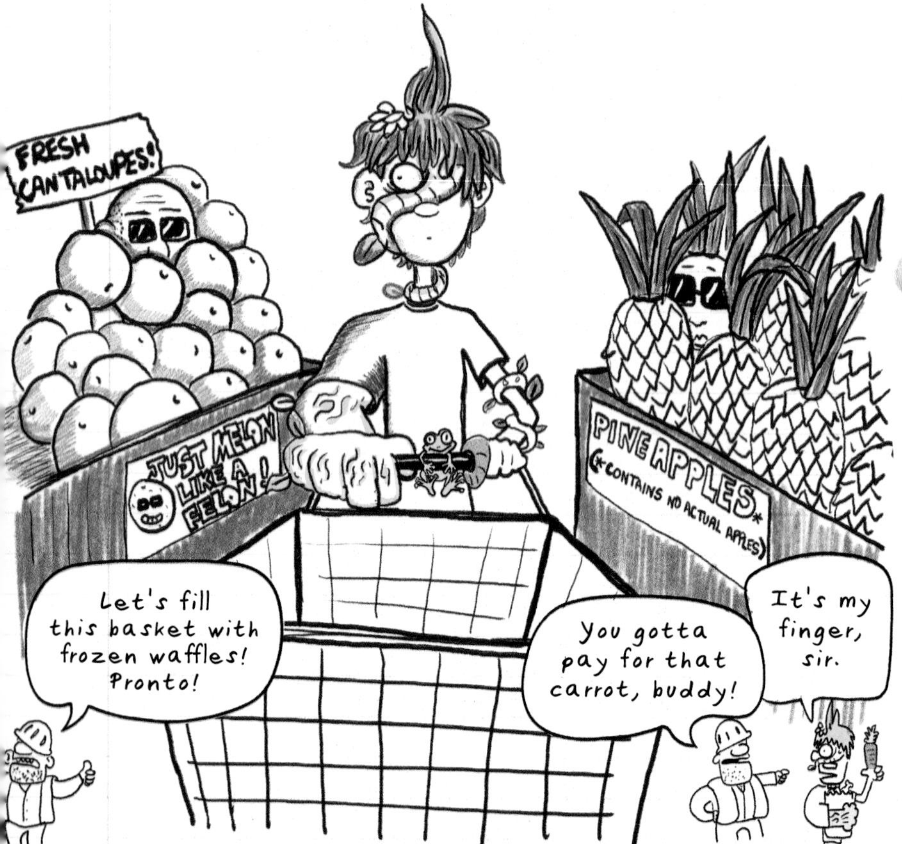
FRESH CANTALOUPES!
JUST MELON LIKE A FELON!
PINEAPPLES*
(*CONTAINS NO ACTUAL APPLES)
Let's fill this basket with frozen waffles! Pronto!
You gotta pay for that carrot, buddy!
It's my finger, sir.

Who were those creeps? I.R.S.? Criminal masterminds? Were they monitoring my junk food purchases? Word must have gotten out about my powers.

Even on the ride home, folks were watching me.

Every turn we took there were eyes on us. Giant, staring, glassy eyes!

Oh wait, that's just an optometrist's billboard.

Mom didn't really notice them, but she said something interesting.

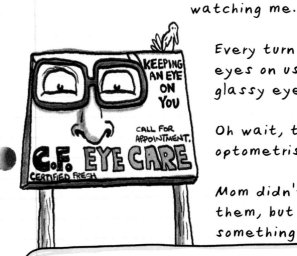

KEEPING AN EYE ON YOU

CALL FOR APPOINTMENT.

C.F. EYE CARE

CERTIFIED FRESH

When we first found you, for months these folks in suits kept showing up with questions. They worked for someone named Ar...Arcade? No. Arcane! Then they just, eventually, let us be.

SUN. NIGHT

It's nearly 10 p.m. now, and after the last few days, one question keeps repeating in my mind over and over and over...

WHO AM I?

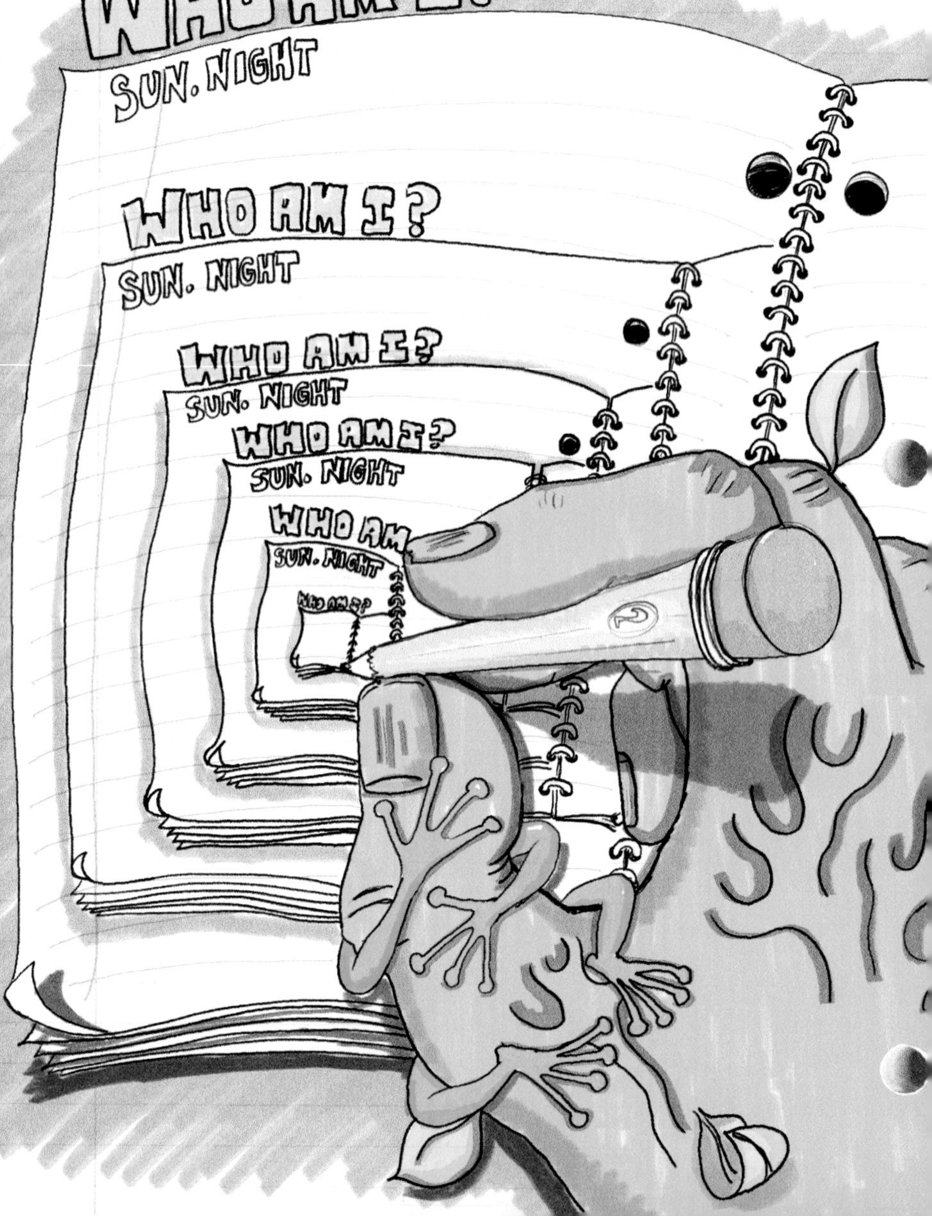
SUN. NIGHT
WHO AM I?
SUN. NIGHT
WHO AM I?
SUN. NIGHT
WHO AM I?
SUN. NIGHT

2:00 A.M.

I just had a nightmare that was totally bananas! I have to sketch it before I forget it.

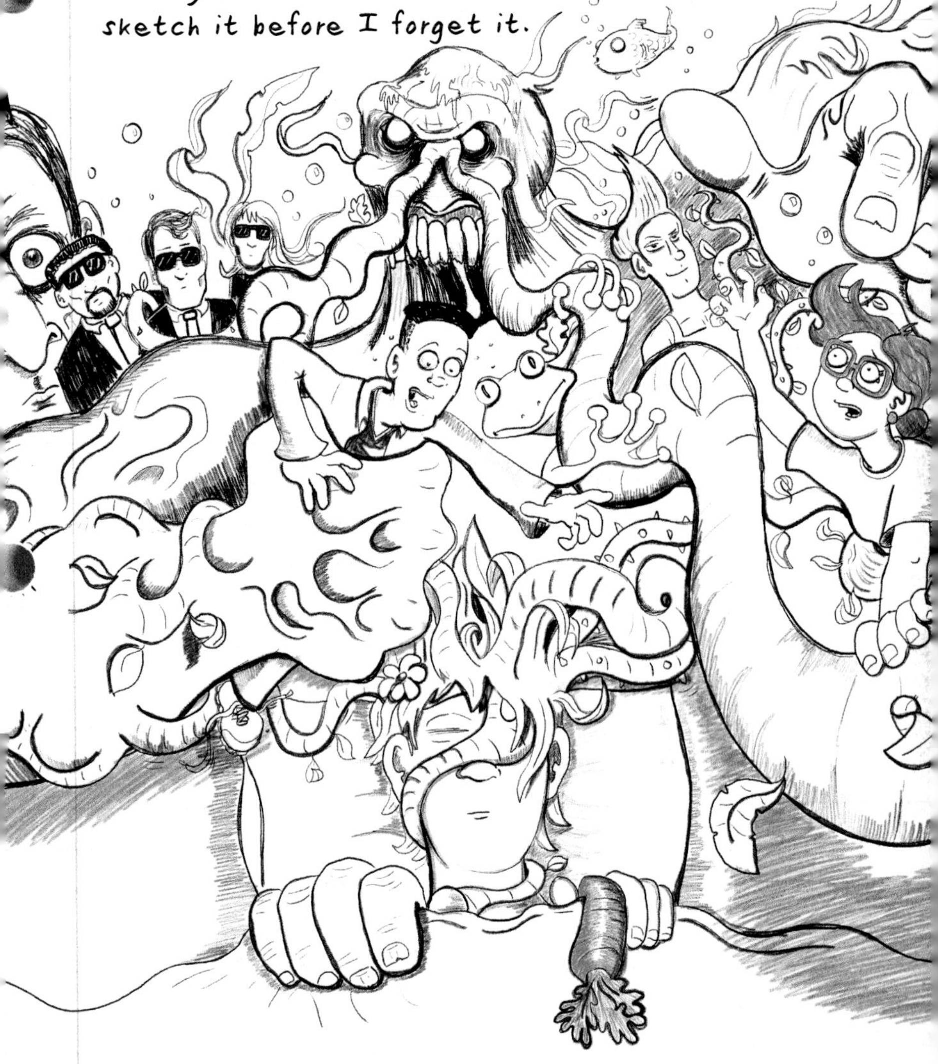

Everyone was in my nightmare—Mr. Finneca, Nils, the shady dudes. Charlotte and Preston, too, and they were screaming for help, tangled up in Swamp Thing's vines...or had I created them? I don't know if I'm gonna be able to go back to sleep after this!

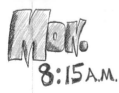

MON.

8:15 A.M.

Feeling blue this morning, so blue I've got my blue pen out. Charlotte is sitting across from me in Mr. Finneca's class. She's mouthing the words "are you okay"?

What does she mean am I okay? Don't I look okay?

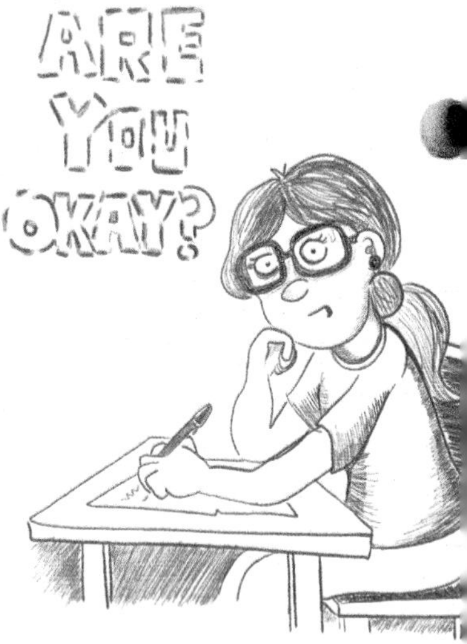
ARE YOU OKAY?

Ugh! Scratch that! I just took a selfie and I most def DO NOT look okay! All the stress and my nightmare-filled slumber has me looking super ragged. #zombieroadkill

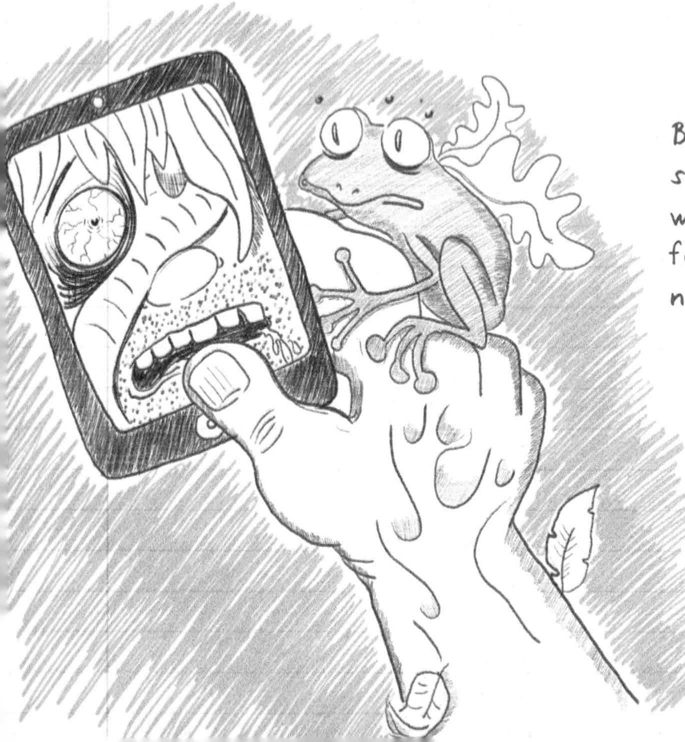

Better go splash some water on my face before next period.

MON. LUNCH

I decided to just do sunshine for lunch today.

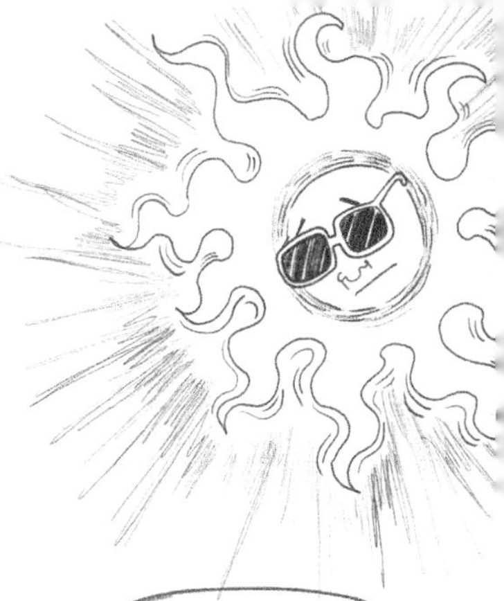

Preston was super excited to see me, but I wasn't in the mood.

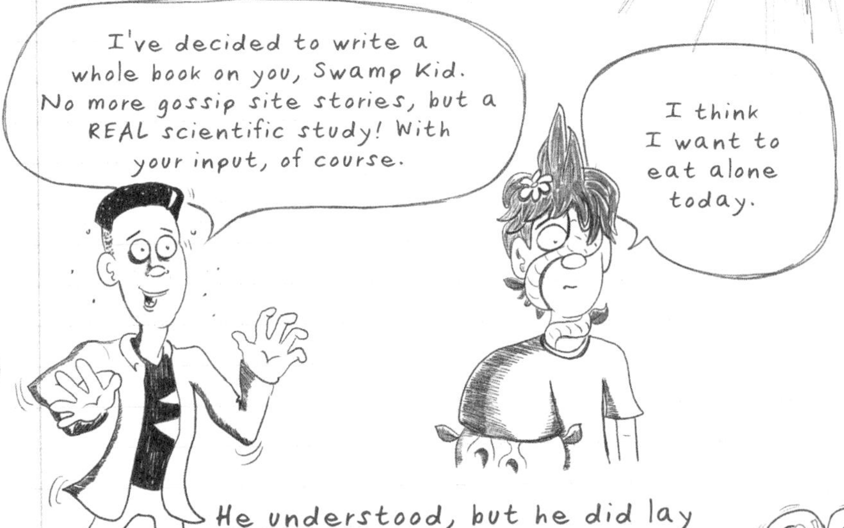
I've decided to write a whole book on you, Swamp Kid. No more gossip site stories, but a REAL scientific study! With your input, of course.
I think I want to eat alone today.

He understood, but he did lay some serious sad-puppy-dog eyes on me as he left. Charlotte was super cool about it, though.

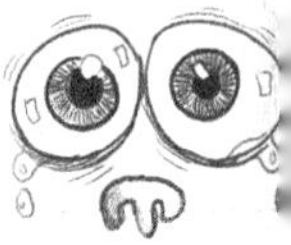

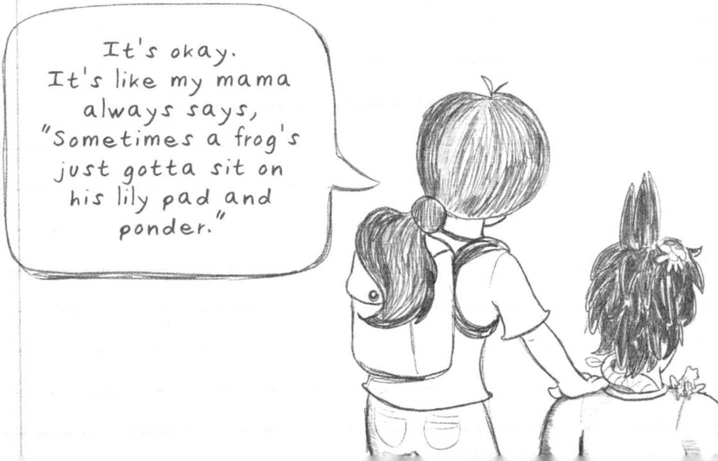
It's okay. It's like my mama always says, "Sometimes a frog's just gotta sit on his lily pad and ponder."

I'm done with the blue ink now and an idea is brewing in this lime green melon of mine...today after school, I go searching for answers... deep in the swamp. Oh wait. Here comes Coach Sanchez again.

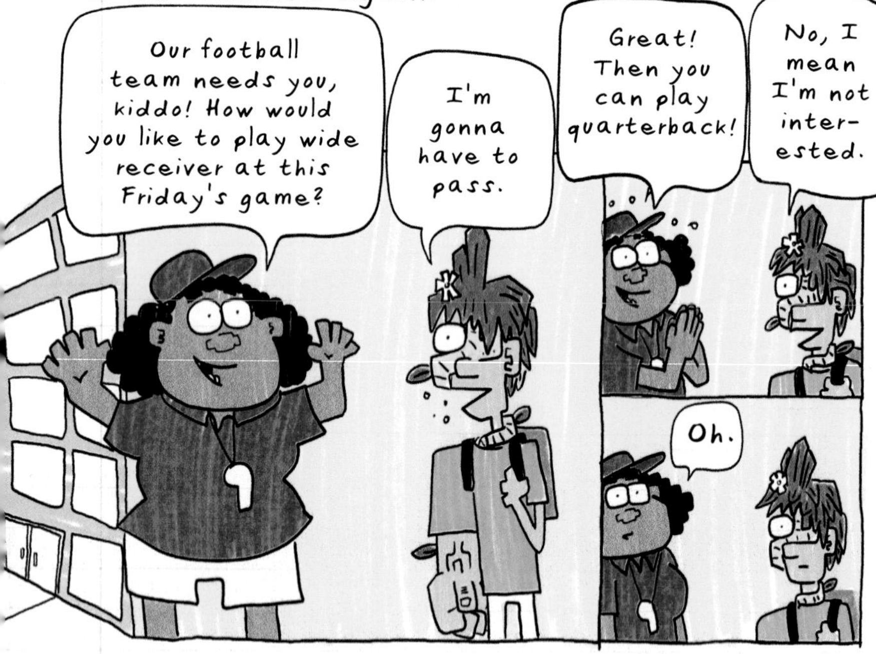
Our football team needs you, kiddo! How would you like to play wide receiver at this Friday's game?
I'm gonna have to pass.
Great! Then you can play quarterback!
No, I mean I'm not inter-ested.
Oh.

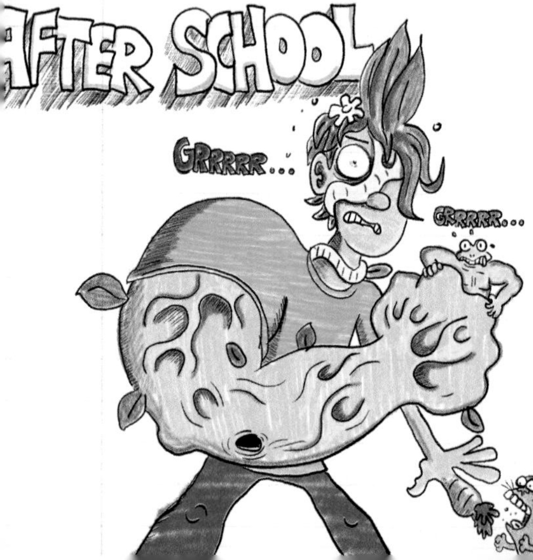
AFTER SCHOOL
GRRRRR...
GRRRRR...

School's out. The halls are clear. I'm about to trek into the bayou to confront my fears. But first, a stop-off at the one organization that can help prepare me for my one-on-one with an angry superhero...

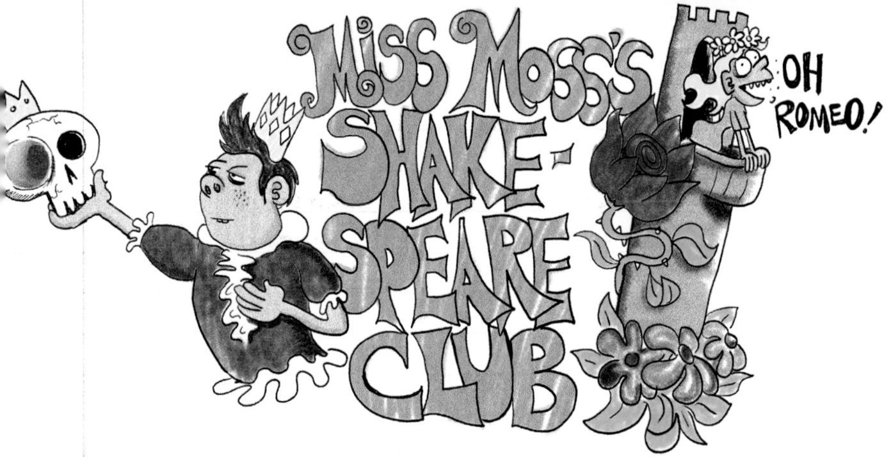
MISS MOSS'S SHAKE-SPEARE CLUB
OH ROMEO!

That's right. The Shakespeare Club meets after school twice a week and if you thought my mad scientist outfit was nerdy...

Ms. Moss was super happy to see me again!

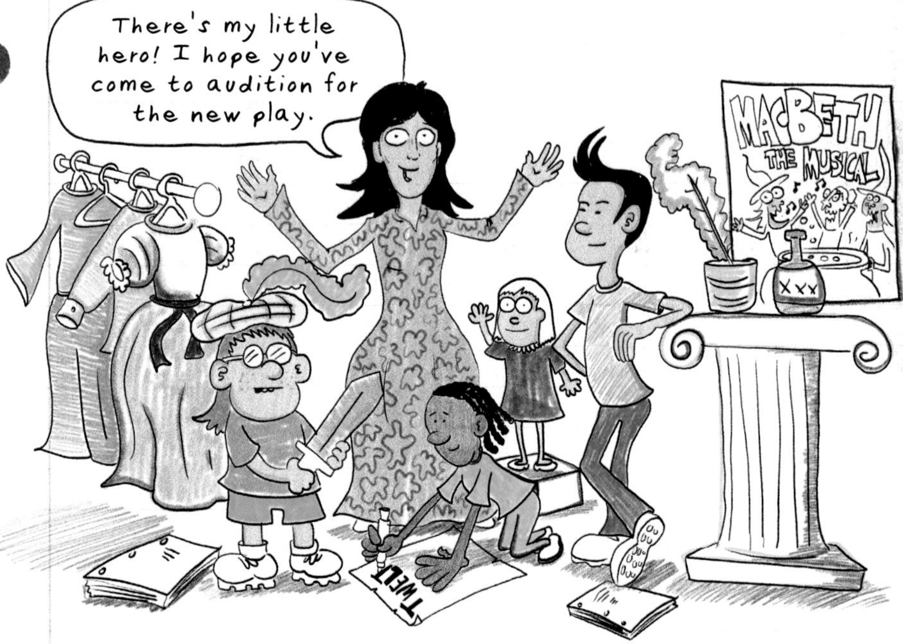
There's my little hero! I hope you've come to audition for the new play.
MACBETH THE MUSICAL

Since she usually casts me as shrubbery, that would be a big NO. But I did need her help.

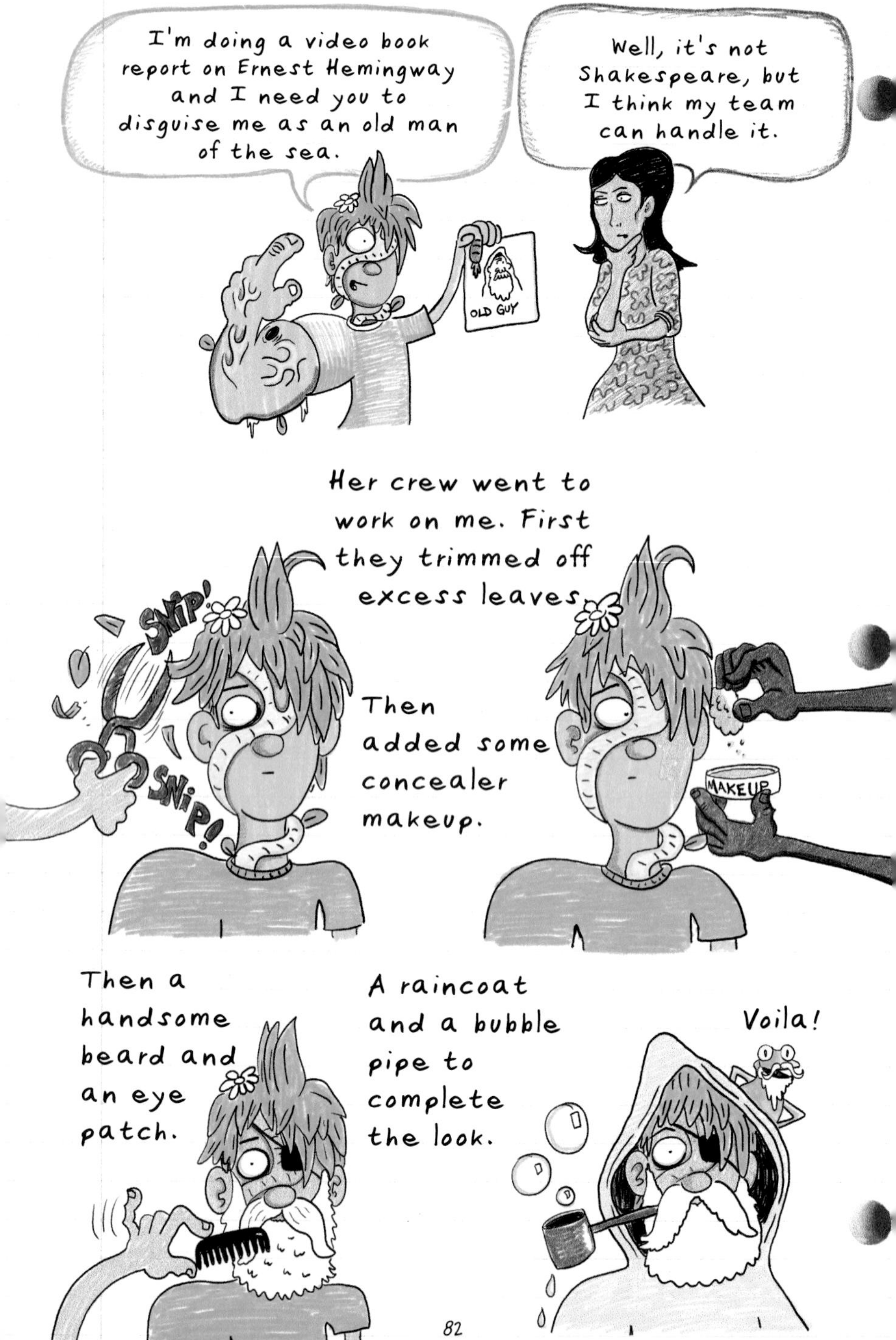

I'm doing a video book report on Ernest Hemingway and I need you to disguise me as an old man of the sea.
OLD GUY
Well, it's not Shakespeare, but I think my team can handle it.
Her crew went to work on me. First they trimmed off excess leaves.
SNIP!
SNIP!
Then added some concealer makeup.
MAKEUP
Then a handsome beard and an eye patch.
A raincoat and a bubble pipe to complete the look.
Voila!

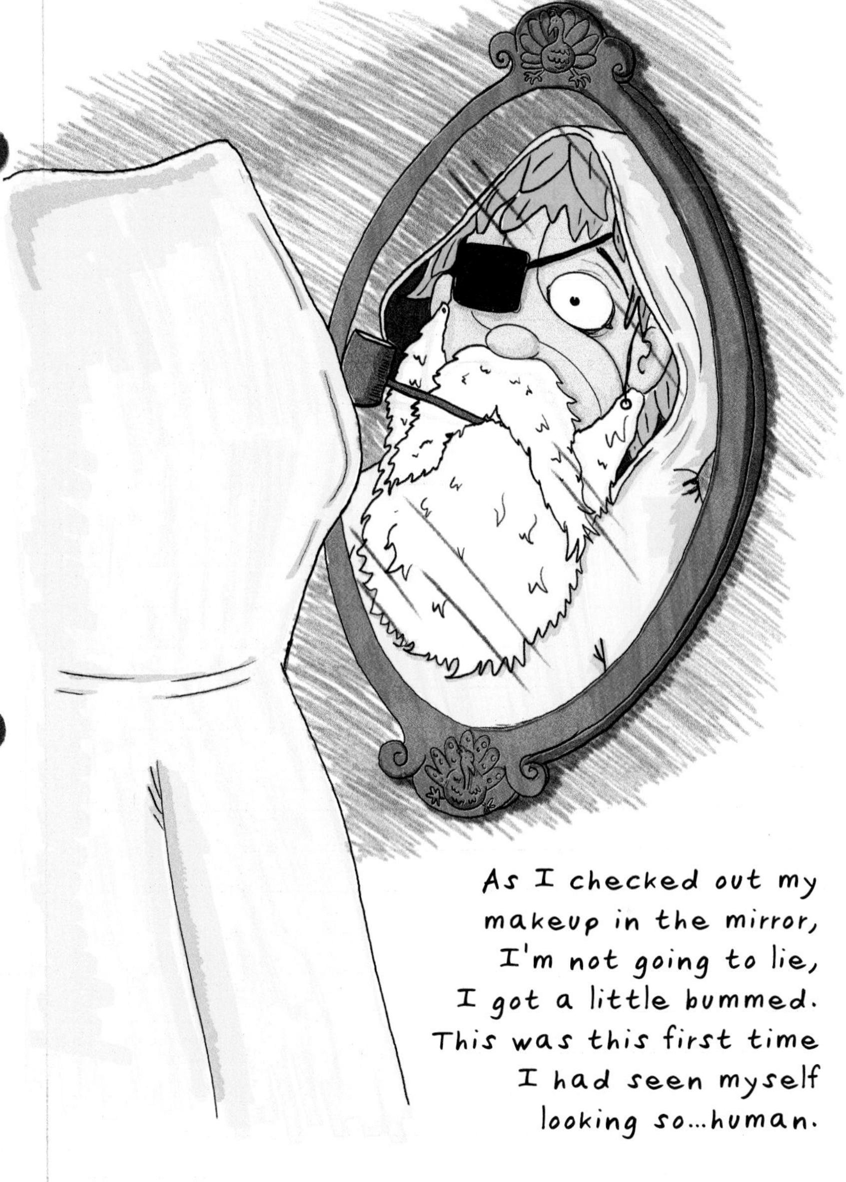

As I checked out my makeup in the mirror, I'm not going to lie, I got a little bummed. This was this first time I had seen myself looking so...human.

Is it weird to wish I could look like an elderly fisherman all the time?

Anyway, it's almost 4:15 now. If I'm searching for you-know-who, I'd better go. I'll update you on what happens tonight. Wish me luck!

MONDAY NIGHT UPDATE NEWS YOU CAN TRUST

Okay, I'm just gonna get into it because a lot happened since school finished. First off, my old-man costume immediately fooled Nils Canebrake.

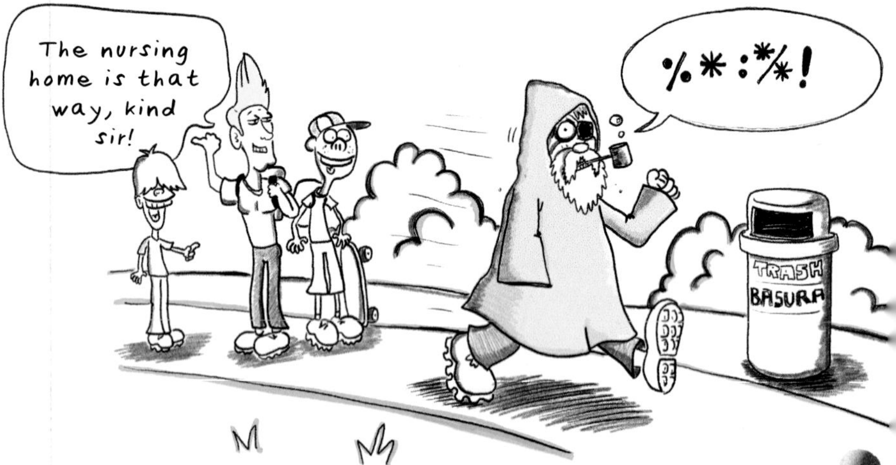
The nursing home is that way, kind sir!
%*:*/*!
TRASH
BASURA

I won't tell you what I actually told him but it's something a salty old sea dog would say. I was only acting, sheesh!

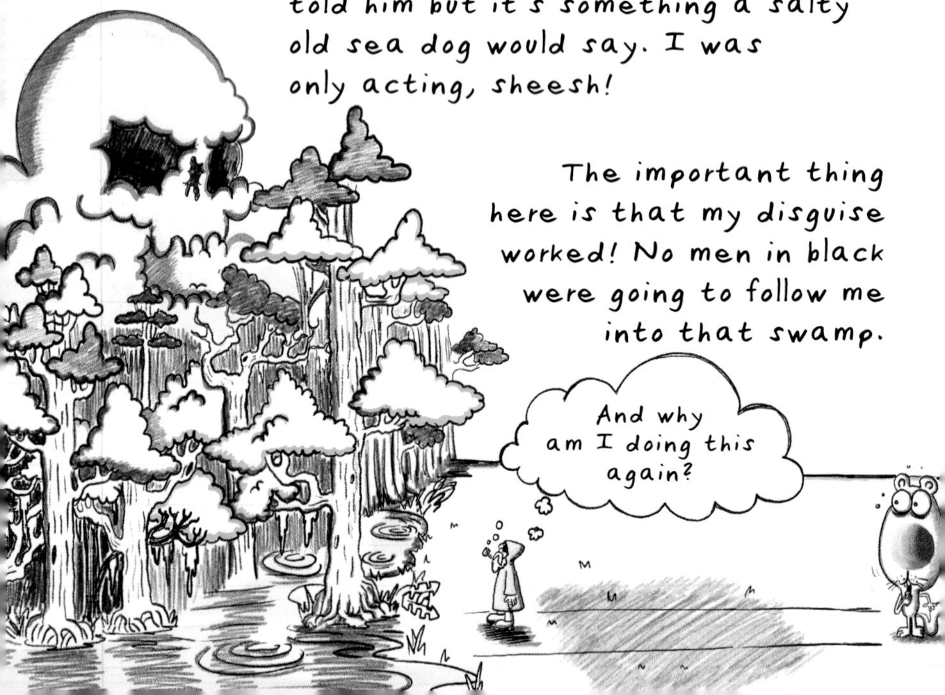
And why am I doing this again?

The important thing here is that my disguise worked! No men in black were going to follow me into that swamp.

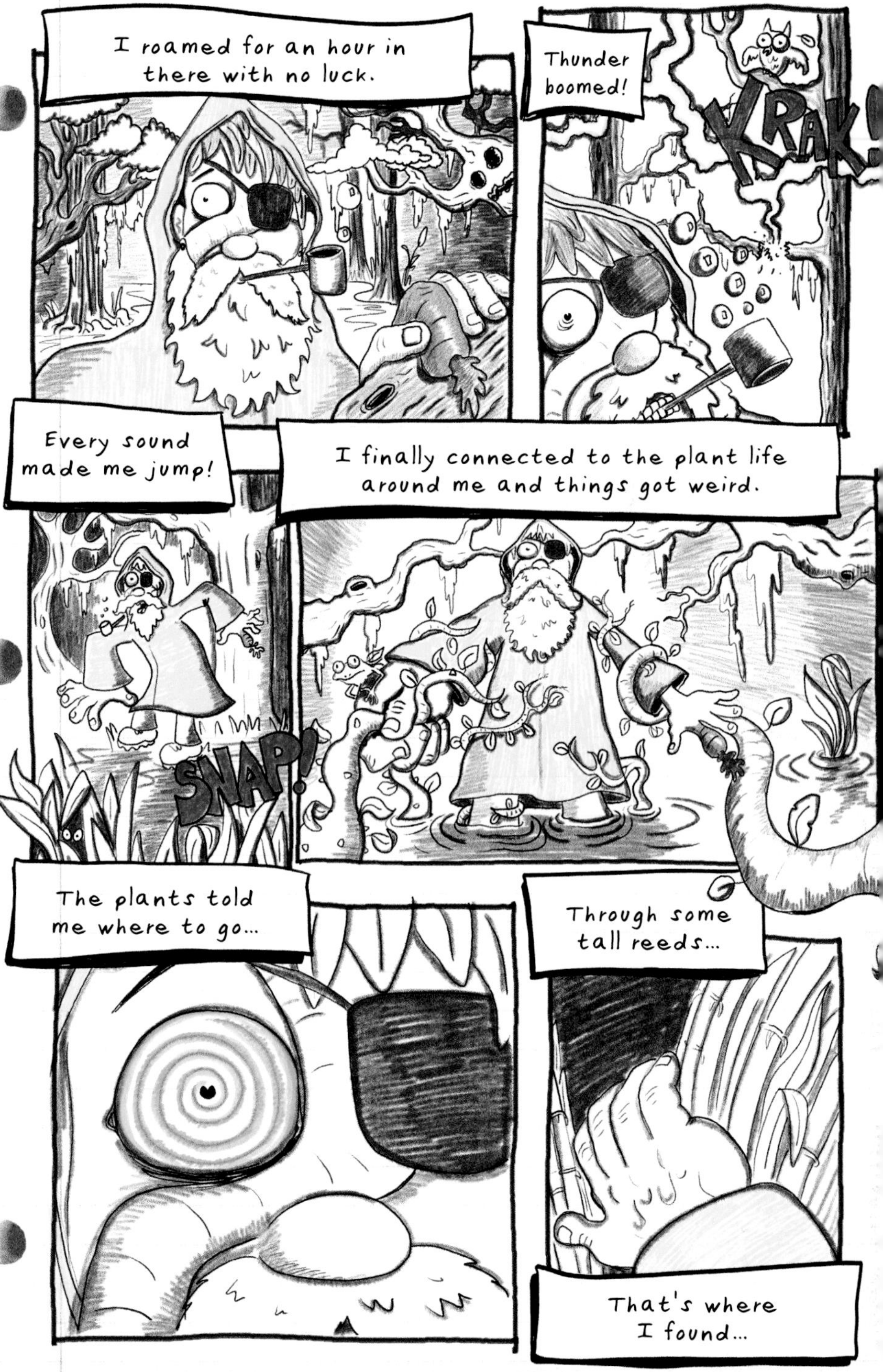
I roamed for an hour in there with no luck.
Thunder boomed!
KRAK!
Every sound made me jump!
SNAP!
I finally connected to the plant life around me and things got weird.
The plants told me where to go...
Through some tall reeds...
That's where I found...

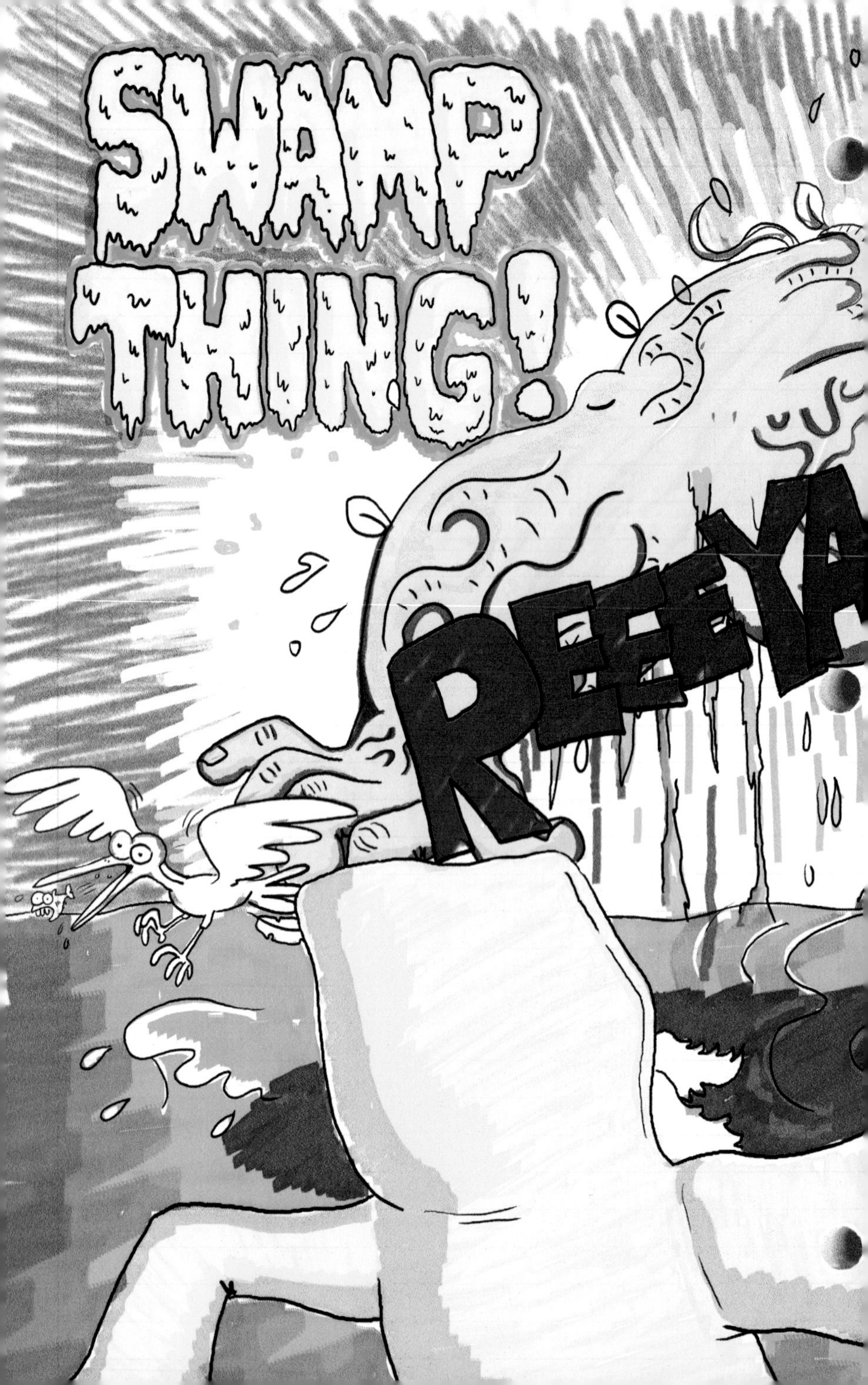
SWAMP THING!
REEEYA

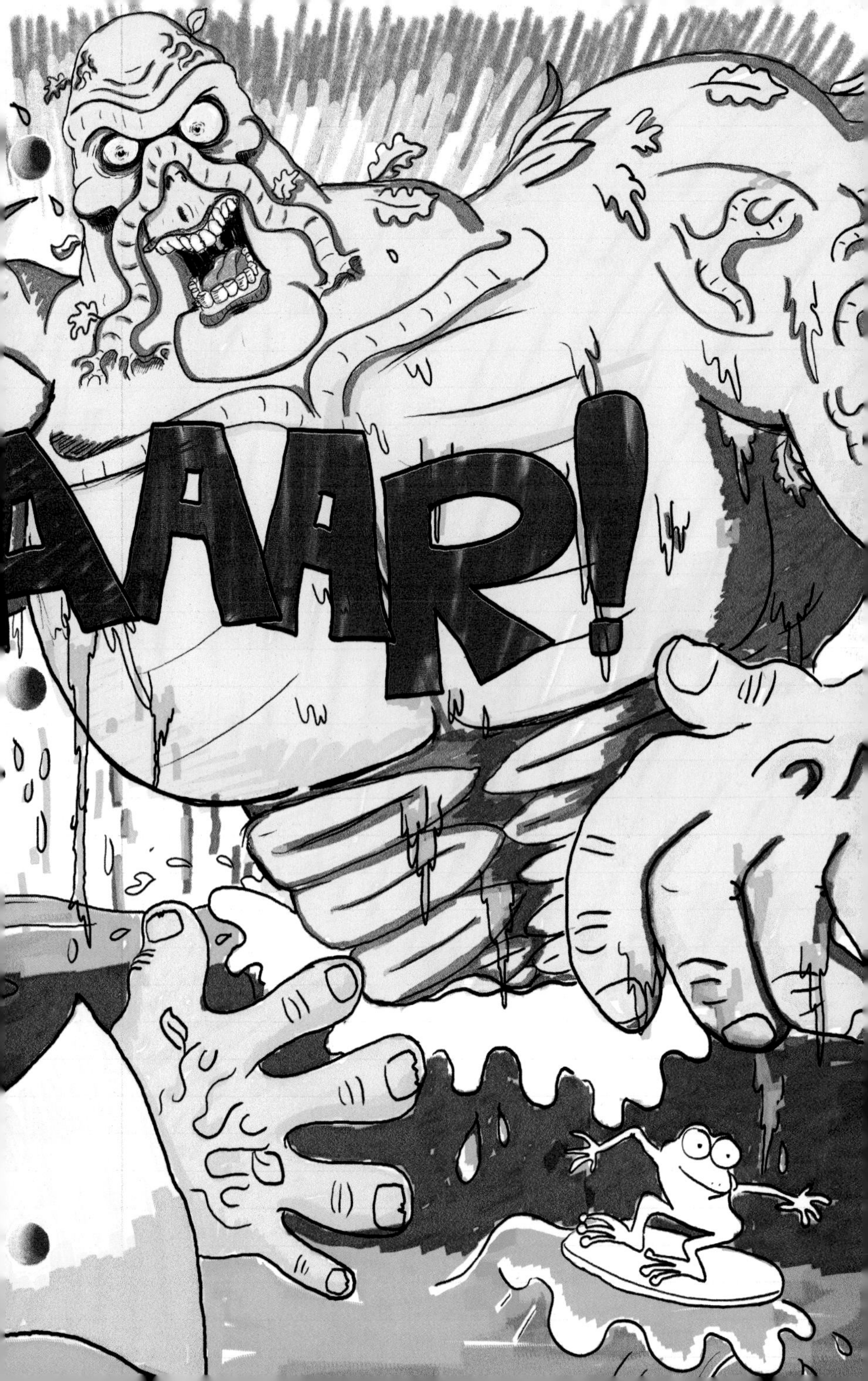
AAAR!

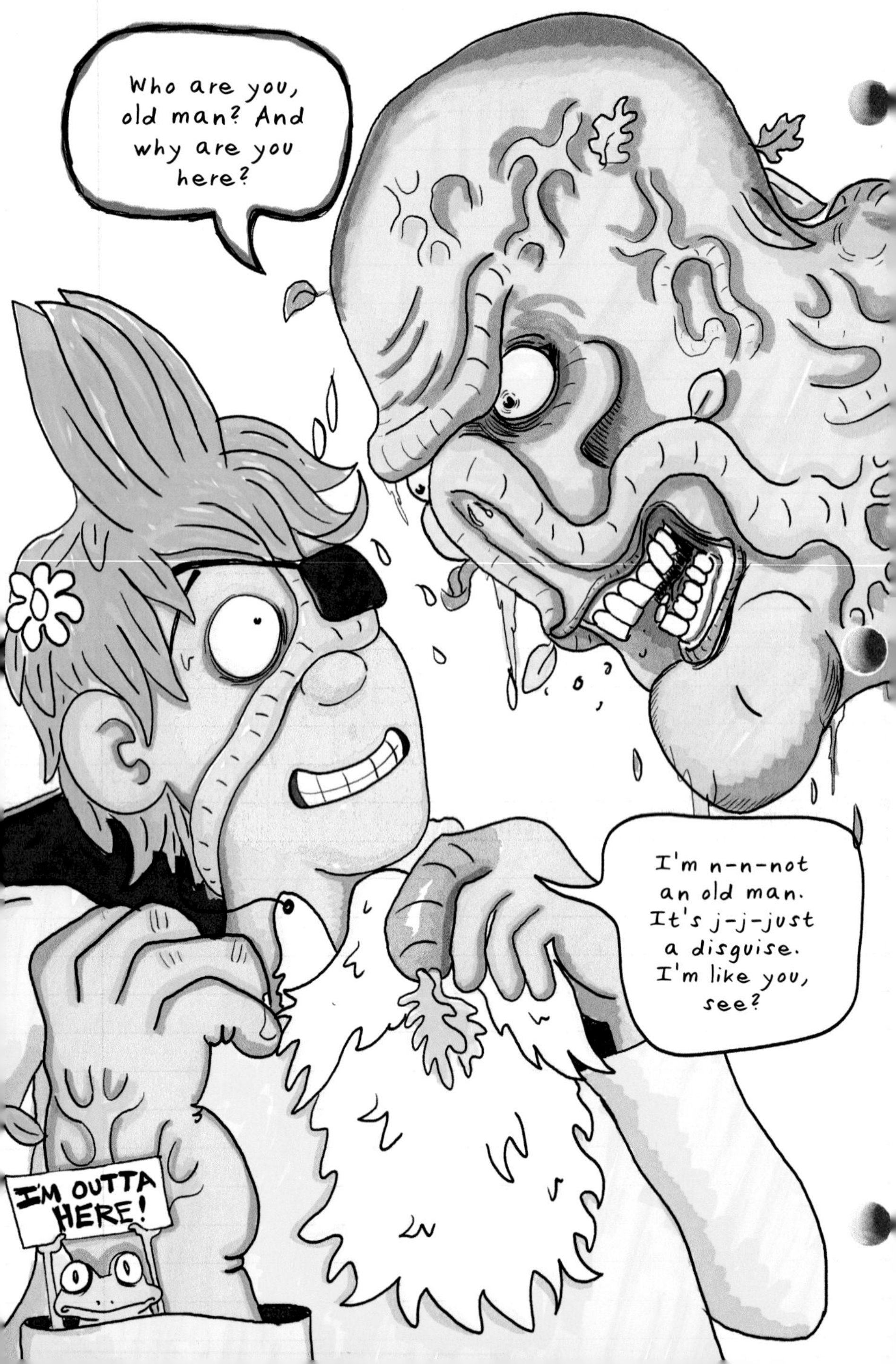
Who are you, old man? And why are you here?
I'm n-n-not an old man. It's j-j-just a disguise. I'm like you, see?
I'M OUTTA HERE!

Using the power of the plant life around me, I stretched my arm into an impressive vine. Of course, it looked like a puny twig next to his physique.

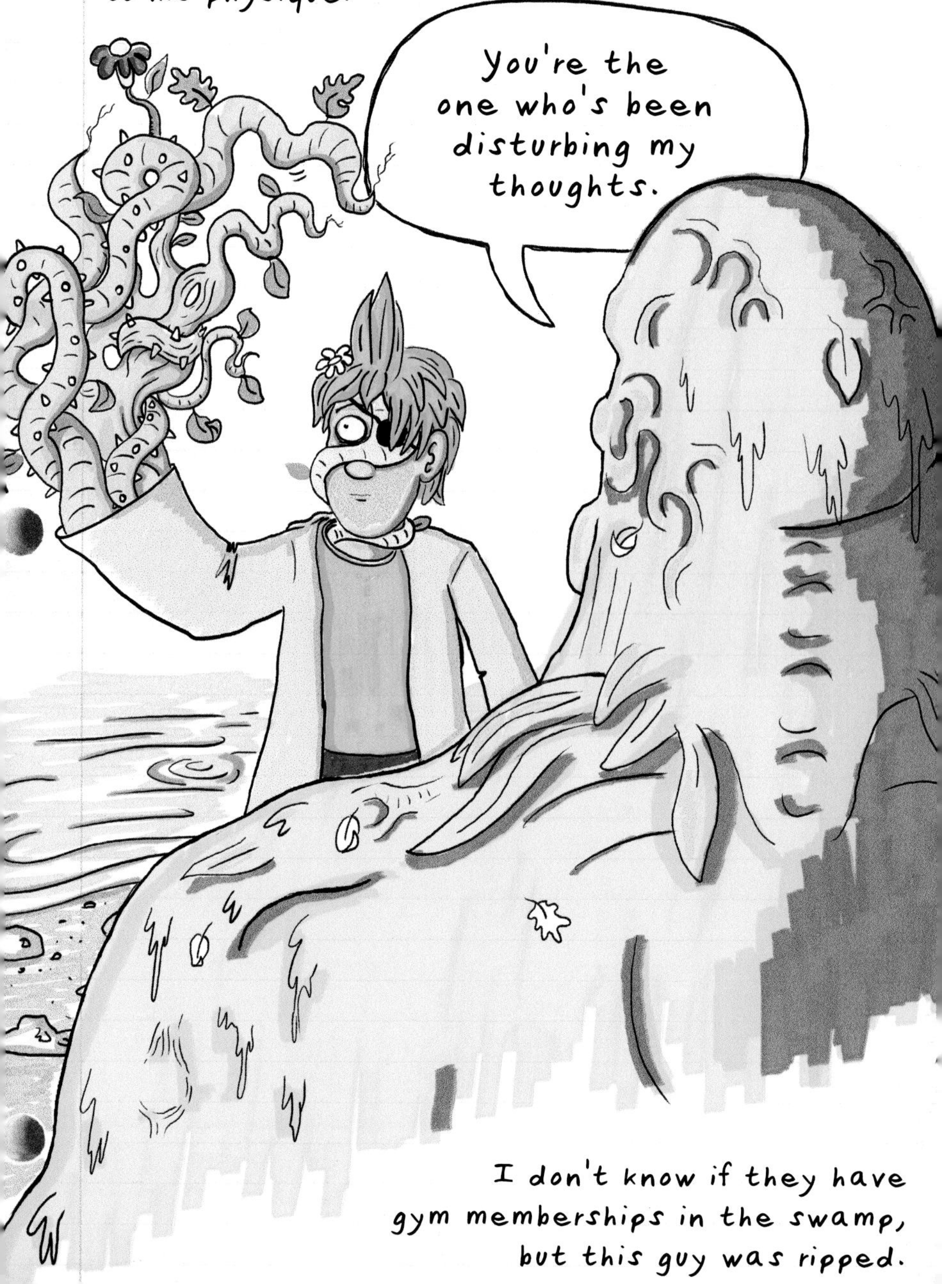

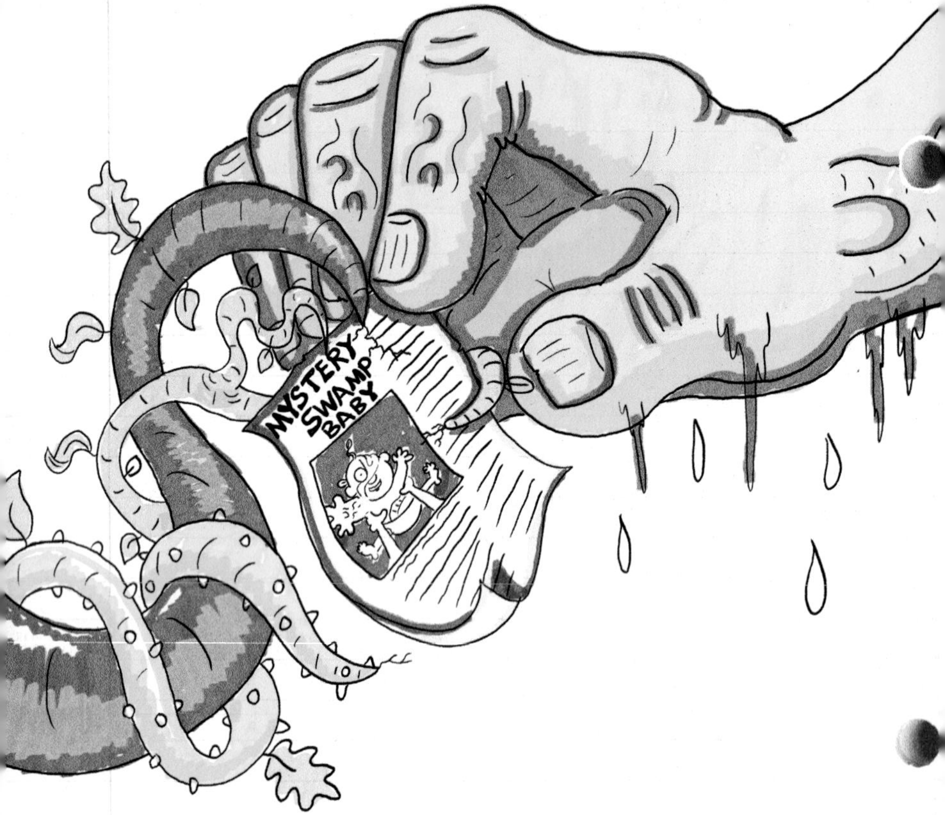
MYSTERY SWAMP BABY

I showed him the newspaper clipping and then hit him with a truckload of questions. Who am I? Why am I like this? What's my connection to the swamp? Why are there shady people following me? And—the most important question—are we somehow related? Swamp Thing stopped me midsentence...

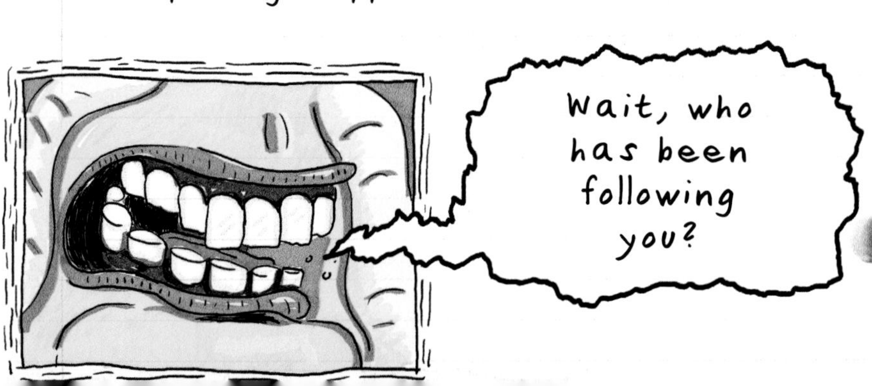
Wait, who has been following you?

I told him that ever since I had discovered I can control my abilities (sort of) folks had been tailing me. And I told him that the name Arcane had been coming up a lot. He did NOT react well to that name.

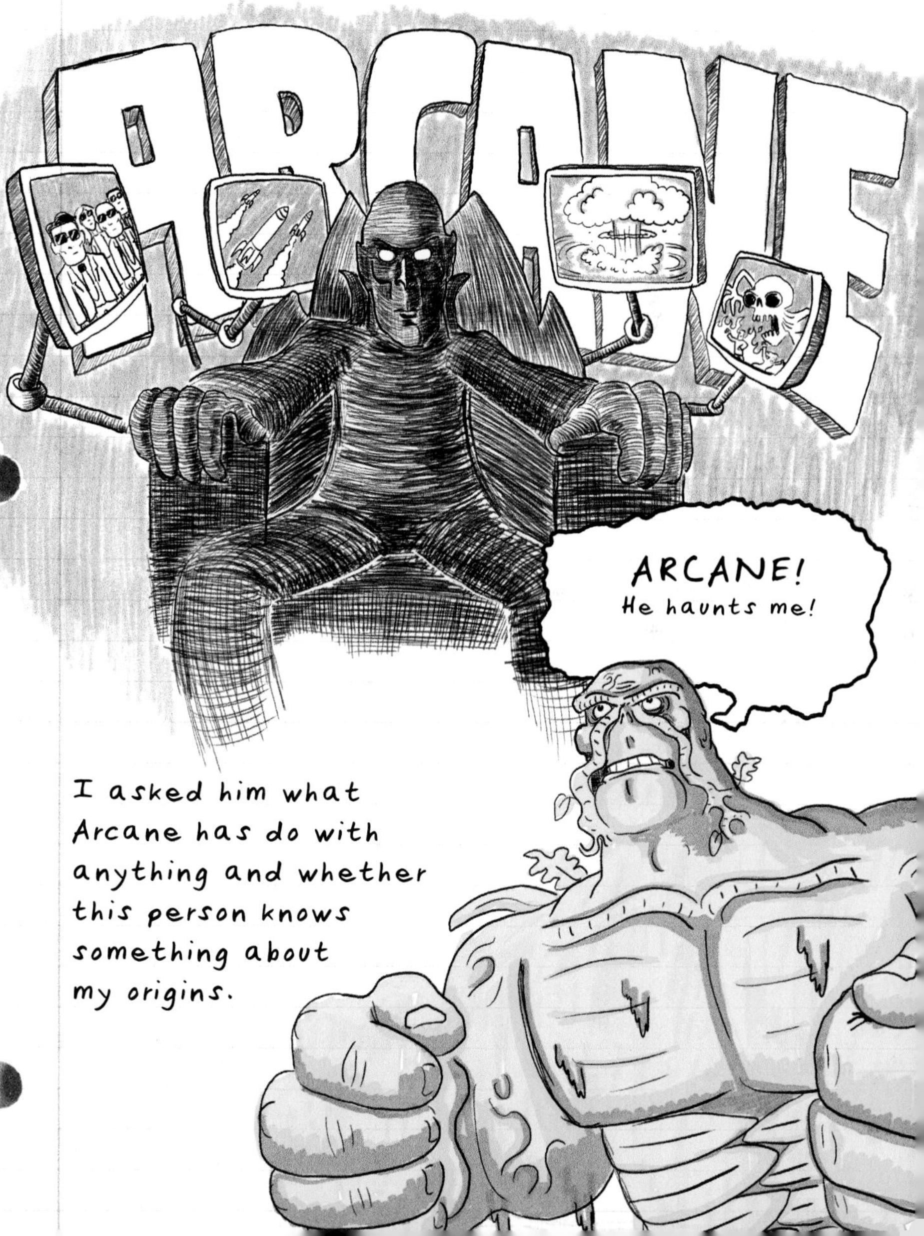
ARCANE
ARCANE! He haunts me!

I asked him what Arcane has do with anything and whether this person knows something about my origins.

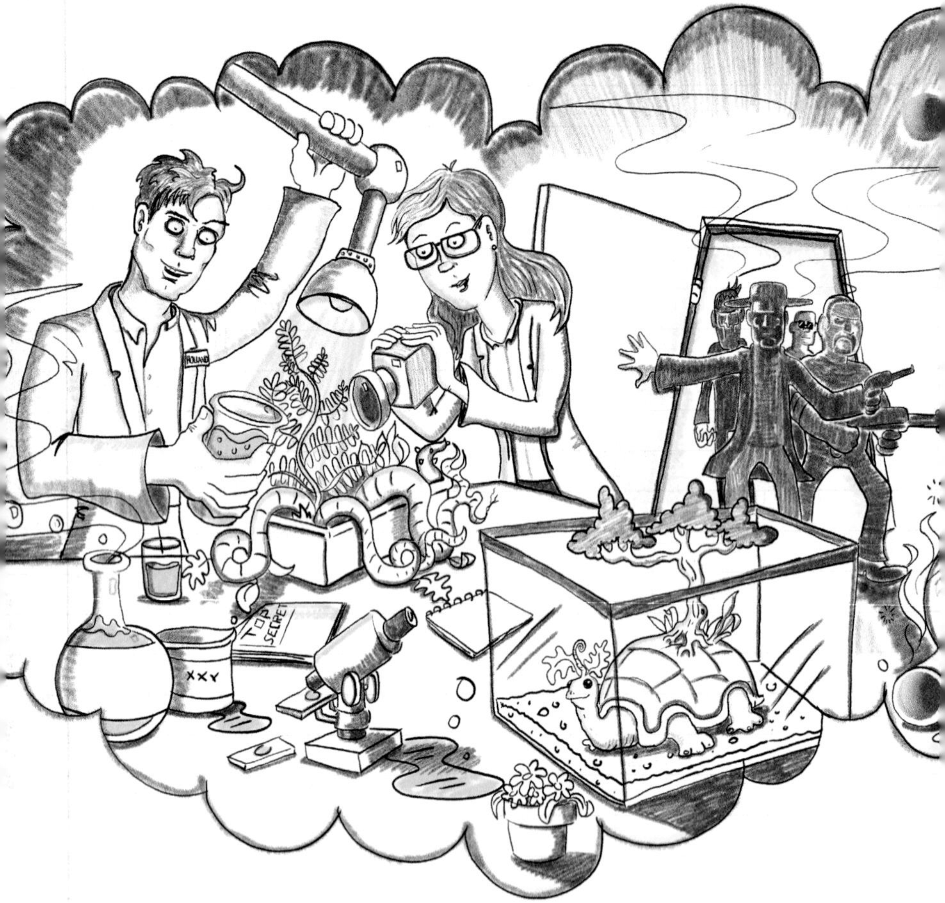
HOLLAND
TOP SECRET
XXY

After a long pause, he told me his story. He was once Dr. Alec Holland. Along with his wife, he had discovered a powerful formula in their swamp laboratory, a serum that held the secrets to tissue regeneration and eternal life. But dark forces had intervened. Men had shown up one night. Bad men. There was an attack and an explosion!

When he crawled out of the swamp, Alec Holland was no longer himself.

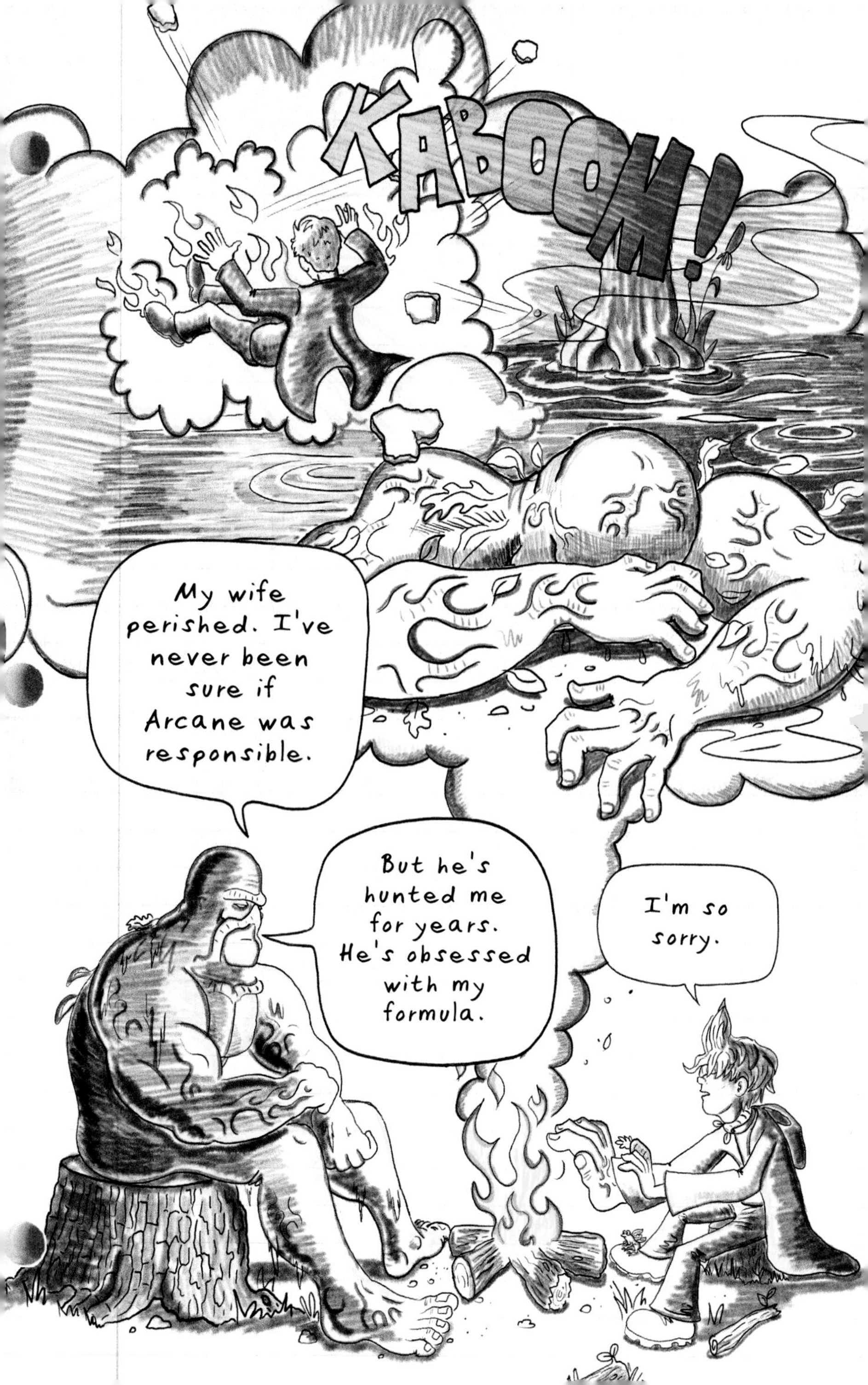
KABOOM!!
My wife perished. I've never been sure if Arcane was responsible.
But he's hunted me for years. He's obsessed with my formula.
I'm so sorry.

But Swamp Thing couldn't explain what I had to do with anything. His best guess was that the formula explosion had affected other life in the area, too. Like Specimen Number Two and me. He had no real answers.

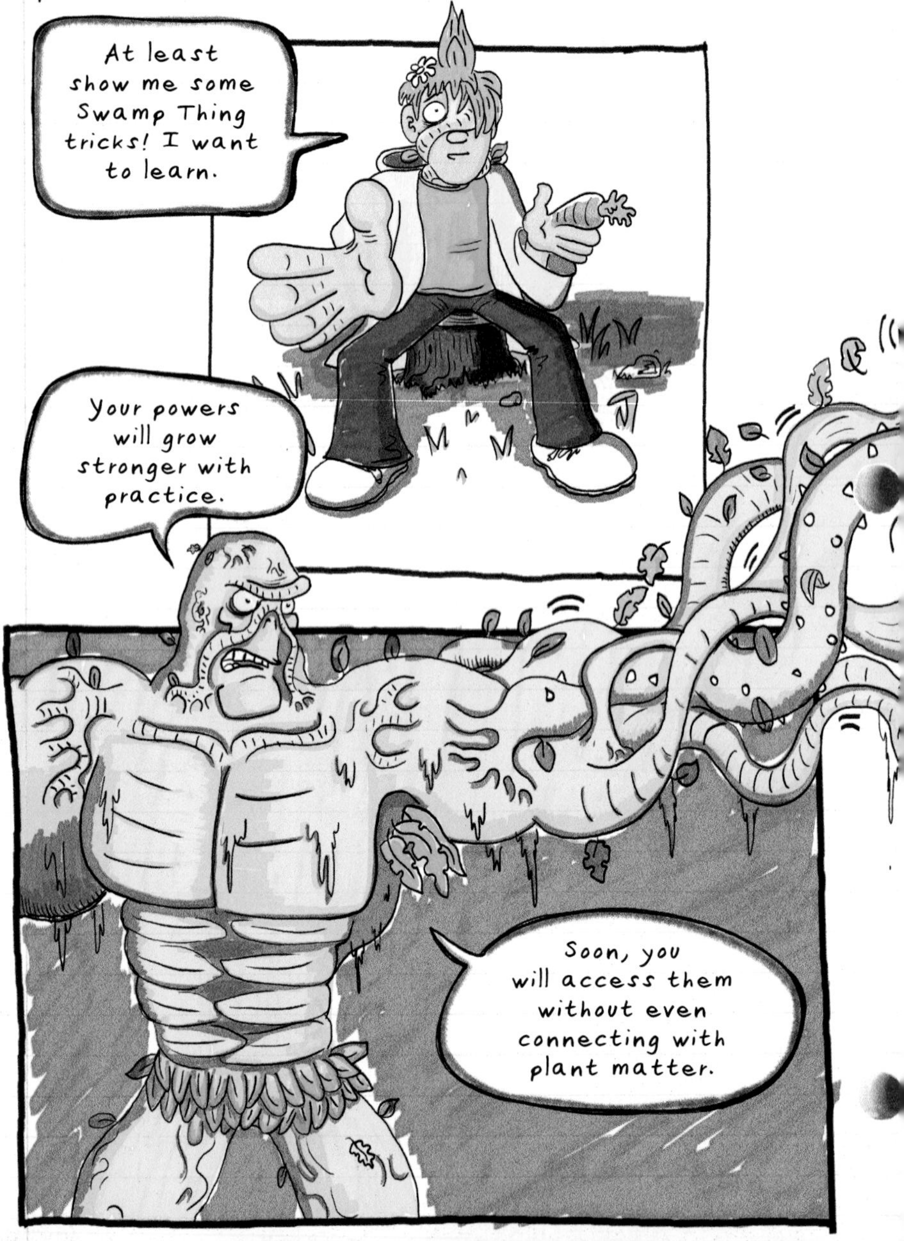
At least show me some Swamp Thing tricks! I want to learn.
Your powers will grow stronger with practice.
Soon, you will access them without even connecting with plant matter.

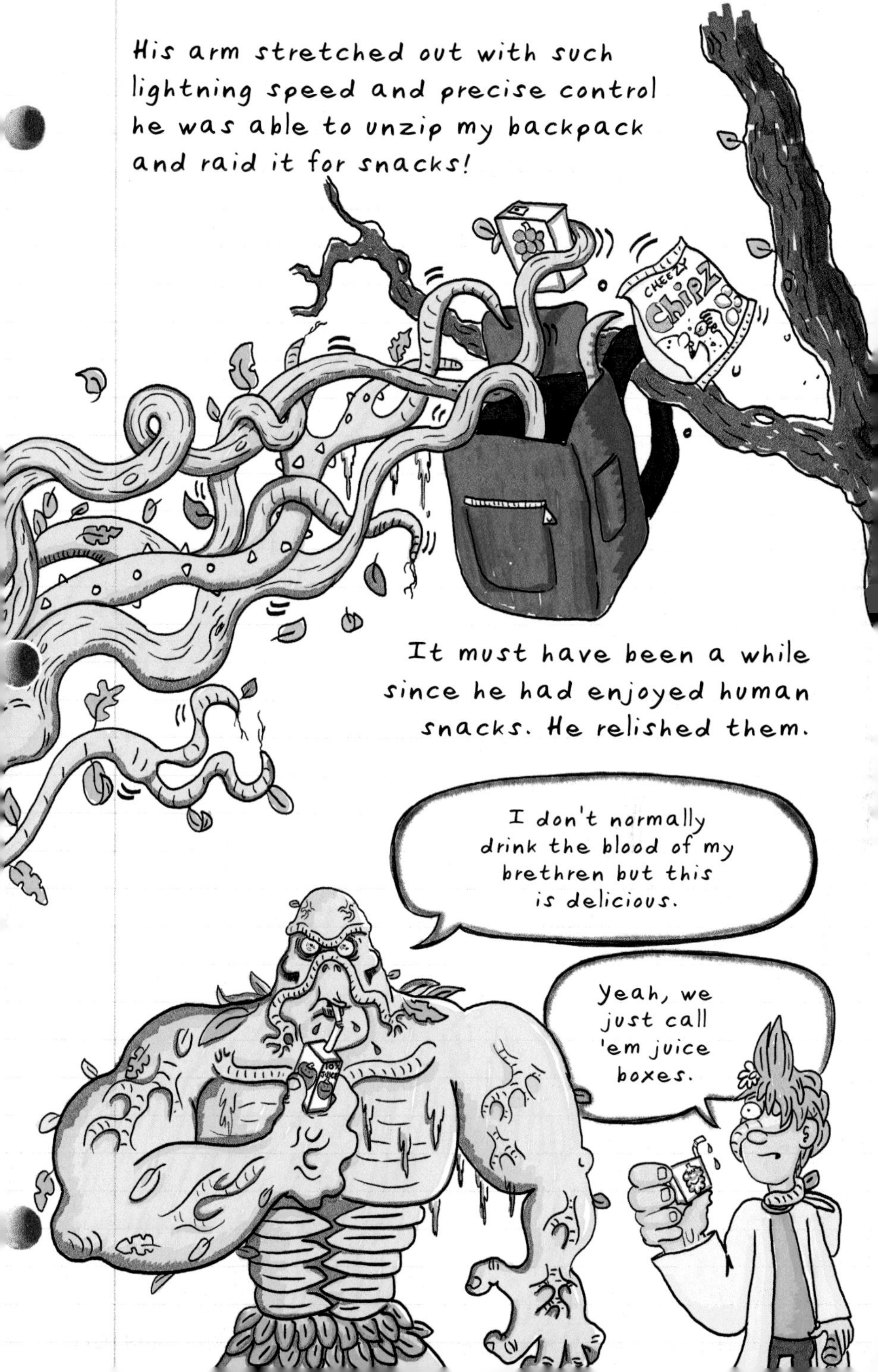
His arm stretched out with such lightning speed and precise control he was able to unzip my backpack and raid it for snacks!
CHEEZY
ChipZ
It must have been a while since he had enjoyed human snacks. He relished them.
I don't normally drink the blood of my brethren but this is delicious.
Yeah, we just call 'em juice boxes.

I could tell Swamp Thing missed life among humans so I tried to convince him to come back with me or, better yet, let me stay! We could be a superhero team, fighting crime!

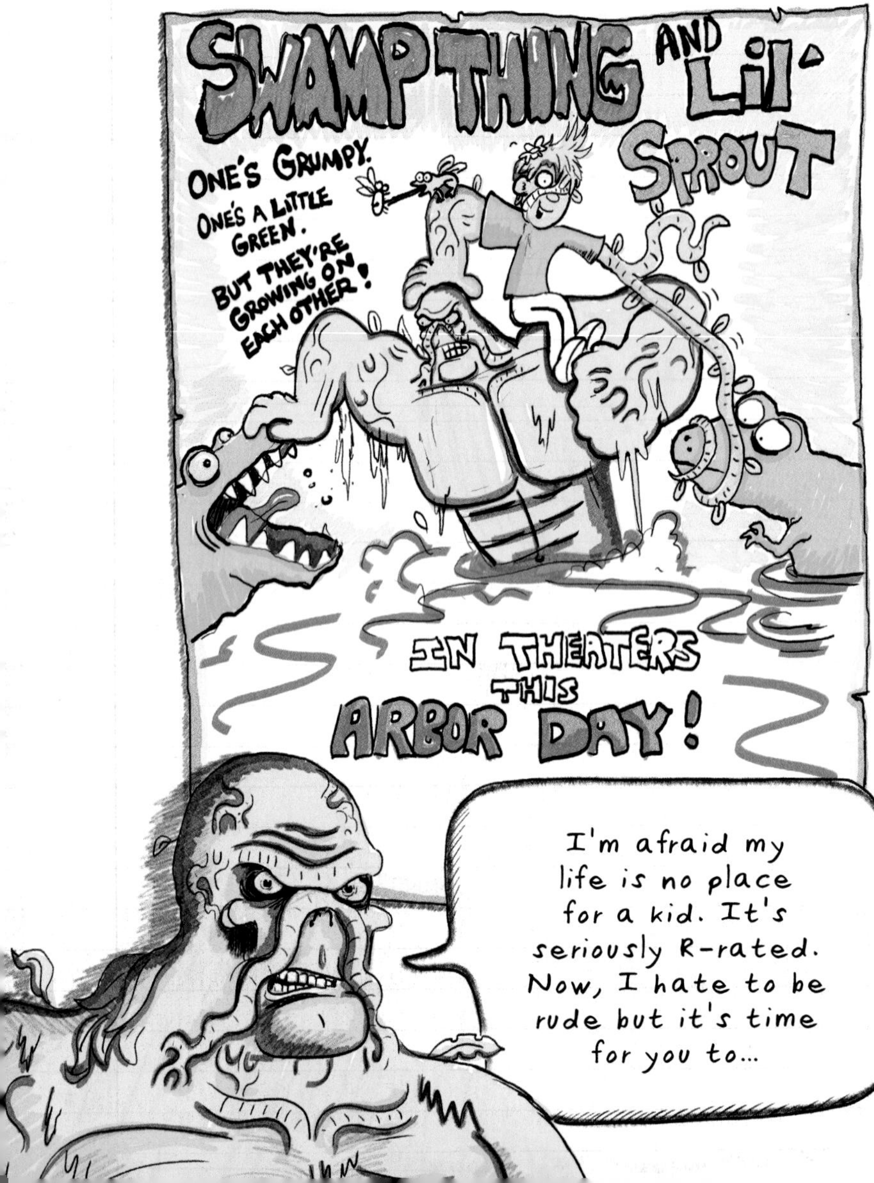
SWAMP THING AND LIL' SPROUT
ONE'S GRUMPY. ONE'S A LITTLE GREEN. BUT THEY'RE GROWING ON EACH OTHER!
IN THEATERS THIS ARBOR DAY!
I'm afraid my life is no place for a kid. It's seriously R-rated. Now, I hate to be rude but it's time for you to...

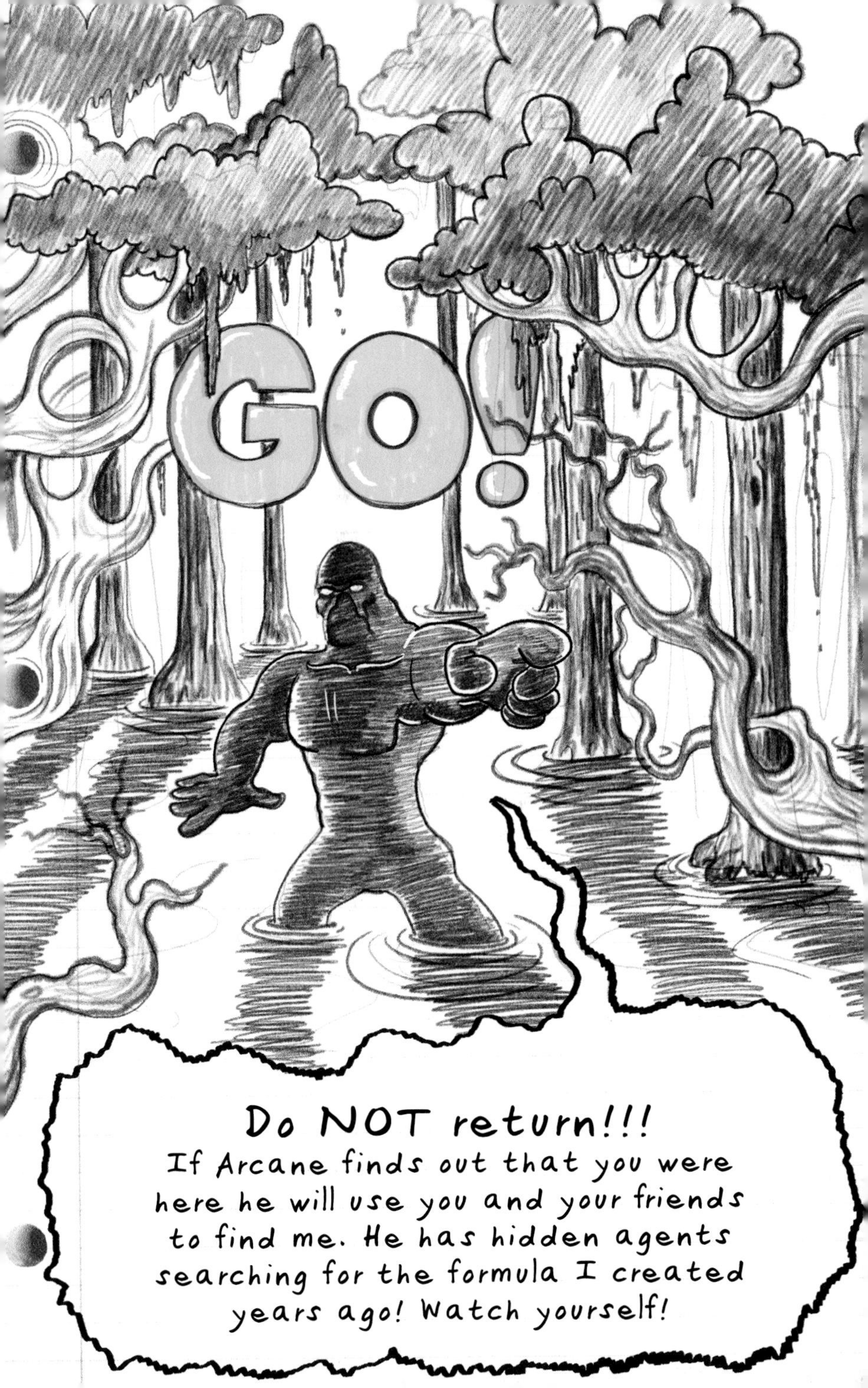
GO!
Do NOT return!!!
If Arcane finds out that you were here he will use you and your friends to find me. He has hidden agents searching for the formula I created years ago! Watch yourself!

MON. MIDNIGHT

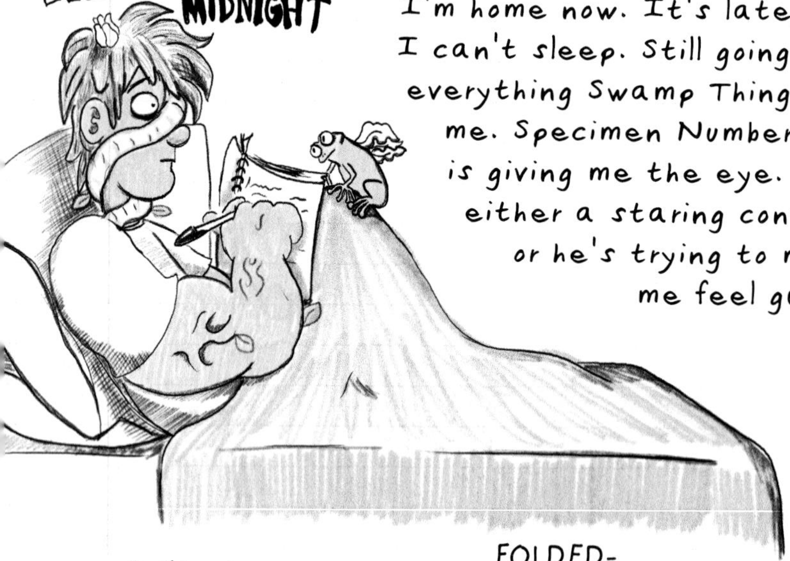

I'm home now. It's late, but I can't sleep. Still going over everything Swamp Thing told me. Specimen Number Two is giving me the eye. It's either a staring contest or he's trying to make me feel guilty.

Guilty because I didn't get home until after dark and my folks were not happy. They're contemplating not letting me go to the football game this Friday which I'm not sure counts as punishment but I won't tell them that.

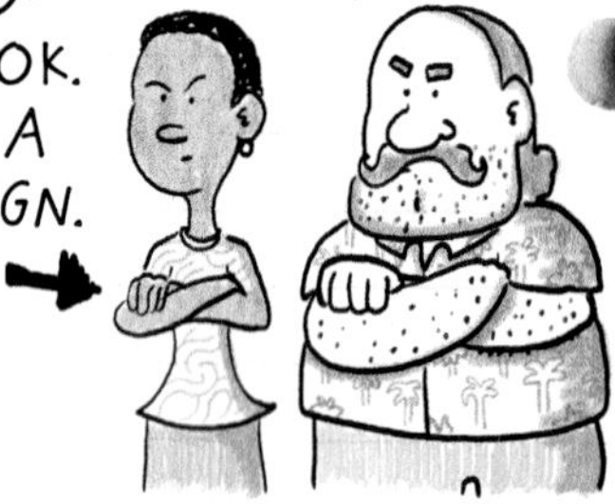
FOLDED-ARM LOOK. NEVER A GOOD SIGN.

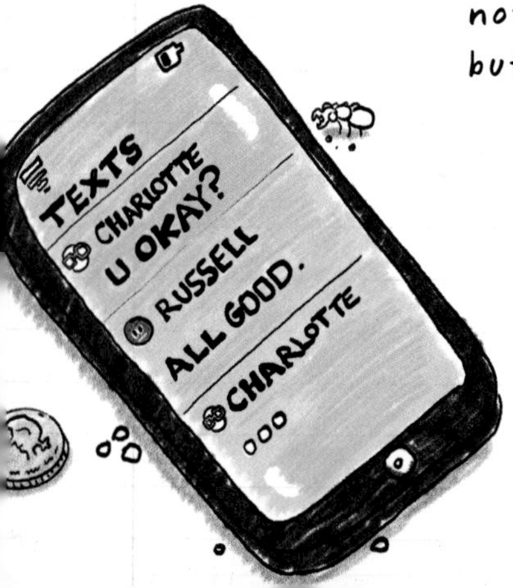
TEXTS
CHARLOTTE
U OKAY?
RUSSELL
ALL GOOD.
CHARLOTTE
OOO

Just got a text from Charlotte. "U okay?" I texted her back—"All good."

I wish I could say I believed that.

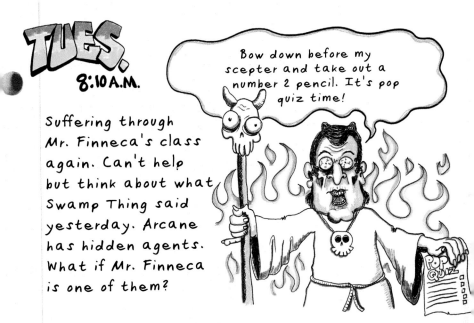

TUES.

8:10 A.M.

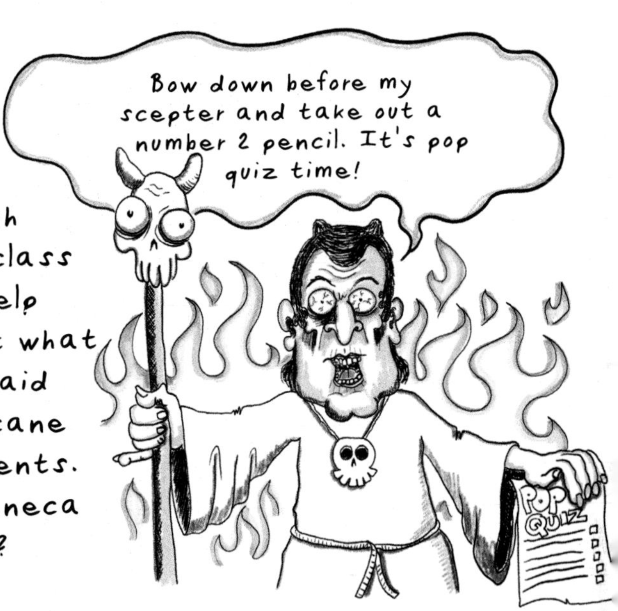
Bow down before my scepter and take out a number 2 pencil. It's pop quiz time!
POP QUIZ

Suffering through Mr. Finneca's class again. Can't help but think about what Swamp Thing said yesterday. Arcane has hidden agents. What if Mr. Finneca is one of them?

OMG, what if Mr. Finneca IS Arcane disguised as a science teacher?

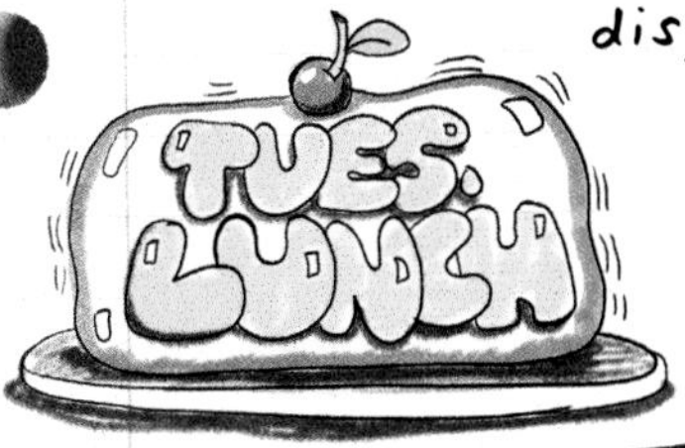
TUES. LUNCH

It's lunchtime now. I just apologized to Preston for being so standoffish.

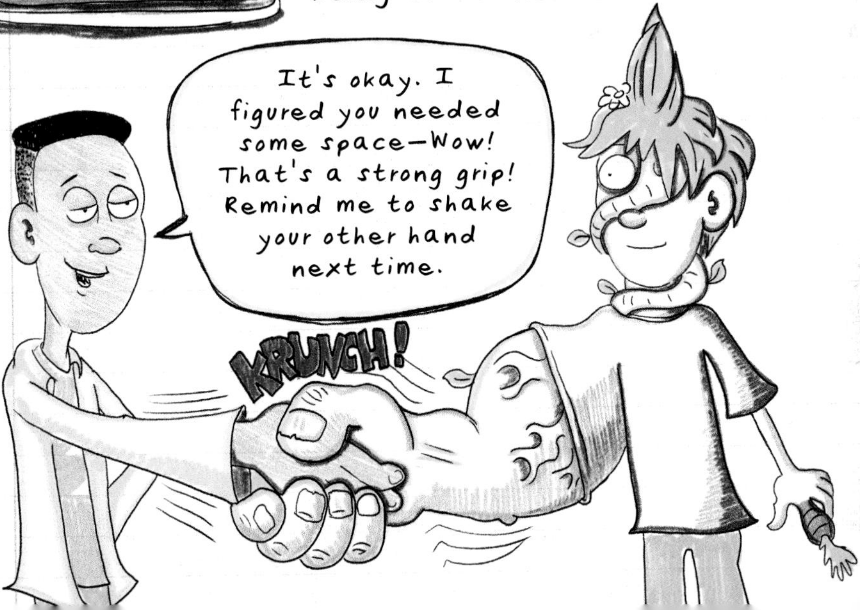
It's okay. I figured you needed some space—Wow! That's a strong grip! Remind me to shake your other hand next time.
KRUNCH!

TUES. AFTER SCHOOL

I just now got a chance to apologize to Charlotte. I kinda wanted to tell her about my adventure but she cut me off before I could say one word...

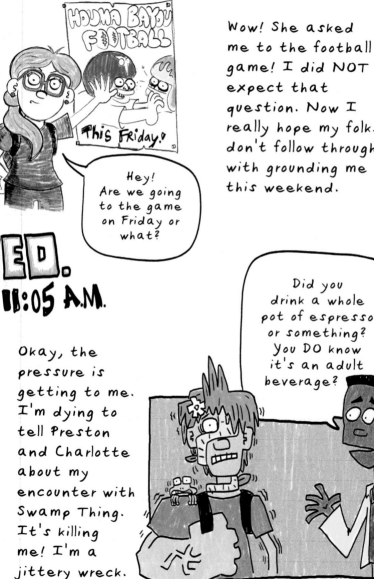

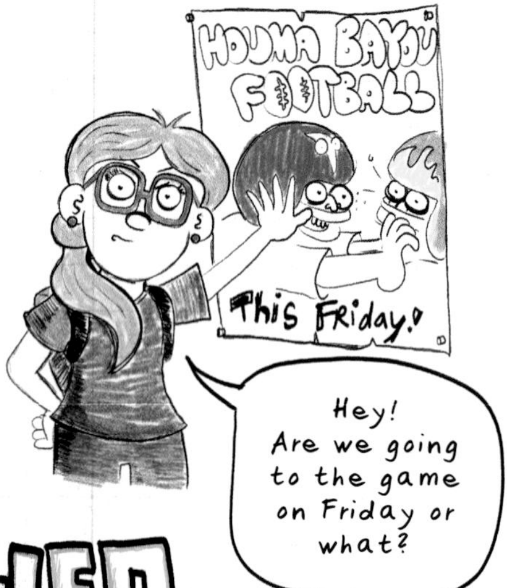
HOUMA BAYOU FOOTBALL
THIS FRIDAY!
Hey! Are we going to the game on Friday or what?

Wow! She asked me to the football game! I did NOT expect that question. Now I really hope my folks don't follow through with grounding me this weekend.

WED. 11:05 A.M.

Okay, the pressure is getting to me. I'm dying to tell Preston and Charlotte about my encounter with Swamp Thing. It's killing me! I'm a jittery wreck.

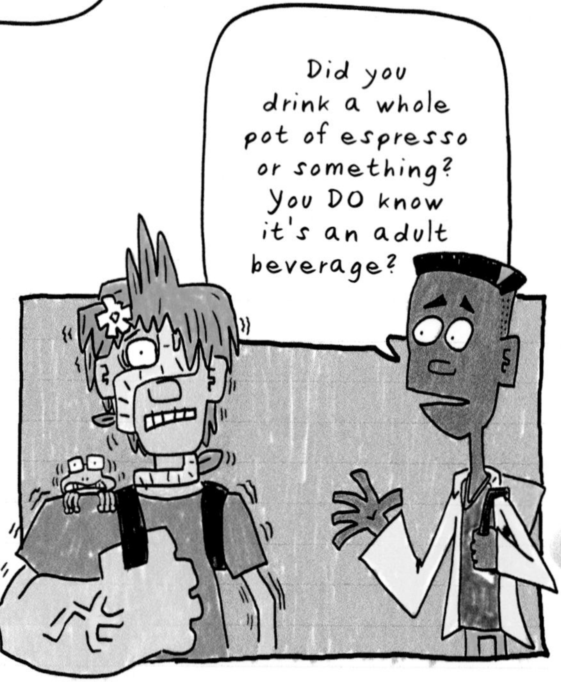
Did you drink a whole pot of espresso or something? You DO know it's an adult beverage?

THURS NIGHT UPDATE

All right! I'm in bed now, doodling.
A lot happened today. A. LOT.

First off, I couldn't take it anymore. After lunch, I called Preston and Charlotte into the library to reveal my little secret.

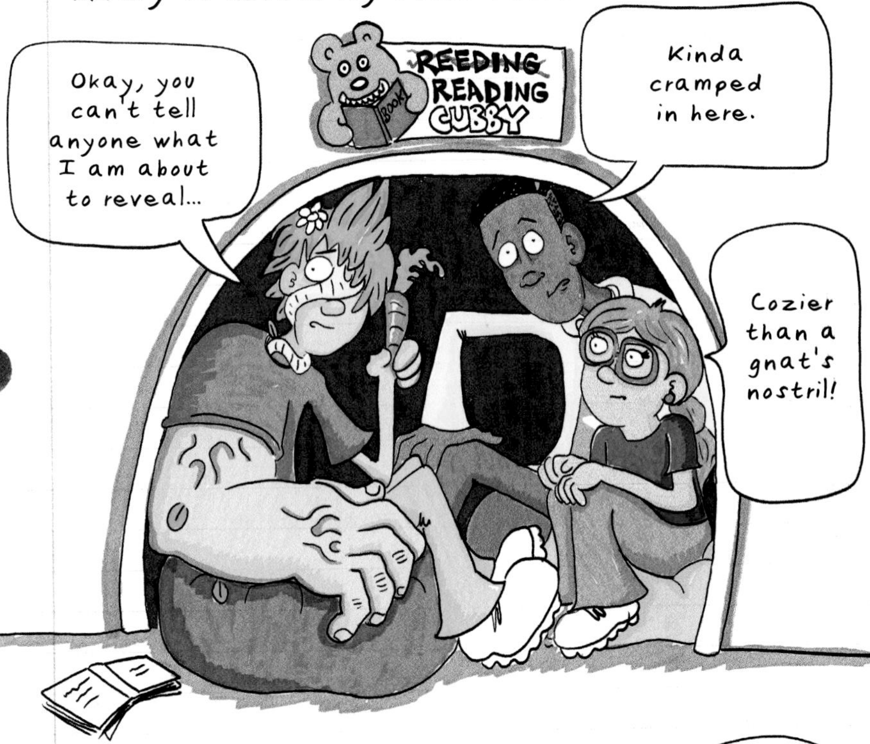
REEDING
READING
CUBBY
BOOK
Okay, you can't tell anyone what I am about to reveal...
Kinda cramped in here.
Cozier than a gnat's nostril!

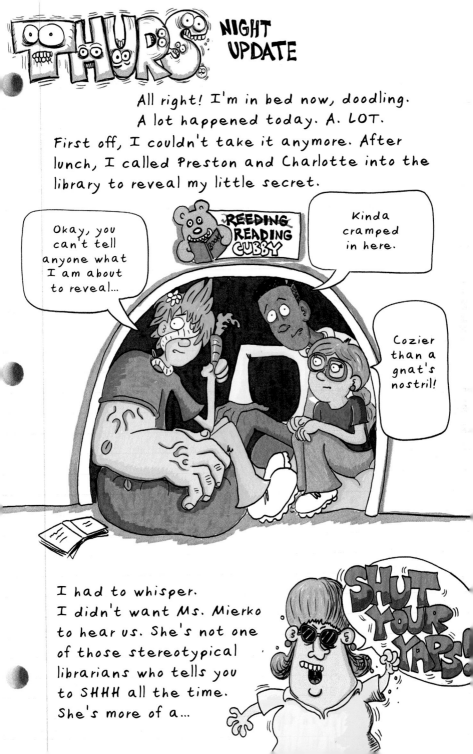

I had to whisper.
I didn't want Ms. Mierko to hear us. She's not one of those stereotypical librarians who tells you to SHHH all the time. She's more of a...

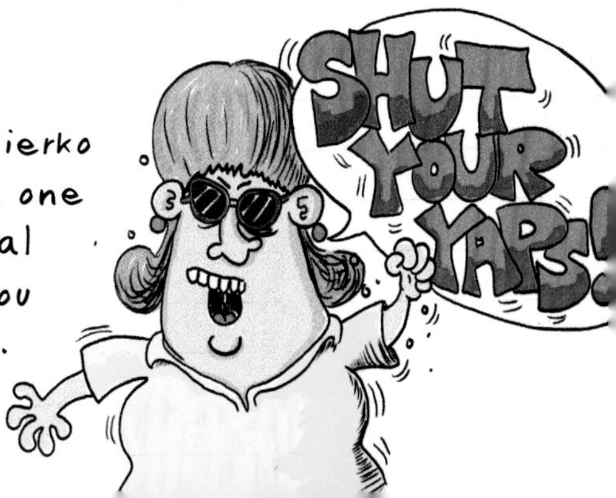
SHUT YOUR YAPS!

But before Ms. Mierko could yell at us, another more intense scream came echoing down the hallway!

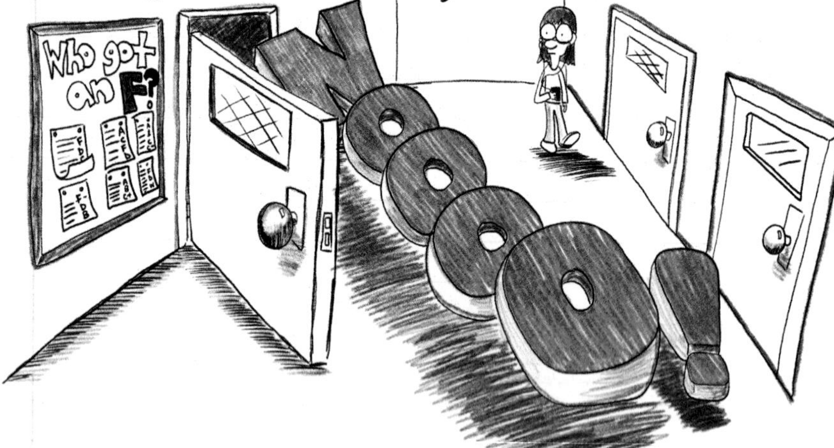
Who got an F?
WOOOO!

It was coming from Mr. Finneca's room!

Turns out, someone had broken into his specimen cabinet and stolen everything! Mr. Finneca was wiggin' out.

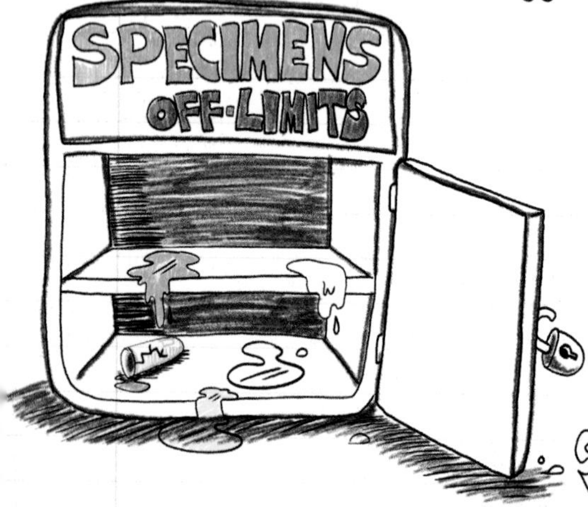
SPECIMENS
OFF-LIMITS

I asked him if one of those specimens happened to be the vine that had shot out of my toe on the day I raced Nils. He got pretty quiet.

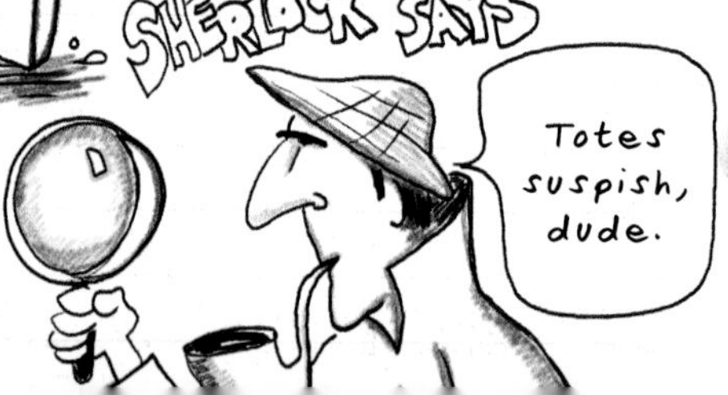
SHERLOCK SAYS
Totes suspish, dude.

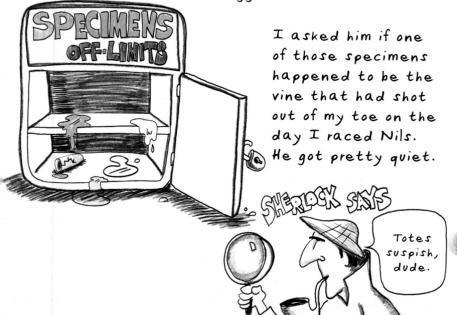

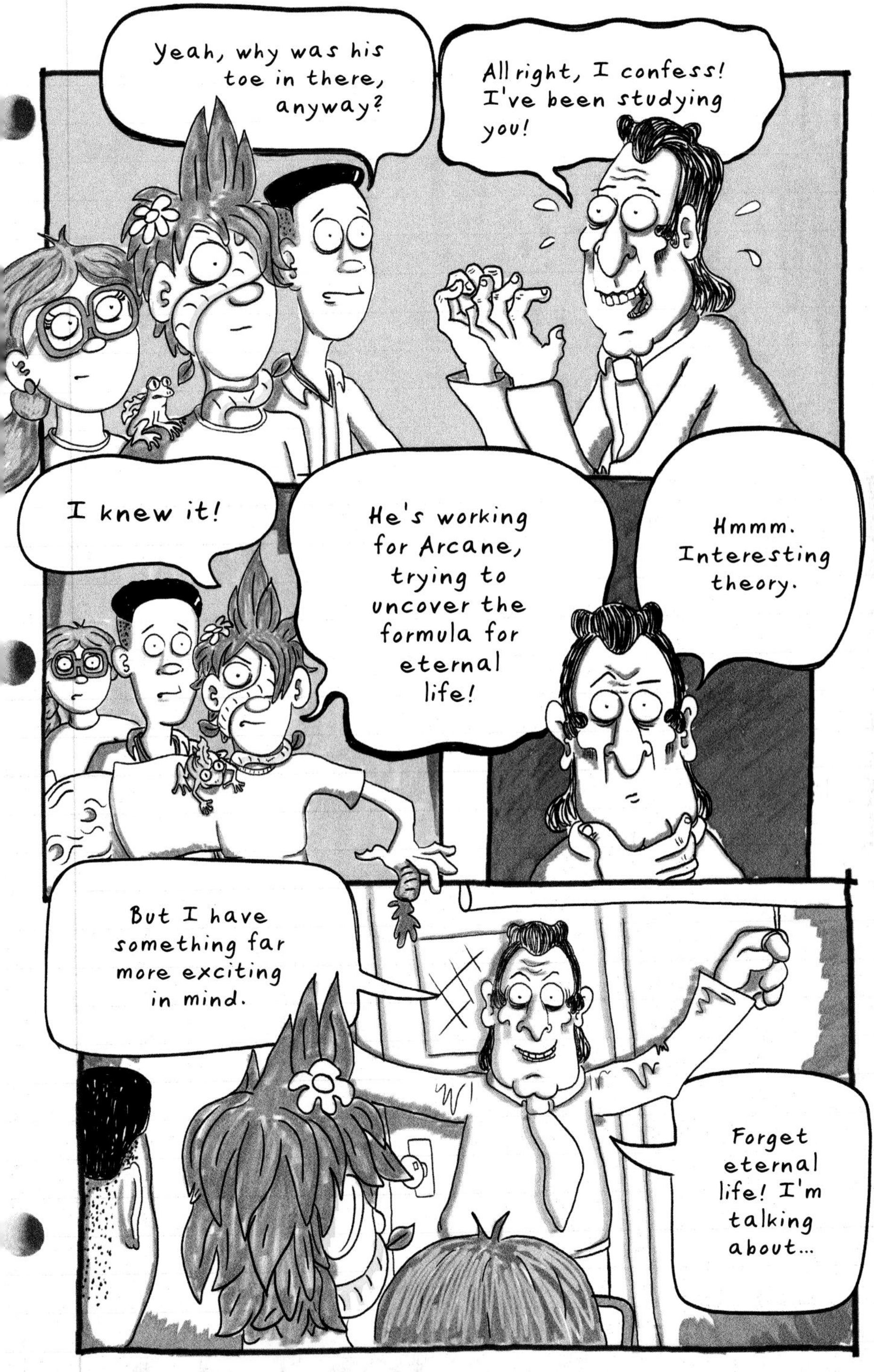

Yeah, why was his toe in there, anyway?
All right, I confess! I've been studying you!
I knew it!
He's working for Arcane, trying to uncover the formula for eternal life!
Hmmm. Interesting theory.
But I have something far more exciting in mind.
Forget eternal life! I'm talking about...

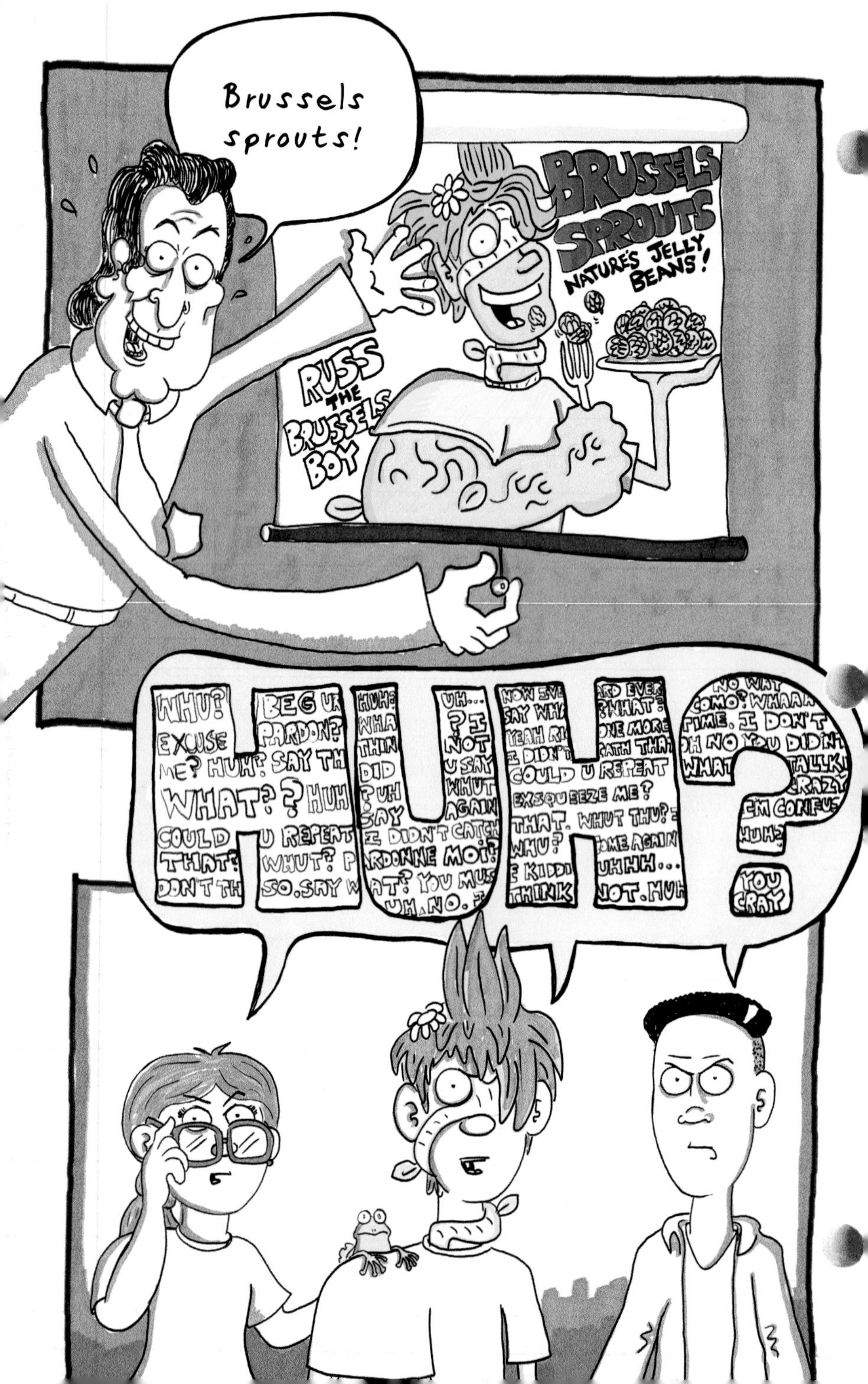

Brussels sprouts!
BRUSSELS SPROUTS
NATURE'S JELLY BEANS!
RUSS THE BRUSSELS BOY
HUH?

Mr. Finneca started raving about how brussels sprouts are a multimillion-dollar industry and that I would be the perfect poster boy to market them to kids all over the world! He'd even been studying samples of my DNA to figure out how to get me to sprout my own sprouts!

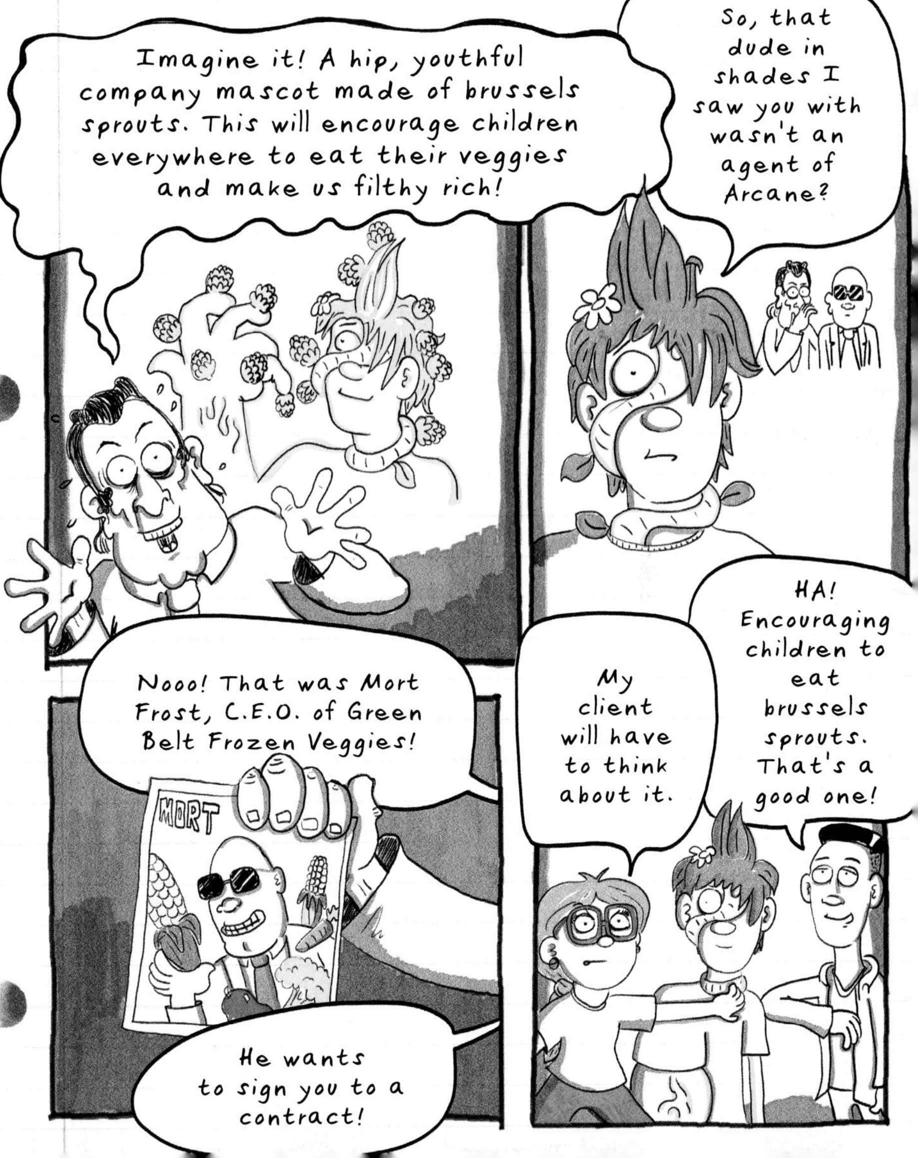
Imagine it! A hip, youthful company mascot made of brussels sprouts. This will encourage children everywhere to eat their veggies and make us filthy rich!
So, that dude in shades I saw you with wasn't an agent of Arcane?
Nooo! That was Mort Frost, C.E.O. of Green Belt Frozen Veggies!
MORT
He wants to sign you to a contract!
HA! Encouraging children to eat brussels sprouts. That's a good one!
My client will have to think about it.

We decided to walk home from school, contemplating Mr. Finneca's, uh, interesting offer.

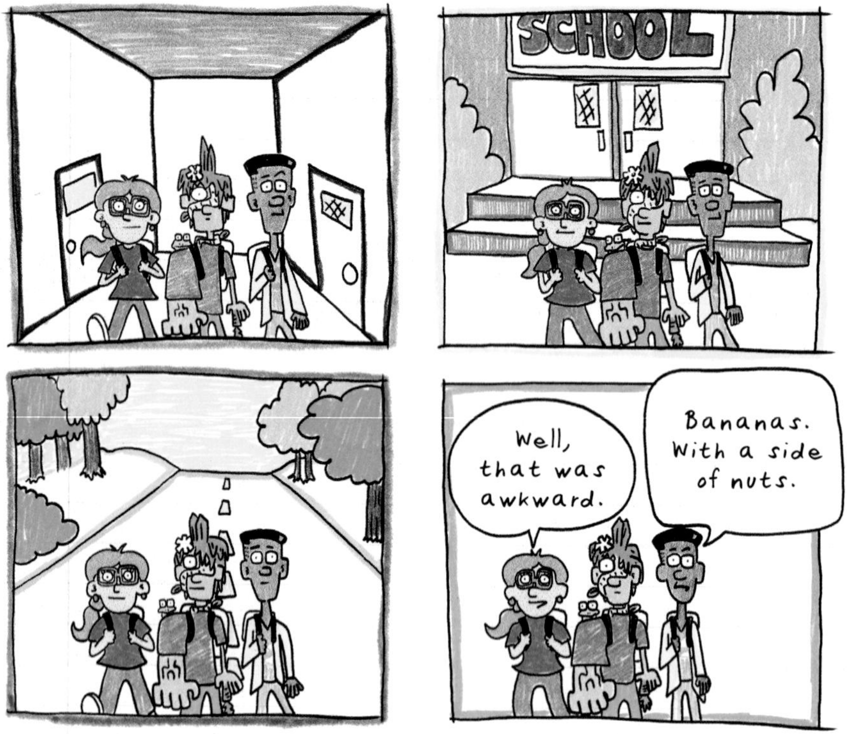
SCHOOL
Well, that was awkward.
Bananas. With a side of nuts.

That's when Charlotte stopped to grill me.

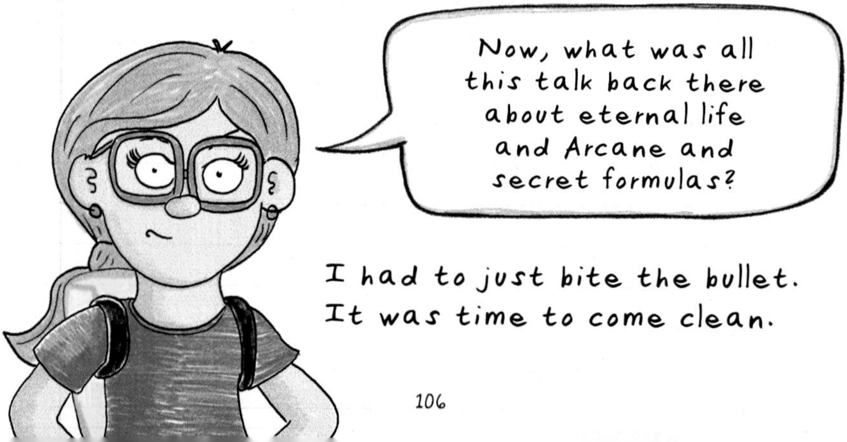
Now, what was all this talk back there about eternal life and Arcane and secret formulas?

I had to just bite the bullet. It was time to come clean.

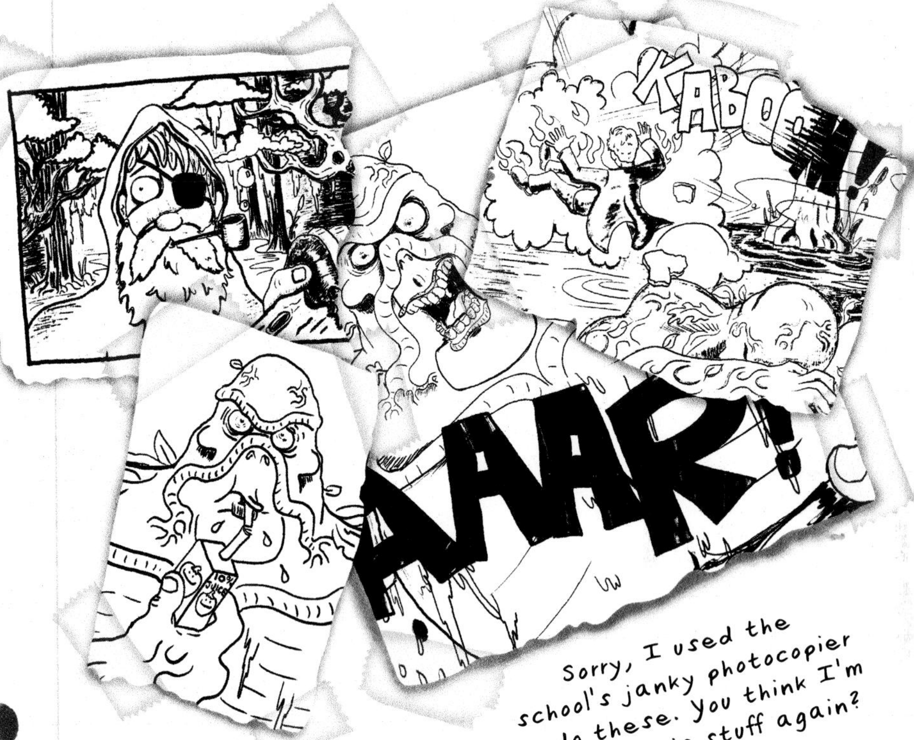
KABOO
AAAR!

Sorry, I used the school's janky photocopier to do these. You think I'm drawing this stuff again? No way!

So I told them about everything. My trip into the bog dressed as the old dude, my meeting with Swamp Thing, the story of his transformation from man into plant matter. And I relayed his warning. That if we weren't careful, Arcane's agents could get ahold of his formula, which could lead to...

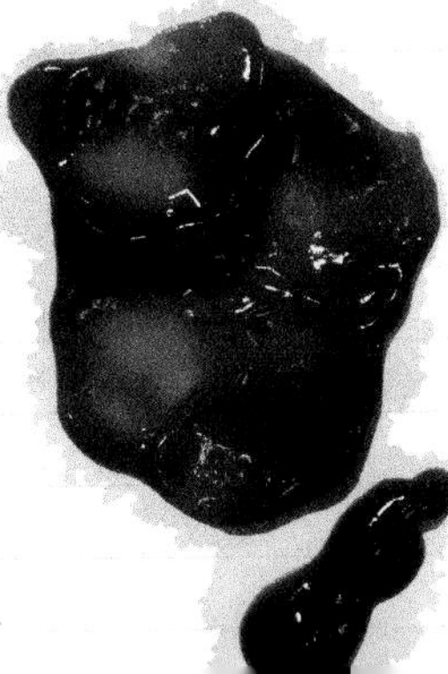

Oops! Sorry. Don't worry. That's not blood. Just a ketchup stain. I'm eating tater tots in bed again.

Preston handled my revelation with dignity and grace...

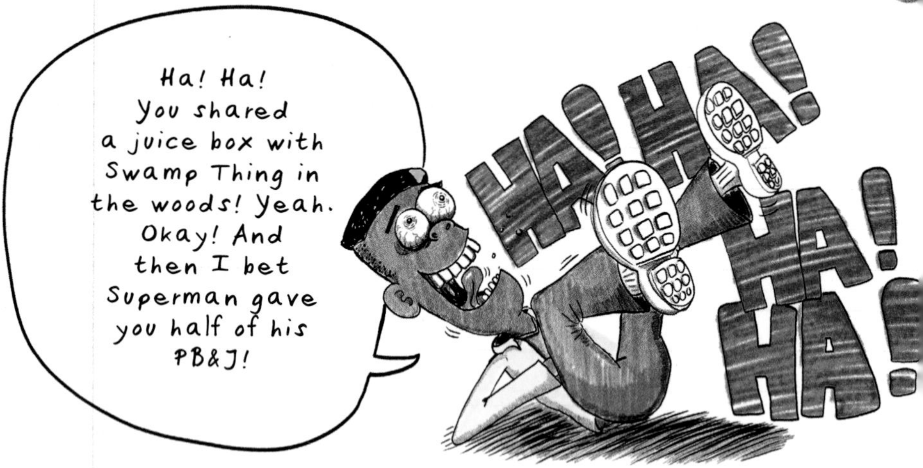

Ha! Ha! You shared a juice box with Swamp Thing in the woods! Yeah. Okay! And then I bet Superman gave you half of his PB&J!
HA! HA! HA! HA!

But Charlotte believed me right away...

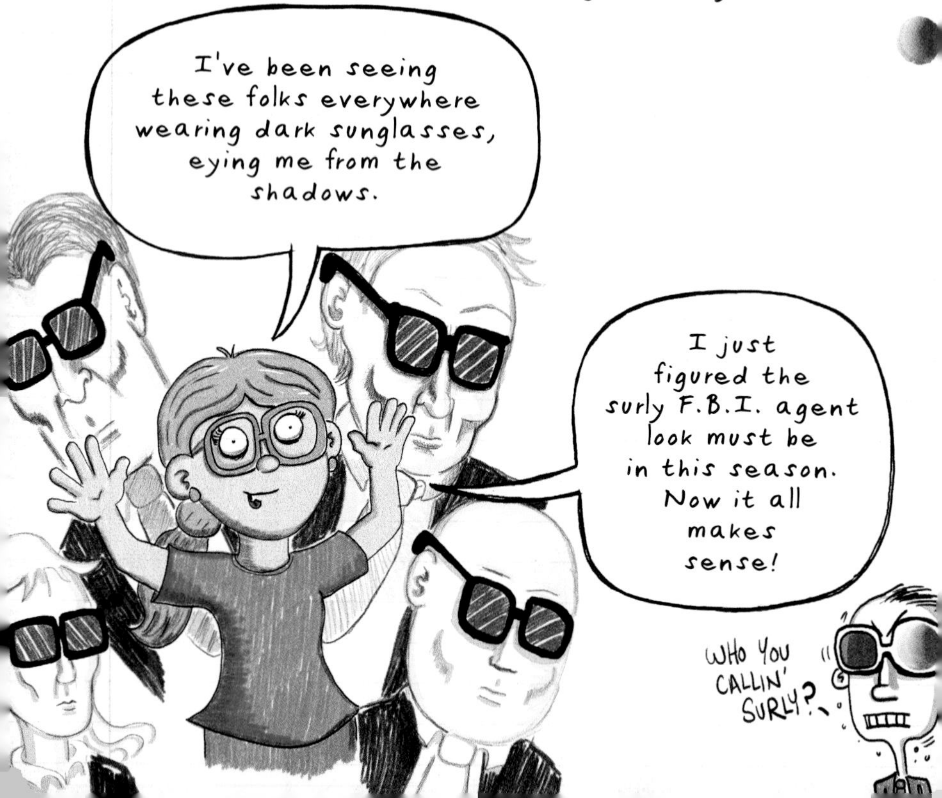

I've been seeing these folks everywhere wearing dark sunglasses, eying me from the shadows.
I just figured the surly F.B.I. agent look must be in this season. Now it all makes sense!
WHO YOU CALLIN' SURLY?

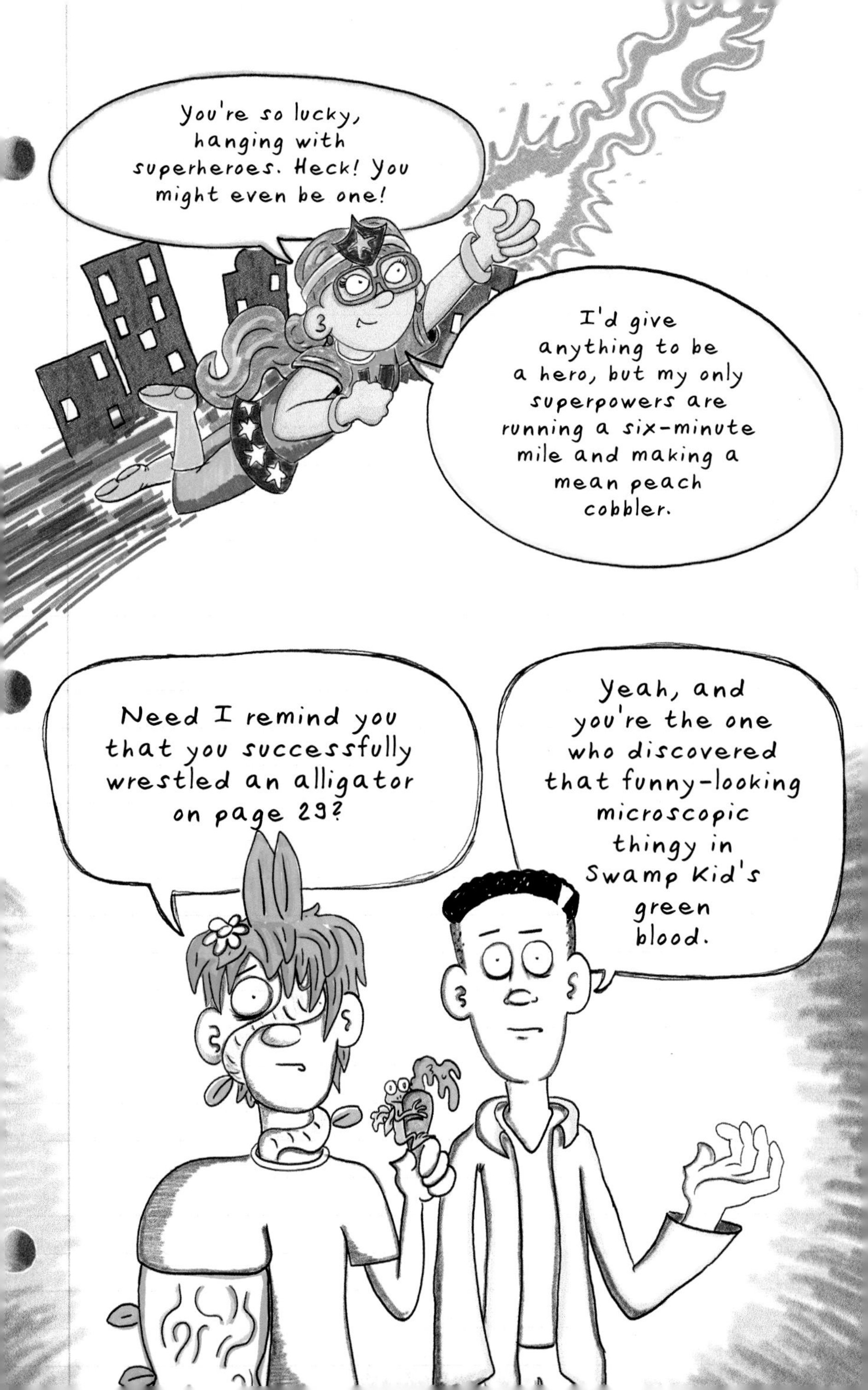

You're so lucky, hanging with superheroes. Heck! You might even be one!
I'd give anything to be a hero, but my only superpowers are running a six-minute mile and making a mean peach cobbler.
Need I remind you that you successfully wrestled an alligator on page 29?
Yeah, and you're the one who discovered that funny-looking microscopic thingy in Swamp Kid's green blood.

It suddenly occurred to me that the funny-looking microscopic thingy might also be in Swamp Thing's blood. If only we had a sample of his D.N.A.

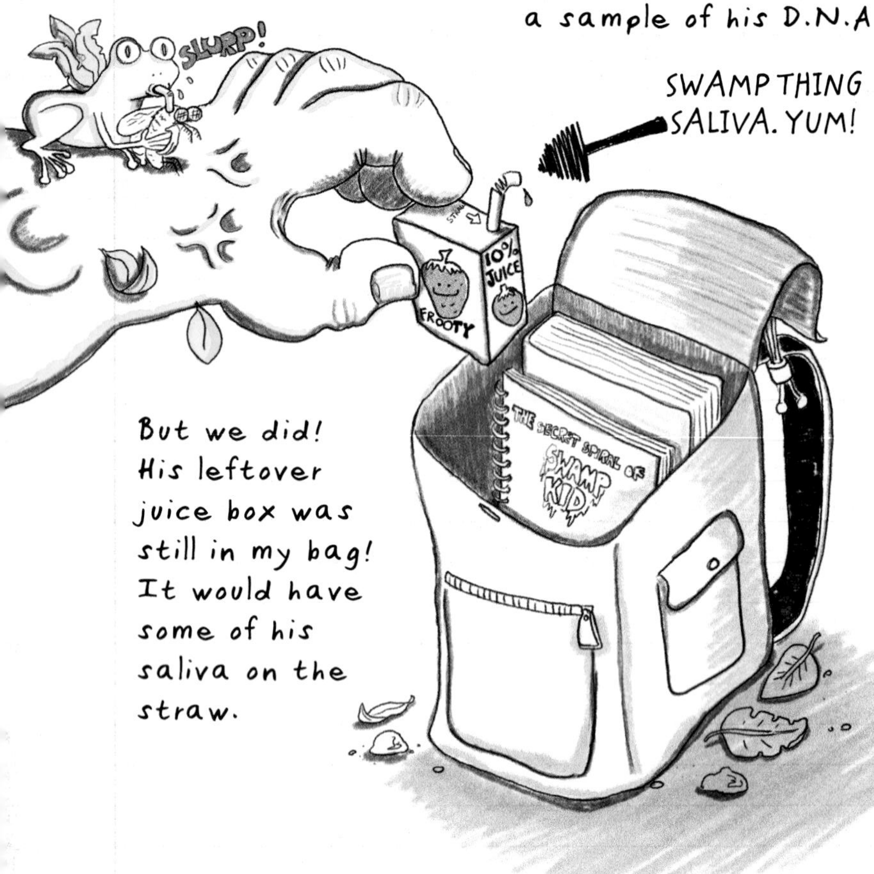
SLURP!
SWAMP THING SALIVA. YUM!
10% JUICE
FROOTY
THE SECRET SPIRAL OF SWAMP KID

But we did! His leftover juice box was still in my bag! It would have some of his saliva on the straw.

If my hunch is correct, the sample will show the same results as my blood test and that means that maybe traces of the formula that Dr. Alec Holland developed still linger in my bloodstream. Could it be possible Arcane can derive the recipe for the formula not just from Swamp Thing's blood but from mine, too? Maybe that explains my sample going missing from the science lab.

THURS. 1:00 A.M.

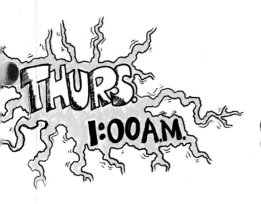

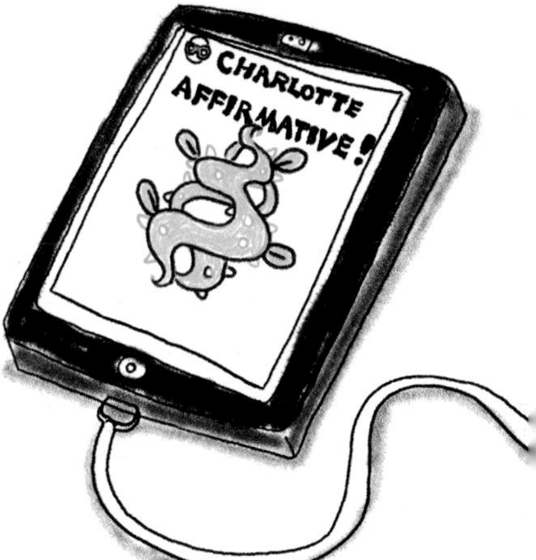
CHARLOTTE
AFFIRMATIVE!

Charlotte just woke me up with an important text. The mystery element definitely did show up when she checked out the juice box sample under the microscope!

Now I'm totally paranoid! Arcane could be after me and my frog. And Charlotte and Preston and anyone else who knows me could be in danger, too!

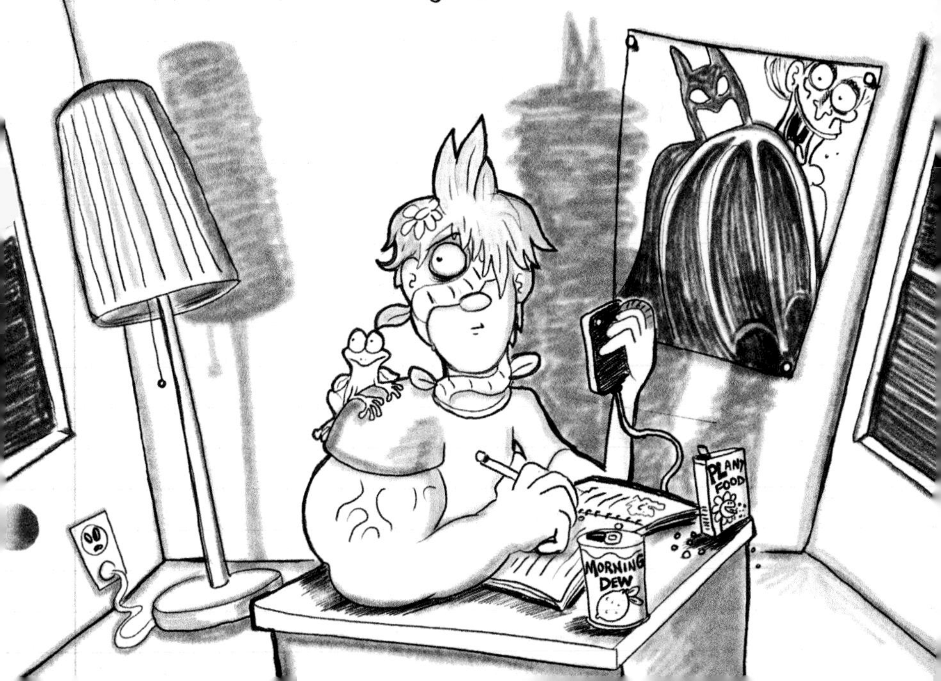
PLANT FOOD
MORNING DEW

FRI

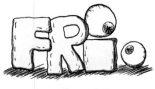

8:11 A.M.

Friday morning. Tonight's the big game and everyone's buzzing about it. I think Mr. Finneca must be a little embarrassed by his big brussels sprouts moment because he's been hiding behind a book all class.

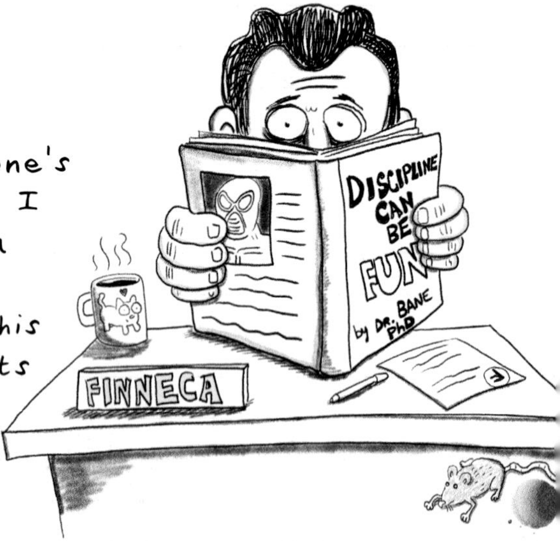
DISCIPLINE CAN BE FUN
by DR. BANE PhD
FINNECA

11:12 A.M.

Something a little wackadoodle just happened. I was walking toward the lunchroom and, like a dope, totally bumped into Nils Canebrake.

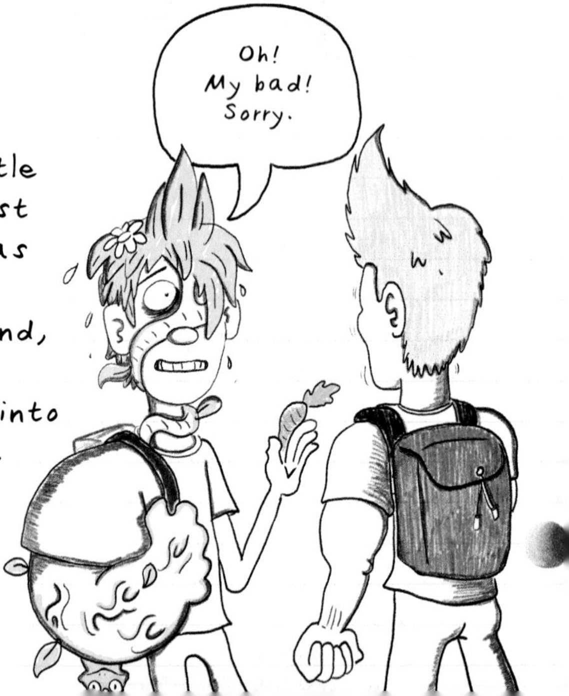
Oh! My bad! Sorry.

Now, it being Nils, I totally expected him to give me some grief and oh, he gave me grief. But it was the quality of his put-down that was subpar.

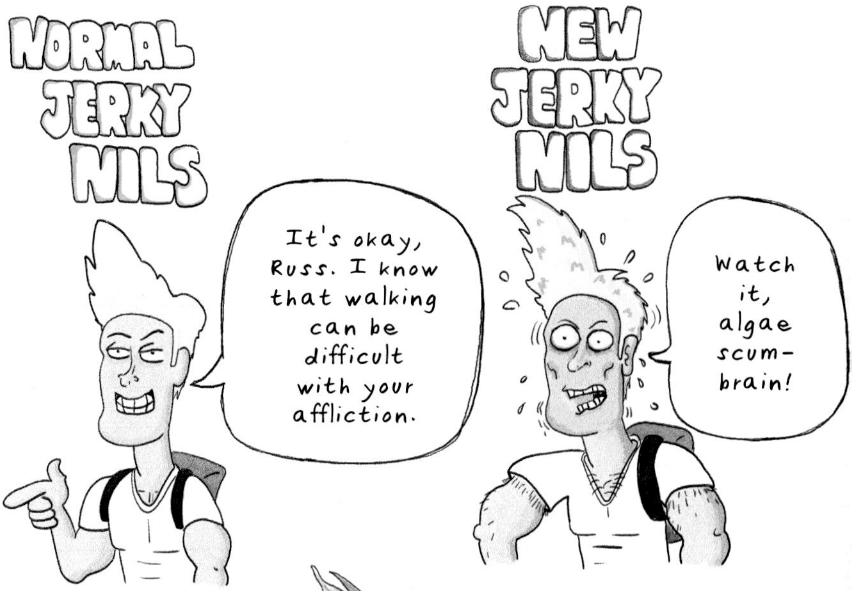
NORMAL JERKY NILS
It's okay, Russ. I know that walking can be difficult with your affliction.
NEW JERKY NILS
Watch it, algae scum-brain!

Algae scumbrain? That was weak sauce coming from Nils. The scariest thing, though, was when he looked back at me. The face he gave me could be this year's number-one-selling Halloween decoration.

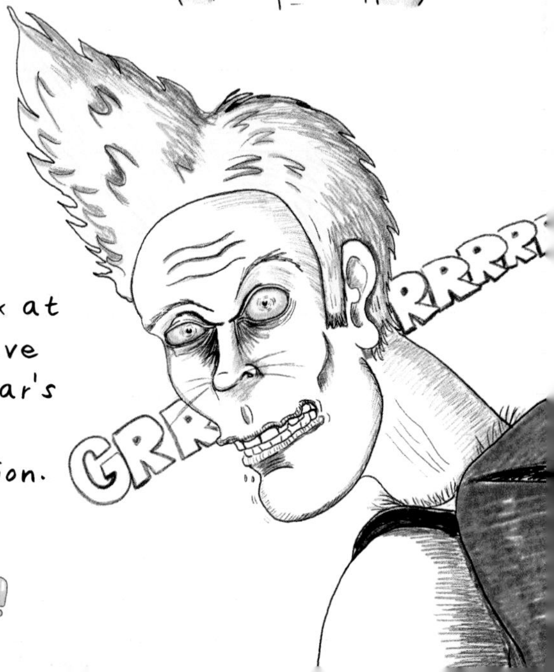
GRR
RRRRR

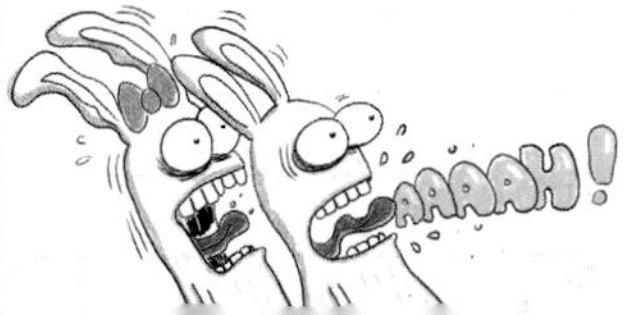
AAAAAH!

FRI. LUNCH

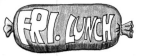

Spent lunch period practicing my powers with Charlotte. She's a righteous sparring partner!!

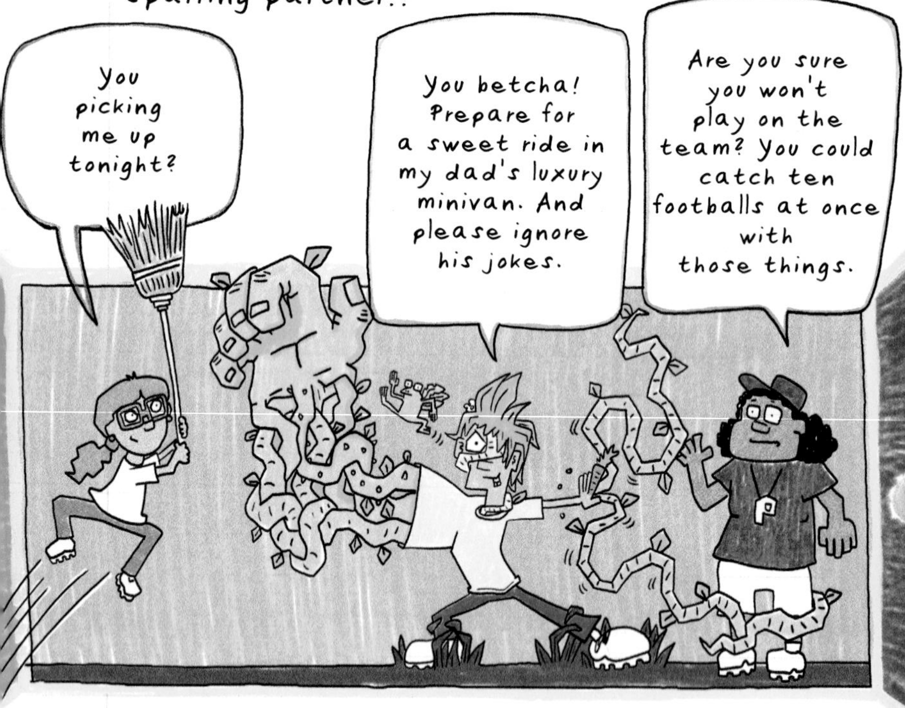
You picking me up tonight?
You betcha! Prepare for a sweet ride in my dad's luxury minivan. And please ignore his jokes.
Are you sure you won't play on the team? You could catch ten footballs at once with those things.

3:55 P.M.

On the bumpy bus now. Headed home. There are totally some shady dudes following us, too. Preston's getting them on video.

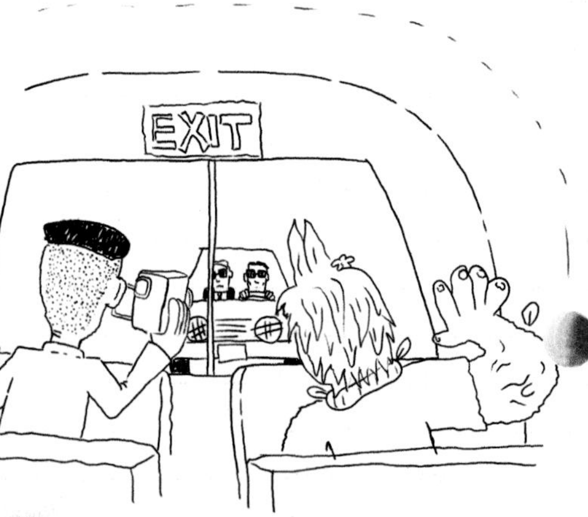
EXIT

6:00 P.M.

Getting ready for my big night out. My parents are already embarrassing me.

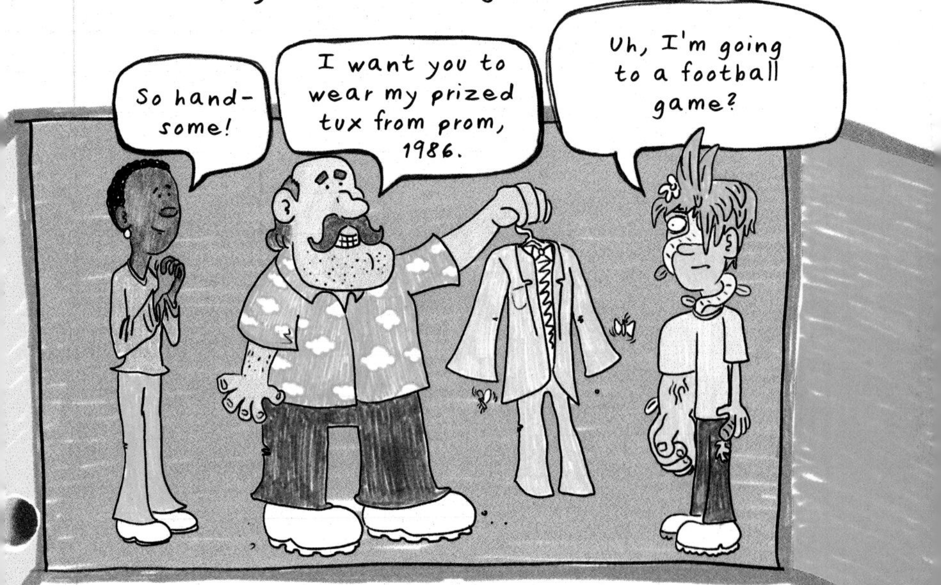
So handsome!
I want you to wear my prized tux from prom, 1986.
Uh, I'm going to a football game?

I chose my own outfit, thank you very much, and took a look in the mirror. Not bad. I don't know what it is but I'm kinda liking my look all of a sudden.

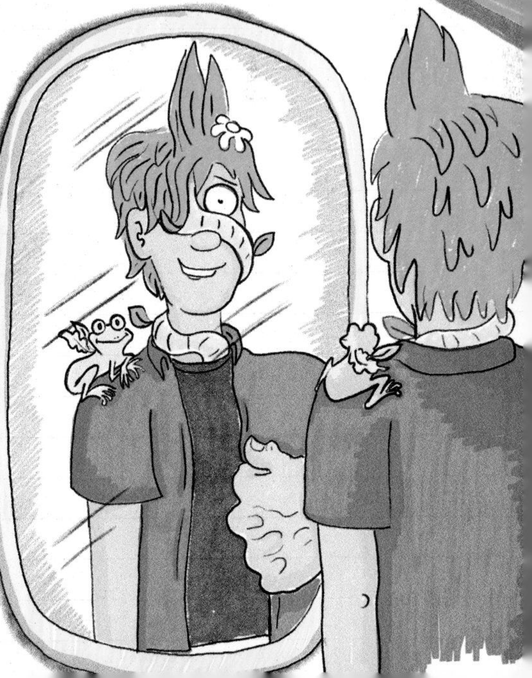

Gotta run! I'll let you know how it goes.

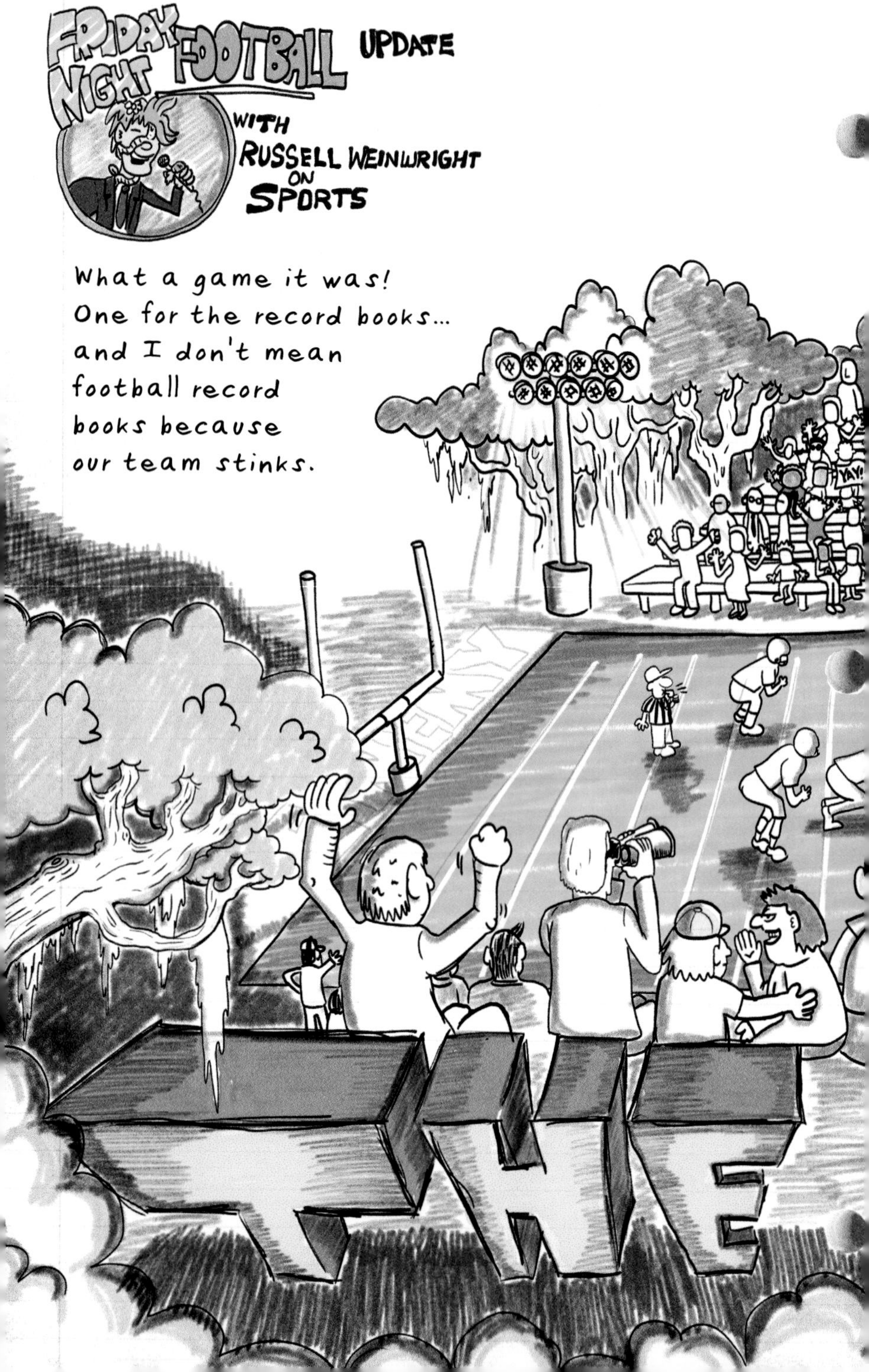
FRIDAY NIGHT FOOTBALL UPDATE
WITH RUSSELL WEINWRIGHT ON SPORTS
What a game it was! One for the record books... and I don't mean football record books because our team stinks.
YAY!
THE

It was a home game against the Baton Rouge Battle Rogues, which is a mouthful. Seriously, Baton Rouge, change your mascot.

The stands were packed!

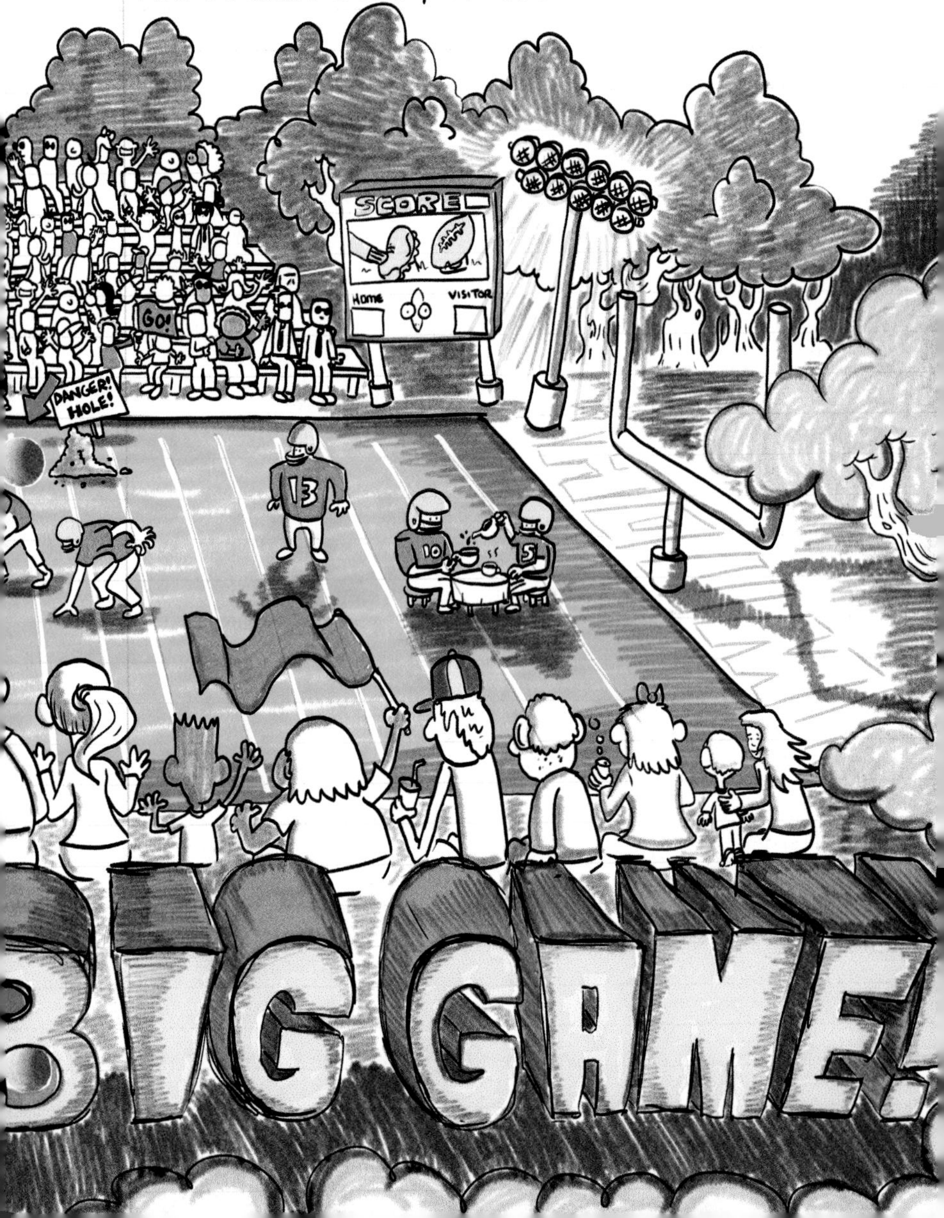
SCORE
HOME
VISITOR
GO!
DANGER! HOLE!
13
10
5
BIG GAME!

First order of business—loading up on snacks!

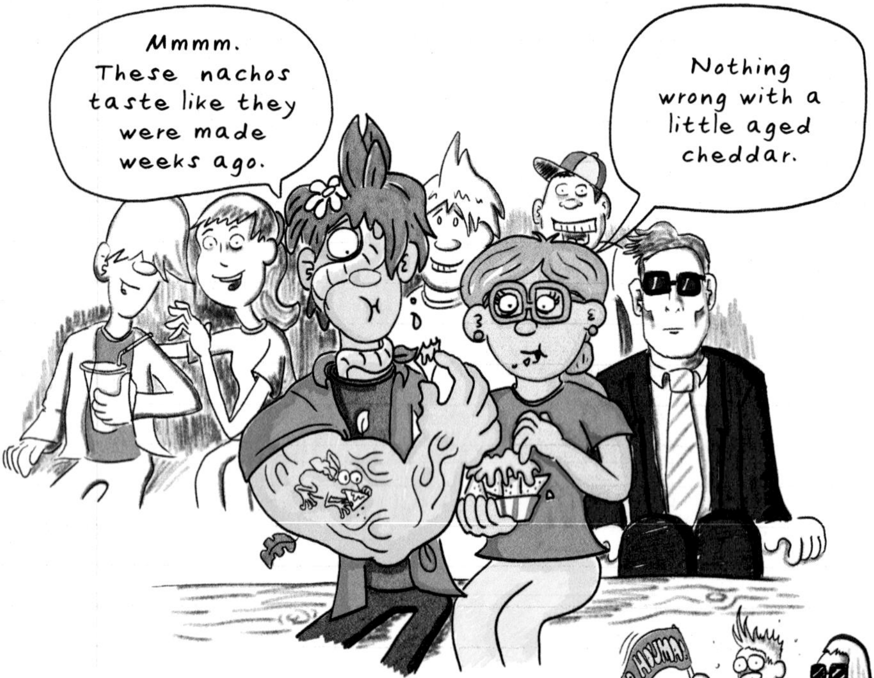
Mmmm. These nachos taste like they were made weeks ago.
Nothing wrong with a little aged cheddar.

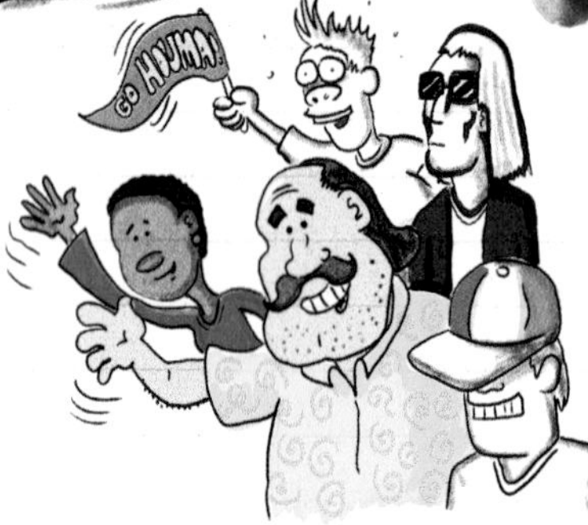

Mom and Dad were sitting ten rows away, but they kept staring and waving at me nonstop.

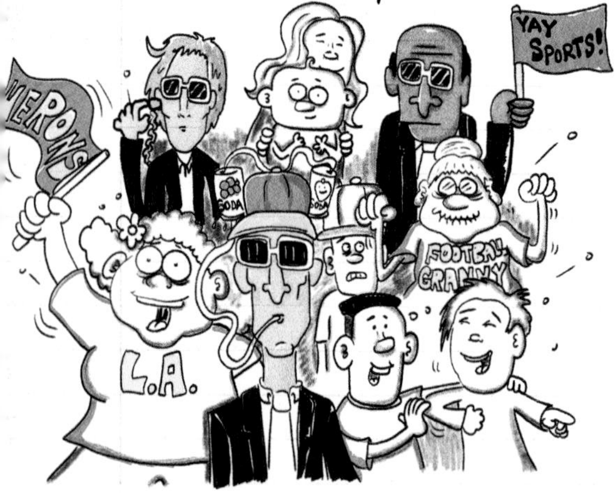
YAY SPORTS!
SODA
SODA
FOOTBALL GRANNY
L.A.

Throughout the stands there were some shady fans that, call me crazy, looked like they just didn't belong.

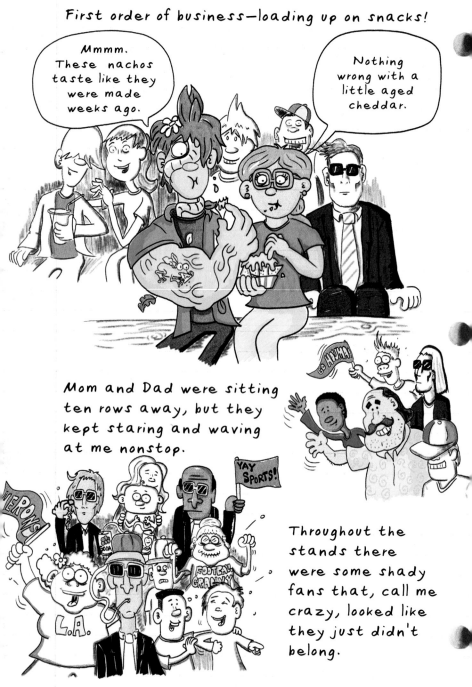

Preston was filming the game for the yearbook committee. He probably should've been paying attention instead of waving at us, though.

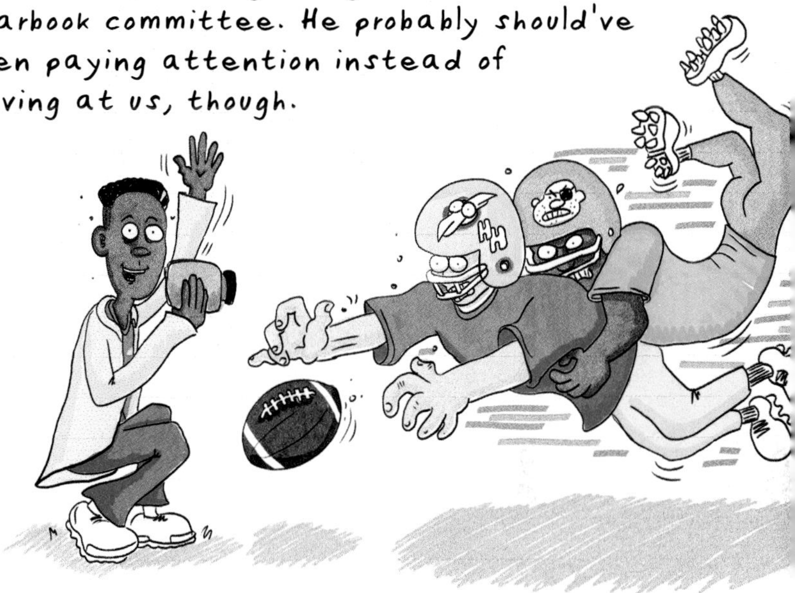

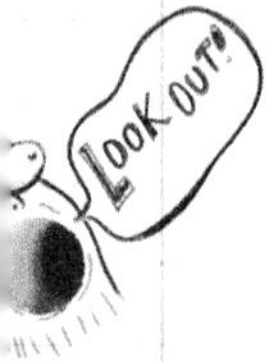
LOOK OUT!

And our creepy school mascot, the Houma Heron, was getting down to some bumpin' Jock Jams on the sidelines.

That bird's got some sweet moves but we all know it's actually Principal Parker under the plumage.

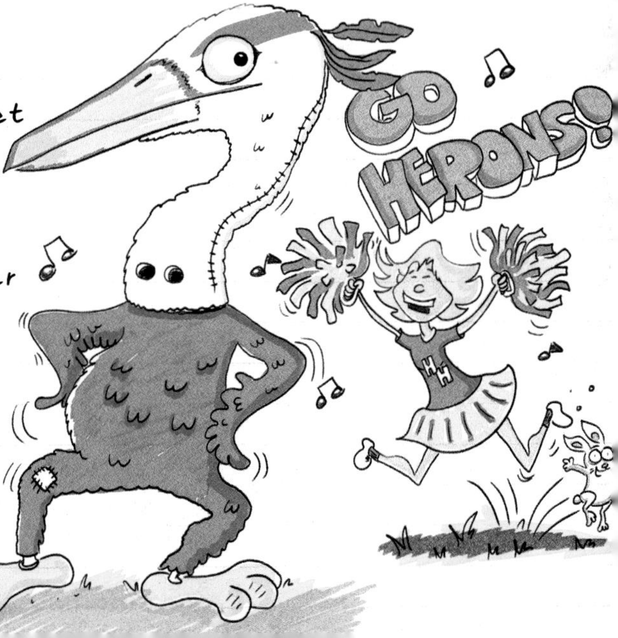
GO HERONS!

All of a sudden there was some sort of commotion at the bench! Coach Sanchez was upset, stuff was getting tossed around, even Mr. Finneca was in the mix! I couldn't tell what was going on, but it seemed like a player was causing a scene.

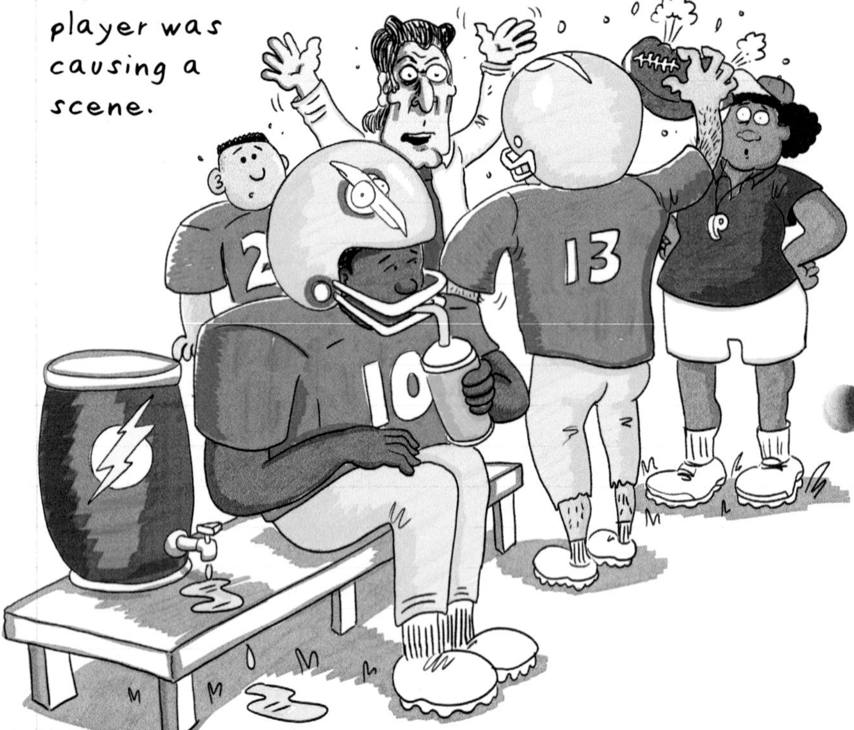

Of course, you know Preston had to get right in there with his camera.

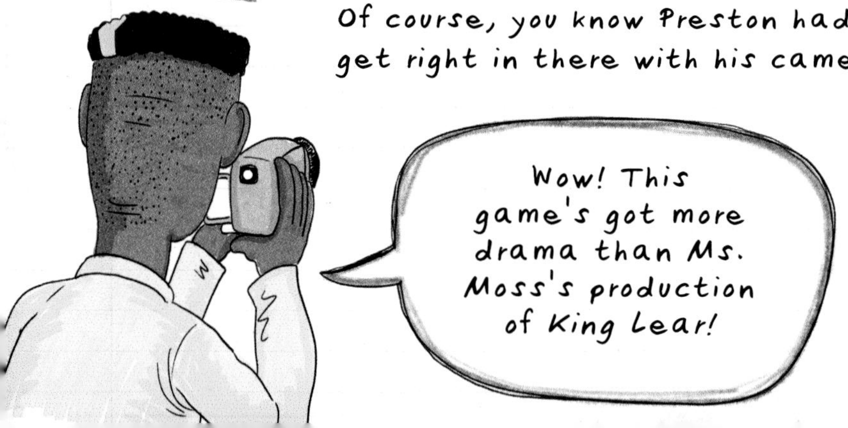
Wow! This game's got more drama than Ms. Moss's production of King Lear!

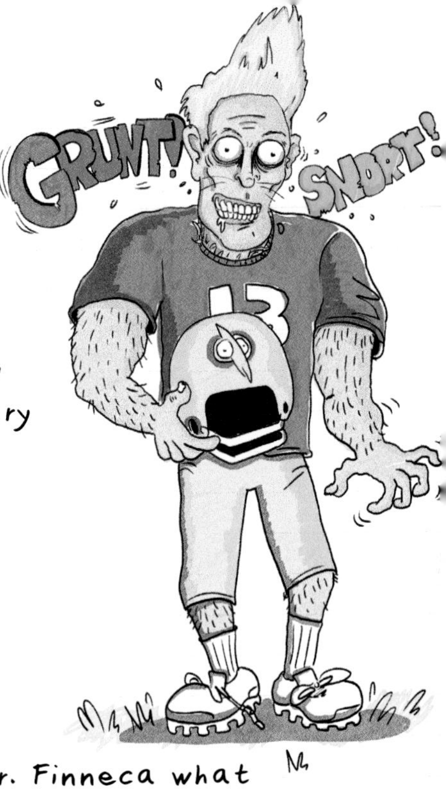
GRUNT!
SNORT!

Here's the really weird part—the person causing all the ruckus was Nils Canebrake. And if you thought he looked scary after school today, you should've seen him tonight. He was muscled up and sweaty and snarling. A regular Dr. Nils and Mr. Hyde!

I ran over and asked Mr. Finneca what was up. Turns out, he had done some snooping and discovered Nils was the one who broke into his cabinet and stole the specimens.

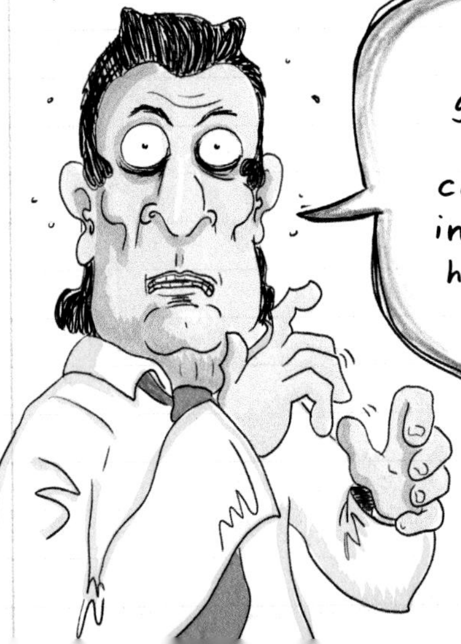
I don't know what's gotten into him! He's not acting like himself. I confronted him and he flew into a rage! I fear he may hurt someone. He's usually such a kind boy.

Uh...yeah, let's not go crazy there, Teach.

The funny thing was, Nils was playing like a pro. Nailing passes and scoring and laying down some brutal tackles. The crowd went nuts for him!

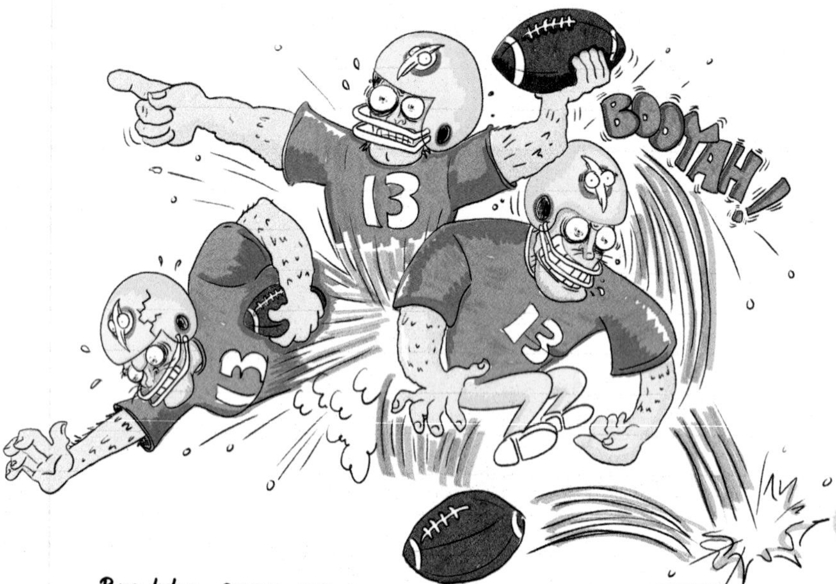
BOOYAH!
13
13
13

Pretty soon we were even winning the game! A first!

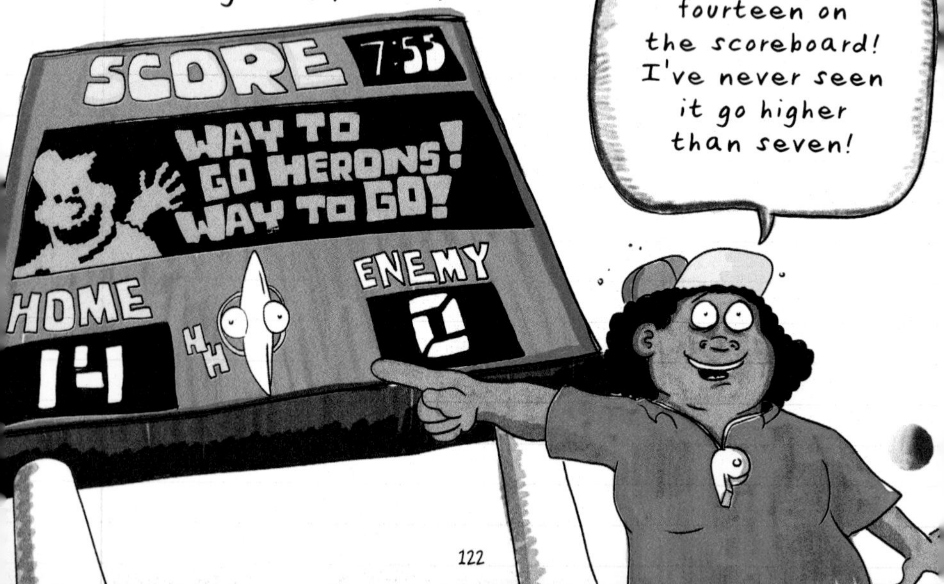
Hey! It says fourteen on the scoreboard! I've never seen it go higher than seven!
SCORE
7:55
WAY TO GO HERONS! WAY TO GO!
HOME
14
ENEMY

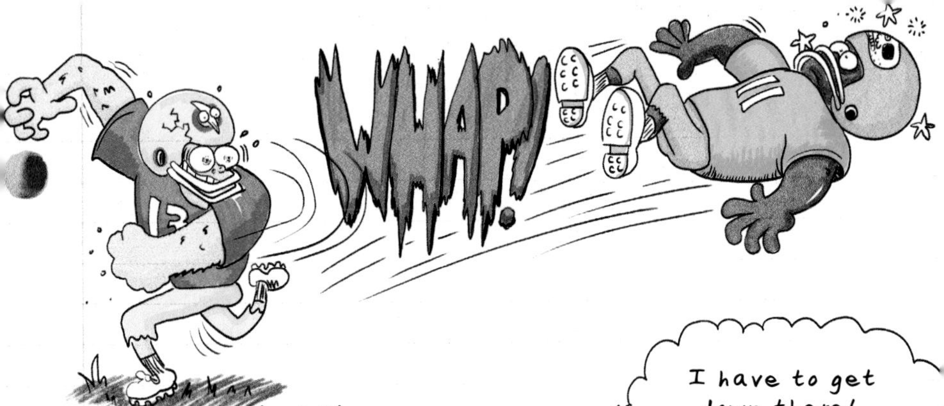
WHAP!

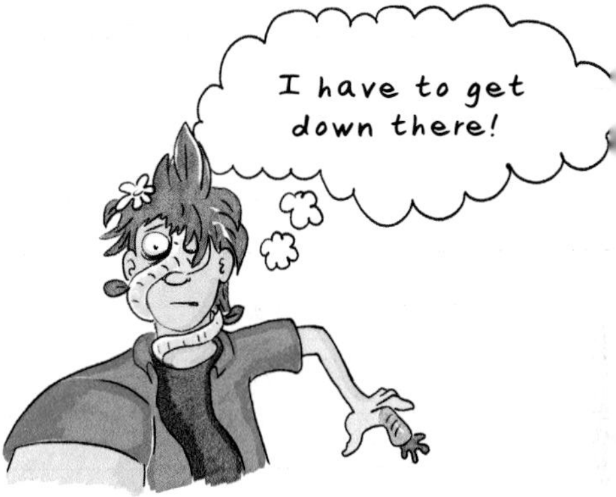
I have to get down there!

After a while Nils was really enjoying the tackling part...like, way too much. He was smacking and throwing around the other team like beanbags, ignoring the angry refs.

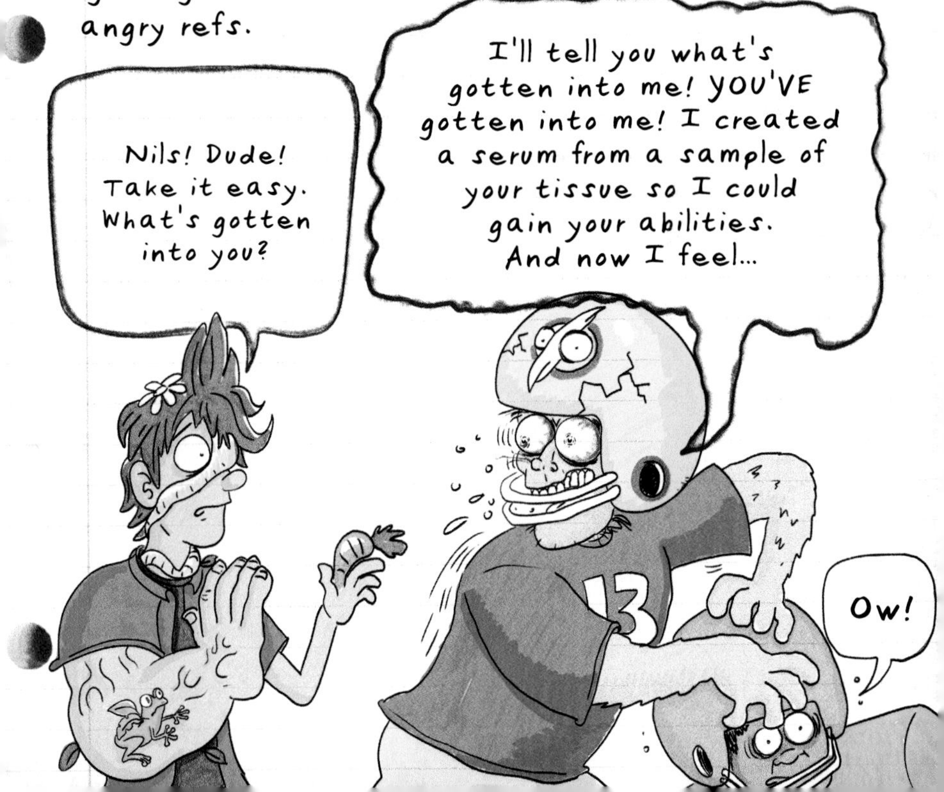
Nils! Dude! Take it easy. What's gotten into you?
I'll tell you what's gotten into me! YOU'VE gotten into me! I created a serum from a sample of your tissue so I could gain your abilities. And now I feel...
Ow!

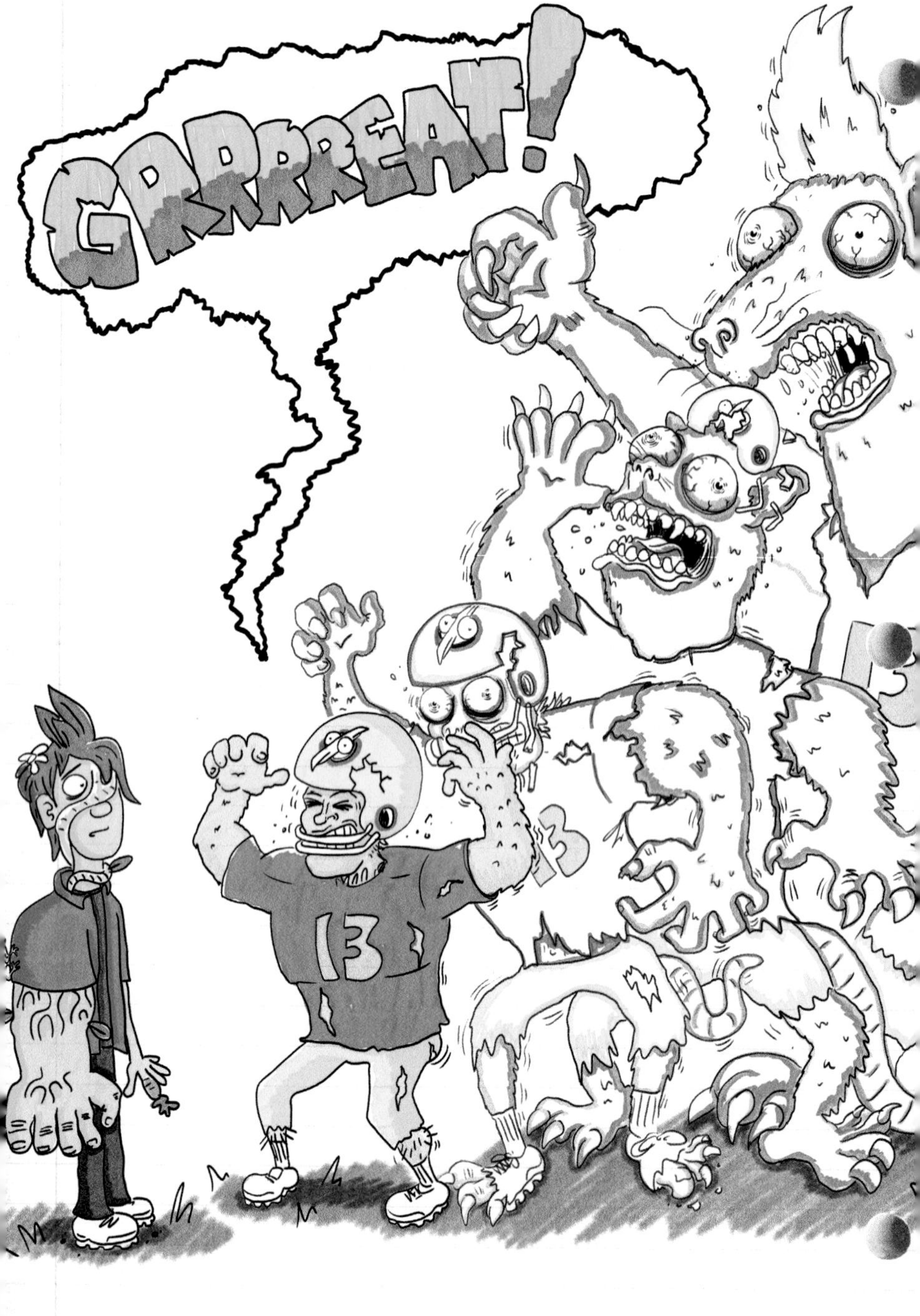
GRRRREAT!

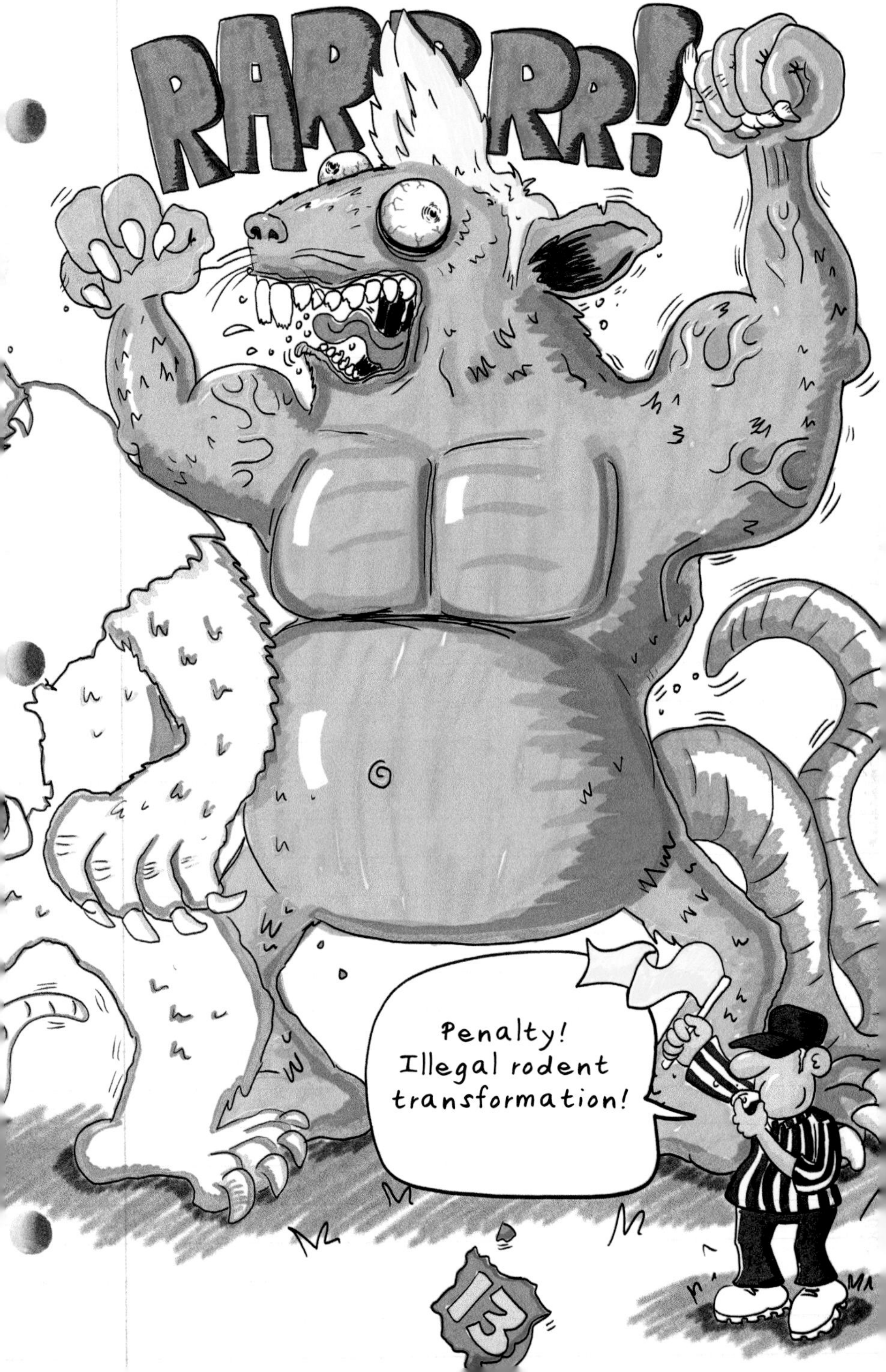
RARRRR!
Penalty! Illegal rodent transformation!

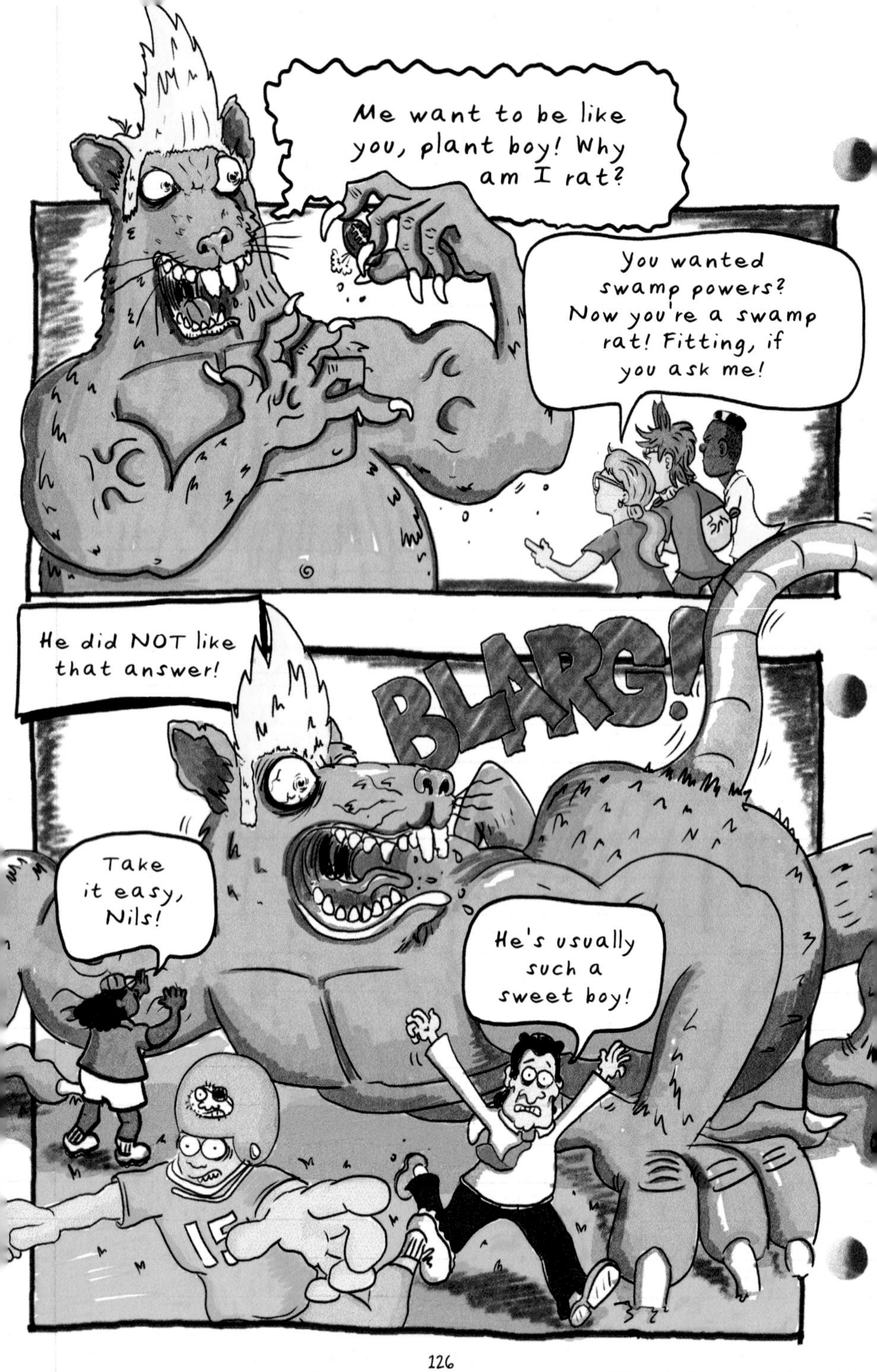
Me want to be like you, plant boy! Why am I rat?
You wanted swamp powers? Now you're a swamp rat! Fitting, if you ask me!
He did NOT like that answer!
BLARG!
Take it easy, Nils!
He's usually such a sweet boy!
15

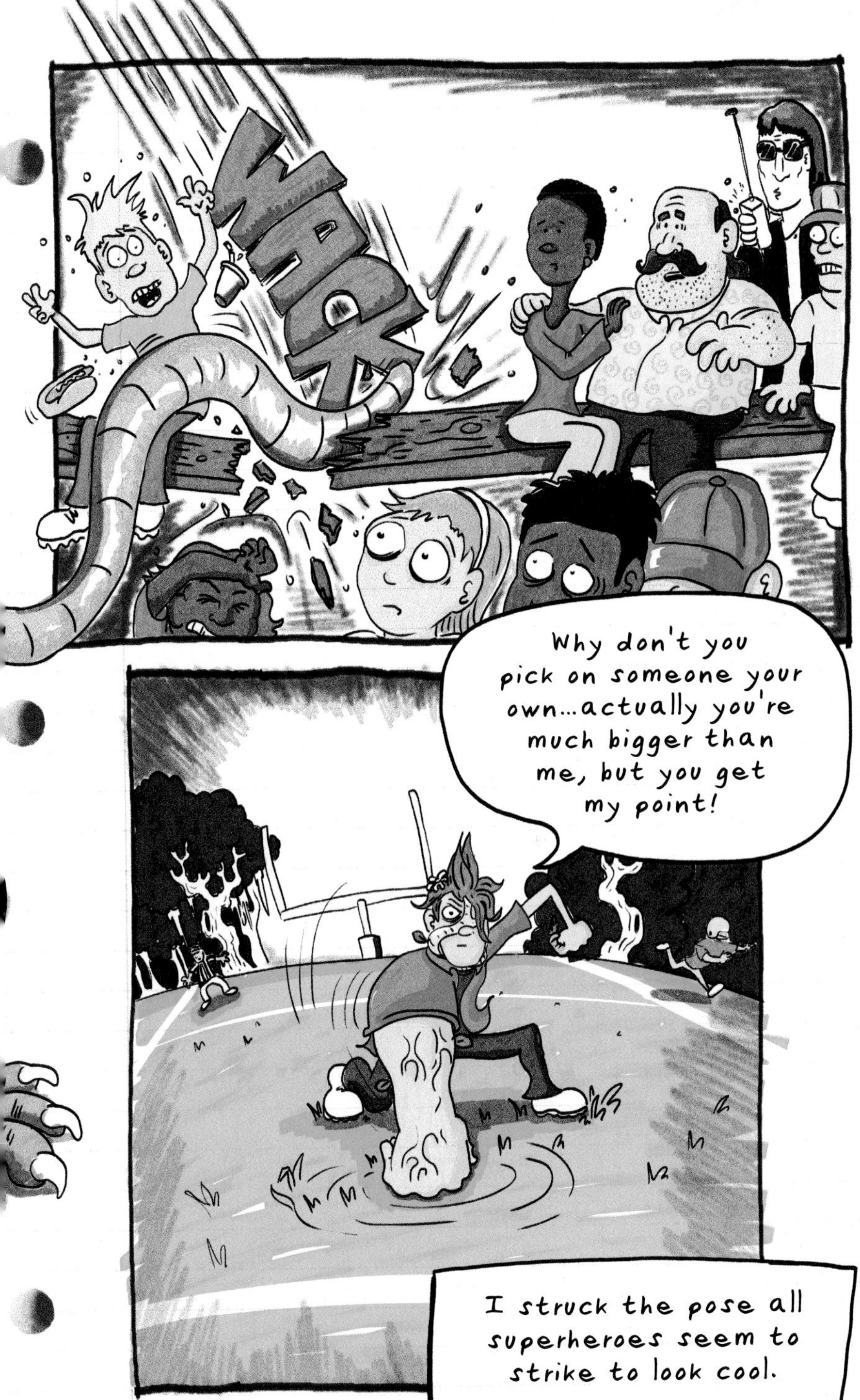
WHACK
Why don't you pick on someone your own...actually you're much bigger than me, but you get my point!
I struck the pose all superheroes seem to strike to look cool.

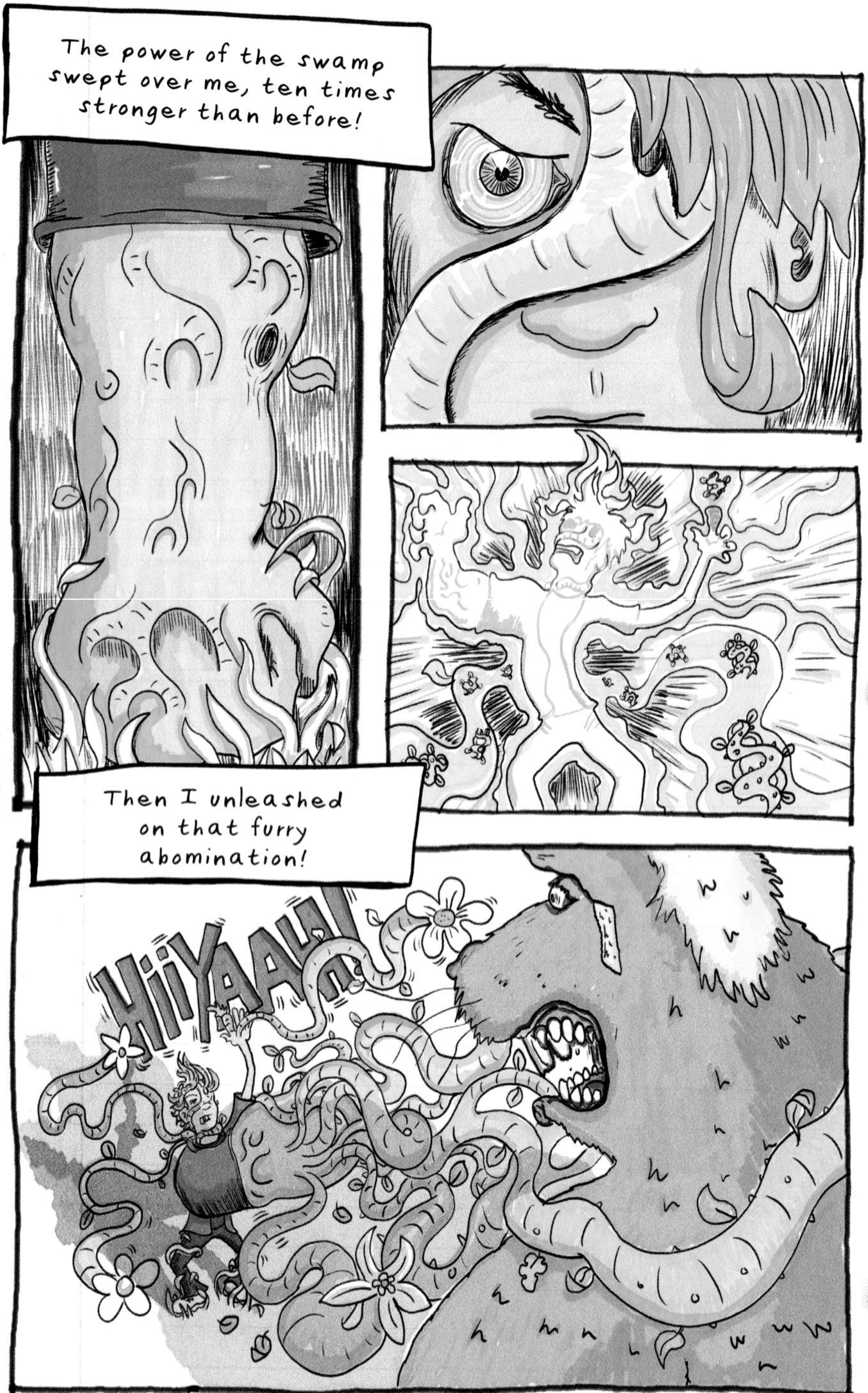
The power of the swamp swept over me, ten times stronger than before!
Then I unleashed on that furry abomination!
HiiYAAH!

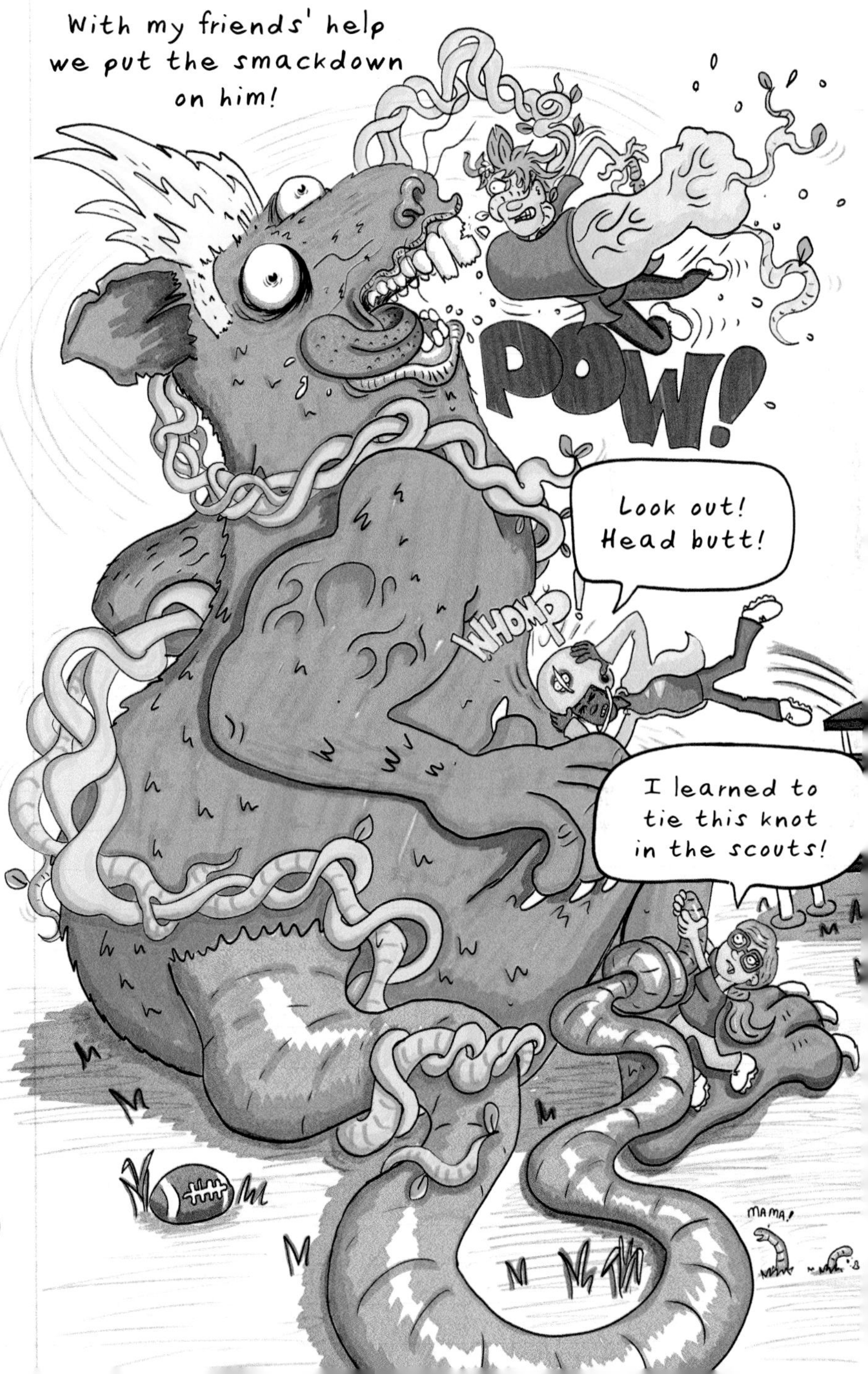
With my friends' help we put the smackdown on him!
POW!
Look out! Head butt!
WHOMP!
I learned to tie this knot in the scouts!
MAMA!

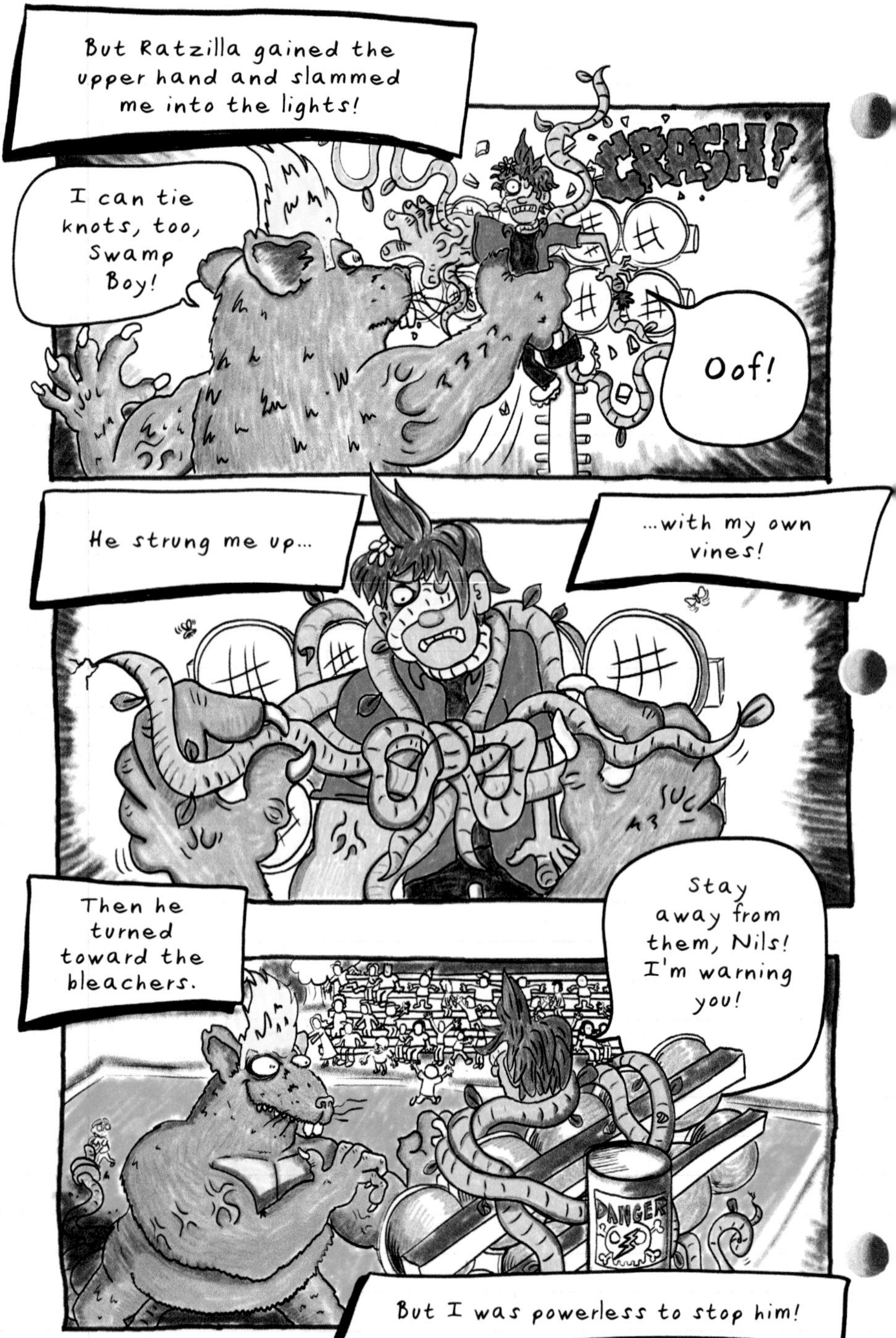
But Ratzilla gained the upper hand and slammed me into the lights!
I can tie knots, too, Swamp Boy!
CRASH!
Oof!
He strung me up...
...with my own vines!
Then he turned toward the bleachers.
Stay away from them, Nils! I'm warning you!
DANGER
But I was powerless to stop him!

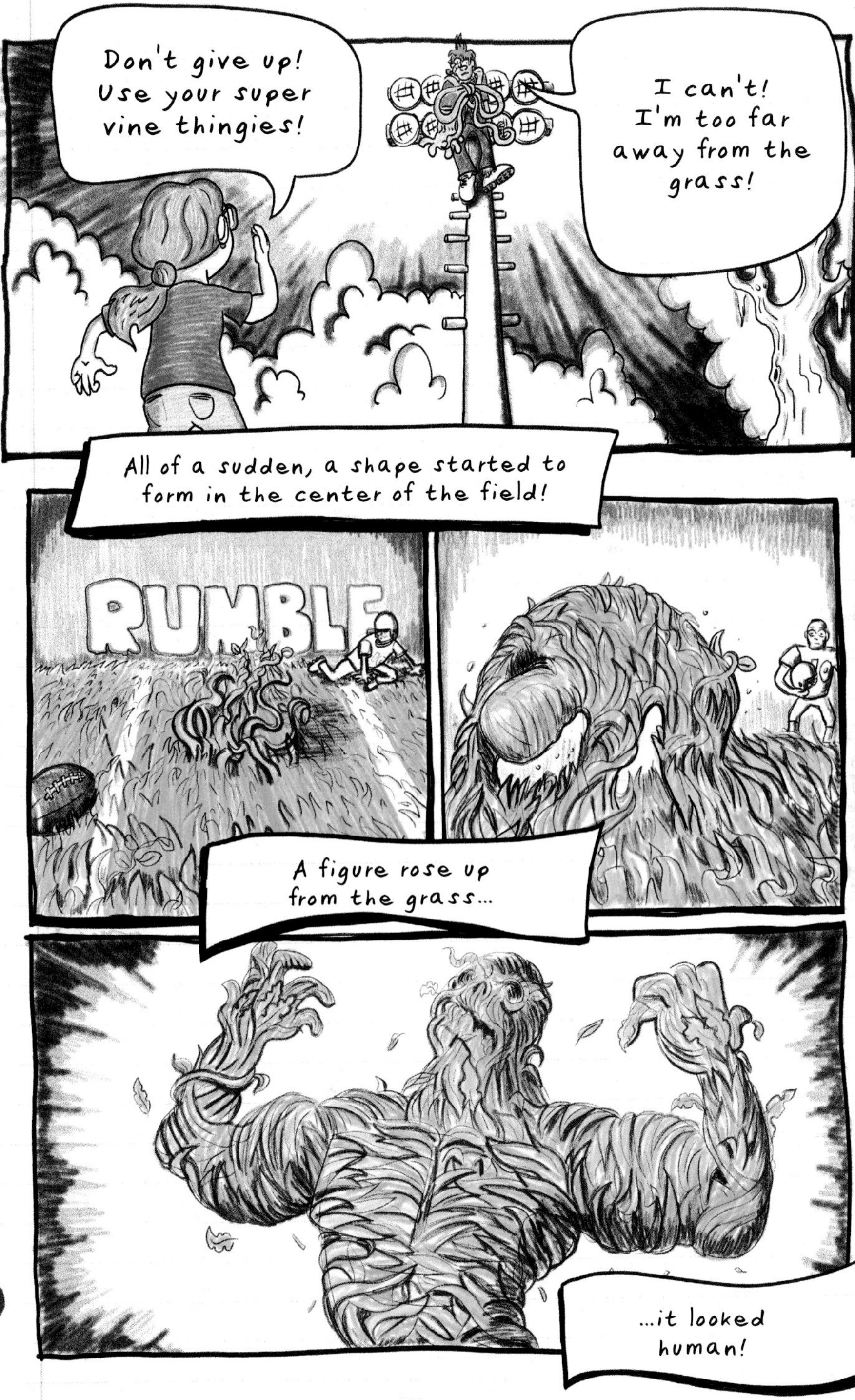
Don't give up! Use your super vine thingies!
I can't! I'm too far away from the grass!
All of a sudden, a shape started to form in the center of the field!
RUMBLE
A figure rose up from the grass...
...it looked human!

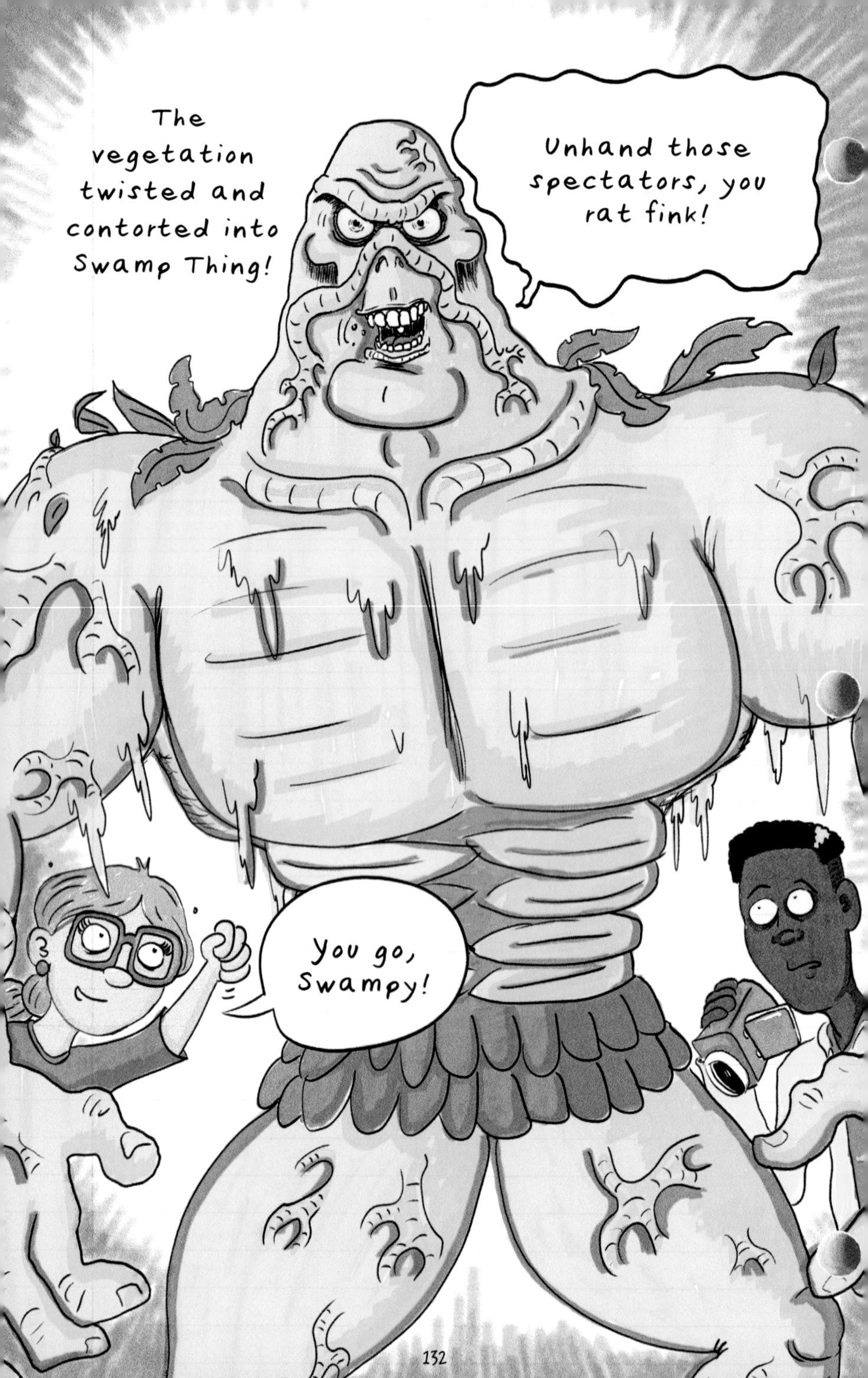
The vegetation twisted and contorted into Swamp Thing!
Unhand those spectators, you rat fink!
You go, Swampy!

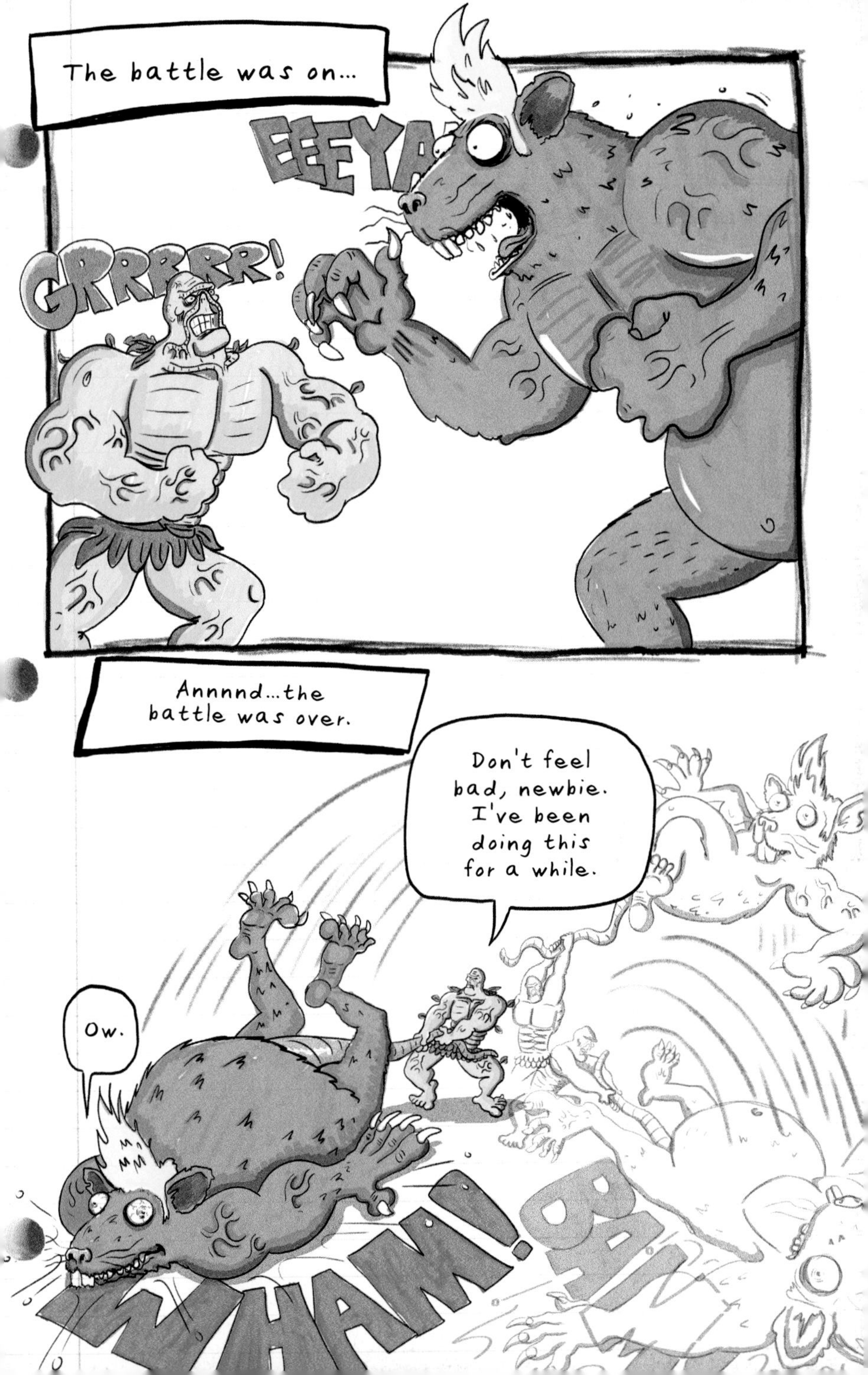
The battle was on...
EEEYA
GRRRRR!
Annnnd...the battle was over.
Don't feel bad, newbie. I've been doing this for a while.
Ow.
WHAM!
BA

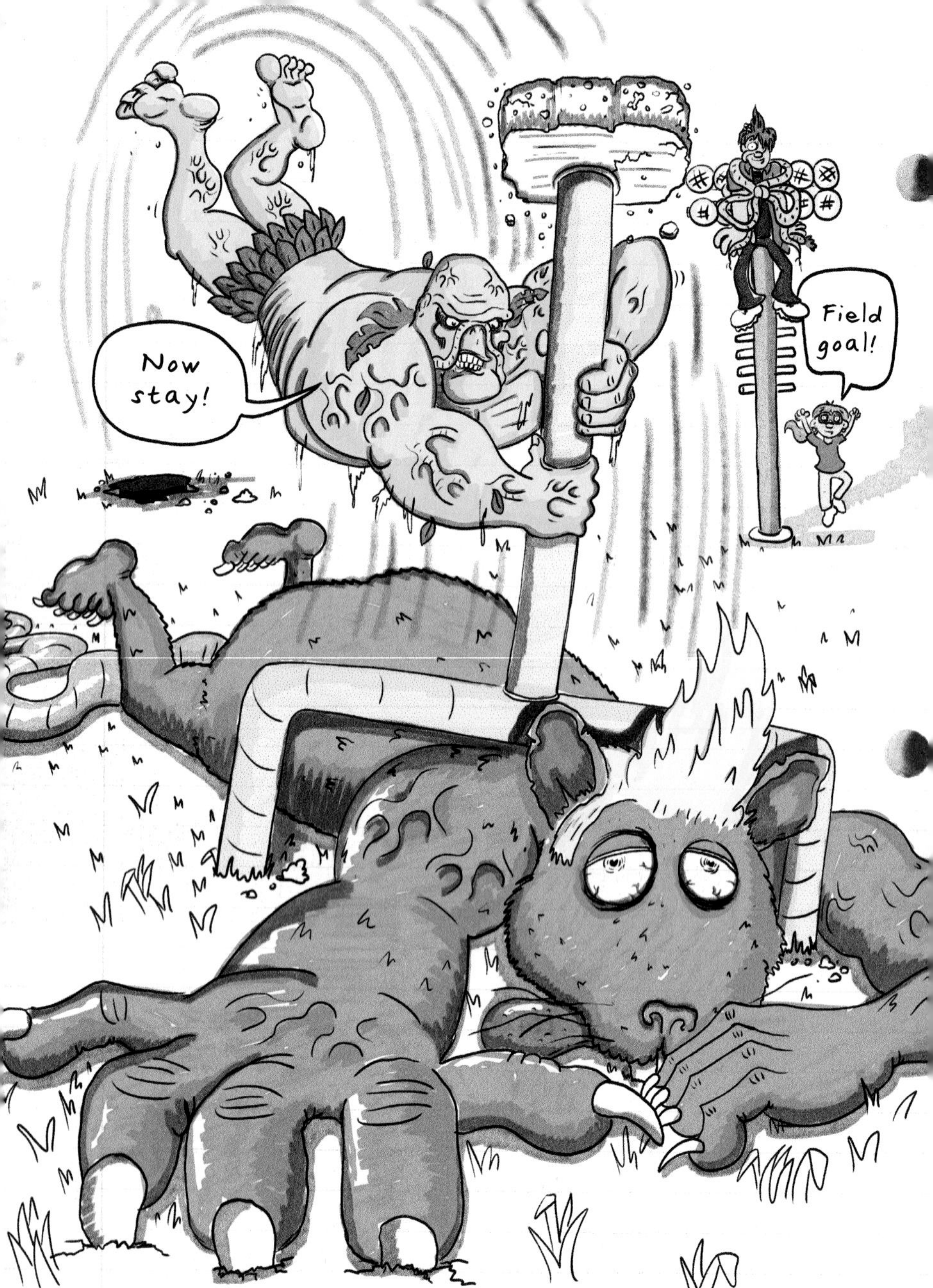
Now stay!
Field goal!

Swamp Thing pinned Nils to the ground with an uprooted goal post. That rat wasn't going anywhere!

Don't go thinking we were out of danger, though. A freaky voice suddenly blared out over the loudspeaker! And a digitized face appeared on the scoreboard!

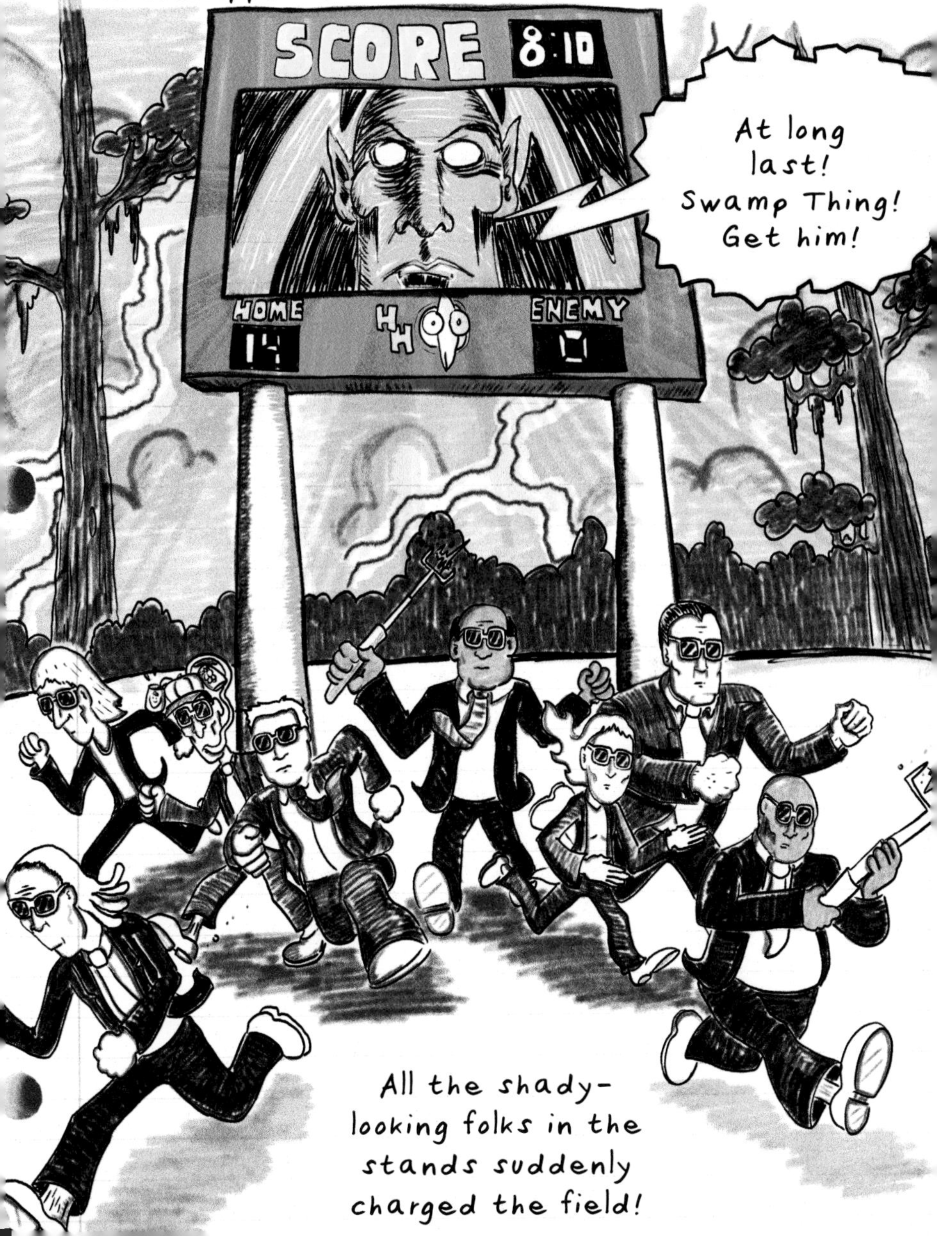

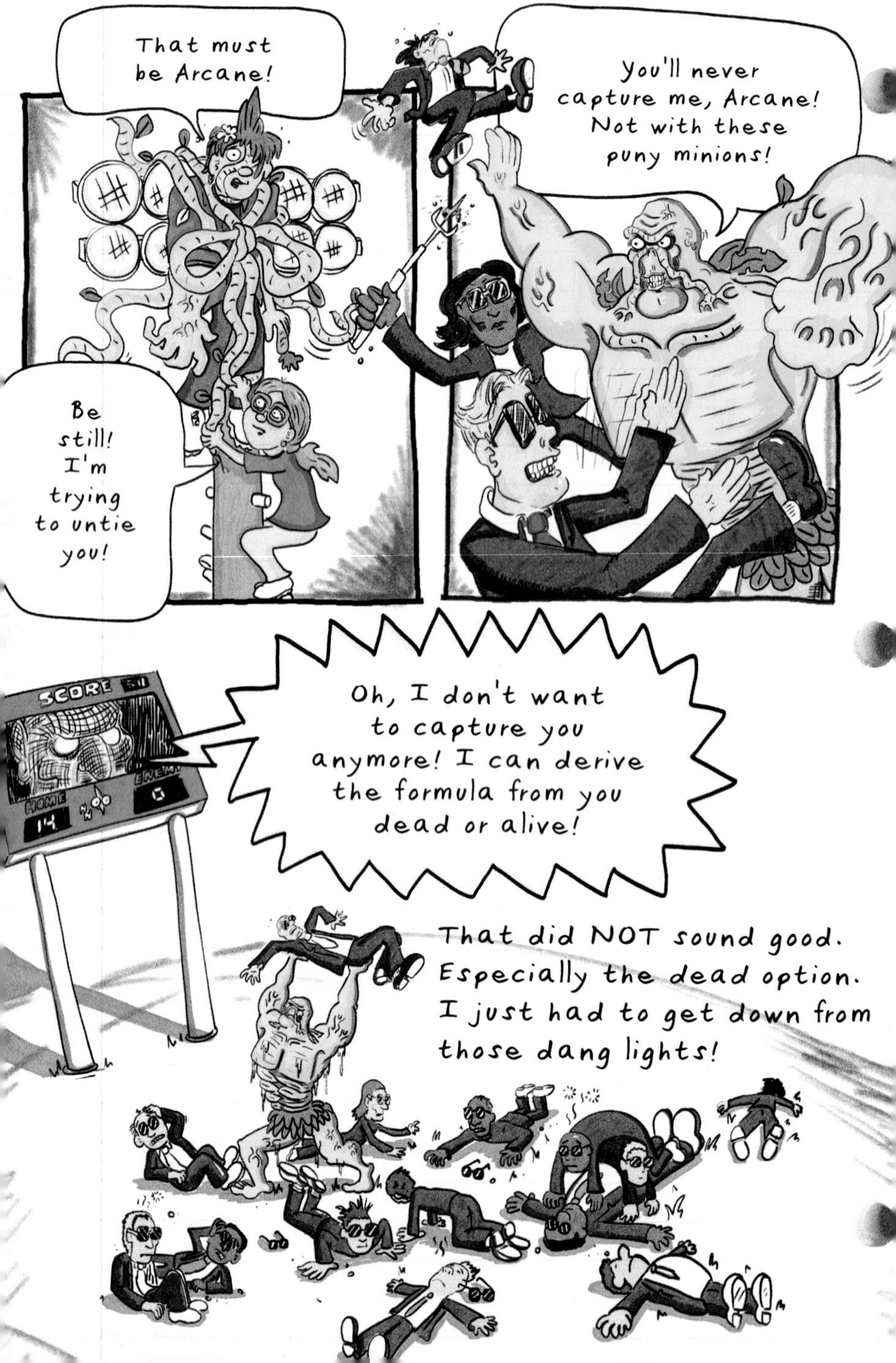

That must be Arcane!
You'll never capture me, Arcane! Not with these puny minions!
Be still! I'm trying to untie you!
SCORE
HOME
ENEMY
14
0
Oh, I don't want to capture you anymore! I can derive the formula from you dead or alive!
That did NOT sound good. Especially the dead option. I just had to get down from those dang lights!

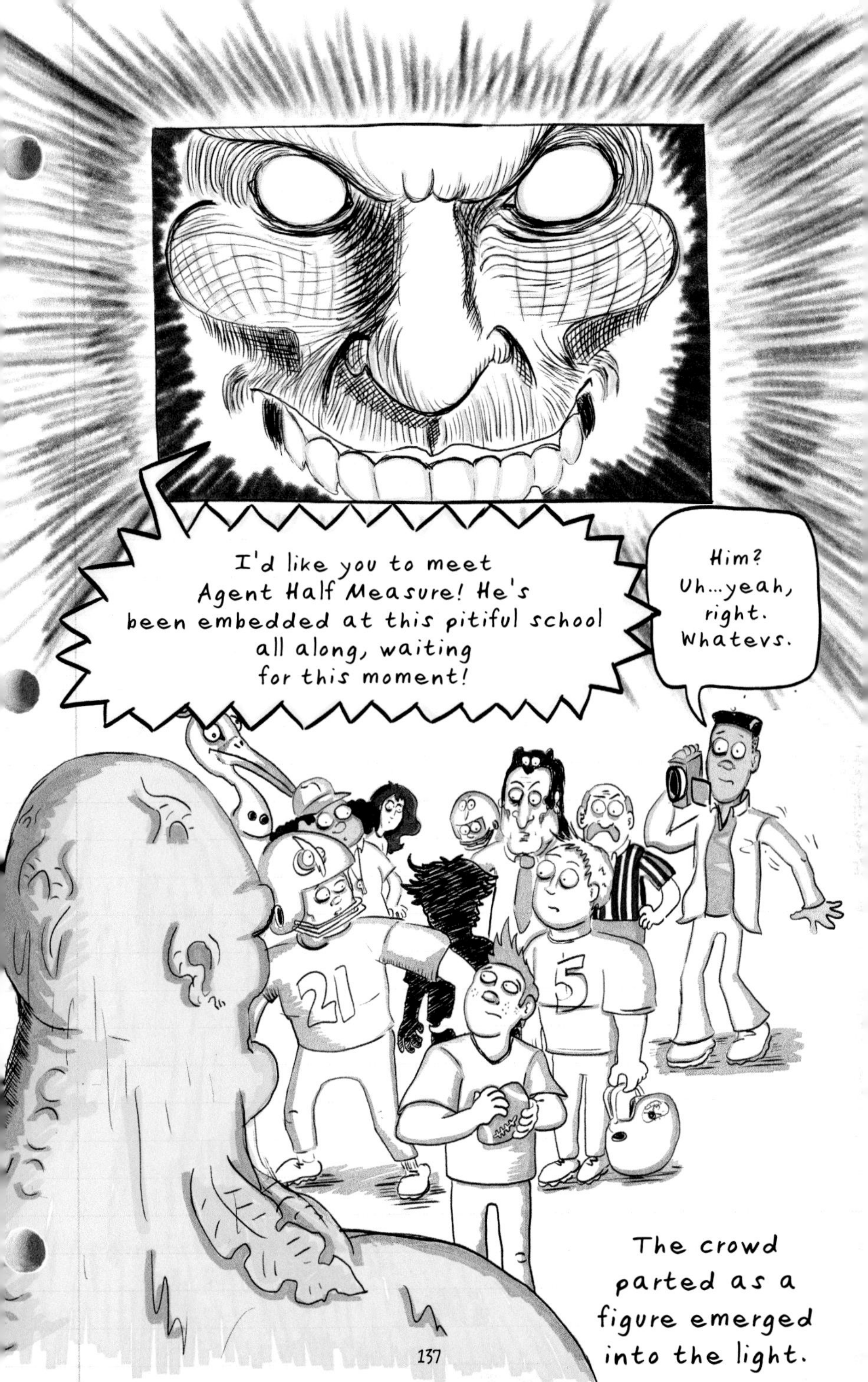
I'd like you to meet Agent Half Measure! He's been embedded at this pitiful school all along, waiting for this moment!
Him? Uh...yeah, right. Whatevs.
The crowd parted as a figure emerged into the light.

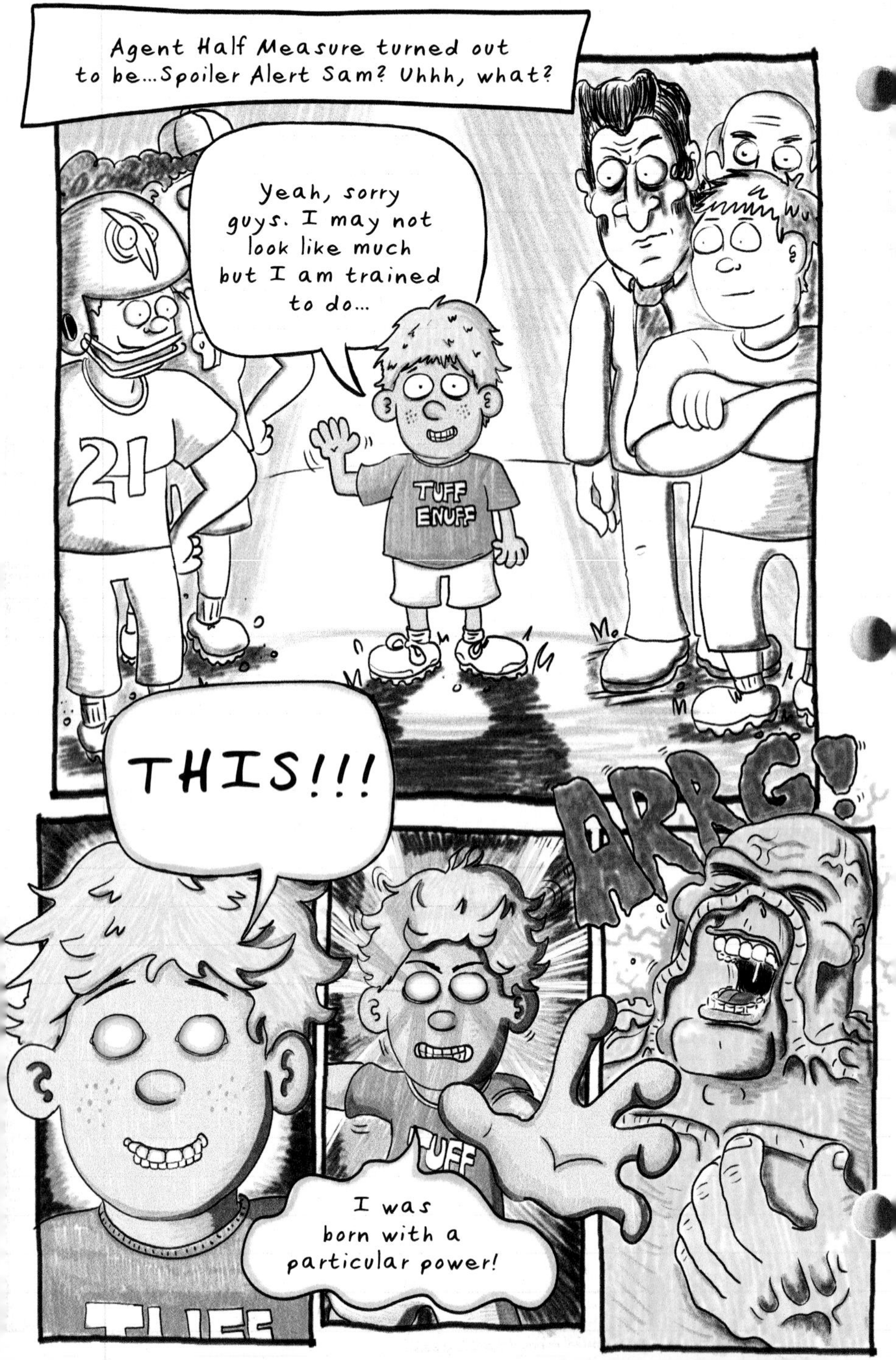
Agent Half Measure turned out to be...Spoiler Alert Sam? Uhhh, what?
Yeah, sorry guys. I may not look like much but I am trained to do...
21
TUFF ENUFF
THIS!!!
ARRG!
TUFF
I was born with a particular power!

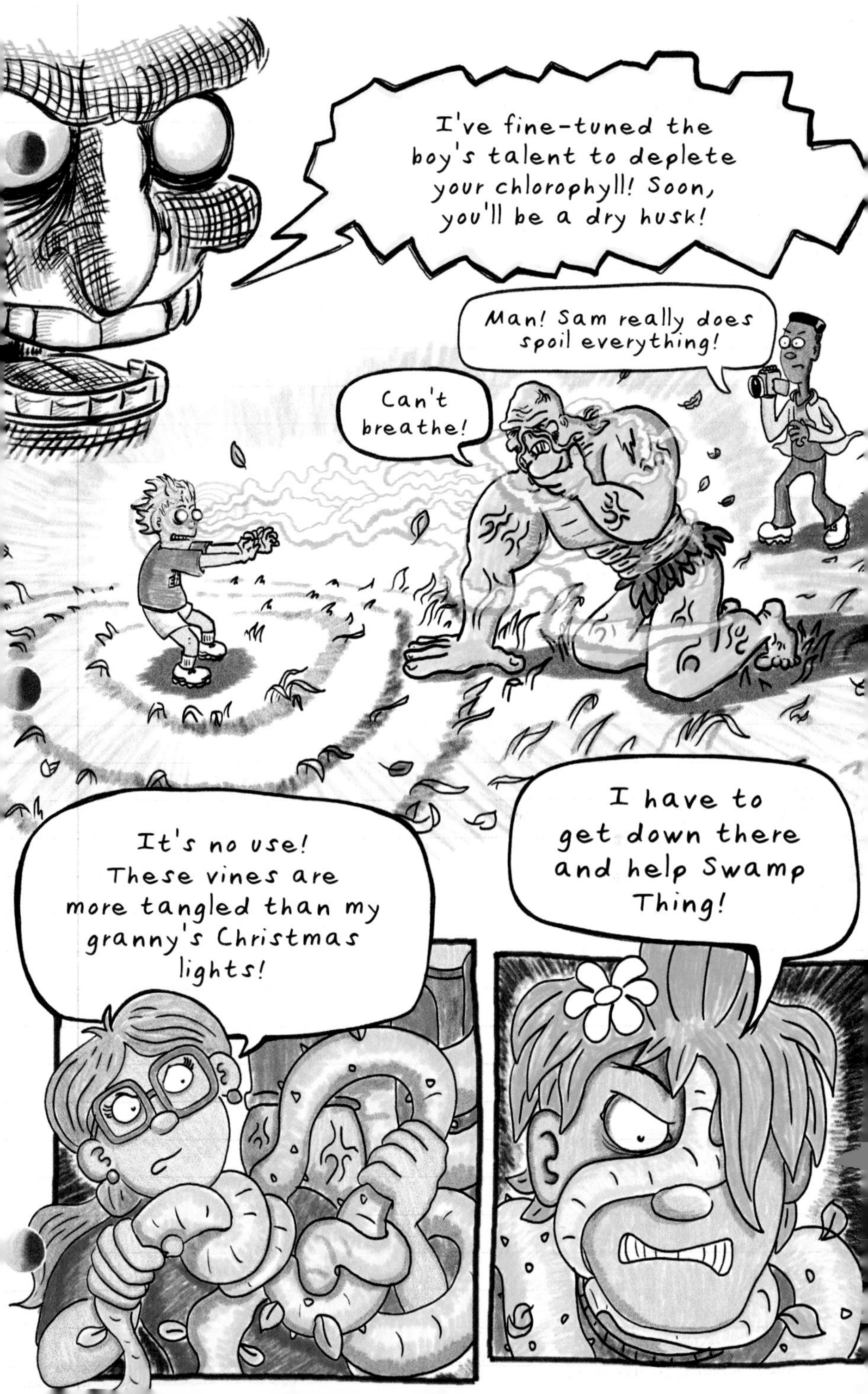
I've fine-tuned the boy's talent to deplete your chlorophyll! Soon, you'll be a dry husk!
Man! Sam really does spoil everything!
Can't breathe!
It's no use! These vines are more tangled than my granny's Christmas lights!
I have to get down there and help Swamp Thing!

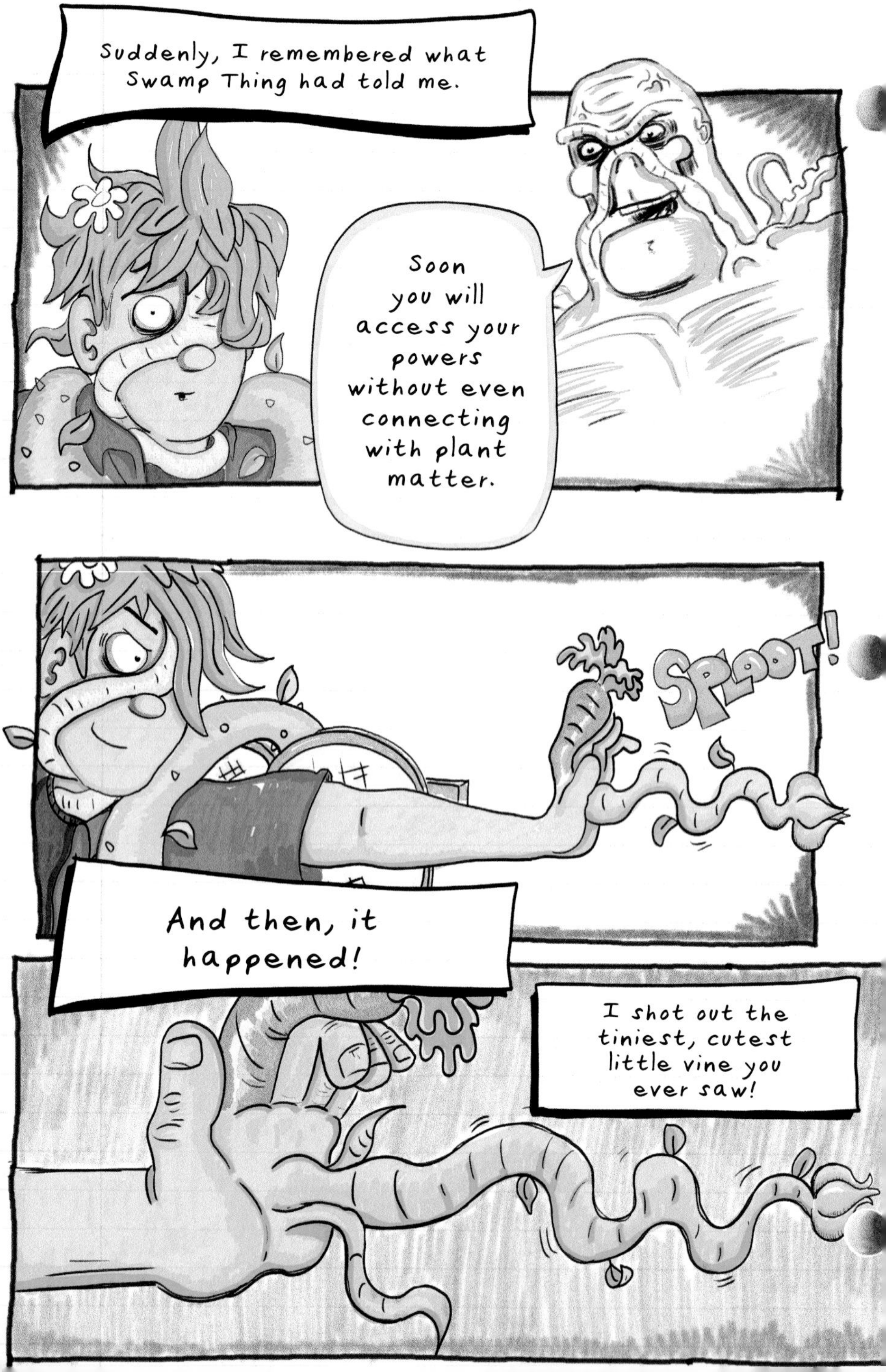
Suddenly, I remembered what Swamp Thing had told me.
Soon you will access your powers without even connecting with plant matter.
SPLOOT!
And then, it happened!
I shot out the tiniest, cutest little vine you ever saw!

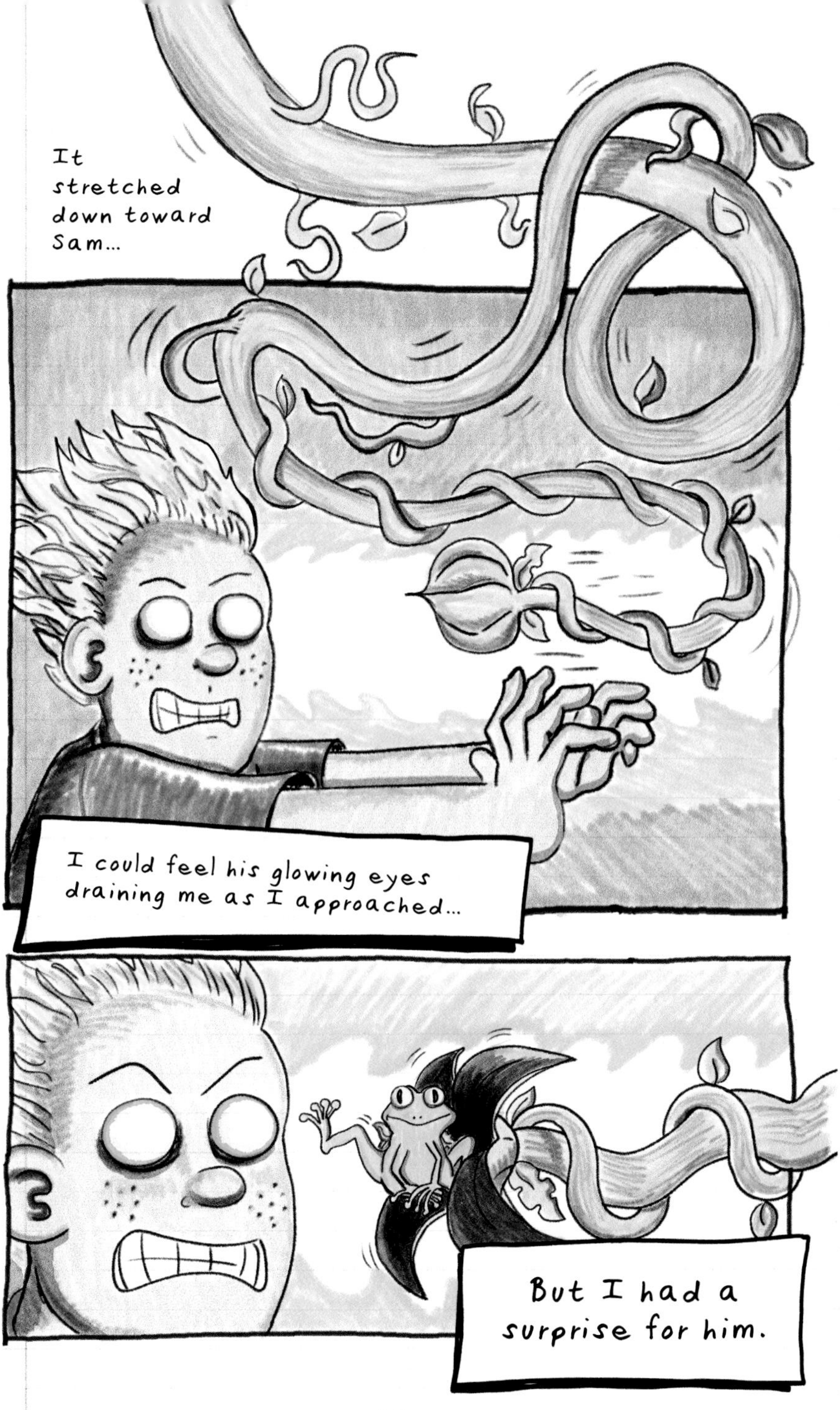
It stretched down toward Sam...
I could feel his glowing eyes draining me as I approached...
But I had a surprise for him.

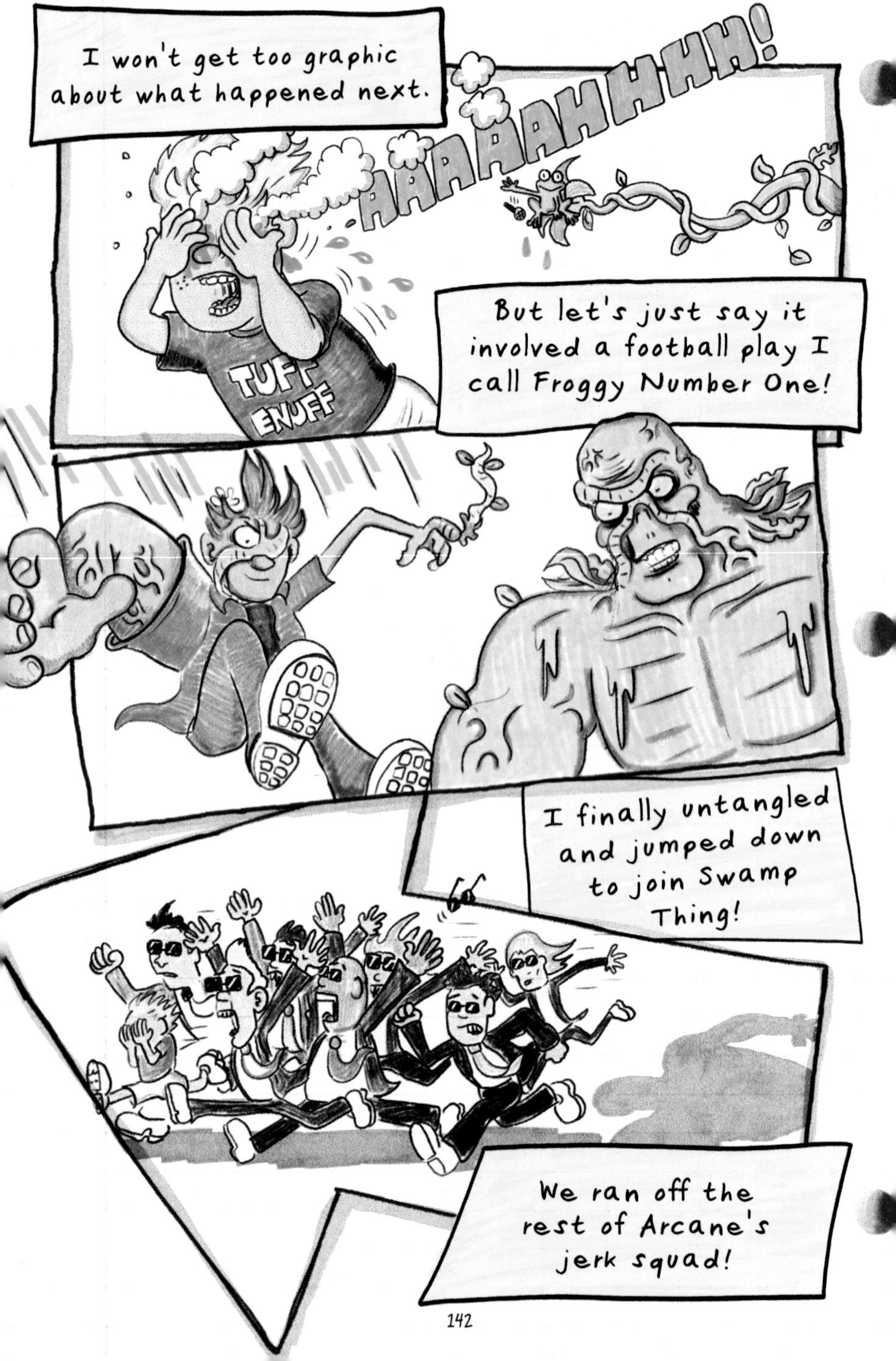
I won't get too graphic about what happened next.
AAAAAAHHHHH!
TUFF ENUFF
But let's just say it involved a football play I call Froggy Number One!
I finally untangled and jumped down to join Swamp Thing!
We ran off the rest of Arcane's jerk squad!

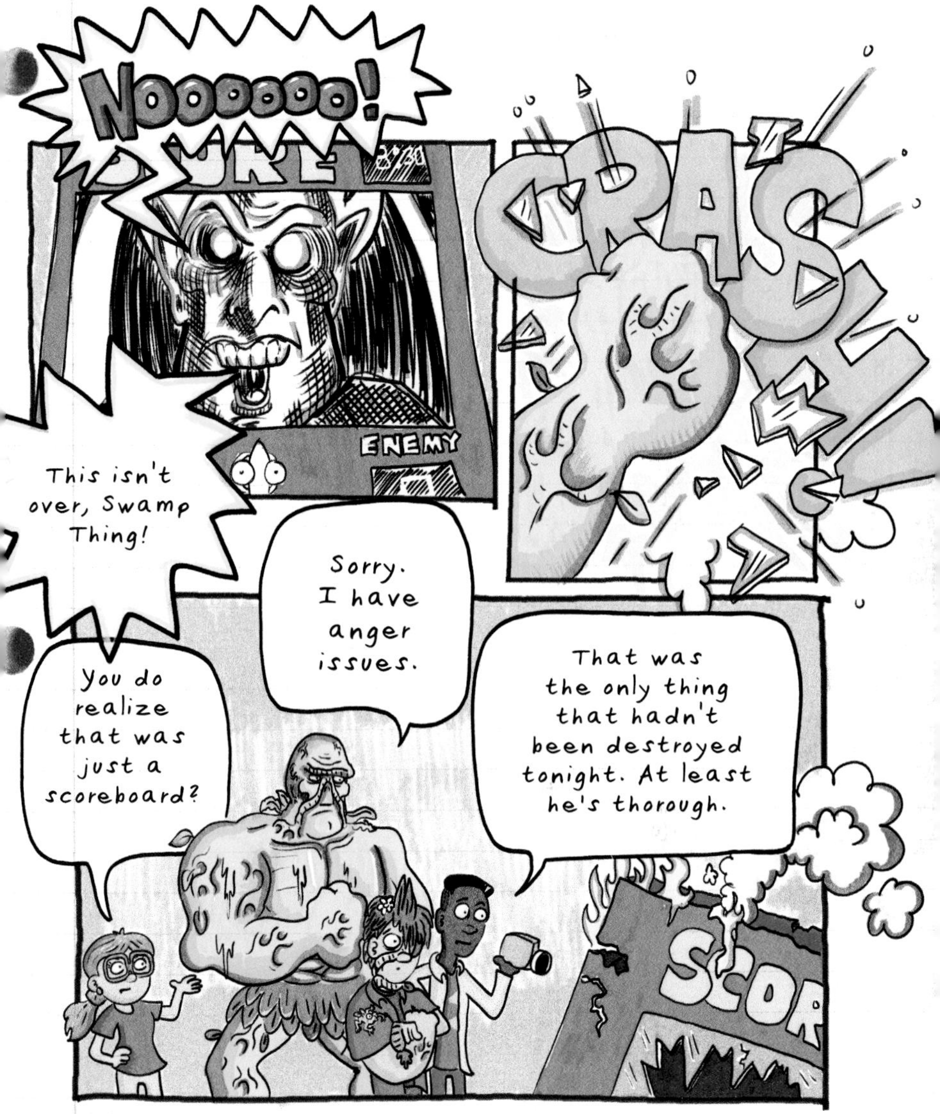
NOOOOOO!
ENEMY
CRASH!
This isn't over, Swamp Thing!
Sorry. I have anger issues.
You do realize that was just a scoreboard?
That was the only thing that hadn't been destroyed tonight. At least he's thorough.
SCOR

Arcane's agents sped off in their black S.U.V.s, along with little Sam. Swamp Thing grunted a "thanks" under his breath and slipped into the woods. It was over.

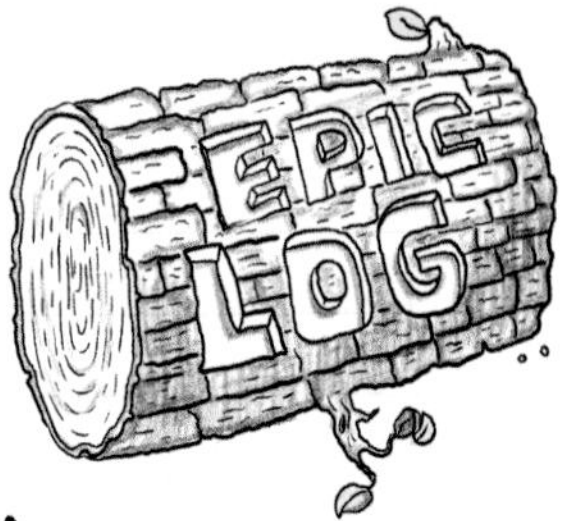
EPIC LOG

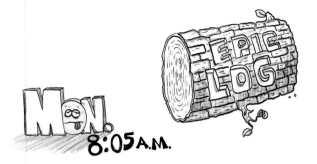

MON. 8:05 A.M.

Okay, I lied. It's not over. It's Monday morning. The dust has settled. I'm about to slip into unconsciousness in Mr. Finneca's class as usual.

Nils showed up briefly to clear out his locker. He got suspended but at least he's back to normal...mostly.

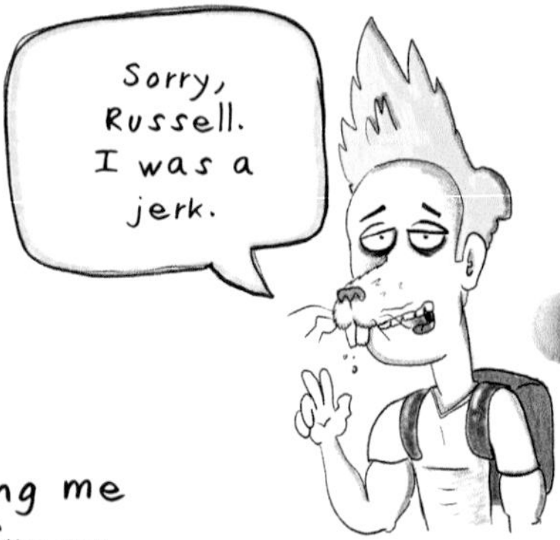
Sorry, Russell. I was a jerk.

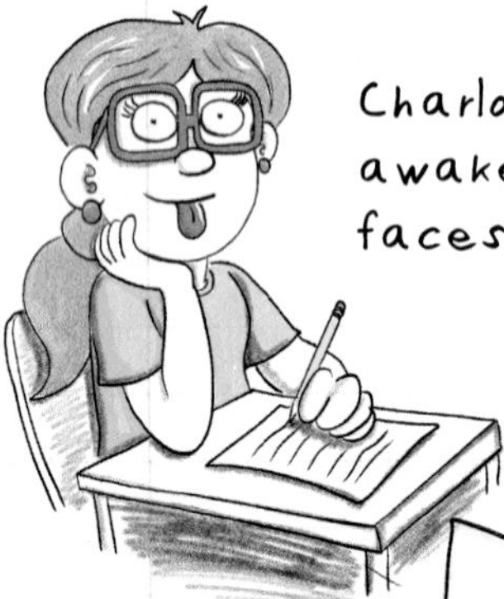

Charlotte is keeping me awake by making funny faces from across the room.

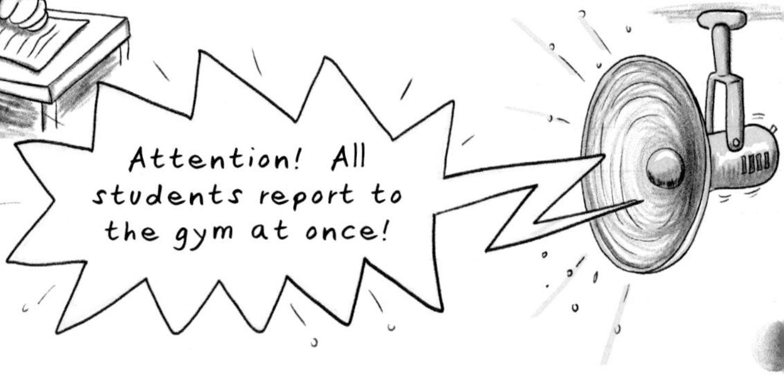
Attention! All students report to the gym at once!

Uh-oh. There's an emergency assembly in the gym. I gotta go! Hope we're not in trouble.

11:02 A.M. UPDATE

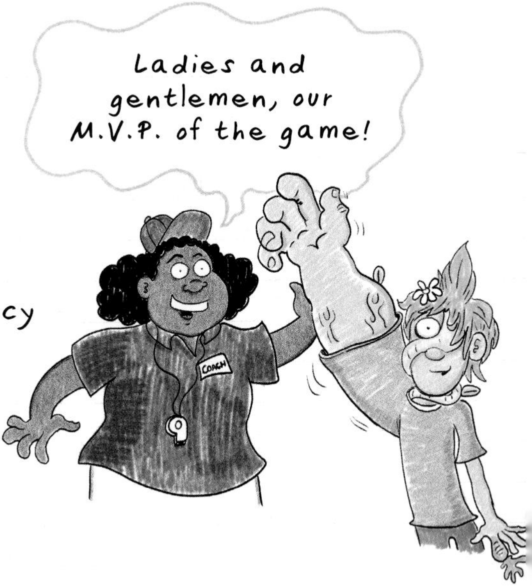
Ladies and gentlemen, our M.V.P. of the game!
COACH

Okay, you won't believe what happened! It wasn't an emergency assembly after all. The whole school was waiting to thank me with a huge celebration! I was ambushed!

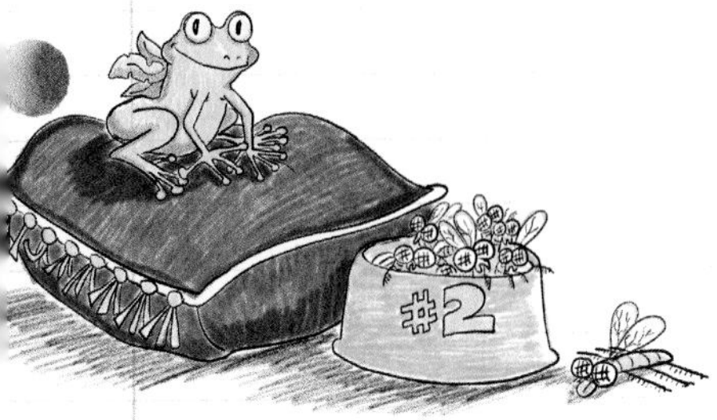
#2

Charlotte and Preston got shout-outs, too. And Specimen Number Two got his own swanky bowl of dead dragonflies. There's even talk of him becoming the new school mascot! What a day!

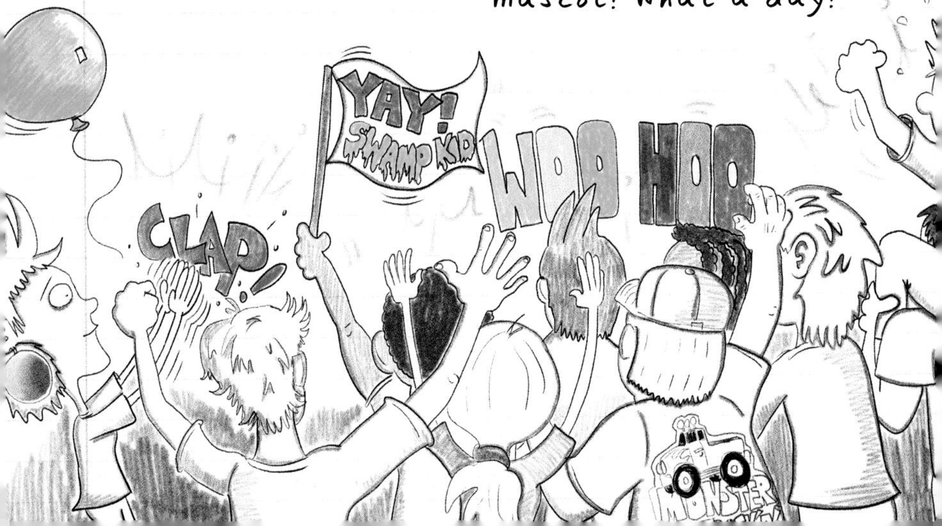
YAY! SWAMP KID
WOO HOO
CLAP!

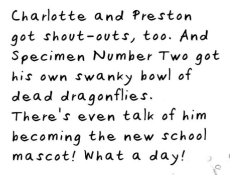

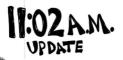

LUNCH

It's lunchtime. Not very hungry. Still stuffed with cupcakes and cookies from the big Me party. I think I'm going to suggest that it become an annual event. Or maybe a whole Me month. Mecember! Just kidding. I don't want to get a big head over this. Of course, it would go nicely with my big arm. Yuk! Yuk!

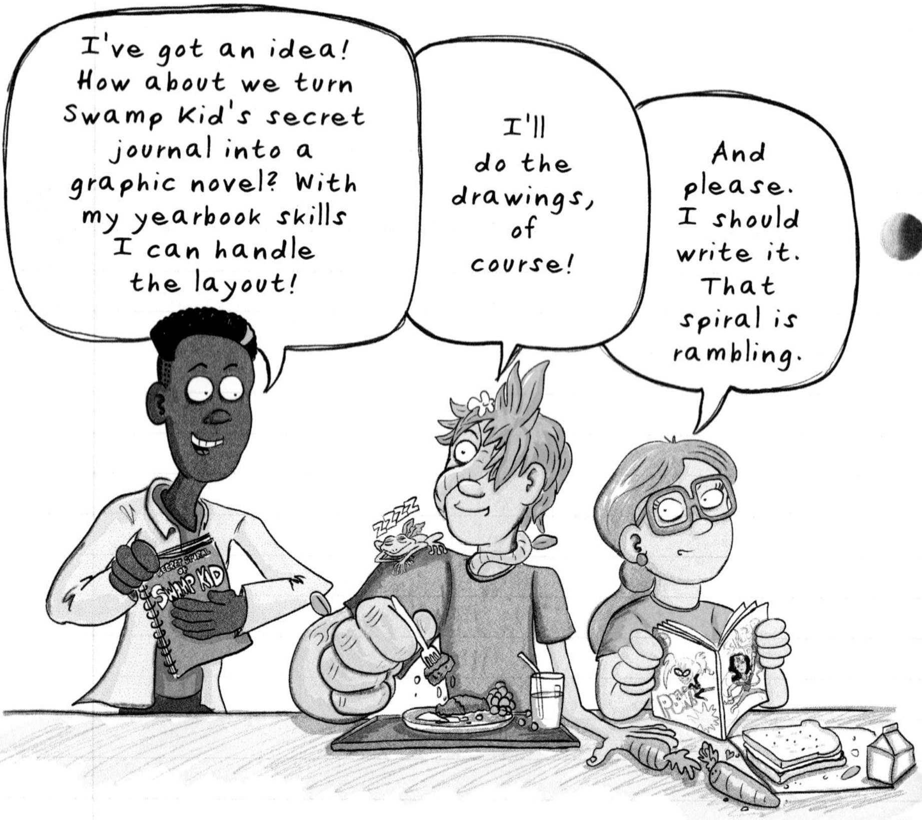
I've got an idea! How about we turn Swamp Kid's secret journal into a graphic novel? With my yearbook skills I can handle the layout!
I'll do the drawings, of course!
And please. I should write it. That spiral is rambling.
SECRET SPIRAL OF SWAMP KID

Everything in this picture looks all happy and wonderful. But don't go thinking life's back to normal and peachy keen.

Danger still lurks. I have to stay vigilant. And so should YOU! Arcane's agents could be anywhere. Or everywhere! Perhaps disguised as a lunch lady in dark shades...

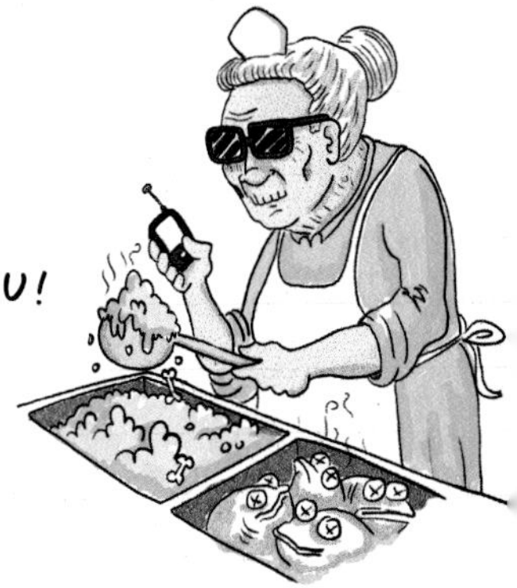

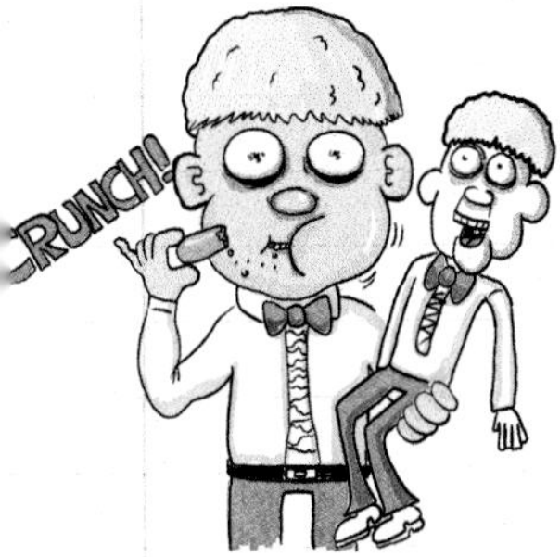
CRUNCH!

Or a kid who really loves ventriloquist dummies and baby carrots...

Or that weird school mascot that won't stop staring at you.

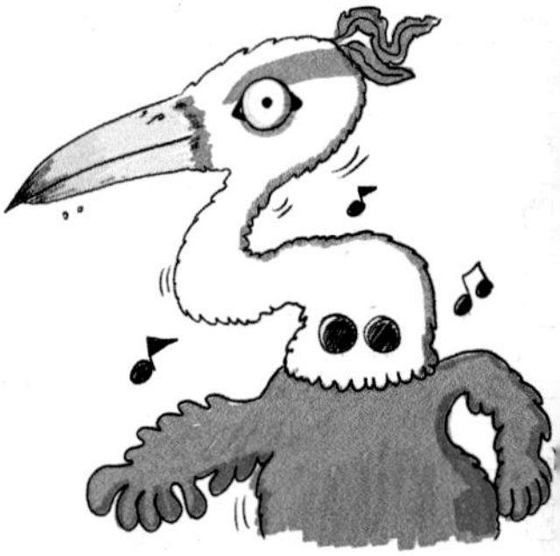

Watch your back. Watch your front! And if evil should ever take hold of your school and destruction seems imminent, remember there is someone you can call. A raging green tide of justice known as

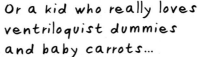

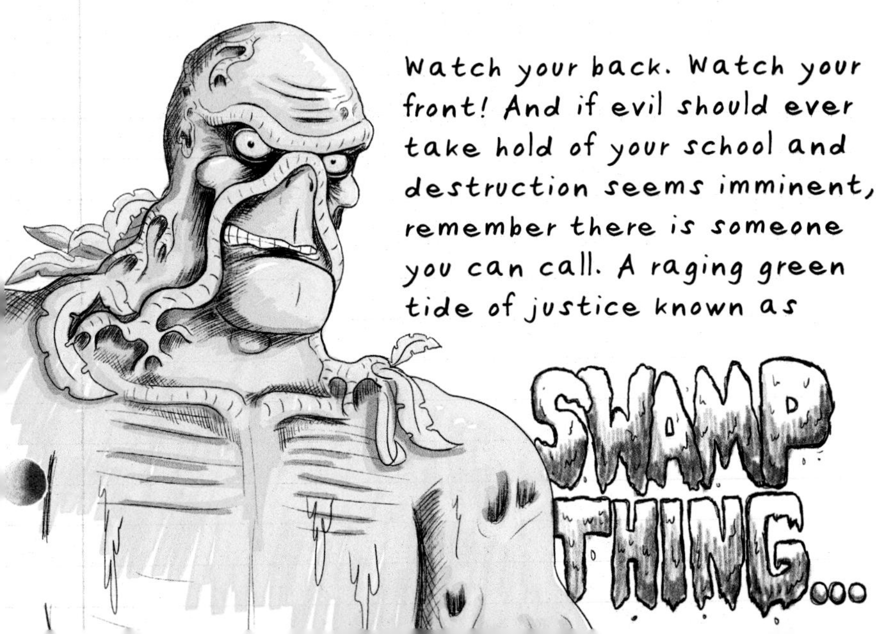
SWAMP THING...

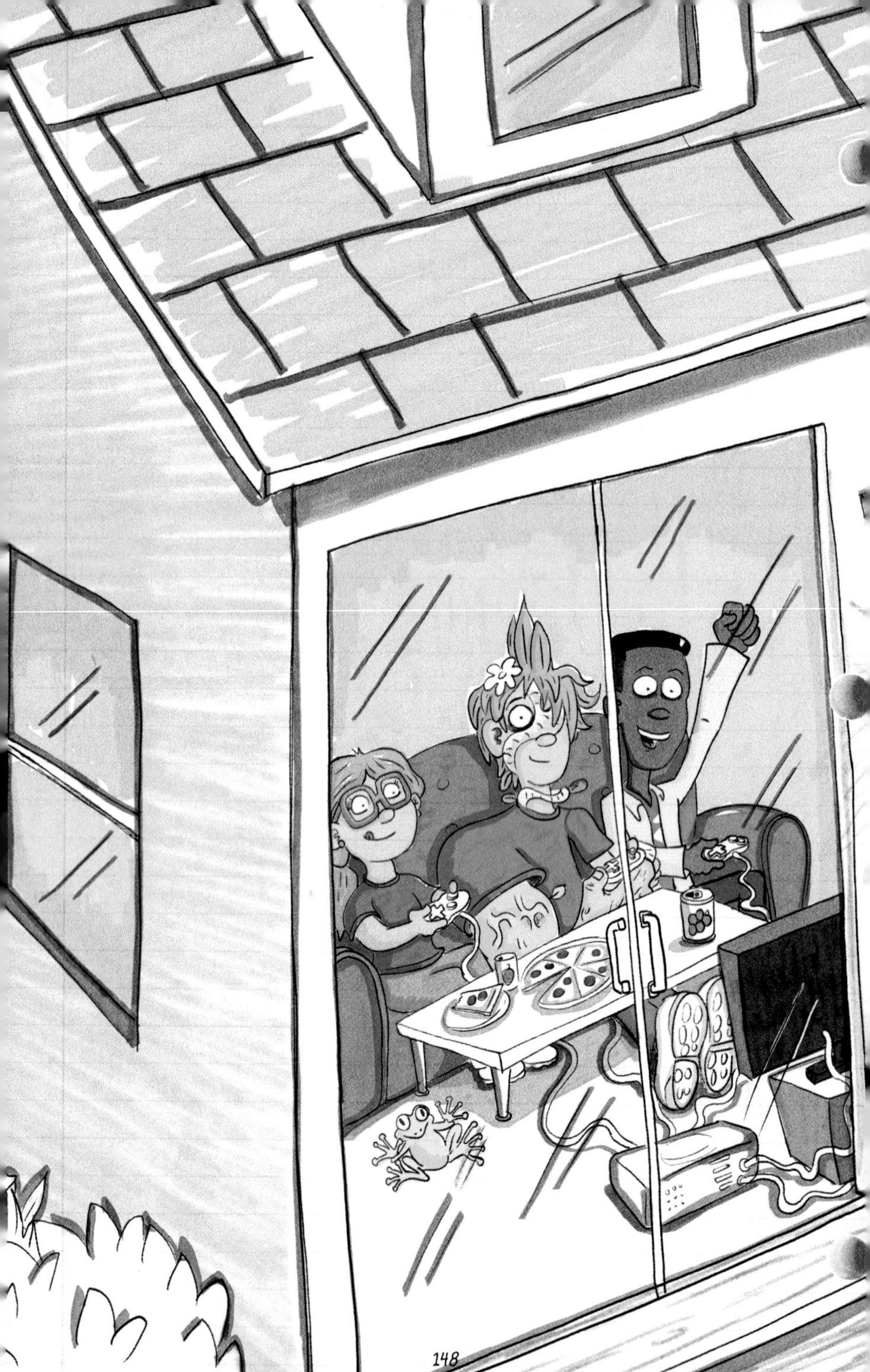

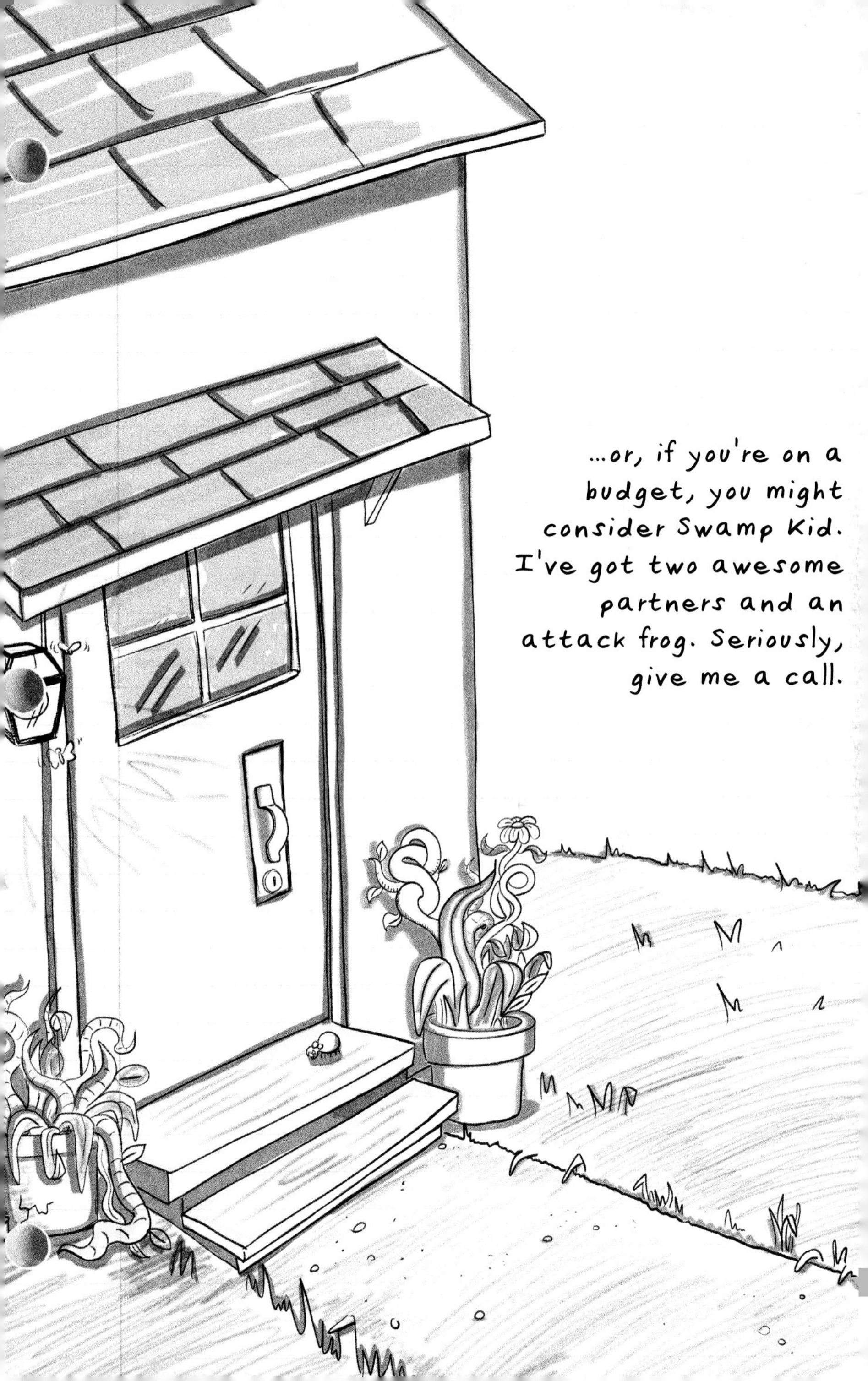
...or, if you're on a budget, you might consider Swamp Kid. I've got two awesome partners and an attack frog. Seriously, give me a call.

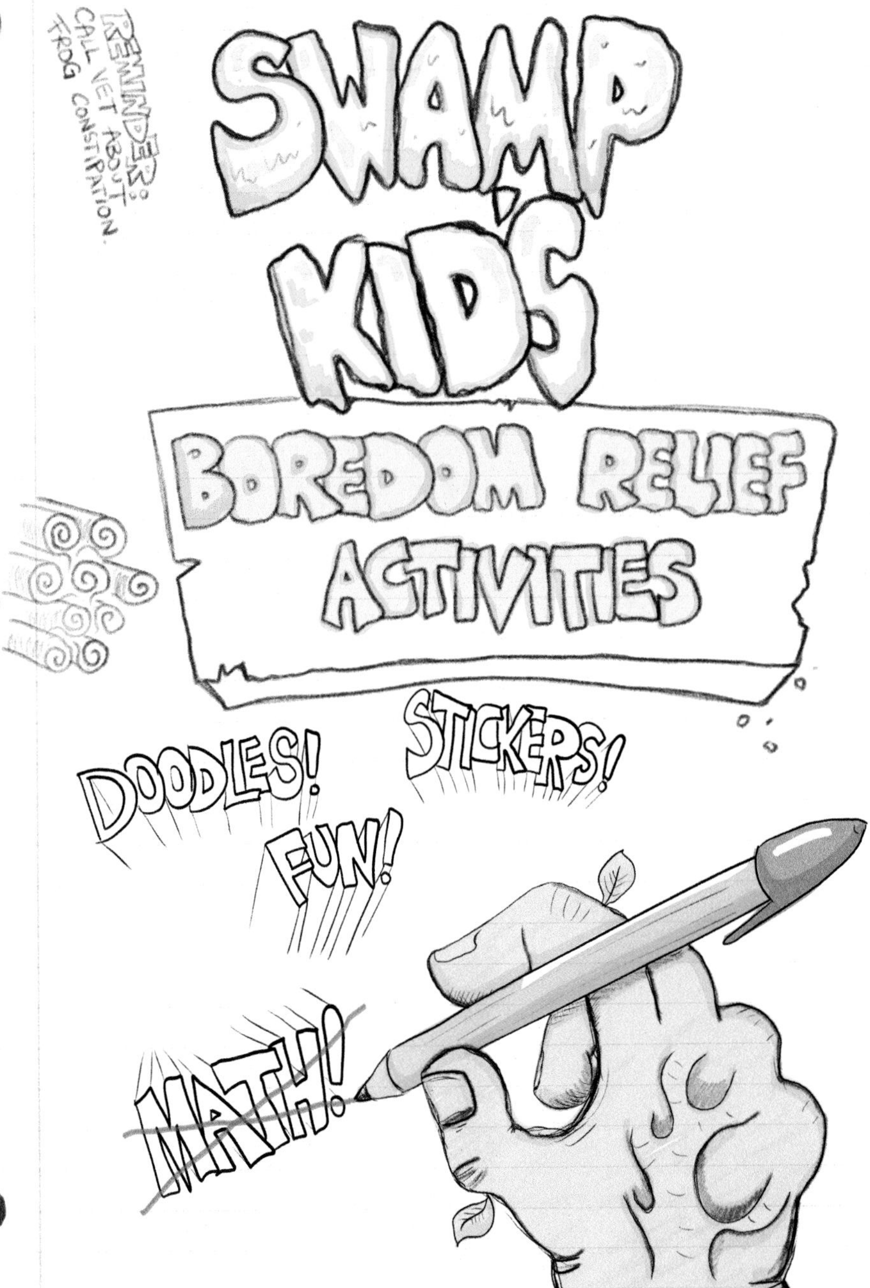
REMINDER: CALL VET ABOUT FROG CONSTIPATION.
SWAMP KID'S
BOREDOM RELIEF ACTIVITIES
DOODLES!
STICKERS!
FUN!
MATH!

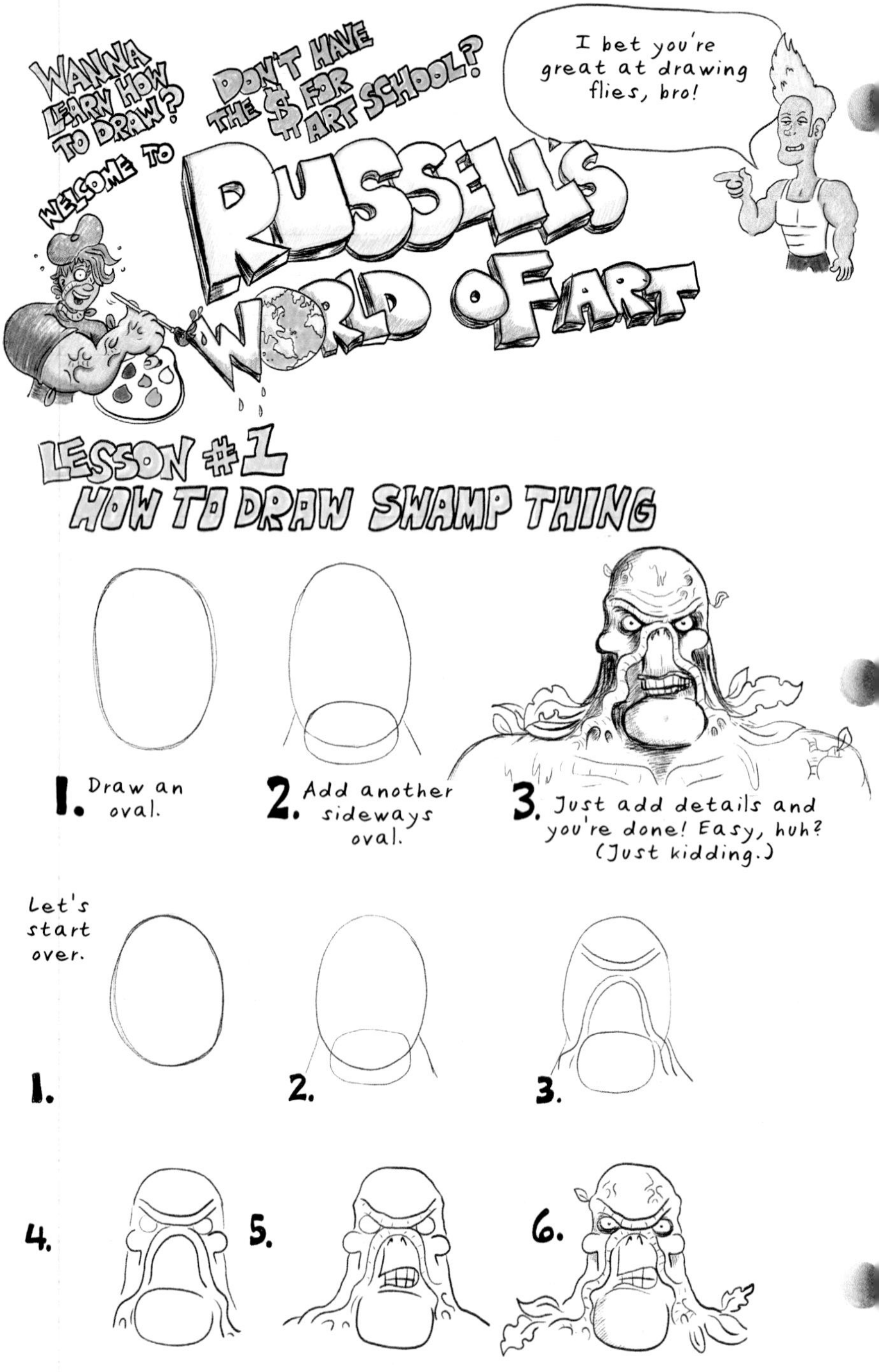
WANNA LEARN HOW TO DRAW?
DON'T HAVE THE $ FOR ART SCHOOL?
WELCOME TO
RUSSELL'S WORLD OF ART
I bet you're great at drawing flies, bro!
LESSON #1
HOW TO DRAW SWAMP THING
1. Draw an oval.
2. Add another sideways oval.
3. Just add details and you're done! Easy, huh? (Just kidding.)
Let's start over.
1.
2.
3.
4.
5.
6.

HOW TO DRAW SPECIMEN NUMBER TWO

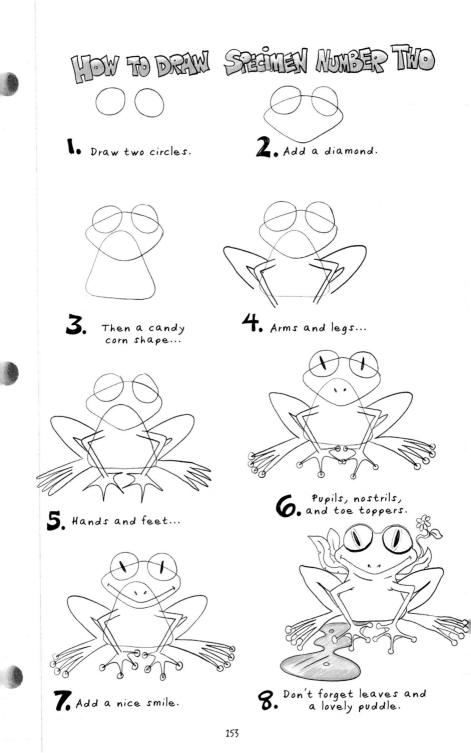

1. Draw two circles.

2. Add a diamond.

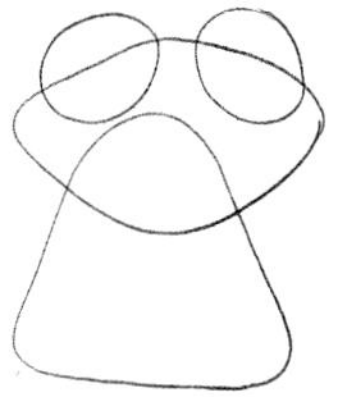

3. Then a candy corn shape...

4. Arms and legs...

5. Hands and feet...

6. Pupils, nostrils, and toe toppers.

7. Add a nice smile.

8. Don't forget leaves and a lovely puddle.

153

EVERYTHING LOOKS COOLER WITH VEINS

IT'S AMAZING WHAT A FEW SQUIGGLY LINES CAN DO FOR YOUR DRAWINGS!

MUSCLES LOOK RIPPED!

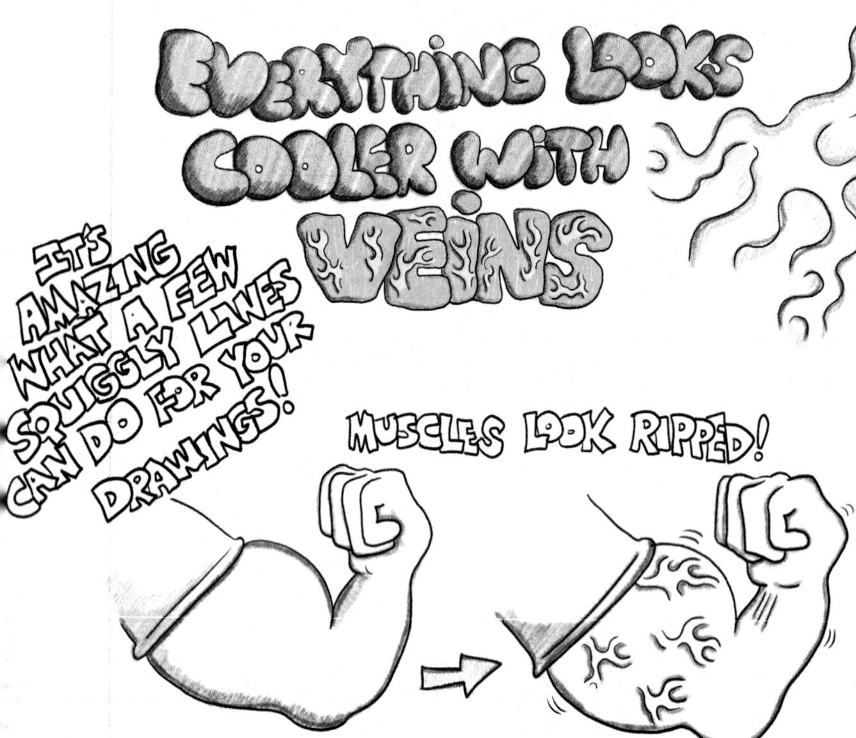

HEADS LOOK INTENSE!

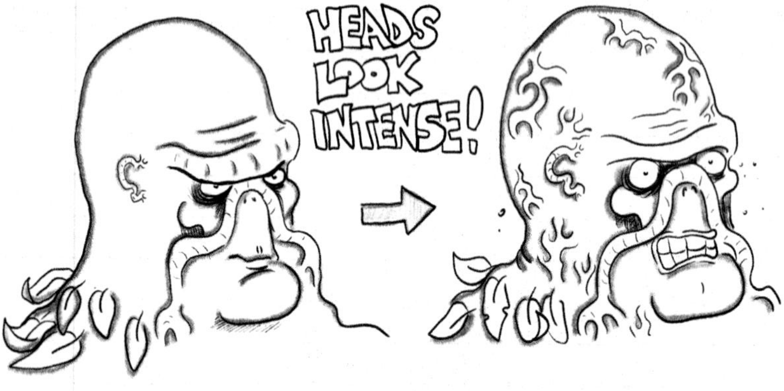

LADY BUGS LOOK JACKED!

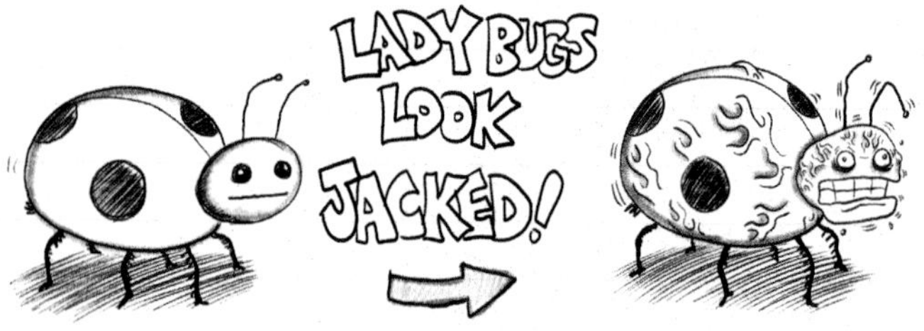

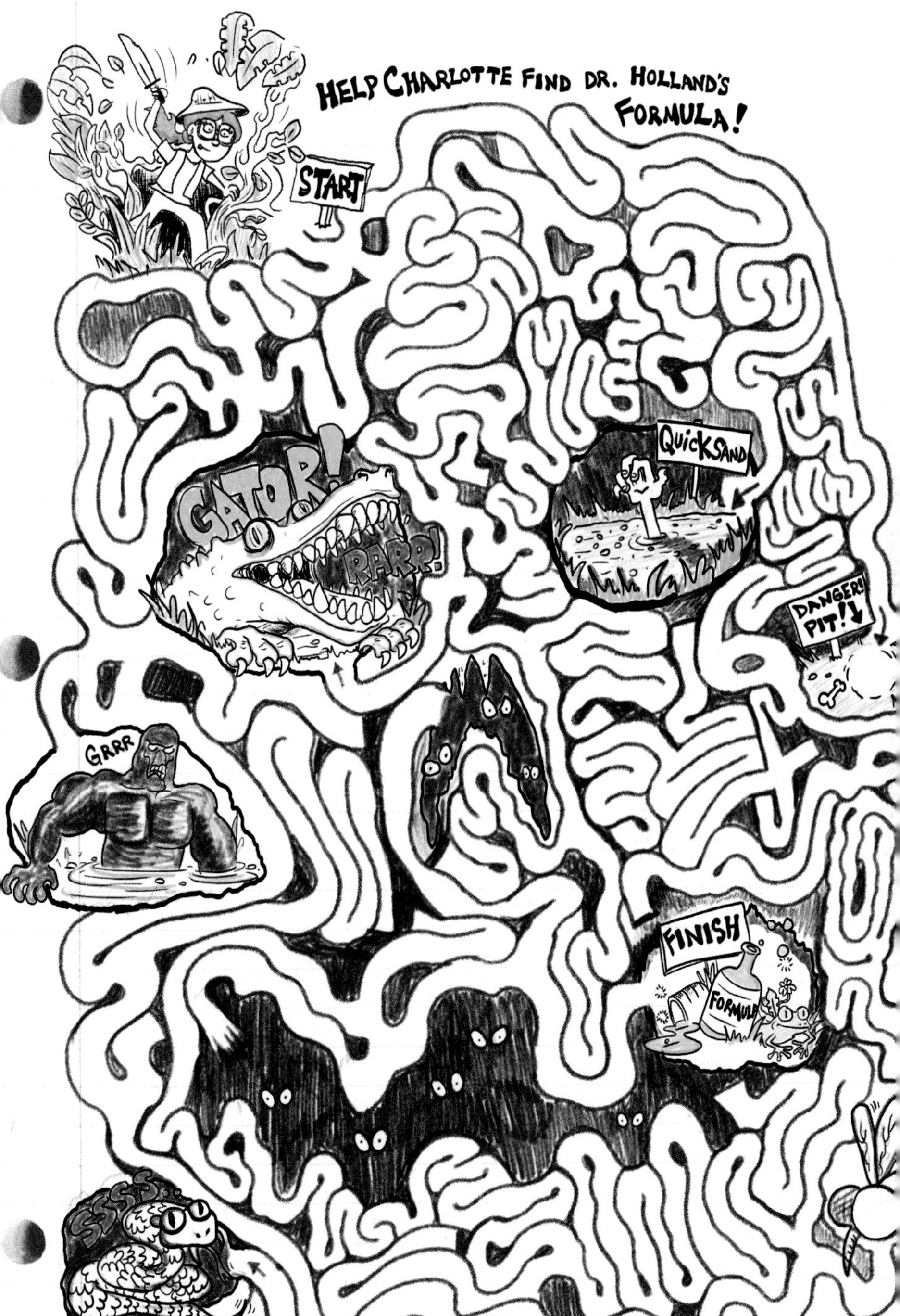
HELP CHARLOTTE FIND DR. HOLLAND'S FORMULA!
START
GATOR!
RARR!
QUICKSAND
DANGER! PIT!
GRRR
FINISH
FORMULA
SSSS

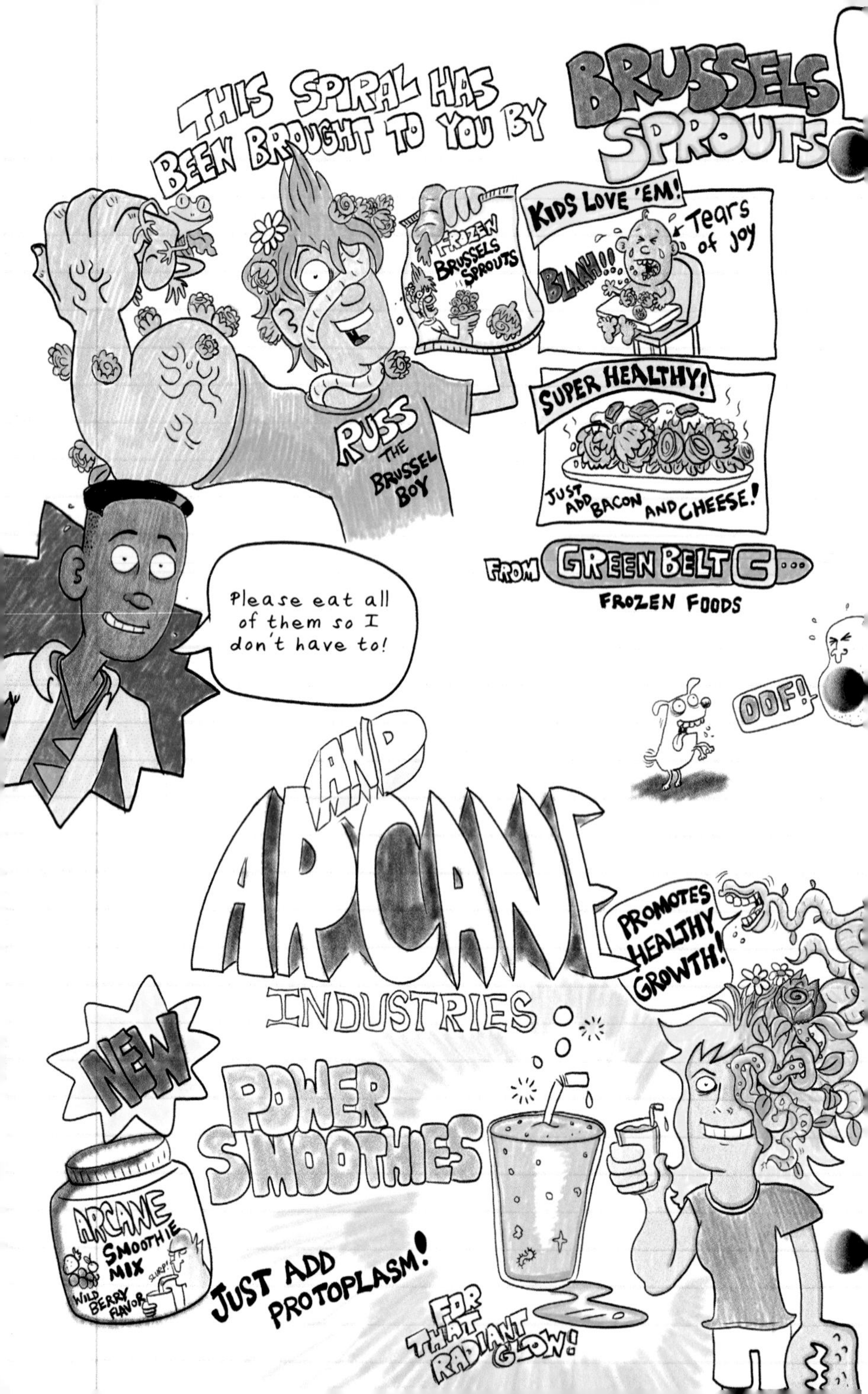

THIS SPIRAL HAS BEEN BROUGHT TO YOU BY
BRUSSELS SPROUTS!
FROZEN BRUSSELS SPROUTS
KIDS LOVE 'EM!
BLAAH!!
Tears of joy
SUPER HEALTHY!
JUST ADD BACON AND CHEESE!
RUSS THE BRUSSEL BOY
FROM GREEN BELT FROZEN FOODS
Please eat all of them so I don't have to!
OOF!
AND
ARCANE INDUSTRIES
PROMOTES HEALTHY GROWTH!
NEW
POWER SMOOTHIES
ARCANE SMOOTHIE MIX
WILD BERRY FLAVOR
SLURP!
JUST ADD PROTOPLASM!
FOR THAT RADIANT GLOW!

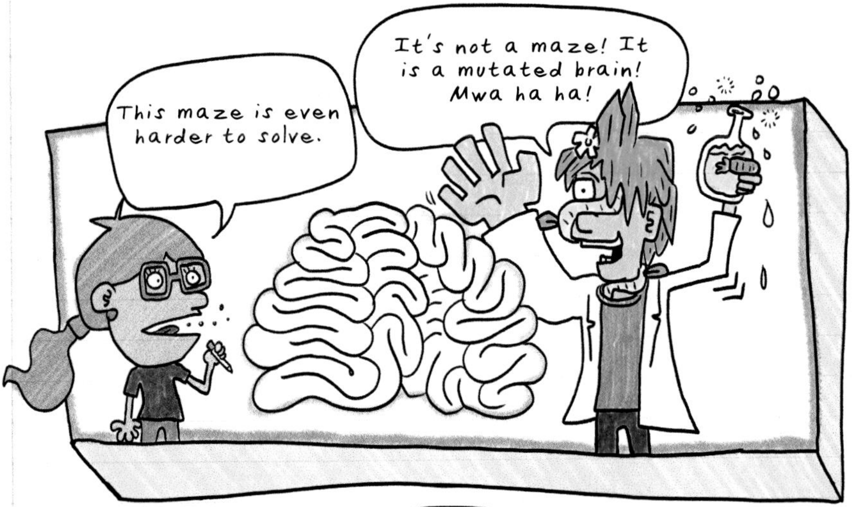
This maze is even harder to solve.
It's not a maze! It is a mutated brain! Mwa ha ha!

THE GOOD OLD DAYS

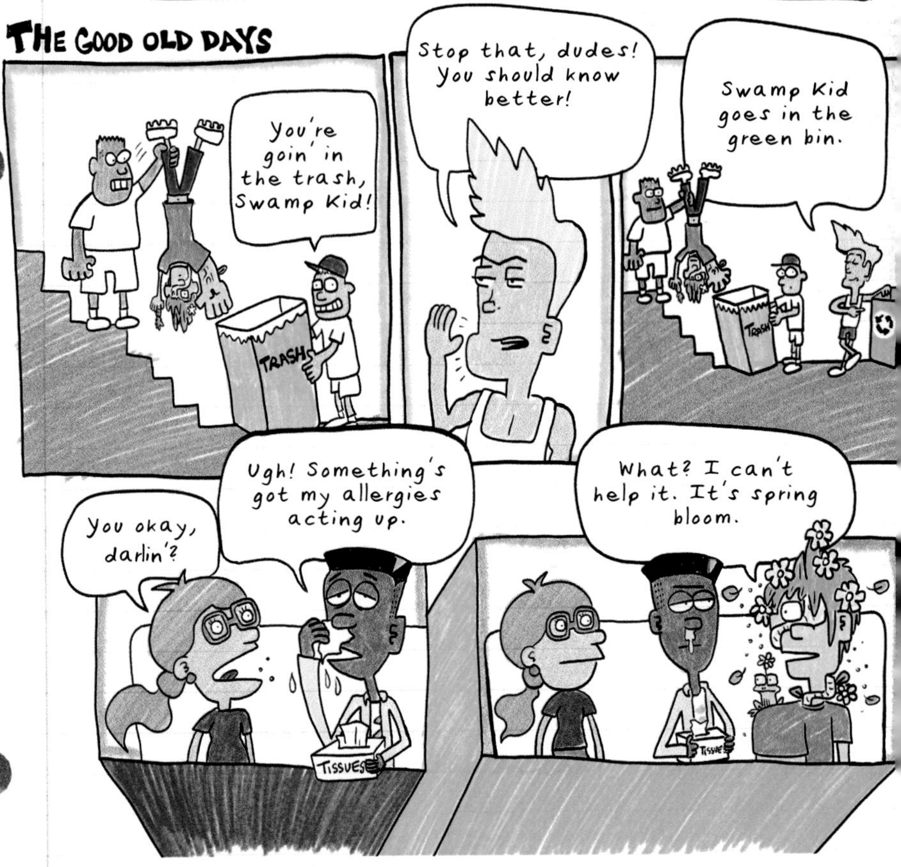
You're goin' in the trash, Swamp Kid!
TRASH
Stop that, dudes! You should know better!
Swamp Kid goes in the green bin.
TRASH
You okay, darlin'?
Ugh! Something's got my allergies acting up.
TISSUES
What? I can't help it. It's spring bloom.
TISSUES

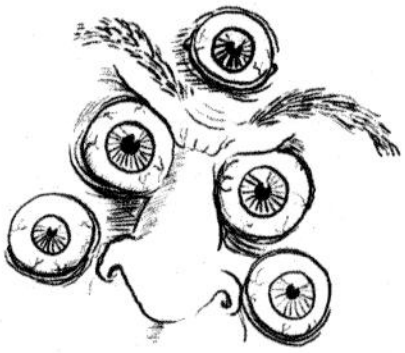

HOUMA HERONS

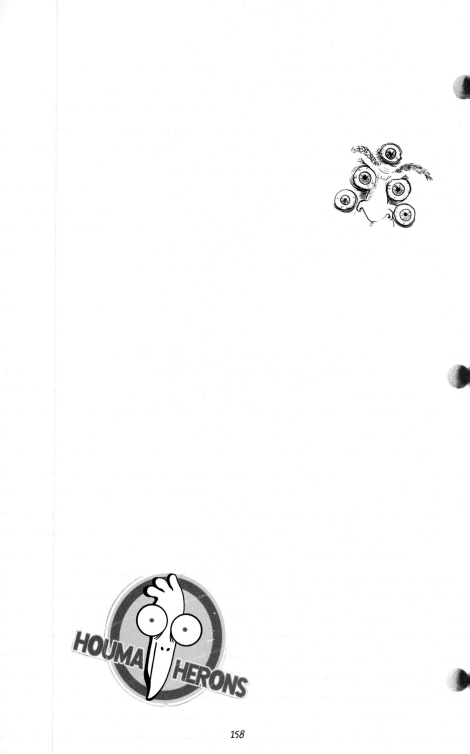

Kirk Scroggs is an author-illustrator best known for the *Snoop Troop* books, *It Came From Beneath the Playground*, and *Attack of the Ninja Potato Clones*, as well as the series *Tales of a Sixth-Grade Muppet* and *Wiley & Grampa's Creature Features*. His website is kirkscroggs.com

Don't miss this exciting adventure from DC Zoom!
Turn the next page for a super sneak peek.

Can Superman keep Smallville
from going to the dogs?

From the *New York Times* bestselling creators of TINY TITANS comes the hilarious story of Clark Kent as he navigates aliens, disappearing hot dog carts, and middle school.

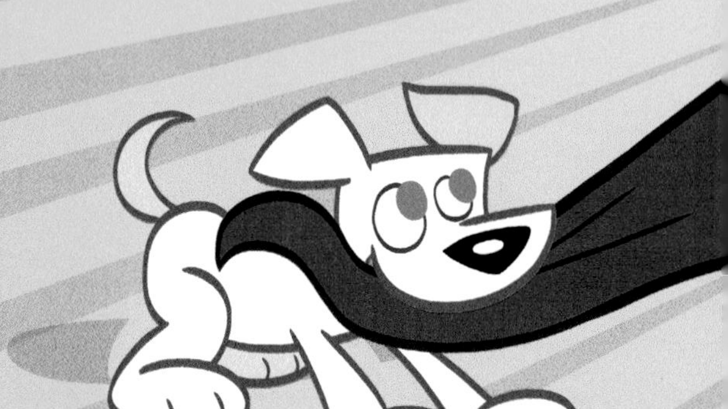
ART BALTAZAR

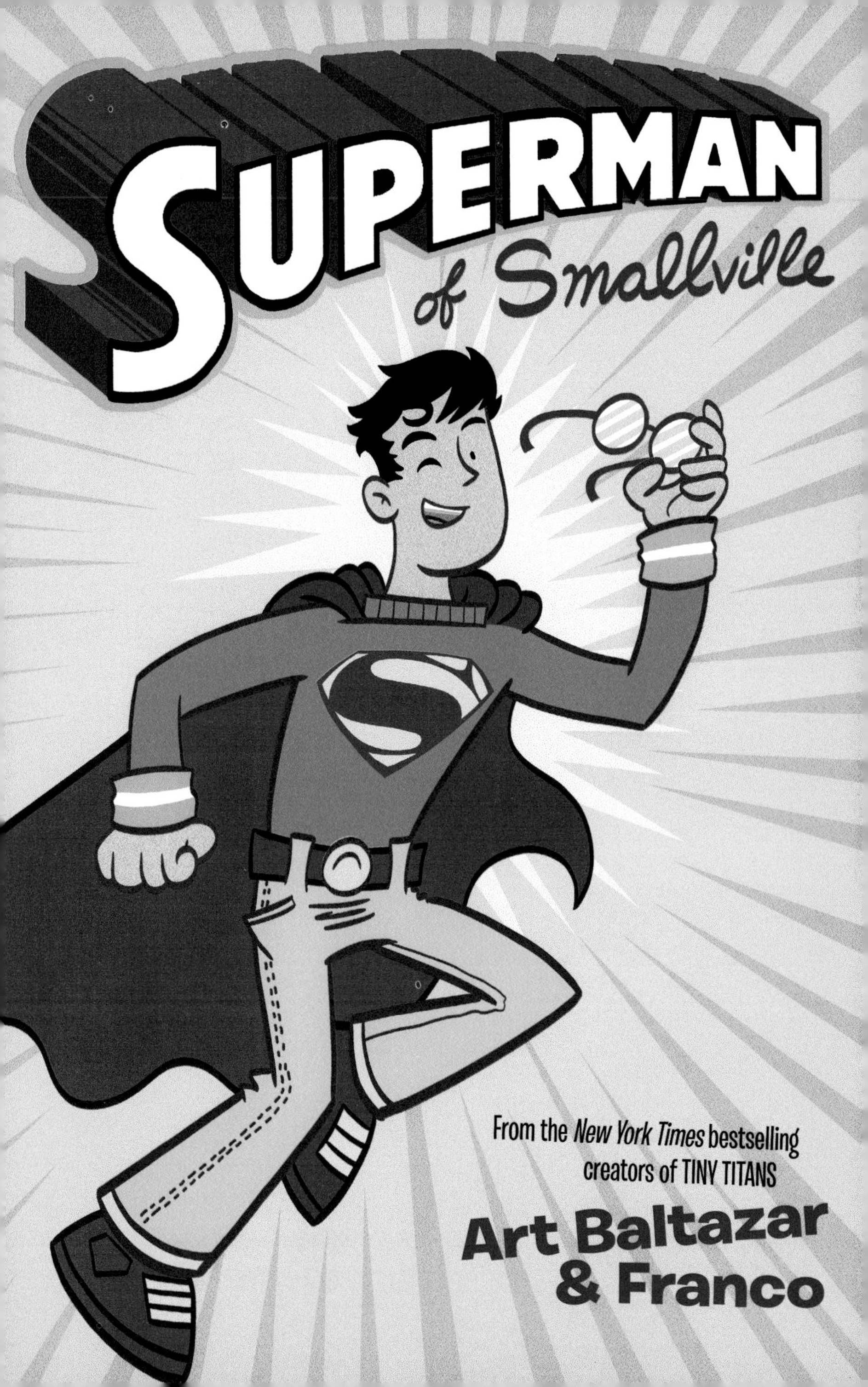
SUPERMAN
of Smallville
From the New York Times bestselling
creators of TINY TITANS
Art Baltazar
& Franco

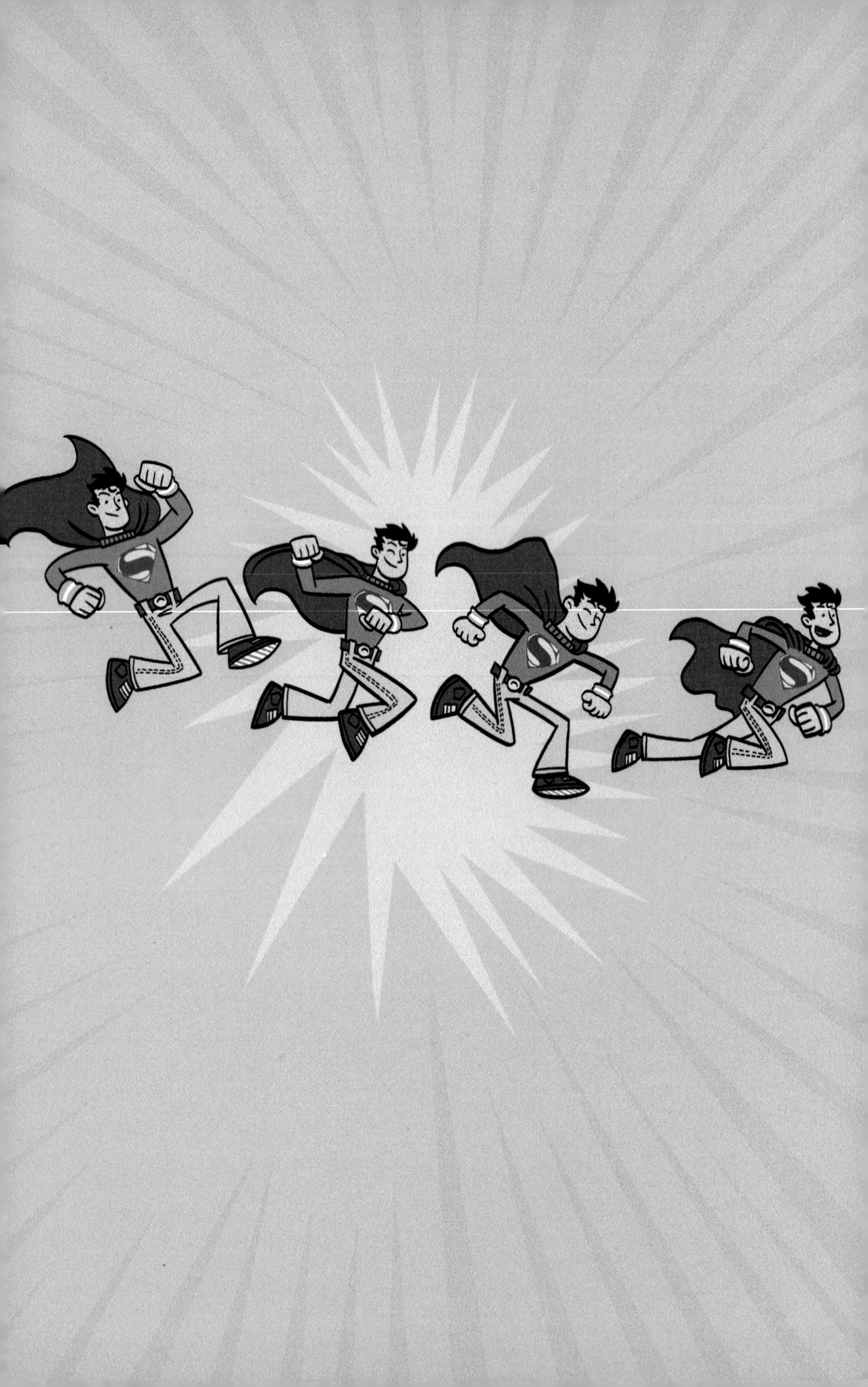

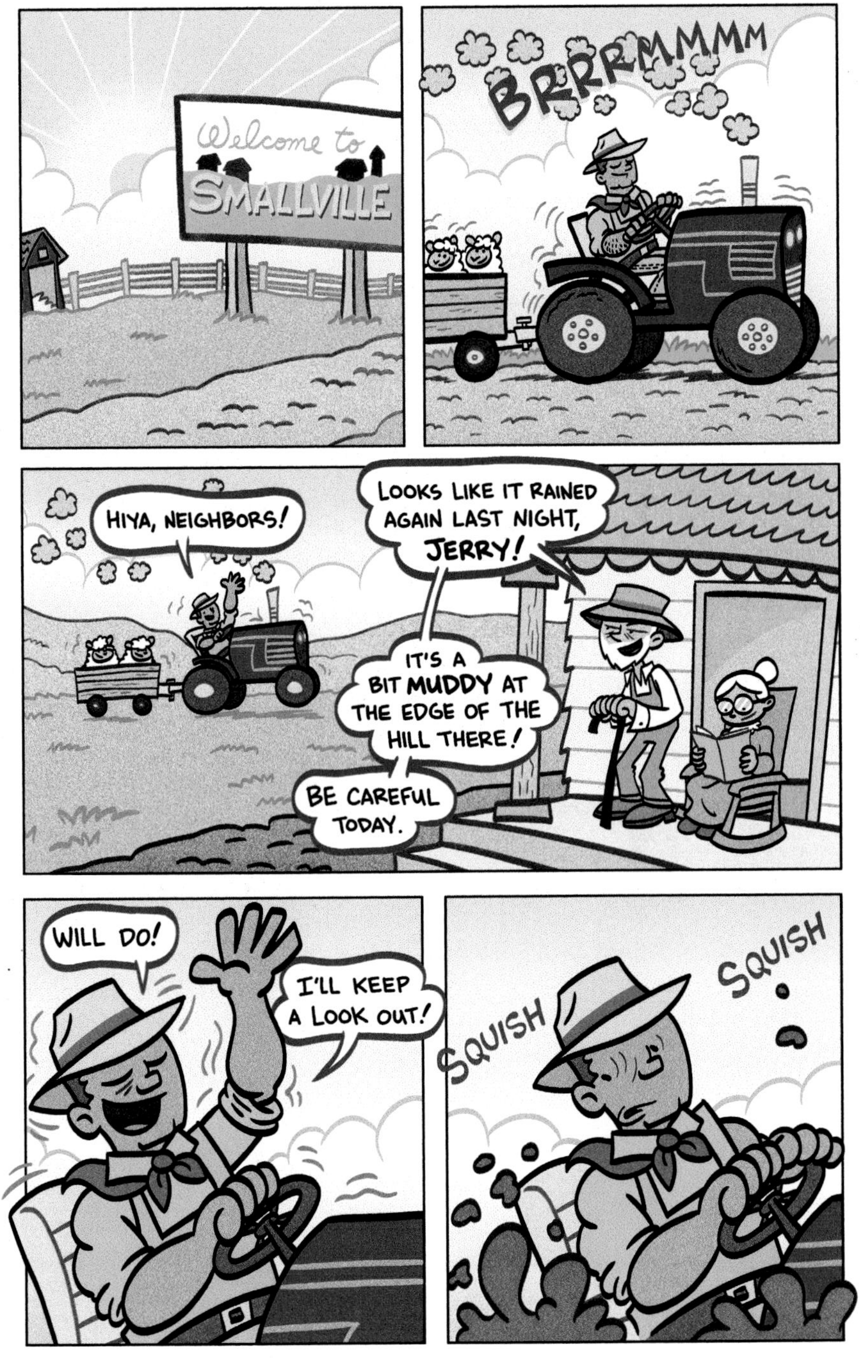
Welcome to
SMALLVILLE
BRRRMMMMM
HIYA, NEIGHBORS!
LOOKS LIKE IT RAINED AGAIN LAST NIGHT, JERRY!
IT'S A BIT MUDDY AT THE EDGE OF THE HILL THERE!
BE CAREFUL TODAY.
WILL DO!
I'LL KEEP A LOOK OUT!
SQUISH
SQUISH

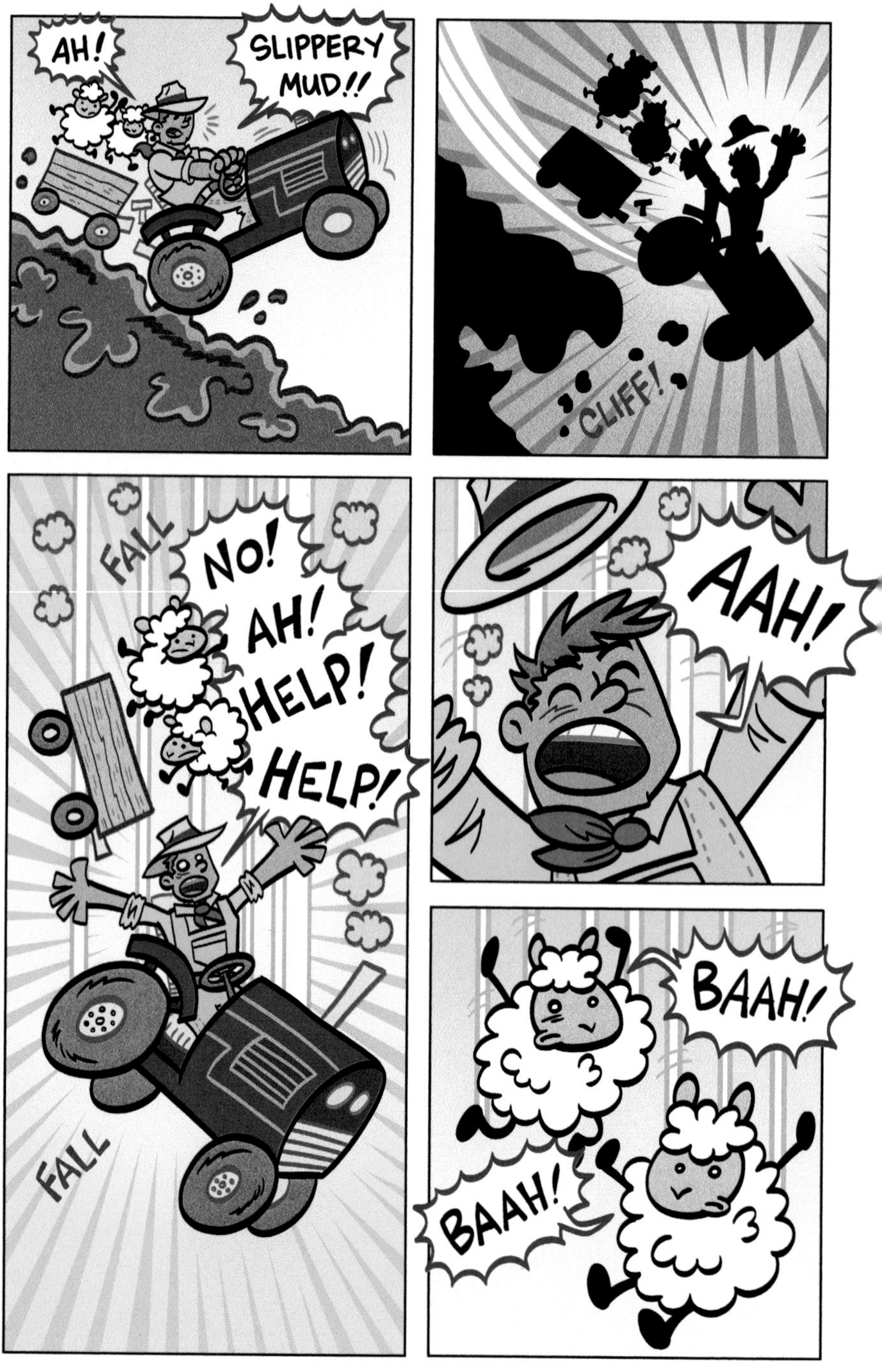
AH!
SLIPPERY MUD!!
CLIFF!
FALL
NO! AH! HELP! HELP!
FALL
AAH!
BAAH!
BAAH!

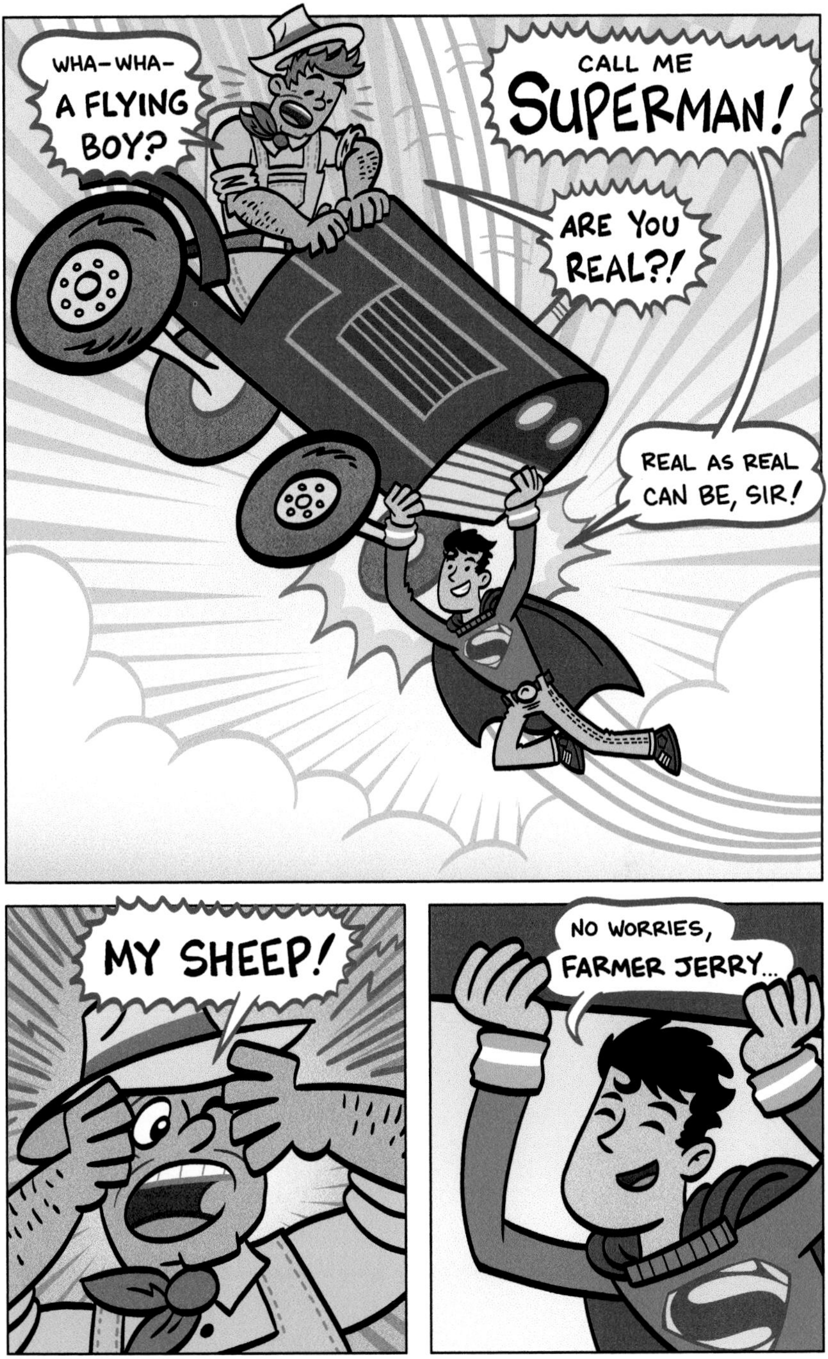
WHA-WHA- A FLYING BOY?
CALL ME SUPERMAN!
ARE YOU REAL?!
REAL AS REAL CAN BE, SIR!
MY SHEEP!
NO WORRIES, FARMER JERRY...

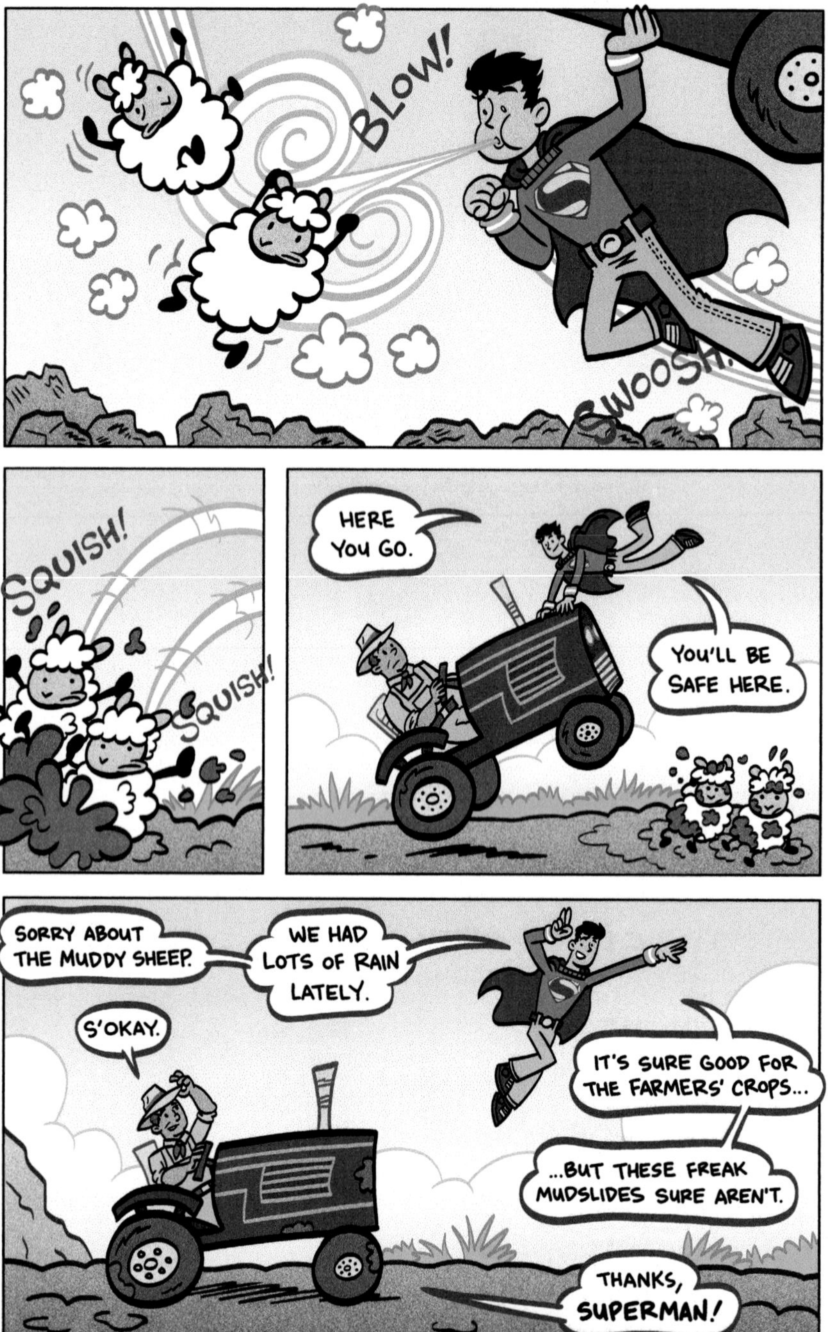
BLOW!
SWOOSH!
SQUISH!
SQUISH!
HERE YOU GO.
YOU'LL BE SAFE HERE.
SORRY ABOUT THE MUDDY SHEEP.
WE HAD LOTS OF RAIN LATELY.
S'OKAY.
IT'S SURE GOOD FOR THE FARMERS' CROPS...
...BUT THESE FREAK MUDSLIDES SURE AREN'T.
THANKS, SUPERMAN!

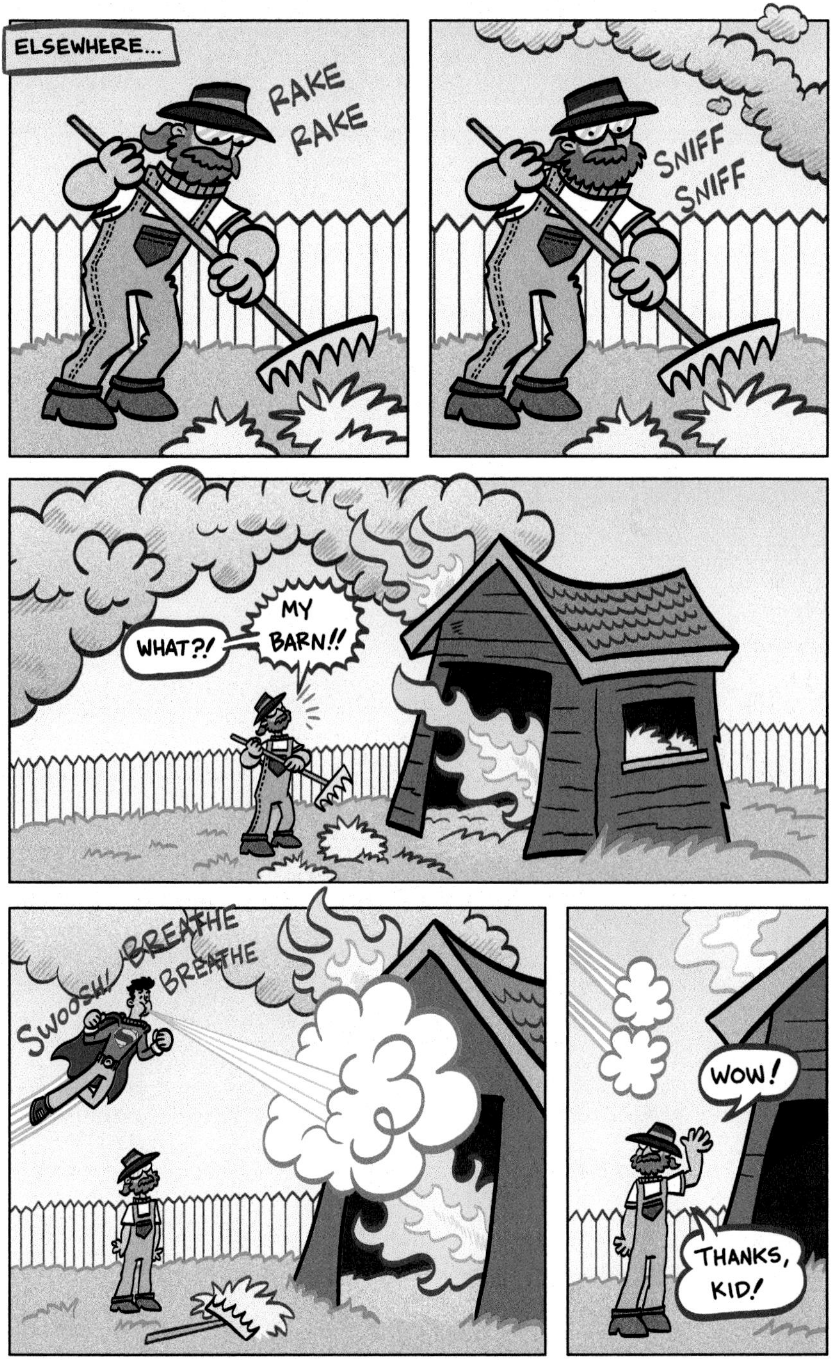
ELSEWHERE...
RAKE RAKE
SNIFF SNIFF
WHAT?!
MY BARN!!
SWOOSH!
BREATHE BREATHE
WOW!
THANKS, KID!

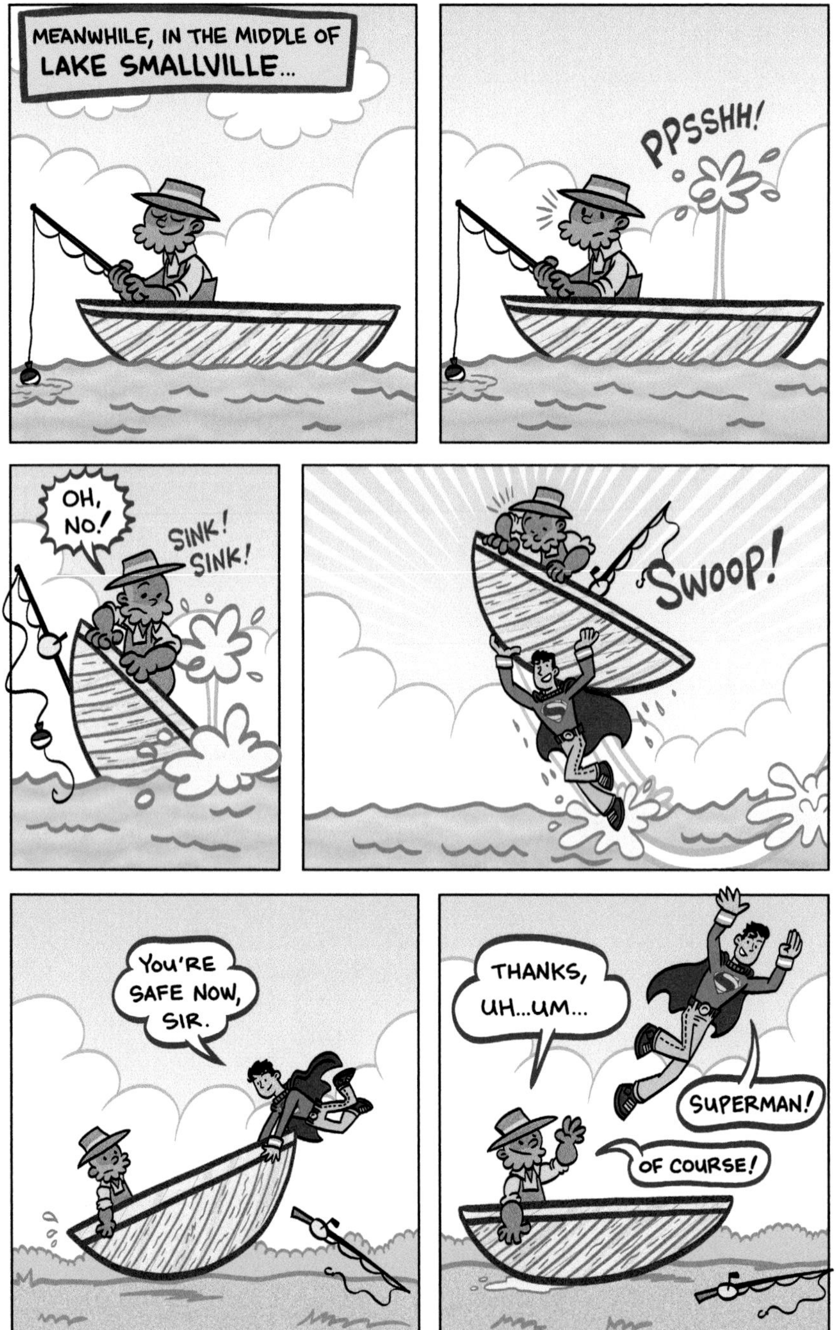
MEANWHILE, IN THE MIDDLE OF LAKE SMALLVILLE...
PPSSHH!
OH, NO!
SINK! SINK!
SWOOP!
YOU'RE SAFE NOW, SIR.
THANKS, UH...UM...
SUPERMAN!
OF COURSE!

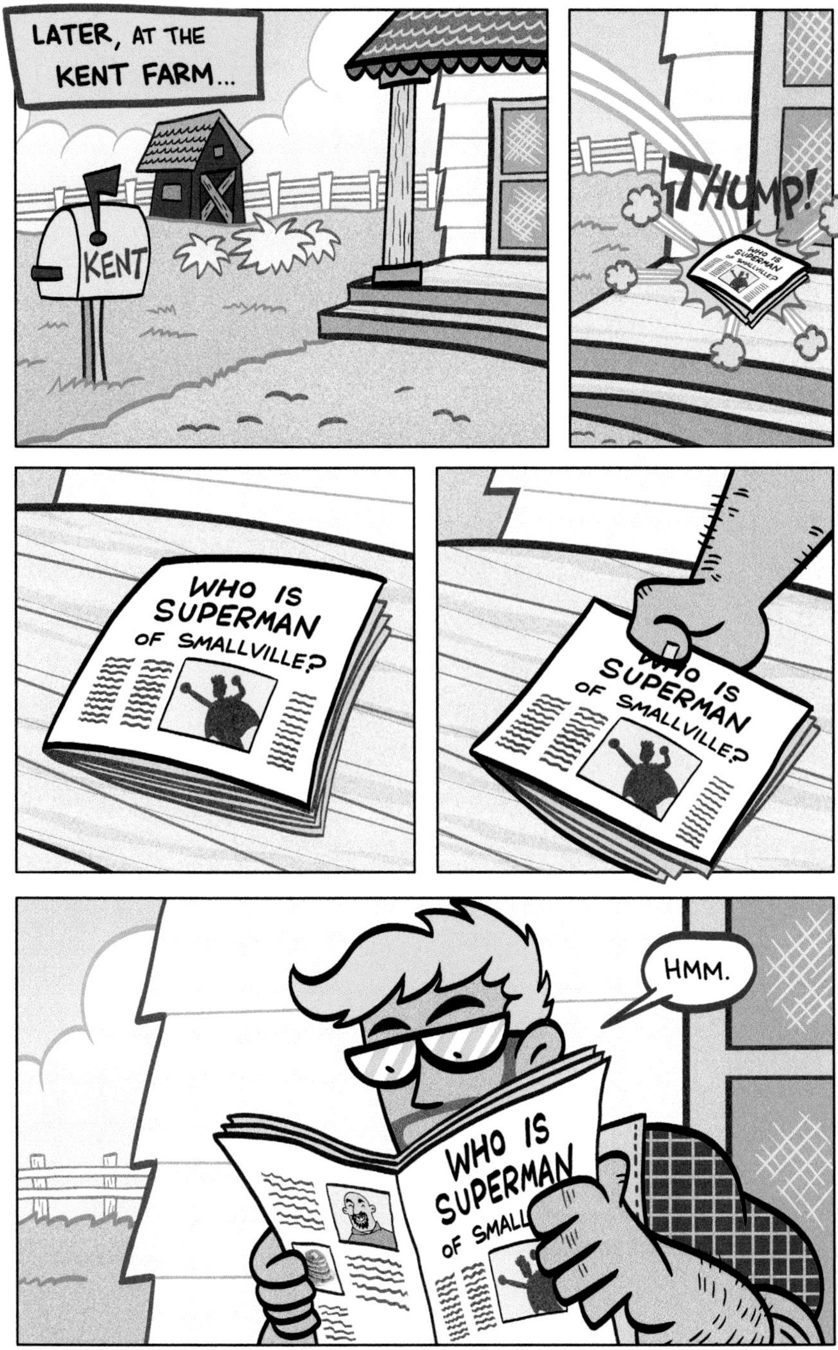
LATER, AT THE KENT FARM...
KENT
THUMP!
WHO IS SUPERMAN OF SMALLVILLE?
WHO IS SUPERMAN OF SMALLVILLE?
WHO IS SUPERMAN
HMM.

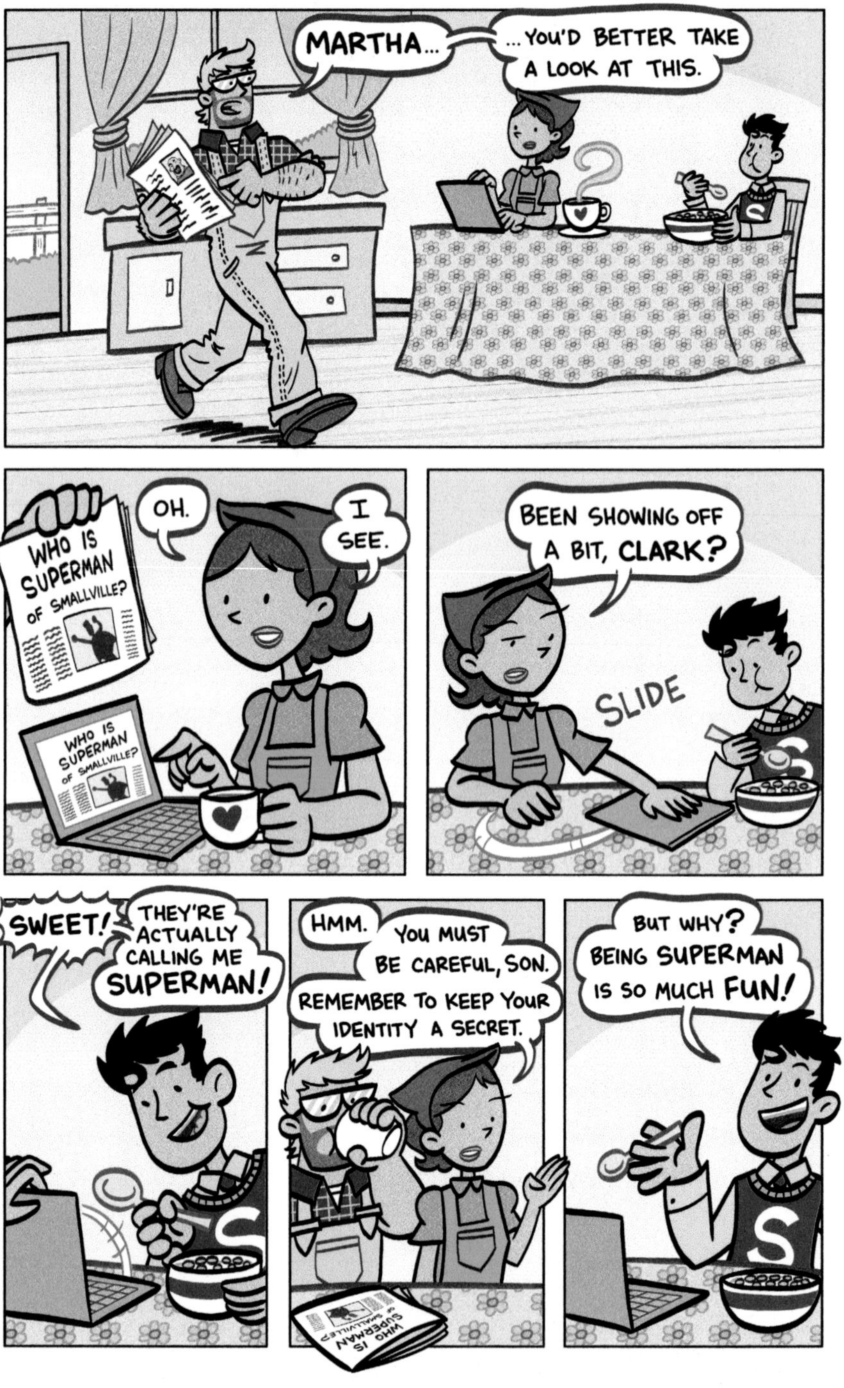

MARTHA...
...YOU'D BETTER TAKE A LOOK AT THIS.
WHO IS SUPERMAN OF SMALLVILLE?
OH.
I SEE.
WHO IS SUPERMAN OF SMALLVILLE?
BEEN SHOWING OFF A BIT, CLARK?
SLIDE
SWEET!
THEY'RE ACTUALLY CALLING ME SUPERMAN!
HMM.
YOU MUST BE CAREFUL, SON.
REMEMBER TO KEEP YOUR IDENTITY A SECRET.
WHO IS SUPERMAN OF SMALLVILLE?
BUT WHY? BEING SUPERMAN IS SO MUCH FUN!

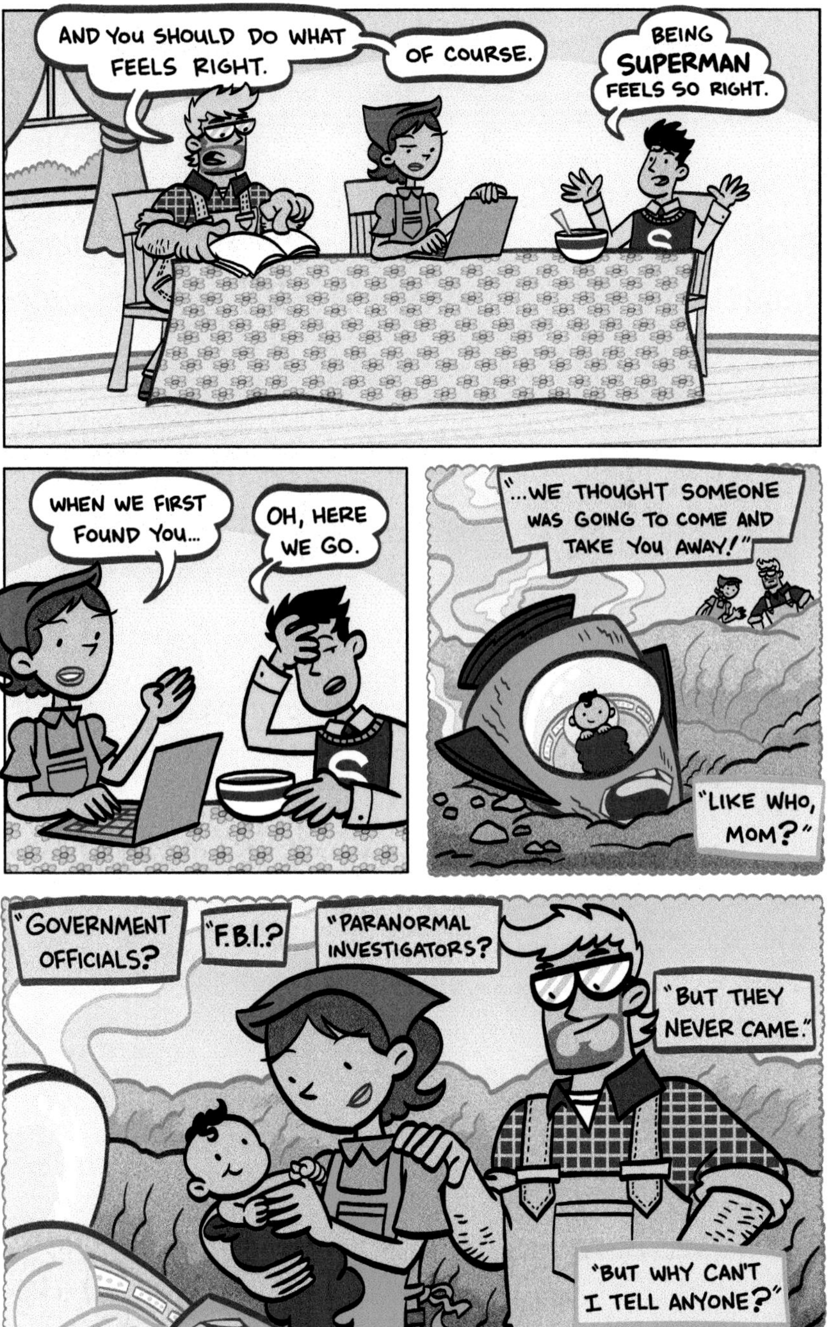
AND YOU SHOULD DO WHAT FEELS RIGHT.
OF COURSE.
BEING SUPERMAN FEELS SO RIGHT.
WHEN WE FIRST FOUND YOU...
OH, HERE WE GO.
"...WE THOUGHT SOMEONE WAS GOING TO COME AND TAKE YOU AWAY!"
"LIKE WHO, MOM?"
"GOVERNMENT OFFICIALS?
"F.B.I.?
"PARANORMAL INVESTIGATORS?
"BUT THEY NEVER CAME."
"BUT WHY CAN'T I TELL ANYONE?"

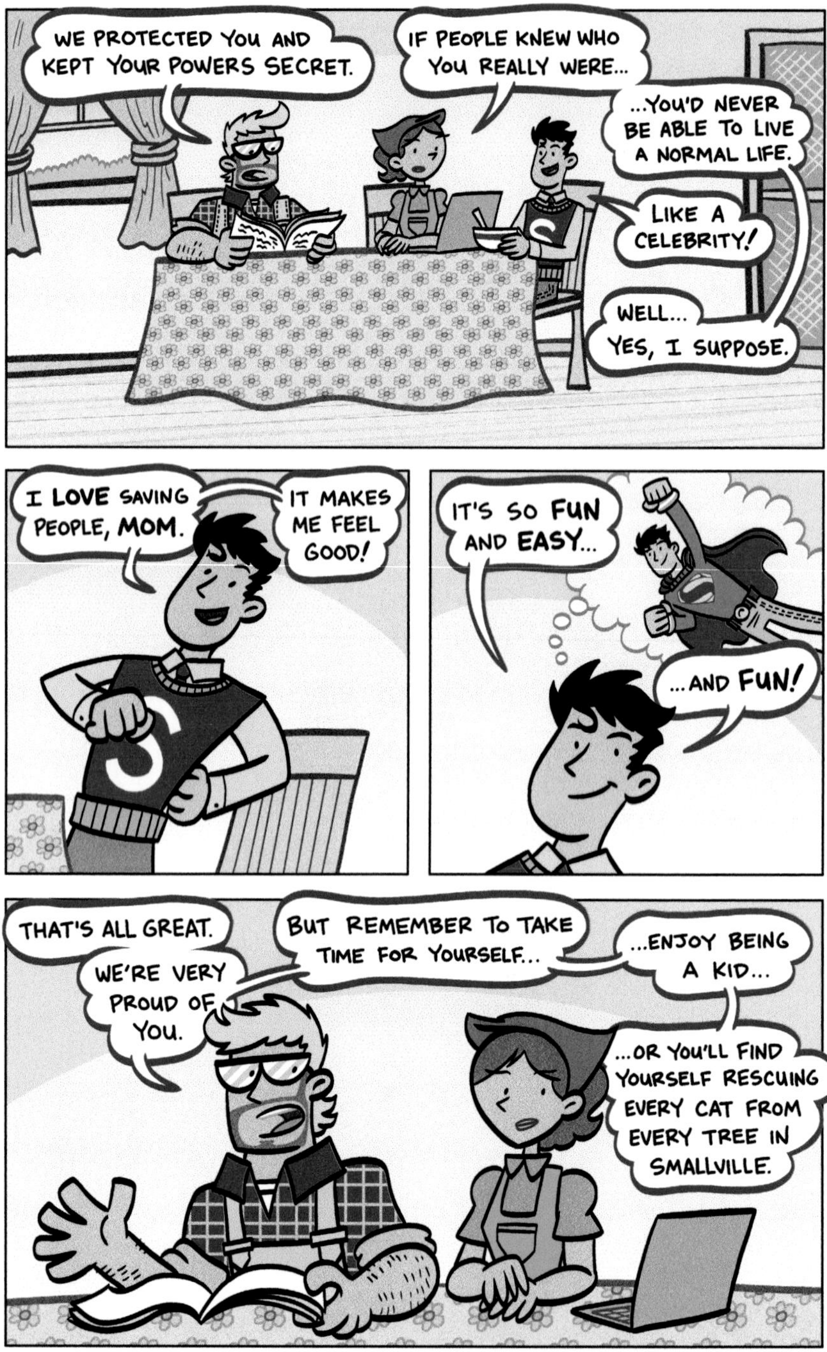
WE PROTECTED YOU AND KEPT YOUR POWERS SECRET.
IF PEOPLE KNEW WHO YOU REALLY WERE...
...YOU'D NEVER BE ABLE TO LIVE A NORMAL LIFE.
LIKE A CELEBRITY!
WELL... YES, I SUPPOSE.
I **LOVE** SAVING PEOPLE, **MOM**.
IT MAKES ME FEEL GOOD!
IT'S SO **FUN** AND **EASY**...
...AND **FUN**!
THAT'S ALL GREAT.
WE'RE VERY PROUD OF YOU.
BUT REMEMBER TO TAKE TIME FOR YOURSELF...
...ENJOY BEING A KID...
...OR YOU'LL FIND YOURSELF RESCUING EVERY CAT FROM EVERY TREE IN SMALLVILLE.

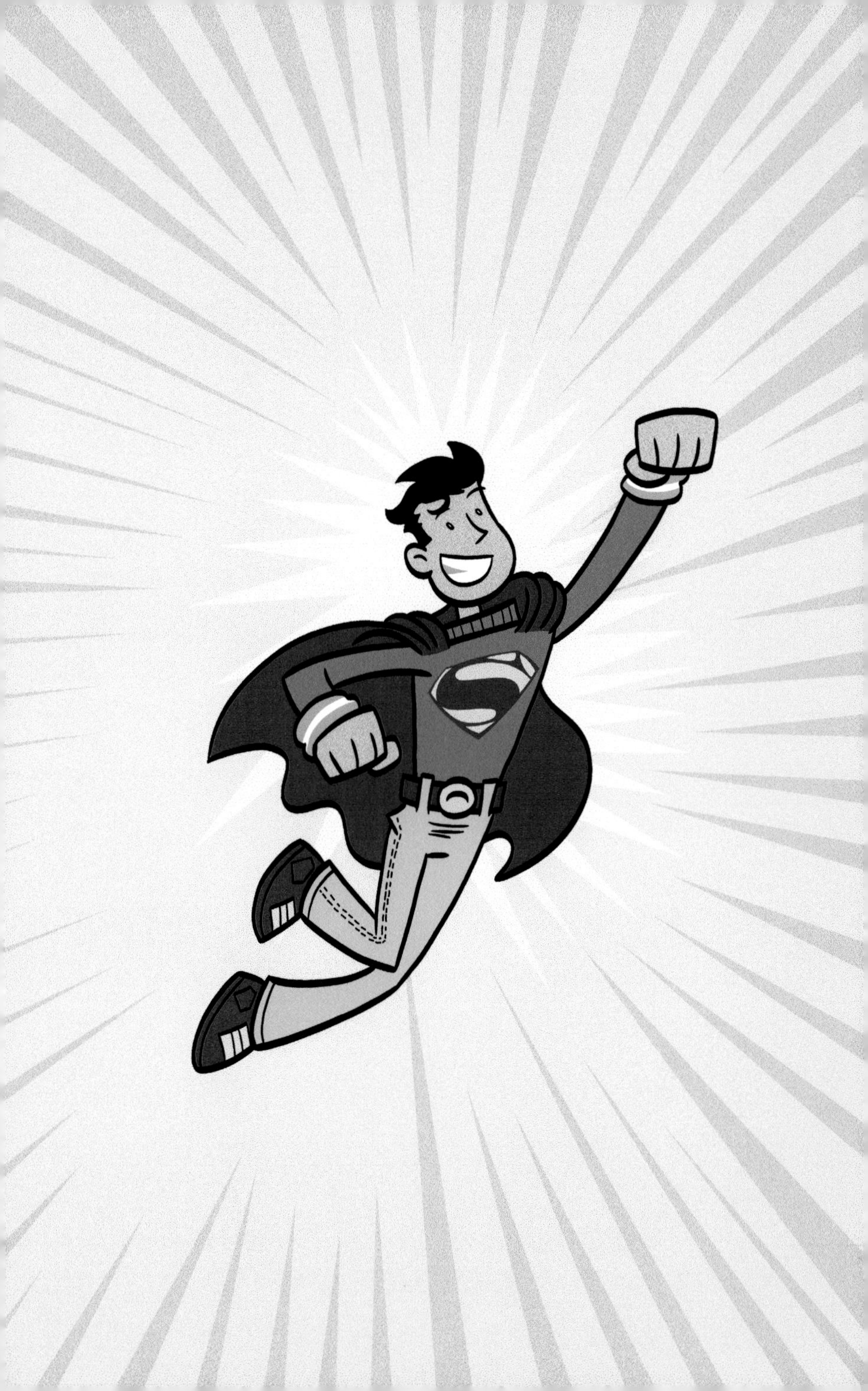

ZERO HEROES

GNARLEY QUINN

ZERO HEROES
DAY-OLD CABBAGE
AQUAMANATEE

NO SLUGGING

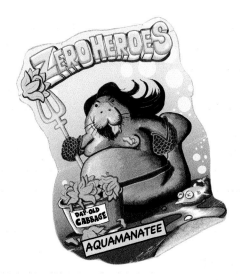

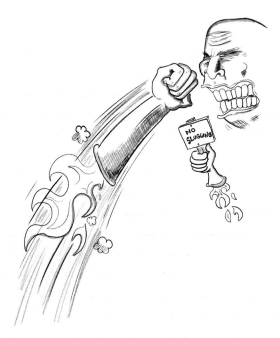

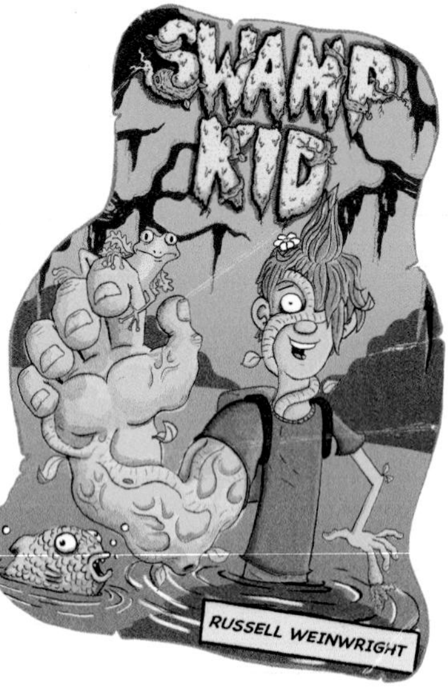
SWAMP KID
RUSSELL WEINWRIGHT

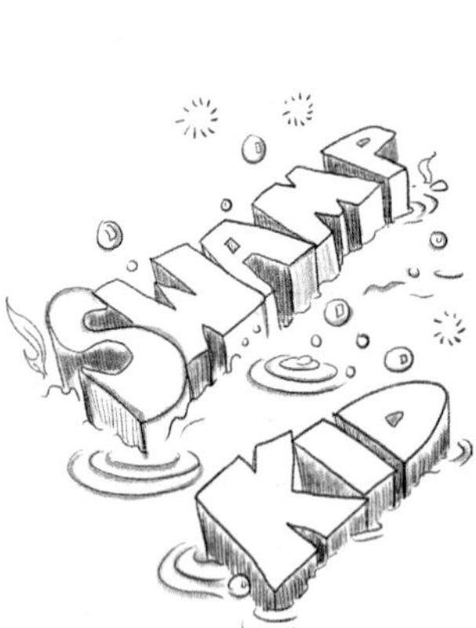
SWAMP KID